It Had to Be You

Ellie Adams

CORGI BOOKS

TRANSWORLD PUBLISHERS
61–63 Uxbridge Road, London W5 5SA
A Random House Group Company
www.transworldbooks.co.uk

IT HAD TO BE YOU
A CORGI BOOK: 9780552166850

First published in Great Britain
in 2014 by Corgi
an imprint of Transworld Publishers

A CIP catalogue record for this book
is available from the British Library.

Addresses for Random House Group Ltd companies outside the UK
can be found at: www.randomhouse.co.uk
The Random House Group Ltd Reg. No. 954009

The Random House Group Limited supports the Forest Stewardship
Council® (FSC®), the leading international forest-certification
organisation. Our books carrying the FSC label are printed on
FSC®-certified paper. FSC is the only forest-certification scheme
supported by the leading environmental organisations, including
Greenpeace. Our paper procurement policy can be found
at www.randomhouse.co.uk/environment

Typeset in 11/14pt Palatino by
Kestrel Data, Exeter, Devon.
Printed and bound by
CPI Group (UK) Ltd, Croydon, CR0 4YY.

2 4 6 8 10 9 7 5 3 1

To Dad,
for sponsoring the arts

Chapter 1

On the night of the 30th Birthday Party of Doom, Lizzy Spellman learnt three things.

Number one: Camera phones are the worst invention in the history of womankind.

Number two: She was never going to get another boyfriend again. After drinking herself to death on Kumala white wine, her body would lie undiscovered for weeks until the semi-hot postman with the Three Lions tattoo on his calf noticed the bad smell, or someone realized that she hadn't been on Facebook for a while.

Number three: It's bloody *murder* going for a wee in a Henry VIII costume.

In retrospect the outfit hadn't been the best idea for a warm June evening, but then Lizzy hadn't had much choice. The party was being held by an old university friend of Lizzy's, and the fancy-dress theme was 'Dead Icons'. She and Justin had been meant to be going as Bonnie and Clyde, but at the last minute her boyfriend had changed his mind and decided he was going as Che Guevara, the Argentine revolutionary.

'I just think it's a bit naff when couples dress up as couples,' he'd told her. 'You can still go as Bonnie, though, if you like.'

He was somewhat missing the point, Lizzy had said. It was like Ant going without Dec. At which point Justin had told her it was she who was missing the point: Ant and Dec weren't dead.

By the time Lizzy had got to Costume Drama! on Saturday morning there had barely been anything left. Half of London, it had seemed, was at a fancy-dress party that weekend. Faced with the choice of Buzz Lightyear, a 'horny witch' and a flammable-looking Henry VIII number, Lizzy had gone for Henry VIII. He was a kind of an icon, wasn't he?

The outfit was a nightmare to take off. Especially when they were on a pleasure boat on the Thames and the toilet was a tiny cubicle with barely room to swing a doublet. By the time Lizzy returned from the loo her friends had disappeared. She took one look across the crowded deck and decided to stay put by the railings. They were bound to turn up soon.

As far as fancy-dress parties went, it was all a bit pretentious. Lizzy had no idea who half the guests were, let alone which dead famous person they were meant to be. She'd already tried to join in a conversation with one group dressed in togas, only to discover they were conversing in fluent Latin.

'I like your costume,' she said to a man with a long curly wig, who was having an illicit fag over the side of the boat. 'I didn't know Michael Bolton had died, though, that's really sad.'

He shot her a contemptuous look. 'Try Galileo, sweedie.' Flicking the butt overboard, he swanned off.

He'd probably had a horrible time at boarding school, Lizzy told herself. She turned back to take in the view, which always made her heart soar. The riverbank was lit up like a line of Christmas lights, the Houses of Parliament looming impressively in the distance. Another party boat was chugging along towards them from the opposite direction. A Union Jack flag fluttered at its bow and it made Lizzy think of Justin. A flock of butterflies rose up in her stomach again.

Tomorrow was their six-month anniversary, and Justin was taking Lizzy out for a special lunch. 'It's a surprise,' he'd told her, eyes twinkling. 'I've got something to ask you.'

His comment had set the proverbial cat amongst the pigeons. Her best friend Poppet thought Justin was going to ask Lizzy to move in with him. Her other best friend Nic was sure he was going to ask Lizzy to do something weird in bed, or at the very least see where she stood on dogging. Lizzy had also made the mistake of telling her mother, and Mrs Spellman was now convinced Justin was going to propose. 'You're both the Right Age, darling,' she'd said when she'd rung Lizzy for the umpteenth time at work that week to ask what Lizzy was going to wear for the occasion.

'We've only been going out six months, Mum! And I'm only twenty-eight!'

'Exactly. You don't want to hang about.' Her mother's

tone had turned ominous. 'Justin's a good catch. If you don't snap him up someone else will.'

'What do you suggest I do, take him engagement ring shopping?'

'I hate it when you get this defeatist attitude. I'm hanging up now.'

Lizzy was a romantic, but there was a difference between this and being a full-blown fantasist. Justin was a sweet and caring man, but he was also logical and organized and always thought everything through. That was why he was managing director of the second-most-successful flagpole company in the south west of England. This was someone who used a spreadsheet to do his weekly food shop; he was hardly going to ask Lizzy to marry him when they weren't even living together yet. Besides, Lizzy's dad was terrible at keeping secrets and Mr Spellman hadn't let slip anything about Justin asking for Lizzy's hand in marriage. To be honest, Lizzy wasn't sure about marriage herself just yet. Despite what her mother said, they weren't living in the fifties and women didn't spontaneously combust if they weren't married off by a certain age.

No, it had to be that Justin was going to ask her to move in with him. The signs were definitely there. When they'd first started going out, his fridge had been a fat-free zone, but recently he'd started buying semi-skimmed milk for Lizzy and Lurpak spreadable butter because he knew she liked it on her toast in the mornings. Even more significantly, he'd cleared out his sports-socks drawer for her to 'leave a few things for when you stay over'. It might not sound like much, but for someone who took his triathlon training as seriously as Justin, this was a pretty big statement.

Lizzy stared across the dark river and couldn't suppress an indefinable shiver. But what if – just if – he *was* going to propose?

A strident Nottingham accent shattered her thoughts. 'Oi, Ginger Bollocks!'

A statuesque Amy Winehouse was tottering across the deck, propping up a swaying Mother Teresa. Arriving in front of Lizzy, Nic adjusted her beehive and swore loudly. 'This Wonderbra is cutting off my blood supply. I'm going to have to take it off.'

'We thought you'd fallen overboard,' Poppet, aka Mother Teresa, said. 'You've been gone ages.'

'You try going to the loo in a codpiece,' Lizzy sighed. 'I think I've dropped a gold sovereign down the toilet.'

'Where's Justin?'

'I've told you, don't *say* it like that.'

'Don't say it like what?' Nic asked innocently.

Lizzy gave her a look. 'You know exactly what I mean! You always call him "Just-in".'

'I really don't know what you're talking about. I can't help the way I pronounce his name, can I?'

'You're such an old trout,' Lizzy said, unable to keep the smile off her face. 'I'll have you know there's nothing wrong with my boyfriend's manhood.'

Poppet produced a bottle of Veuve Clicquot from under her habit. 'Who wants bubbles?'

'Where did you get that?' Lizzy asked.

'Stole it from the bar.' She smiled angelically. 'No one suspects Mother Teresa.'

'It's the only way we're going to get pissed when the

house white is thirty quid a bottle.' Nic caught a nearby William Shakespeare checking out her legs. 'What are you looking at?'

'Nothing,' he spluttered.

The champagne was surreptitiously passed round. 'HMQ?' Lizzy asked between swigs. 'HMQ' was their code for 'Hot Man Quota'.

'Three out of ten and that's being generous,' Nic said. 'What is it with posh people and no chins?'

'I think I saw a hot pope who looks a bit like Matt Damon,' Poppet said.

'You think everyone looks like Matt Damon.' Nic got her phone out. 'Come on, let's get a picture.'

'Don't tag me in it, I look horrible,' Poppet fretted. 'I knew I should have come as Mata Hari!'

'Poppet,' Nic said patiently. 'Have you *seen* Lizzy? Are you and Justin planning to have sex later in that thing?' she asked Lizzy. 'Only it's going to take him all night just to get through the layers.'

'Someone talking about me?' Justin materialized from the crowd in front of them with a beer in each hand.

'We were discussing the logistics of you having sex with old Henry VIII here,' Nic told him. 'Have you ever gone to bed with someone in a codpiece?'

'Ha ha,' Justin said weakly. He always kept a distance from Nic, as if she was a wild animal that was liable to attack at any moment.

'We'll leave you lovebirds to it.' Nic flashed an evil grin. 'Come on, Pops, let's go and find Matt Damon.' She strutted off, pulling Poppet behind her.

Justin handed Lizzy a beer. 'Is Matt Damon here?'

'No, silly, someone who looks like him.' Lizzy smiled at her boyfriend. He could be so literal.

They sipped their drinks and made eyes at each other. Lizzy felt a glow of happiness. Justin did look handsome in his Che Guevara beret, especially with the tan he'd got from his golfing weekend in Marbella.

Failing to get his arm round Lizzy, he settled for kissing the tip of her nose instead. 'I can hardly see you in there under that beard,' he said fondly. 'You are funny.'

'Funny "ha ha" or funny peculiar?'

'Well, you *are* a bit eccentric, Lizzy. You could have come as someone sexy, but instead you turn up as an obese tyrant. You don't care what people think.'

'Oh,' she said, feeling a bit deflated. 'Well, I only came as Henry because, you know, you changed your mind at the last moment.'

'It's all right,' he said. 'I *like* being the one with the crazy girlfriend.'

'You do?'

Justin twanged her beard affectionately. 'Just not *too* crazy. Try to stay off the white wine tonight.'

He nuzzled her neck. 'Are you looking forward to lunch tomorrow?'

'Sure am! Are you?'

'Oh yes,' he said with a knowing smile. Lizzy felt her stomach go again. *Oh God!*

They might be at a party with everyone who'd ever appeared on the panel for *University Challenge*, but one thing always united people. 'Karaoke's about to start,' Justin said. 'Do you know what you want to sing?'

'We were thinking about "Waterfalls". Or Poppet's

quite keen on "Whole Again", but Nic hates Jenny Frost.'

He frowned. 'I meant us.'

'Oh, sorry. I thought you didn't like doing the whole,' Lizzy made finger quotes, '"couples doing couples" thing.'

'Yeah, with fancy dress.' He gave her a nudge. 'What's your favourite duet? You can choose anything you want.'

'"Summer Nights" is always a good one.'

Justin screwed his face up. 'Too cheesy.'

'"Islands in the Stream"?'

'Same. It needs to be something more contemporary.'

'How about Beyoncé and Jay-Z, "Bonnie and Clyde"? At least we get the couples theme in somewhere.'

'It's got loads of rapping in it.'

'I thought you said you used to MC round all the clubs in Basingstoke when you were younger?'

Justin looked vaguely irritated. 'I just haven't had the chance to practise for ages. I know! Let's do that "You've Lost That Loving Feeling".'

'Didn't you want something contemporary? It's not exactly very romantic either,' Lizzy joked.

'*Top Gun* is number three in my top five films!' He was all buoyed up again. 'I'll go and put our names down.'

The deck below was packed. Someone had just finished murdering Bruno Mars and now it was Lizzy and Justin's turn.

'I'll go first,' he told her. 'You can come in on the chorus.'

Lizzy had no idea he'd take it so seriously. They'd had a powwow at the side of the stage to get "in the zone", and Justin was now strutting round with his microphone. She watched him blow a kiss to the crowd as the intro started; who'd have thought there was such an entertainer lurking inside him?

A minute later Lizzy was just wondering whether to get down and leave him to it when Justin suddenly turned round and threw himself down in front of her. 'Baby, baby . . .' he crooned.

'I'd get down on my knees for yoooo,' the crowd sang along.

It all happened in a split second. Lizzy and Justin's eyes locked. There was a shout from the crowd.

'Oh my God! He's going to propose!'

The music suddenly cut off. A chant started up. 'Ask her, ask her, ask her!'

Lizzy caught a glimpse of Poppet's face across the sea of people in the room. Her mouth had formed into a little 'O'.

Justin scrambled to his feet. 'Well, the thing is . . .' His microphone screeched horribly.

'Just ask her!' someone cried.

'The thing is . . .' He gave a weak smile. 'I guess this has just taken me a bit by surprise.'

'No it hasn't, you were going to propose tomorrow!' shouted a girl dressed as Joan of Arc who Lizzy had never met before. *What the hell?*

'I was?' Justin asked.

Joan of Arc pointed at Poppet. 'That's what she said in the queue for the loo.'

'I was joking!' Poppet wailed. 'Me and Nic were just

saying how hilarious it would be if he actually did ask Lizzy to marry him!'

Standing beside Poppet, Nic put her head in her hands.

'So you *have* been talking about it with your friends?' Justin said uncertainly.

'No! I mean, yes, but not seriously! In a kind of "Oh my God, can you imagine!" way, like Poppet said. It's what girls do, isn't it? Anyway,' Lizzy added lamely, 'my mum said it first, not me.'

'Your *mum* thinks I'm going to propose?'

Lizzy gave him a desperate smile. 'You said you had something special to ask me at lunch tomorrow?'

'Speak up!' someone cried. 'I missed that!'

Justin's face had turned the same colour as his khaki jumpsuit. 'I was going to ask if you wanted to go on a mini break.'

'A *mini break*?' Lizzy's words echoed round the room.

'Yeah,' he said uncertainly. 'Did you really think I was going to ask you to marry me?'

'No! But, well, I thought you might be going to ask me to move in.'

'What? No way! What I mean is,' he said hurriedly, 'it's a bit too soon to be thinking about that.'

He'd subconsciously taken a step back from her. Lizzy started having the strangest out-of-body experience. *I'm not standing up here*, she thought to herself. *This isn't happening.*

The room had gone deathly quiet. Justin turned to Lizzy. 'You're a really nice girl and we have lots of fun,' he told her. 'But you're moving *way* too fast.'

'So why ask me on a mini break?' she asked feebly.

He gave a helpless shrug. 'Everyone else seemed to be going on them. I got a really good deal on this hotel with a golf course and it had a nice spa. I thought you could go there while I played a few rounds and went to the gym . . .' He trailed off.

Lizzy's throat had dried up to the point where she was no longer capable of producing saliva. 'So basically you're saying I was your plus one on a sports holiday?'

'I wouldn't put it exactly like that,' he said uncomfortably. 'We'd get to spend some time together as well.'

Lizzy searched in vain for Poppet and Nic. But all she could see were the mesmerized faces of their audience looking back at her.

Justin's eyes were flicking towards the emergency exit. 'You've got the wrong end of the stick,' he told Lizzy. 'I just thought a mini break would give us the chance to spend some proper time together, you know, and see how things go. But all this talk of marriage . . .'

'But my mum said it, not me,' she said miserably.

He wasn't listening. 'If you're thinking like this now, what are you going to be like in a year's time? Planning our children's names?'

He caught sight of Lizzy's guilty expression. 'Oh come on!' she protested. 'We've all had the old "what we'd call our kids" conversation.' She appealed to the crowd. 'Haven't we?'

Her words faded into the deafening silence. Justin shook his head violently. 'You've forced me into a corner. I'm sorry, Lizzy, but you were never the girl that I was going to marry.'

There was a collective *'Ouch!'* across the room. Justin put his hand on her arm, like a vet about to put an elderly dog out of its misery. 'I'm sorry,' he said again. 'It's over.'

Lizzy could feel the blood rushing into her ears. A hundred pairs of eyes were boring into her, sealing her hot humiliation. What happened next was so left field and unexpected it took everyone by surprise, most of all her. She put her hands on Justin's shoulders and pulled him towards her. A look of surprised relief crossed his face as he thought she was about to give him a magnanimous hug, then Lizzy headbutted him, hard.

Chapter 2

It was bad enough getting dumped by your boyfriend in front of a room full of people. Especially when one of those people records the whole thing on their camera phone. But by far the worst thing is when that person decides to put the footage on YouTube.

By midday on Sunday 'Girl Who Gets Jilted at 30th Birthday and Headbutts Boyfriend' had three hundred thousand hits and rising. To compound Lizzy's shame, the ginger beard had muffled her voice, so it was only Justin who you could hear. It was all there in excruciating detail: Lizzy in her floppy hat looking like a confused Weeble, Justin delivering his devastating line: *I'm sorry, Lizzy, but you were never the girl I was going to marry,* Lizzy's head jerking forward like a giant woodpecker, and Justin staggering backwards holding his hands over his bloody nose. The footage ended abruptly at that point, but the damage had been done.

Lizzy was still hiding under her duvet, where she'd been for nearly twelve hours straight.

'Are you sure I can't get you anything?' Poppet was perched on the end of the bed in a hoody of Lizzy's that was too big for her. She hadn't stopped apologizing all night.

'I'm fine.'

'This is all my fault! If only I hadn't said anything! Do you really hate me?'

'Of course I don't hate you.' Lizzy's voice didn't feel like her own. Nothing felt like it was her own. Was this how a person felt when they were suffering from post-traumatic stress syndrome?

'Are you sure you haven't hurt your head?' Poppet asked.

'No.'

It was true. Somehow Lizzy had known instinctively where to headbutt Justin and cause the maximum damage whilst leaving herself without even a mark. It was like something primeval had reared up out from the depths of her soul. Lizzy had never so much as bitch slapped anyone in her life. It was shocking to discover she was capable of such off-the-wall violence.

She heard Poppet gasp. 'You've got another ten thousand hits on YouTube! What if you go bigger than "Gangnam Style"?'

An hour later Lizzy's identity was leaked when someone uploaded a Facebook picture of her with a triple chin on to one of the gossip websites. Journalists started to cluster outside her block of flats and rang the doorbell constantly, until Poppet bravely went outside and disabled the bell by bashing it with a wok she'd found collecting dust at the back of the cupboard.

Afterwards she tried coaxing Lizzy out from under the duvet with a cup of tea, but Lizzy wasn't having any of it.

'I just want to be left alone. How did these people find me?'

'Why don't you take the hat off, at least?' Poppet suggested. 'It must be really hot under there.'

Lizzy made a *meurgggh* noise.

'I know, I'll make you some toast! The sell-by date on the bread is last week but I'll just cut the mouldy bits off.'

Lizzy heard Poppet leave the room again. It did smell like something had died under the duvet. *My dignity*, Lizzy thought. She was still in the Henry VIII costume, as if it were armour protecting her from the full horror of what had happened.

She shuffled miserably round the mattress trying to find a cold spot. There had been no word from Justin. They were meant to have been sitting down for their romantic lunch by now and planning their mini break. Instead, Lizzy was newly single, humiliated on a national scale and wearing a pair of polyester breeches that had disappeared right up her bum crack.

How had this *happened*?

Part of her was still expecting Justin to rock up with a sheepish smile on his face. He would admit he'd just freaked out and hadn't really meant it, and that he'd deserved the bloody nose. Or else a camera crew would spring out of the wardrobe and tell Lizzy she'd been the victim of a TV prank. Lizzy would take it all with good grace and coolly remark that she didn't want to marry Justin anyway. She'd come out of the whole thing really well and it would make Justin realize what he'd lost and decide that maybe he *did* want more than a mini break. Henry VIII would become the nation's most popular choice for fancy dress and everyone would live happily ever after. (Once Lizzy had made her errant boyfriend suffer for the appropriate amount of time.)

Justin didn't come round. There was no camera crew hiding, no matter how many times Poppet searched the flat. By 3 p.m. 'Girl Who Gets Jilted at 30ᵗʰ Birthday and Headbutts Boyfriend' had reached six hundred thousand hits and Lizzy had twenty thousand new Twitter followers. People were retweeting the link as far as Uzbekistan and China. Someone had set up a fake Twitter account @DumpedHeadbuttGirl and was tweeting things like, 'Butt out you lot, my love life is none of your business,' and 'All the single ladies, all the single ladies! *weeps silently and stabs Beyoncé poster in eye with pencil*.' Someone else had even created a Vine set to the eighties power ballad 'Love Is A Battlefield', where the infamous moment was on slow-motion constant repeat.

'That one's actually quite funny,' Poppet accidentally said in front of Lizzy, before swiftly pressing 'hide'.

At 4.15 p.m. Nic called from the airport. Poppet put her on speakerphone.

'Has she spoken yet?' Nic asked.

'The odd word,' Poppet sighed. 'She's still refusing to come out from under the duvet.'

'Lizzy, you listen, OK? Justin is a *massive wanker* who didn't deserve you in the first place.'

'She's worried he's going to press charges for GBH,' Poppet told her.

'He's lucky you didn't kick him so hard in the bollocks he's blowing them out through his nose. He hasn't got a leg to stand on. Look, they're calling my flight. I'll call you when I land.'

Lizzy continued to lie there in the fetid dark, trying not to breathe in the noxious fumes from her own body. *Welcome to Duvetland! A place where humiliated exes come to fester.*

'Oh dear,' Poppet suddenly said.

Lizzy stuck her head out. 'What is it?'

Her friend smiled nervously. 'You're on the *Mail-Online.*'

Lizzy grabbed the laptop. She was at the top of the infamous 'Sidebar of Shame'. The caption read: 'Hell hath no fury! PR Lizzy Spellman Unmasked as "Girl Who Gets Jilted at 30th Birthday and Headbutts Boyfriend" Goes Viral.'

'Don't get upset!' Poppet implored her. 'Remember that YouTube video of that American girl who was walking along texting in a shopping mall and she fell into a fountain! That was *way* more embarrassing.'

It was official: Lizzy's life was OVER.

Chapter 3

Lizzy woke with a start. What a horrible nightmare. The fancy-dress party, the YouTube viral, the gang of paparazzi outside her flat. It had felt so *real* . . .

A horn went off right by her ear, nearly giving Lizzy a heart attack. It was her 'Sherwood Forest' text alert. It was from Nic.

How are you feeling? Has Twat Face got in contact to say sorry yet?

Oh God! It hadn't been a nightmare! The events of the last twenty-four hours flashed through Lizzy's mind like the reel from a horror film. Her laptop was on the bed next to her, still open on the last *Daily Mail* article about her: 'Unmarried Women in Japan Hold Candlelit Vigil for Lizzy Spellman'.

There was no way she could go to work. She sent her boss a text and crawled back under the covers. She'd have to hire someone to do *her* PR at this rate.

Poppet called on her way to a client meeting. 'Have the reporters gone yet?'

'There's even more of them,' Lizzy said wearily.

'They've started putting twenty-pound notes through the door trying to bribe me to talk to them.'

'Why don't you watch something that isn't the news? It will take your mind off things,' Poppet said soothingly. 'I'll call you at lunch.'

Lizzy rang off and switched on *This Morning*. Phillip and Holly had their serious faces on. A violet-haired woman was sitting on the sofa opposite them. The caption on the screen read 'Mary DuVille, author of *Single Women Need Self Love First*'.

'Lizzy Spellman will be in a very dark place right now,' Mary DuVille intoned. 'Being rejected by the man you thought you were going to marry affects the psyche at a primeval level.'

'How can Justin have done that to her in front of a room full of people?' asked an outraged Holly. 'It's totally out of order!'

Mary DuVille looked grave. 'From what I can see, Lizzy displays all the symptoms of a classic fantasist. It's a common problem for women who are on the threshold of their thirties and are panicking about being left on the shelf.'

Phillip Schofield gazed solemnly into the camera. 'Are you like Lizzy Spellman and have been told that you're not "The One"? If so, please get in touch and call the number on the screen now. Next up – how to wow dinner guests with the perfect rum baba!'

Lizzy woke from a new nightmare slumber where she was trapped inside a bridal shop and there were dozens of faces pressed against the window laughing at her. Someone was banging on the front door. 'Go away!' she shouted hysterically. 'I've got nothing to say to you!'

Her mother's voice sliced down the corridor like a scythe. 'Elizabeth! Open up. We've only got fifteen minutes' parking on the car.'

'Leave me alone!'

'Don't be so ridiculous. Are you going to open up or am I going to have to ask your father to force the door and put his shoulder out?'

Muttering obscenities, Lizzy hauled herself out of bed and trudged down the hallway. She opened the front door and saw her parents framed on the doorstep in a blinding display of camera-bulbs. They threw themselves in and shut the door behind them.

'I hope they don't use those pictures, I didn't have time to do the back of my hair.' Lizzy's mum pulled off her sunglasses. 'Oh, darling, you look *dreadful*.'

'I feel dreadful,' Lizzy said, and burst into tears.

That was the thing about parents. They had been the last people Lizzy had wanted to see – her mum anyway – but they had come in and immediately made everything better.

By the time Lizzy had got out of the shower her dad had done the washing up and her mum had tidied away all the old Sunday papers in the living room, stripped Lizzy's bed and laid out an outfit for her to wear.

'We're taking you out for lunch,' her mum informed her.

Luckily her dad had had the foresight to bring his golfing umbrella in, which he opened up in the reporters' faces as they charged out to the car. The three of them were now ensconced in a nearby Pizza Express. Lizzy was wearing a Topshop scarf round her head and had insisted on sitting away from the window so no one could recognize her.

'Don't be silly. It's not like you're Princess Diana back from the dead.' Her mum looked at the menu. 'Are we having garlic doughballs?'

'I thought you were on the 5:2 diet,' Lizzy said.

'It's one of my "off" days. Oh come on, darling, don't start crying again.'

'Poor old Lizard's had a horrid time,' her dad said gently.

'I know that, Michael!' Mrs Spellman softened her tone. 'I'm just *saying* there's no point her lying round feeling sorry for herself.'

'This is a c-c-catastrophe,' Lizzy gulped. 'How can I ever face anyone again?'

'This is not a catastrophe,' her mother told her. 'Orphans starving in Africa is a catastrophe. Thousands of people losing their homes in flash floods is a catastrophe. That awful Gordon Halliday getting elected as councillor for Bromley West *is* a major catastrophe. I know it feels like your world has ended.' She handed Lizzy a Kleenex from her handbag. 'But you have to get some perspective.'

The annoying thing was that her mum was right. Lizzy just wasn't in any fit state to accept it yet. She blew her nose loudly, making an elderly couple on the next table jump. 'How did you find out?'

'Lauren called us,' her dad said.

'*Lauren's* seen it?' Lauren was Lizzy's sister who lived in New York.

'And we went over to David and Jacqui's last night and it was all they could talk about. David kept on replaying it on YouLube.' Her mum gave Lizzy a reproachful look. 'I'm not very impressed with my daughter being involved in a public brawl. I know you were upset, but there was no need to resort to physical violence.'

'What about the time you kicked Dad on the shin with your stiletto when we were younger and he had to go to A & E because the wound went septic?' Lizzy sniffed.

'That was different. I was under extreme provocation. Your father and Uncle Alan had been on the whisky and they were being extremely silly.' Mrs Spellman jangled the bracelet of her wristwatch. 'How was I to know the steel tip would go through a pair of trousers *and* his merino wool sock?'

'Justin's lucky I wasn't there or I would have bopped him on the nose myself,' Mr Spellman said. 'He's an idiot for not wanting to marry you.'

'I didn't think he was going to bloody propose!' Lizzy shouted.

Her parents looked at her as if she was mad.

'Sorry,' she muttered. 'I'm just feeling a bit sensitive about it at the moment.'

Her mother was trying to catch the waiter's eye. 'Well, *I* never wanted him in the family anyway.'

Lizzy stared at her. 'Mum, you're the one who said he was going to ask me to marry him in the first place!'

'Did I? I don't think so.'

'You've been saying it all week!'

Mrs Spellman shook her head dismissively. 'You must have got muddled up. I always thought Justin had a suspicious mouth.'

'What on earth does that mean?' Lizzy's dad asked.

'It was always a bit tight and anxious-looking. Like he'd done something wrong and knew he was about to be found out at any moment. You know.' She screwed her lips up. '*Suspicious!*'

Mr Spellman rolled his eyes. 'What I will say,' he told Lizzy, 'is marriage proposal or no marriage proposal, no decent man would do that to his girlfriend in public. Especially not to my Lizard.'

'Thanks, Dad,' Lizzy said gratefully. Her parents might be bonkers but they always made her feel better.

'Onwards and upwards, darling,' her mother declared. 'You'll go back to work tomorrow and we'll have no more of this silliness. What do the Spellmans always say?'

'A smile a day keeps the naysayers away,' Lizzy and her dad chanted dutifully.

'That's more like it.' Mrs Spellman waved her menu in the air. 'There he goes, blatantly ignoring me again! That's London for you.'

On the way home her mother made them pull over at a Tesco Metro to buy Lizzy some groceries.

'Your father and I were very alarmed at all the empty wine bottles in the flat,' she told Lizzy as they went down the fruit and veg aisle.

'I had a party last weekend,' Lizzy lied.

'I don't remember you saying . . . How about a nice pineapple? Did I tell you Jacqui's started juicing? She's been doing that Jason Vale book, you know that diet guru all the celebrities go to.'

'I haven't got anywhere to put a juicer in the kitchen, Mum.'

Mrs Spellman gave her A Look. 'You seem to find somewhere for all those wine bottles.'

The girl at the checkout gave Lizzy a sympathetic smile and produced a rather battered box of Celebrations from under the till. 'These are on us. Same thing happened to my mate. She thought her boyfriend was going to propose on Christmas Day and all she got was one of those crappy foot spas. Sometimes you've just got to eat through the heartbreak.'

'That's very kind of you, but she'll never get another boyfriend if she's fat and covered in spots,' Mrs Spellman told her. 'Oh look, Lizzy, your father's waving. He must be getting antsy about being parked in the bus lane.'

As they drove up to the flat the gang of reporters had doubled in size. They surged forward as they spotted the Spellmans' Volvo Estate. Another round of flash-bulbs went off.

'This is unacceptable.' Lizzy's dad started to unbuckle his seatbelt, but her mum stopped him.

'I'll take care of this, Michael.'

Her mum climbed out of the car. A microphone was shoved in her face. 'Mrs Spellman, as Lizzy's mother, you must know the trauma your daughter is going through. How is she coping?'

'She is coping perfectly fine, thank you. And for the record, she didn't want to marry him anyway!'

'I thought he was going to ask me to move in!' Lizzy wailed from the back seat.

'I'm the first to admit Lizzy has her faults,' Mrs Spellman told the assembled pack of reporters. 'But she didn't deserve any of this. Lizzy is a kind, loving, wonderful daughter. A little messy, yes, and she drinks far too much, but that's what these ladettes do these days, isn't it?' She rolled her eyes, playing up to her audience. 'And don't get me started on her finances!'

Lizzy whimpered gently and started to slide down the seat. It seemed her mother wasn't done yet. Grabbing the microphone, Mrs Spellman beamed at the bank of reporters.

'If anyone knows any nice single men, do send them her way! *Somebody* out there must want her!'

Chapter 4

Lizzy's boss was already in when she got into the office the next morning. Antonia was at her desk wearing a beaded kaftan and surrounded by ringing phones.

'A-ha!' she cried. 'Our resident celebrity!'

Lizzy cautiously removed her sunglasses and unwound her headscarf. 'Sorry I'm late. I had a bit of a nightmare getting in.'

That was an understatement. Besieged by the reporters still on her doorstep, Lizzy had been forced to flag down a passing cab to escape. The previous customer had left behind a copy of the *Metro* and in it, there was a full-page interview with Lizzy's now ex-boyfriend. 'I had to follow my heart and it wasn't with Lizzy. I wish her the very best.' His face still looked rather battered from where Lizzy had delivered the killer blow, but as Poppet had pointed out, how could he complain about a broken nose when he'd broken Lizzy's heart?

'With all the coverage you've been getting you could have at least got a product placement in,' Antonia told her. 'Talk about pissing away a golden opportunity.'

'Sorry,' Lizzy mumbled. 'Next time I get dumped by my boyfriend and it goes global, I'll make sure I remember.'

'You may think all this is funny, darling, but your clients are very concerned about how it's going to affect them. We're meant to be the ones creating the news, not making it. We can't have you running off and hogging all the attention.' Antonia stood up and heaved her Anya Hindmarch tote over her shoulder. 'I'm off to meet Jocasta for a crisis summit. We're not to be disturbed under *any circumstances*.'

The phones were still ringing off the hook. 'Aren't you going to answer those?' she asked Lizzy.

The morning was horrific. Lizzy's clients were convinced she was leaving them to become a TV star. She had to try and placate them, as well as attempting to do her usual workload and fielding constant phone calls from journalists. It was hard not to appreciate the irony. Normally these people wouldn't give her the time of day. Now they were falling over themselves to get an exclusive interview with her.

By midday the press had cottoned on to where Haven PR was. When Antonia came back to the office she had to drive through a pack of them to get to her parking space.

Lizzy had just got off the phone to a very nice woman from the *Huffington Post*, who wanted to do a sympathetic interview about what had happened. 'It would be your chance to put your side of the story across,' she told Lizzy.

33

'Tell them we want a big plug for the new herbal constipation product or we're not playing ball,' barked Antonia.

Lizzy emailed the *Huffington Post* woman back to politely say that unfortunately she wouldn't be able to do it.

At 6 p.m. even Antonia could see how frazzled Lizzy was and offered to drive her to the tube station in her Range Rover. By the time Lizzy arrived at San Marco, the Italian restaurant she and her friends had been going to for years, she was in need of a stiff drink. Giuseppe, the rotund owner who bore an uncanny resemblance to the porn star Ron Jeremy, greeted her in a high state of excitement.

'Lee-zee! We don't get many famous people in here.'

'Very funny,' Lizzy said wearily.

'It sucks to be jilted, hey?' Giuseppe nudged her in the ribs. 'I have nephew from Tuscany who is single. He have bad Internet connection so might not have seen video. You want me to call him?'

'That's really sweet, Giuseppe, but I think it's a bit too soon.'

The restaurant owner nodded solemnly. 'Heartbroken of course. You need time to grieve. Come! I give you a booth so no one stare.'

Poppet was already waiting with a carafe of wine. 'It's on the house. Giuseppe is really worried about you.'

Lizzy necked a glass of Pinot Grigio in one go.

'Are you going to keep those sunglasses on?' Poppet asked. 'Only I think they're just going to attract more attention.'

Nic arrived ten minutes later on her phone, wheeling her overnight case behind her.

'Let's talk to them tomorrow. I'll send you the budget breakdown. OK, bye.' She flopped down next to Lizzy. 'I am gagging for a drink.'

'How was Berlin?' Poppet asked.

'Brussels. Boring. I hate that place.'

Nic was the global sales and marketing manager for a well-known hotel chain. It never ceased to amaze Lizzy that someone she'd once watched projectile-vomit Baileys through both nostrils now had such an important job.

Giuseppe materialized at the table like a jolly genie. 'What can I get you ladies?'

'The usual please: two garlic breads with extra cheese and we'll have some of those amazeballs stuffed olives on the counter,' Nic instructed. 'Then Poppet will have the Sicilian – no onions – Lizzy will have the truffle risotto and I'll have the seafood linguine. No anchovies, remember, G Man. I hate those little bastards.'

'Your wish my command.' He bowed and rushed off.

Lizzy looked gratefully around the table. 'Oh girls, I don't think I've ever been so pleased to see you.'

Mr Spellman called Lizzy and her friends 'the Three Amigos', because as he said, 'If one's around you know that the other two aren't far behind.' Lizzy had first laid eyes on Nic in the student union at Southampton University. Nic, sporting an undercut a decade before Miley Cyrus, had been challenging the captain of the rugby first team to see who could finish a pint of Aftershock first. A fresher at the time, Nic had set a new university record while the captain of the rugby team had been rushed to hospital to have his stomach pumped. Nic had been next door in halls to Poppet, who Lizzy had thought was some sort of secretary because she had turned up on the first day of term in a suit and carrying a briefcase. They'd all gone out for a pub crawl round the city's dodgiest bars, where Nic had got them chucked out of three places for mine-sweeping drinks and Poppet had actually wet herself twice from laughing so much. From then on the three of them had been inseparable.

They might have clicked on a mental level, but physically they couldn't have been more different. Nic was tall and broad-shouldered like a netball player. She was aggressively make-up free, unlike Poppet who bought a new MAC Lipglass virtually every week. Poppet's real name was Anisha, but she'd got the nickname Poppet at uni because she was tiny and doll-like. Half-Indian and half-Persian, Poppet had inherited her high grooming standards from her mum, who always wore beautiful saris and red lipstick and was one of the most glamorous women Lizzy had ever met.

'We've been really worried about you,' Poppet told her. 'I think it's amazing you've actually gone to work. I wouldn't be able to leave the house.'

'I'm sure that will make her feel loads better,' Nic said dryly. 'This will all blow over,' she told Lizzy. 'Remember Rebecca Loos tossed off a pig, and she's happily married and living in obscurity now.'

Giuseppe came back with the olives and Lizzy dived in. She'd already mindlessly munched her way through four breadsticks. 'I'm meant to be on the heartbreak diet,' she sighed. 'My mother is right. Not only am I single, I'm going to be *obese* and single for the rest of my life.'

'Don't be silly,' Poppet said loyally. 'You won't stay single. Trust me, there will be loads of men out there, just waiting to snap you up!'

'The bunny-boiler who got dumped on stage in a Henry VIII costume?' Lizzy said gloomily. 'I don't exactly see them lining up, do you?'

She was officially damaged goods. It didn't matter that she'd managed to have two semi-successful relationships (three if you counted Aussie Andy, although he'd been away travelling for six months of it which meant they'd only really properly gone out for four months). Her track record had been wiped out in one fell swoop. Men would see her as the praying mantis of marriage. Her picture would be held up as a warning in pubs and sports changing rooms across the land.

'Still no word from Justin?' Poppet ventured.

Lizzy shook her head miserably. 'I went on Facebook earlier to de-friend him and found out he'd already done it to me.'

Poppet looked outraged. 'He didn't even allow you that one dignity!'

'The guy's a complete dickhead.' Nic hoovered up a breadstick. 'He drank alcopops for God's sake. That is someone with serious issues about their sexuality.'

'C'mon, he drank a Smirnoff Ice *once* when he was really hungover from the all-day cricket,' Lizzy protested.

Nic looked at her strangely. 'Why are you defending him? Justin hung you out to dry, Lizzy.'

At that moment Giuseppe appeared brandishing their garlic bread. No one spoke until he'd gone again.

'You're right,' Lizzy sighed. 'It's just so *weird*. Justin's Alpro Light is still in my fridge. We had tickets to go and see Professor Green. He'd already asked me to go to his Christmas party! Why make all these plans if his heart was never in it? It was like I was with the guy for six months and I never really knew him.'

'No one knows anyone in six months,' Nic said darkly. 'They're just sizing each other up and deciding whether to stay or not.'

'Oh great, thanks!'

'It's better you find out now than in a few years' time when he leaves you standing at the aisle.' Poppet's eyes widened. 'I didn't mean it like that.'

'Meanwhile I'm left looking like a deluded fantasist.' Lizzy picked miserably at an olive. 'Why *didn't* Justin want to marry me, anyway?'

'You said you didn't want to marry him either,' Poppet pointed out.

'That's not the point.' How could someone know that early on that they didn't want to marry her? Was she really that repulsive first thing in the morning? Were her little idiosyncrasies really so annoying that they'd cancelled out any thoughts Justin might've had about proposing? What about growing together as people and learning to love each other's imperfections? To be told 'No thanks' by someone who hadn't even found out a quarter of the stuff about you was *brutal*.

'What's wrong with me?' she asked despairingly. 'Have I got a flashing sign above my head saying "FOR FUN TIMES AND MINI BREAKS ONLY"?'

'Bollocks!' Nic yelled in the manner that Len Goodman from *Strictly Come Dancing* shouted 'Seven!' 'There's nothing bloody wrong with you!'

'So why didn't he want to marry me?'

'I'll tell you exactly why. Guys like Justin have their perfect, boring little lives with their perfect, boring little routines. They'll end up marrying some perfect boring girl with perfect boring shiny hair, because she won't upset the equilibrium and make them realize how totally and absolutely *nothing* they are!' Nic waved her glass around so violently the contents sloshed out. 'This isn't about Justin not wanting to marry you! It's about the fact that deep down he knew that *you* didn't want to marry *him*!'

'Go Nic!' Poppet shouted happily.

'There are millions of bland and boring blokes like Justin. *You* on the other hand,' Nic told Lizzy, 'are a wonderful, unique, brilliant, warm, funny, lovely person.'

'There's only one Lizzy Spellman!' Poppet chanted.

'Don't let that no-mark twat bring you down!' Nic actually slapped the table.

Lizzy looked at Poppet's sweet little face and Nic, all fierce-browed and indignant, and felt a rush of love. They were the best friends in the world. Who needed a man? Who *cared* if she was a global laughing stock when she had these two?

'To friendship!' Nic said.

'And codpieces!' Poppet cried.

Lizzy held her glass aloft. 'To friends and codpieces!' 'Alcopops.' Nic looked smug. 'Just saying.'

It turned out that Nic was right. The next day the news broke that a Lib Dem MP had been caught in a dogging circle, and a Hollywood couple had split up amidst allegations of adultery. When Lizzy cautiously peeked out of the living room curtains the reporters had gone. For now at least, the storm had blown over.

The tight knot that had been sitting in Lizzy's chest since Saturday night suddenly loosened. She stood in front of her bedroom mirror in her dressing gown, able to think properly for the first time in ages.

The last few days had taken their toll. There were dark circles under her eyes and what appeared to be a Worzel Gummidge wig had crash-landed on her head. *Had* she lost a bit of stress-related weight? Lizzy turned sideways. If she stood in a certain way, breathed in and pushed her hips forward, her stomach did look a bit flatter.

If Lizzy had to describe herself she'd say she was Miss Average, but she didn't mean it in a derogatory way. She was just normal: five foot five, shoe size six and generally hovering around the size twelve mark (or a size ten in GAP). Her bum and her sunny smile were probably her best assets, her wobbly belly not so much. Her corkscrew blonde curls had been the bane of her life when she was younger, but these days Lizzy just bunged on the anti-frizz and hoped for the best. Justin had always said he'd found girls with curly hair sexy, even if he had remarked once that Lizzy looked like Louis XIV after she'd got out of the shower.

Justin. What was he up to at that very moment? It was a Wednesday, so he was probably at his early-morning Pilates class. Lizzy imagined him in his Lycra cycling shorts, quads quivering with concentration. Those quads, no longer hers to run her hands over. Never again would she start a sentence with the words: 'My boyfriend Justin . . .' She would never again catch eyes with him across a crowded pub and know it was a given that they were going home together. They would never take it in turns to stand outside a newsagent while the other one went in and bought the drinks. (Always a bottle of water for Lizzy and a Lucozade Sport for him.) Well, not unless she started dating another triathlete who was obsessed with rehydrating their electrolytes. She could go for months without bumping into her next-door neighbour. *I'll probably never see Justin again.*

She expected a new wave of anger or sadness, but all she felt was relief. Nic was right. Who *could* trust a man who drank alcopops?

At that moment a new resolve took hold. Lizzy eyeballed her reflection in that way people did in films at life-changing moments. She was a Spellman! Spellmans didn't lie around feeling sorry for themselves! She would rise like a phoenix from the ashes and start juicing in the mornings, and go on to meet the man of her dreams, while Justin would get dumped by a boring girl with shiny hair and spend the rest of his life in mourning. Ceremoniously pouring her exboyfriend's Alpro Light down the sink, Lizzy went to get ready for work.

Chapter 5

Haven PR was situated in a converted townhouse just off Fulham Broadway. Antonia had worked in HR until she'd suffered some sort of breakdown and jetted off to an ashram in India where she'd famously had twenty-one colonics in twenty-one days and experienced a spiritual rebirth. On returning home she'd dumped her first husband and announced she was setting up a holistic PR agency. Antonia now lived round the corner from the office with her second husband, a young German called Erik, and their thunderous-of-thigh toddler daughter, Christiana.

Lizzy had been working for a large corporate agency when she'd first met Antonia at a product launch. Admittedly not entirely sober after three glasses of white wine on an empty stomach, Antonia's outlook had struck a chord with Lizzy. Restless in her current job, the idea of working in a smaller agency with proper client contact had really appealed to Lizzy. Antonia obviously had a real vision of where she wanted Haven PR to go.

It wasn't until Lizzy actually started her new job that she had realized Antonia was expecting *her* to make that vision come true.

Lizzy's official job title was account manager, but she also found herself dealing with the finance, budgets and staff contracts because the account director, whose job it was to oversee those things, had been signed off with long-term stress. Posh people, Lizzy had realized, treated work as something they went to when they felt like it, which wasn't very often. Having apparently witnessed the dawn of time in India, Antonia now put all her faith in the universe. 'Don't blow a gasket,' she'd trill when she'd only been in for half a day that week and Lizzy was about to spontaneously combust trying to hold everything together. 'The planets will give you all the answers.'

Despite the chaotic way Haven PR was run and the fact that she hadn't had an appraisal in eighteen months, Lizzy couldn't see herself doing any other job. She'd gone into PR because she believed in people's dreams. There was nothing better than seeing something come to fruition after months of blood, sweat and the odd tear. PR could be unpredictable and frustrating, but Lizzy loved the challenge.

Unfortunately, as time went on and Lizzy seemed to be running Haven almost single-handedly, it was becoming more, not less, of a challenge.

Even one day off had produced a catastrophic build-up in Lizzy's inbox. It was doubtful she'd ever be able to even go to the toilet again.

The leggy beauty on the opposite desk had been on

her blinged-up iPhone for the past twenty minutes. It clearly wasn't a work conversation because Lizzy had just heard her ask someone to get some pills for a party.

'Bianca?'

She waved a pair of neon-yellow nails at Lizzy. 'Be with you in a minute, sweets.'

Bianca was Haven's account executive, and fresh out of a degree at Bristol University. Generously, she managed to fit her job at Haven around her social life and various modelling assignments.

'Seriously, darl, tell her to fuck off. The girl's a skank. You know what Damo said when he took her to Monaco.'

'What did you want, sweets?' she asked Lizzy a full ten minutes later.

'Have you done the mail-out yet?' Sending out a mass email to journalists about new products was an integral part of the job.

'I was just about to.'

'Can you make it a priority please?' Lizzy asked nicely.

Bianca flashed a megawatt smile. 'Coming right up.'

Lizzy watched her assistant pick up her phone and read a new text message. Bianca was so laid-back she was practically dead. She'd barely batted an eyelash over Lizzy's YouTube trauma. Bianca's sister had done a season on *Made in Chelsea* and Bianca her-self had made a brief cameo when she'd thrown a glass of champagne in someone's face on a yacht in Hvar.

'Bianca?'

'Yes, sweets?'

'The mail-out!'

Bianca was saved from certain death by hole-punch

as Lizzy's landline started ringing. As usual the Baxters were punctual to the second for their weekly conference call.

Brian Baxter and his wife Debbie were Lizzy's clients and the brains behind Man Down, a herbal tonic for the ill and exhausted modern male. Or man flu, as it was more commonly known. Thanks to Lizzy's heroic promotion in the trade press, Holland & Barrett had just started stocking the range. Not that the Baxters were about to let Lizzy rest on her laurels.

'Have you seen the new *GQ* today?' Brian didn't bother with pleasantries.

'I've got it right here.'

'Me and Debbie are extremely naffed off to see Man Down hasn't got any coverage again this month.'

'I did say that a four-page interview and photo shoot might be a *little* optimistic.'

'They've interviewed David Cameron before, haven't they?'

'Well, yes,' Lizzy said inadequately. 'Yes, they have.'

'I want to see Man Down up there with all the luxury brands, Lizzy. I want to see it in the next James Bond film being stocked in Bond's frigging toilet bag. You don't see 007 failing to save the world because he's in bed with blocked nasal passages, do you? That's a good line actually, write it down.'

'What's the update with the launch?' A squeaky voice cut in, making Lizzy jump. Brian dominated their conversations so much she sometimes forgot Debbie existed.

'It's all looking good. *Holistic Monthly* and *Well Woman* have confirmed they're coming down, and the *Aylesbury*

Herald have also said they'll hold a double-page spread for us. I'm also speaking to a couple of online sites and sending the products out to our key bloggers.'

The Baxters were bringing out a new product called Santa's Little Helper for Christmas. Lizzy was organizing a soft launch in Aylesbury town centre in August. It had to be that far ahead to meet all the key magazines' lead times.

'Have you looked into the Red Arrows doing a fly-by?'

'In all honesty, Brian, I'm not sure the budget will stretch to that.'

The call concluded a gruelling forty-five minutes later. 'Double-check the Red Arrows won't do a freebie, yeah?' Brian instructed. 'Tell them we'll throw in a year's free supply of Man Down.'

Lizzy hung up and massaged her temples. Managing client expectations could be a nightmare.

It was a beautiful summer's evening as Lizzy left the office. Poppet had texted to say she was going out for work drinks in Soho. Did Lizzy want to join them?

She was just considering it when a man walking past did a sharp double take, reminding Lizzy that the spectre of 'Girl Who Gets Jilted . . .' was still alive and present. Not relishing the thought of being gawped at by a pub full of people, she texted Poppet back saying she was going to collapse in front of the TV and watch *Come Dine With Me* on catch-up.

She was struggling through the door with two Sainsbury's bags when her phone went off. Lizzy's heart sank when she saw the caller.

'Hi, Lauren!'

'You've got two minutes. The market's in freefall and my bids are getting hit faster than a red-headed stepchild.'

At twenty-four, Lauren was the youngest of the Spellman children. As a child she had reached Grade 8 at piano and represented her county in sport at everything. These days she was a trader for a bank in New York and got up at 4.30 a.m. every morning to go to boot camp before work. Everyone in the family was terrified of Lauren, although Lizzy's mum pretended she wasn't.

Aside from the fact they were sisters, Lizzy had nothing in common with Lauren. Lauren was ruthlessly single-minded and had no sense of humour – apart from being the only person Lizzy knew who actually laughed at *Tom and Jerry*. Mrs Spellman always said she'd known her work was cut out when she'd gone into Lauren's bedroom when Lauren was two, and had found her youngest daughter changing her own nappy.

Lauren wasn't a bad person; she just had zero empathy skills. Privately Lizzy had always wondered if her sister might have a mild touch of Asperger's, which was probably why she'd ended up doing so well in the City where they dealt with numbers and not humans.

'Holding up?' she barked. Lauren talked in short staccato sentences. Time was money on the trading floor, she would tell her family. People needed an answer there and then.

'Um, I'm fine. I mean it's been pretty hellish, but . . .'

'So you're OK?'

'Yeah,' Lizzy said. 'I guess I'm OK.'

'You need a life plan,' her younger sister told her. 'Have you looked at those pension options I sent you?'

'I am going to get round to it,' Lizzy said lamely. 'It's just been really busy at work.'

'Oh. My. God. You're a financial time bomb and one day it's all going to explode in your face. *And* I bet you're still getting pissed every night with Nic and Poppet.'

'I am not.' Lizzy looked guiltily at the bottle of Chenin Blanc she'd just bought from the supermarket.

'Most of your Facebook updates are about going on hungover McDonalds runs.' Lauren broke off to shout at someone in the background. Lizzy heard the word 'Asia' and what sounded like 'Nike'.

Her sister came back on the phone. 'You know what your problem is, Lizzy?'

'I've got a feeling you're about to tell me.'

'You've never grown up. You've never matured from your fifteen-year-old self. You need to stop getting drunk and start saving.'

'You try living in London.'

'Don't give me that. You're happy to fail at life, but you need to start *trying* at life. You could begin by giving up sugar. You'd see instant results: men, work, your weight; everything. Look, I've got to go. Glad you're feeling better. Bye.'

Chapter 6

It had been two weeks since 'Girl Who Gets Jilted . . .' had gone viral. Since then there had been a new political scandal, a BBC news presenter had been snapped topless on holiday showcasing a surprisingly large pair of whoppers, and an oil spill off the Gulf Coast had caused the *Daily Mail* to go into meltdown about the country running out of petrol, just stopping short of telling their readers to start stockpiling tinned food. Lizzy was no longer being asked for her autograph on the bus, and her Twitter follower count had dipped back into treble figures. Lizzy was now officially old news. 'Your fifteen minutes of fame are over, my friend,' Nic told her. 'Now you know how *X Factor* contestants must feel.'

The only downside to being back in anonymity was that journalists were ignoring her calls again. Lizzy was leaving another voicemail about Night Night Baby when Antonia burst through the door with a White Company bag clamped under one meaty arm.

'Darling, don't think that for a moment! You are a

wonderful talent!' She went into the meeting room and shut the door.

Lizzy knew who her boss was on the phone to. Jocasta Reynolds-Johnson was Haven biggest client. Zen Ten, her organic skincare range, was stocked in Waitrose and other outlets across the UK. Jocasta ran her business out of an industrial park in the Cotswolds and actually wasn't very Zen at all. She was always ringing up on the edge of a meltdown shouting about how stressed she was. Most of Antonia's time was taken up placating Jocasta and trying to keep her from going to another agency.

Antonia emerged fifteen minutes later. 'Jocasta's about to blow a gasket.'

'What's happened?' Lizzy asked.

'Some distribution cock-up. I think I calmed her down. Fuck! We simply *cannot* afford to lose Zen Ten.' She wiped her forehead. 'Speaking of which, I've just taken on a new client. One of my dearest friends Tils has come up with the most inspired idea ever. It's going to totally revolutionize the market.'

'Oh?' Lizzy didn't like the gleam in her boss's eye.

Antonia reached into the White Company bag and pulled out something that looked like a headband with two antennae attached to it. 'Meet your new project! This little beauty is called a Happy Halo.'

'Are they deelyboppers?' Lizzy said confusedly.

'Dear girl, they are so much more than that! Come on, we're meeting Tils at Highroad House in half an hour.'

*

Highroad House was a members' club in nearby leafy Chiswick that Antonia practically lived at. 'Tils' turned out to be a nervy blonde perched on an oversized sofa surrounded by boxes of the aforementioned Happy Halos. She launched straight in to explaining the concept to Lizzy.

'So I got the idea from this *amazing* shaman I met on a retreat in Mexico.'

Her eyes gleamed fanatically. Lizzy started to get a horrible sinking feeling.

'Each antenna has a crystal inside. When it wobbles, it sends vibrations from the crystal through the body to rebalance your chakras and unblock stuck energies. It's also *rilly* good for healing unhappy auras.'

'Look how black Lizzy's aura is,' Antonia said. 'It's all the alcohol she drinks.'

'Then this is exactly what you need!' Tilly cried. 'Here, try one with the pink crystals.'

Lizzy put a Happy Halo on, painfully aware that there was a table of rather attractive silver foxes having a lunch meeting next to them. The cheap plastic headband dug into her head.

'The healing element sounds great,' she said carefully, 'but I don't really understand. Why deelyboppers?'

'To move the energy around, dumbo!' Antonia roared.

'And everyone loves a deelybopper, don't they?' Tilly said. 'You can heal yourself *and* have fun at the same time!' She pushed a piece of paper across the table to Lizzy. 'Each one comes with a certificate of authentication to show Shaman Ron has personally blessed each crystal.'

Lizzy stared at Shaman Ron, who looked like a tanorexic Father Christmas. No wonder he was so happy; he was probably laughing all the way to the bank.

'How many did you buy?' she asked.

'The initial order is twenty thousand.' Tilly peered hopefully at Lizzy. 'Do you think *Vogue* will do something on it?'

On the way out Antonia turned to Lizzy. 'Between you and I, this is like, a favour, yah? Tils had a *rilly* hard time after her shit of a husband left her for his life coach and she needs a break, OK?' She grinned nastily. 'I'm relying on you to pull this off, Lizzy.'

Chapter 7

Lizzy had written hundreds of press releases in her time. Revolutionary new cement powders, fluorescent birdseed, a natural Viagra. There had even been a brief stint looking after the British Tomato Growers' Association. Whatever had come her way, Lizzy had always taken pride in thinking up inventive ways to pitch to a suspicious and often openly hostile media. Seven years into her career she feared she'd found the product that had finally defeated her.

She'd been writing the Happy Halo press release for two days now. No matter what spin she put on it, it still sounded like a crock of outlandish shit.

'It's PR, not ER!' Antonia told her. 'Just sprinkle some of your magic on it!'

The only magic Lizzy needed was a vanishing act. She was going to be the laughing stock of the PR world. That was if 'Girl Who Gets Jilted . . .' hadn't made her enough of one already.

'Have you put it out yet?' Antonia bellowed across the office.

'I'm just about to.' Closing her eyes, Lizzy pressed 'send'. Too late for any more changes: it was now winging its way into the inboxes of some of the most influential journalists in the industry.

She went to the loo and had a gloomy wee. They should have told bloody 'Tils' the Happy Halo was a dud from the start.

When she got back to her desk there were the standard out-of-office responses, plus an email from someone called Elliot Anderson. Lizzy wasn't familiar with the name; he must have been added to her media list. With a tentative feeling of hope she opened it.

To: Lizzy Spellman
From: Elliot Anderson
Subject: RE: All Hail The Happy Halo!

Dear Lizzy,
You may spend your life peddling meaningless drivel but some of us have real jobs to be getting on with. Why don't you try and get one yourself, instead of conning innocent people into buying this crap?
Best wishes (not),
Elliot

It struck exactly where intended. Lizzy was tired, worn-down and humiliated. She didn't need some pompous idiot telling her that her life was shit!

From: Lizzy Spellman

To: Elliot Anderson

Subject: RE:RE: All Hail The Happy Halo!

Dear Elliot,

It sounds like you're in dire need of a Happy Halo! Please let me know if you'd like me to send over any images or samples.

Best Wishes (and cheer up),

Lizzy

She sat back and pressed 'send'. The euphoria lasted all of a second. 'Shit,' Lizzy muttered. Rule number one of PR: never fire off a sarky reply to a journalist, even if they are an obnoxious git!

'Any response yet?' Antonia boomed.

'Um, a few tentative enquiries!' Lizzy consoled herself with the thought that at least she'd never heard of this Elliot Anderson. With any luck he'd be a complete nobody.

'*The* Elliot Anderson?' Poppet gasped. 'As in Elliot Anderson off the news? Gorgeous Elliot Anderson, who's engaged to the fashion designer Amber de la Haye?'

'Don't tell me that!' Lizzy wailed. 'I'd convinced myself he worked for *Salmon and Trout Weekly*!'

Poppet pulled her iPhone out of her bag. They'd met at a cheap and cheerful bistro for a quick bite after work. She got Elliot's Wikipedia page up and showed Lizzy. 'I can't believe you haven't heard of him!'

'I've got BuzzFeed! Why would I need to watch the news?'

Poppet began reading. '"Elliot Nathaniel Anderson (born 4 February 1981) is editor at large at the *Financial Times* and economics correspondent on the ITV *News at Ten*."' She gave Lizzy a significant look. '"Anderson's presenter career started by chance when ITV's *News at Ten* economics editor – due to break a world exclusive – was taken ill just before broadcast. Anderson, who happened to be in the ITV building for another interview, stepped in and proved a natural in front of the camera." Ooh, look! And his dad was a lord!'

She showed Lizzy a picture. Elliot Anderson had thick, dark-red hair and was about thirty years younger than Lizzy had envisaged.

'He was number three on *heat*'s "Hottest Gingers" last year, behind Eddie Redmayne and Prince Harry. There's even a Facebook page set up for his right eyebrow, it does this sexy arch thing when he has an especially serious point to make.' Poppet giggled coquettishly. 'I'm a member actually.'

Lizzy put her head into her hands. 'If Antonia finds out about this I'm done for. She's got about three Amber de la Hayes handbags.'

Amber's own-name fashion label was much in demand. Celebrities fought over her to dress them for the red carpet and the last collection at Selfridges had sold out within hours. She was a big animal-rights campaigner, and her use of ethically sourced materials made her a favourite of PETA and the fashion pack.

Poppet was poring over a photo of the couple. 'That's them at the BAFTAs this year. Don't they look beautiful together? You can tell they're made for each other.'

Lizzy made herself look. Amber de la Haye was smiling radiantly at the camera, stunningly elegant in a simple black gown. Lizzy gazed into the stony face of Elliot Anderson and thought he looked like a complete arse.

Chapter 8

It was Saturday. Poppet was at her niece's birthday party and Nic had gone up north to see her mum. Everyone else Lizzy knew seemed to be either doing couple stuff or training for half marathons. There were a million things she could be getting on with on her 'To Do' List, like looking at her pension options and cleaning the manky salad drawer in the fridge, but instead she called home.

Her dad answered. 'Hullo, Lizard!'

'Hi, Dad. I was thinking I might come home for the night.'

'Excellent, we're having a barbecue and your brother's coming with Hayley.'

'Why didn't you ask me?' Lizzy felt a bit hurt.

'We just assumed you'd be out gallivanting with your glamorous London chums! It's splendid you're coming. We're starting at two p.m. sharp, you know what your mother's like.' Her dad lowered his voice. 'You'd better pick up another bottle of wine on your way over, Jacqui and David are coming.'

Lizzy's parents had lived in the same semi-detached thirties villa in Bromley all Lizzy's life. Despite the fact that Bromley was the biggest borough in London and had rail links to the city in under seventeen minutes, Lizzy's mum regarded the capital as a dangerous, unscrupulous place that operated in an entirely different solar system.

'That's London for you!' she would cry, whenever there was anything on the news, from rising house prices to knife crime to global warming and fox attacks. Lizzy had been frequently warned over the years that she was getting 'London ways'.

It was gone one o'clock by the time Lizzy staggered up the front drive with bags of shopping. Her mother had called as she'd got off the train and asked her to pop into Tesco for a 'few things', which had included four large bottles of sparkling water and a multi-pack of kitchen roll.

Her hands had frozen into claws, so Lizzy banged her head on the glass until her dad answered.

'Hello, Lizard! Have you forgotten your key again? Let me take those for you.'

Everyone was already in the back garden: her mother, the next-door neighbours David and Jacqui, and Lizzy's older brother Robbie and his girlfriend, Hayley.

'Uh-oh, here comes Bridget,' David announced. Everyone fell about laughing.

'I'll think you'll find Bridget Jones is an outdated concept,' Lizzy said with as much dignity as she could muster. 'These days it's perfectly acceptable to be a singleton.'

Robbie got up and high-fived her. 'DJ Lizard in da house!'

'MC Robster on da decks!'

They took on suitable gangster poses as they fell into a rap. 'Hey! Yo! Bromley bluds! We ain't no pussies and our name ain't muds! So look out when Lizard and the Robster are in town. Cos everybody is gonna get down!'

Jacqui looked impressed. 'I really like it. Is it Kanye's new one?'

'It's just this silly song Robbie and Lizzy used to do when they were younger,' Hayley said, sounding annoyed. She stood up and physically wedged herself between them. 'How are you?' she asked Lizzy. 'I was *so* embarrassed for you. *Everyone* we know has seen the video.'

Robbie gave his sister a wink. 'I don't think it was *everyone* we know.'

Mr Spellman appeared with a tray. 'Long Island Iced Tea, anyone?'

They sat down with their drinks and Hayley gave Lizzy a pitying smile. 'We all thought Justin was a keeper,' she said in the same faux-concerned tone. 'You must be *gutted.*'

Lizzy gritted her teeth into a smile. Hayley-bloody-Bidwell. Even though she'd been two years below Lizzy at school, Hayley treated her as if she were some sad sack of a soul who still hadn't figured out what it was all about. In the winner's corner: Hayley and her relationship with Robbie. In the loser's corner: Lizzy and the pitiful ongoing saga that was her love life.

It wasn't the fact that Hayley had been in the annoying

gang at school, or that all the boys had fancied her. It wasn't even the conflicting emotions Lizzy experienced on the rare occasions she saw her brother these days: the initial happiness, swiftly followed by the mild dismay that Hayley-bloody-Bidwell was always with him. It was the fact that now, as Lizzy looked at Hayley with her perfect hair and perfect skinny jeans with her perfect ballet pumps, she realized Hayley was one of those girls Nic had been talking about. The type that would get someone like Justin. And that made Lizzy feel really *sad* because her brother wasn't like Justin. Robbie had always been smart and funny and cool and different. In fifth form his classmates had voted him 'Person most likely to be in a famous band'. How the hell had he ended up living in a new-build outside Tunbridge Wells with Hayley-bloody-Bidwell?

Nic said Hayley's appeal was that she had nice tits and because blokes never got over wanting that trophy of having the hot girl from school. Lizzy thought it was because her brother was laid-back to the point of being pathologically lazy, and when Hayley had come along and got her French manicure into him, Robbie had just gone along with it for an easy life. But she had to admit Nic was right on one point: Hayley *did* look good in a vest top.

Now they'll get married and because Hayley is younger than me – something she never tires of pointing out – and because she doesn't like the taste of alcohol, she'll outlive me by decades and tragic Great Aunt Lizzy will gradually be erased from the Spellman family history. On my deathbed Hayley-bloody-Bidwell's face will be the last face I see.

'Why are you staring at my breasts, Lizzy?'

Lizzy snapped out of her daydream. The whole table was looking at her.

'I was, er, just admiring your top. Mango, isn't it?'

'No, Zara.' Hayley shot Robbie a look. *Great*, Lizzy thought. Not only was she a washed-up spinster, she was now a washed-up depraved lesbian spinster who was liable to attack Hayley at any moment.

Her mother came out of the house with a tray of nibbles. 'Picky bits!'

'P-p-p-picky bits!' Lizzy and Robbie chorused, earning another look of disapproval from Hayley.

Mrs Spellman's 'picky bits' were an institution in the family. They covered an astonishing array of culinary accomplishments, from crisps and dips to cakes and canapés, to leftovers, and things in the freezer that needed using up. Lizzy and her siblings had often been sent to school with packed-lunch combinations like cold broccoli and trifle. 'Your father and I are just having some picky bits for dinner tonight,' her mother would say when Lizzy phoned home during the week.

'How's work going?' David asked.

Lizzy swallowed the last of her Thai fishcake. 'Busy. We've just taken on a new account.'

'Lizzy is practically running the place,' her mother announced. 'With any luck she'll be able to retire on her pension in ten years!'

'Are you all right?' her dad asked, as Lizzy started coughing violently. 'Oh crumbs, I think the sausages are on fire!'

By the time the sun had reached the furthest corner of the patio everybody apart from Lizzy's mum and

Hayley was drunk. Jacqui had fallen off her chair twice. David had just spent half an hour regaling them with tales of when he used to work in the music industry.

'Top you up, Lizard?'

'Go on then. Thanks, Dad.'

There were worse ways of spending a Saturday afternoon than in the sun being stuffed full of food and booze. Lizzy gazed fondly at her parents. They were pretty awesome. Why didn't they all hang out more often?

Mr Spellman continued round the table with the bottle. 'More wine, Hayley?'

She put her hand over the top of her glass. 'No thank you. I've had enough.'

'Very sensible.' Jacqui sighed. 'I suppose that's how you keep your figure.'

Lizzy was suddenly feeling very light-headed. That was the problem with white wine. You could chuck it back until the cows came home and then you hit The Wall.

'I just don't think it's very attractive to see a drunk woman. Men don't really like it.' Hayley gave Lizzy a patronizing smile. 'Maybe that's why you have problems settling down.'

'Or maybe the problem is with the blokes Lizzy meets,' Robbie said nicely.

Hayley gave him a warning look. 'You know, it might be a good idea for you to go and see some sort of counsellor,' she told Lizzy. 'My friend Sam went to see this woman after she kept getting dumped by blokes. She's been with her new one nine months now!' She shrugged daintily. 'Anyway, it's something to think about.'

Until now Lizzy had always managed to rise above Hayley's jibes. But she had enough alcohol sloshing round inside her to sink a battleship, and she was fed up with people declaring open season on her love life.

'Let me give *you* something to think about,' she said, vaguely aware of a voice of reason frantically jumping up and down telling her to SHUT UP NOW! 'You know I think you're a great girl, Hayley. I'm really happy you're going out with my brother. I really am. I am, Mum! Don't look at me like that!'

In Lizzy's bleary drunken state Hayley's features seemed to be melting into a giant puddle of MAC make-up. 'The problem here, Hayley,' she continued, 'is that you've always been defined by a man. And you can be so much more! You don't need a man to be fulfilled in life! Amelia Earhart didn't need a *man* to fly solo round the world! Florence Nightingale didn't defer to a *male* doctor when she was saving thousands of soldiers' lives! You think Sandra Bullock needs a *man* just because things didn't work out with Ryan Reynolds? She didn't hang about waiting for a *man* to get her pregnant, she went straight out and adopted a baby by herself!'

'Hear hear!' Jacqui cheered. 'Bloody men! Shits, the lot of you!'

Hayley was glaring at Lizzy from across the table. 'Because *you're* single and such a big success?'

'Hayley, Hayley, Hayley.' Lizzy groped for her hand and knocked over the salad dressing. 'I'm not trying to upset you. I'm just saying us women need to realize our full potential. You could be anything you wanted! Think about how good you were at netball at school!'

'You're suggesting I become a professional netball player?' Hayley asked sarcastically.

'If that's what makes you happy, then yes! The point I'm trying to *make* is . . .' She lost her train of thought. 'What is my point?'

'You were saying Hayley should retrain as a professional netball player.' David's eyes strayed over Hayley's chest again. 'I think it sounds like an excellent idea.'

'The point I'm trying to make, Hayley, is that you need to get a life.'

'Lizzy,' her dad reprimanded.

'I'm not being horrible! I'm just saying what's in my heart because I want the best for Hayley. And because . . .' Lizzy slurred, holding her glass aloft, 'I am a modern *feminist*.'

The next morning Lizzy walked into an Arctic chill in the kitchen.

'I was wondering when you might surface.' Her mother didn't look up from *You* magazine.

Lizzy shuffled over to the fridge to get the orange juice. It felt like she'd been in a physical fight.

'Um, so what happened after . . .' The evening was a blank past 8 p.m.

'After you passed out under the table? Your father tried to make you go to bed but you refused and threw your shoe over the fence.' Her mum's lips were so pursed they'd practically vanished. 'I said to your father, "She learnt that kind of behaviour in London! We didn't bring our daughter up to crawl round blind drunk on all fours and throw her espadrille into other people's gardens!" In case you're wondering, it's drying in the airing cupboard. David very kindly brought it round this morning, apparently it was in the bottom of their water feature.' She shot her daughter another look.

'I'm really sorry, Mum,' Lizzy said miserably. 'I didn't mean to cause any trouble.'

'Why do you always have to go over the top? Your father is just as bad for encouraging you.' Mrs Spellman got off her bar stool. 'You're having milk thistle for your liver, no two ways about it.'

Lizzy watched her mum reach into the cupboard above the kettle. 'Does Hayley hate me?'

'I wouldn't imagine she's your biggest fan at the moment.'

'She just got on my nerves. How come she's allowed to say mean things and get away with it? Come on, even you must think she's got Robbie under the thumb!'

'Hayley is your brother's girlfriend and we have to respect that,' her mother said crisply. 'Drink this.'

'Urgh, it tastes gross.'

'You've no sympathy from me. Are you staying for lunch?'

It was a tough choice; getting on public transport with the hangover from hell or facing her mother's wrath. 'I'll stay if that's OK.'

'We're having picky bits from last night and *no* alcohol. I'm not living in a house populated by drunkards.' Mrs Spellman paused by the door on her way out. 'And I'd think about sending Hayley a text to say sorry.'

Lizzy groaned inwardly. She'd thought the Happy Halo press release had been hard to write.

Chapter 9

It was proving impossible to get anyone to take her seriously. Even the trade journalists, who'd seen every wacky product on the market, told Lizzy she was fighting a losing battle with the Happy Halo. The worst phone call of all was to the woman at one of the glossy Sunday magazines.

'Hi?' she said aggressively, as if Lizzy had had the nerve to ring her in the middle of a three-week beach holiday.

'Um hi, it's Lizzy from Haven here. How are you?'

'Fine. What do you want?'

'I sent you a press release this morning, and I was just calling to see if you'd like me to send you any images or samples.'

'I get sent hundreds of press releases every day. What was it about?'

Lizzy swallowed. 'The Happy Halo.'

'The Happy what?'

'The Happy Halo? It's an amazing new product we've just taken on. It *looks* like a pair of really fun deelyboppers, but in fact each "bopper" has a crystal inside that sends out good vibrations through the body. It's brilliant for cleansing dirty auras.'

Silence.

'Each crystal has been personally blessed by this amazing shaman called, er, Shaman Ron,' Lizzy said desperately. 'He's really ahead in his field . . .'

For a horrible moment she thought the journalist had hung up. 'Hello? Can you hear me?'

'Loud and clear.' The woman's voice had sounded muffled. 'And what sort of coverage did you see the Happy Halo getting?'

'Well . . . if you were doing any fashion pieces on the next big thing in headgear . . .'

'Headgear?' the woman wheezed.

'Yes, maybe something about looking good and healing yourself at the same time . . .'

There were loud shrieks of laughter down the line.

'Am I on loudspeaker to your office?' Lizzy asked wearily.

There was another round of hysterical laughter before the phone was finally put down on her.

'No joy with the fashion angle?' Antonia said breezily. 'You'd better think up another way to pitch it then.'

To top off the humiliation, Lizzy was being made to wear a Halo in the office at all times. According to Antonia, it was to really 'live the experience'. So far all Lizzy was experiencing was a constant feeling of motion sickness.

At least there had been no comeback from Elliot Anderson. Lizzy had done some more Google stalking and had felt mildly sick to find out he really was quite important. His family had started the prestigious Beestons private bank, which had its HQ in a huge white building just off the Strand, and was second only to the world-famous Coutts. Elliot had studied economics at Oxford, where he'd got a First and had turned down an expected career in banking to go into journalism. He'd won various plaudits for his reporting and in 2011 had been named as one of the ten most powerful people under thirty in the UK. Not the kind of person you wanted to cross swords with. All Lizzy could do was console herself with the thought he was probably far too busy and important to bother with lowly PRs like her. Hopefully by now he would have forgotten all about her email.

On Thursday night she went to meet her friends at a new cocktail club in Soho. Nic and Poppet were already sitting at a table, surrounded by a sea of Mojitos.

Poppet was moaning about the son of a family friend, who'd 'conveniently' turned up at her niece's birthday party.

'What was he like?' Nic asked, handing Lizzy a drink.

'He had the hands of a small child and kept quoting science facts from Professor Brian Cox.' Poppet shuddered. 'And he had a handkerchief.'

Lizzy tucked her iPod headphones away in her handbag. 'What's wrong with having a handkerchief?'

'It's totally gross,' Nic said. 'If you want to have any chance of being intimately sexual with someone, why would you empty the contents of your nose in front of them, and then keep it in your pocket? People don't want to be reminded of other people's orifices! I wouldn't pick my knickers out of my arse in front of someone I fancied. It would be like holding a ringing bell over my head and saying: "Look! Look at my ginormous hungry bottom! Now imagine me taking a dump!"'

'Eww,' Lizzy said. 'I see what you mean.'

'All my parents want me to do is marry a nice Indian boy,' Poppet sighed. 'And all I want to do is marry Matt Damon.'

Nic pulled a face. 'Even after *Behind the Candelabra*?'

Poppet's obsession with Matt Damon made even One Direction fans look a bit fair-weather. She had every DVD he'd ever starred in and was probably the only person in the universe aside from Matt Damon's mum who thought *We Bought a Zoo* would be an enduring classic. Then there was the famous time she'd booked herself on a mini break to Edinburgh after reading somewhere it was the actor's favourite city in the UK. Unsurprisingly she hadn't had a random romantic encounter with Matt Damon in the street, and had spent the rest of the trip in her hotel room consoling herself with the complimentary shortbread.

Lizzy looked down at the plethora of cocktails in front of her. 'Why have we got so many drinks?'

'Happy Hour ends soon.' Nic did a huge yawn. 'And I can't be arsed with going back to the bar.'

While Poppet reapplied her lip-gloss Lizzy told them all about the barbecue of shame at her parents' and her run-in with Hayley. 'Twat,' was all Nic said afterwards.

Poppet zipped her make-up bag back up. 'How are Robbie and Hayley these days?'

'Fine, unfortunately,' Lizzy sighed. 'I think I can safely say she's got Robbie firmly by the balls.' She paused. 'Not that I want to think about my brother's testicles.'

'Pops and I were having a discussion before you got here,' Nic announced. 'We think it's time for you to get back in the game.'

'Not *on* the game,' Poppet snickered.

'I think I'll have to pay someone to sleep with *me*. Did you read some of the *MailOnline* comments? "Lizzy Spellman – Bridezilla in waiting!" Or how about: "She looks like she smells of ham"?'

'Stop thinking like a victim,' Nic told her. 'You need to capitalize on your situation. I bet you'd get loads of hot men giving you sympathy sex.'

'So from now on all I get is sex with guys who feel sorry for me?'

Nic ignored her. 'You need to move on from Justin's penis. As long as he's the last person you've had sex with, the penis thread will always be there.'

The penis thread was one of Nic's many theories about relationships. It didn't matter how much you thought you were over a man, or even if you were the one who'd done the dumping: until you slept with someone else there would always be that invisible link between you and your ex. The first rule of a break up: the penis thread had to be severed as quickly as possible, even if you didn't fancy the bloke you had sex with. 'Otherwise it will always be there, lurking there in the background,' Nic would say in a sinister tone, 'tying you together and stopping you from moving on.'

'How about Internet dating again?' Poppet suggested. 'You got a good response last time.'

'Yeah, from 67-year-old pensioners on mobility scooters!'

'Why don't you and Lizzy both sign up?' Nic picked a mint leaf out of her drink. 'I hate to break it to you, Pops, but Jason Bourne isn't going to come swinging through those doors for you any time soon.'

'I'm not sure Internet dating is for me. It's all so contrived and unromantic.' Poppet gazed out wistfully into the street. 'Why can't people meet how they used to, and leave it to fate?'

'People haven't got time to wait for fate these days, and online dating immediately sorts out the wheat from the chaff. If you get a dud you can tell him to jog on at the click of the button.'

'I just want to meet someone the old-fashioned way, like they do in films. Come on, Nic! Don't you dream about meeting "The One" in the pouring rain at a bus stop?'

Nic looked horrified. 'I wouldn't date a man who used *public transport*.'

While Poppet would happily live in a cardboard box under London Bridge if it meant being with her One True Love, Nic had a very different view of men. In her eyes they were there on a purely functional basis: i.e. procreation, syncing new iPhones, and someone to take things to the tip. She got everything else she needed from her work and her friends.

Poppet wanted a whole football team of kids, or as she put it, 'a netball team of daughters'. Lizzy thought she might have one, but the having-children-thing freaked her out a bit, and knowing her luck, she'd probably fall pregnant first time round with sextuplets.

Nic didn't want a family. She adhered to the mantra of her heroine, the TV historian Dr Lucy Worsley, who had once famously said that she'd been 'educated out of normal reproductive function'. Nic said it wasn't exactly the same, in that Lucy Worsley was uber-posh and Nic had gone to the second roughest school in Nottingham, but the sentiment was there. Having kids simply wasn't part of her plan.

Nic's plan was actually very simple: concentrate on her career until forty, when she would join one of those dating agencies where people had to earn over six figures, and become one half of a significant new power couple. Until then she was happy to satisfy her sexual urges by occasionally shagging one of the green bibs from her British Military Fitness class because – she was fond of saying – at least she knew they had good stamina.

It was Lizzy's turn to go to the bar. The HMQ was quite high tonight, she reflected as she waited to get served, at least a seven out of ten. In the aftermath of 'Girl Who Gets Jilted . . .' Lizzy hadn't even allowed herself to harbour any thoughts about the opposite sex, but there was a very cute guy next to her at the bar, wearing a T-shirt that showed off his nice arms. Rather encouragingly, he was actually smiling at her.

'Hello,' he said. 'Having a good night?'

'Yes thanks,' she smiled back. 'How about you?'

'Pretty good. Who are you here with?'

Lizzy waved vaguely. 'Just some mates.'

They continued to make a bit of small talk. *This is what flirting feels like*, Lizzy thought joyously. Nice Arms picked up his drinks and gave her a wink. 'I'd love to stand here chatting but I'd better get back to my girl-friend. Have a good night with your friends.'

It might have been a non-starter but Lizzy returned to the table feeling considerably brighter. Maybe she wasn't a complete write-off after all.

Nic had her iPad out on the table. 'Let's get you signed up for some Internet dating. If *that* doesn't work then we'll just put you on a swingers' site.'

They started running through the options.

'*Guardian* Soulmates?' Poppet suggested.

'A bit pretentious,' Lizzy said. 'They always ride fixed-gear bikes and read books by people I've never heard of.'

'My Single Friend?'

'What century are you in, Pops?' Nic said incredu-lously. 'No one uses that any more.'

'OK then, Plenty of Fish?'

'Married men and perverts.' Nic didn't elaborate on how she'd arrived at this theory. 'Tinder's good if you want fast, meaningless sex.'

'Tinder is just one massive selfie-off,' Lizzy said. 'Everyone's showing off their six-packs and that's just the girls.'

Nic picked up her phone. 'Oh God, what does Simon want *now*?'

Simon Hargreaves was Nic's demanding boss, who she spent half her life on the phone to. 'I'll have to take this. Carry on without me.'

'How about Muddy Matches?' Poppet suggested after Nic had gone outside. 'You might meet a lonely earl and go and live in his castle!'

She broke off. A dreamy look had come over her face. Lizzy turned round to see a couple at the next table kissing, locked away in their own private world. The man was cradling the woman's face in his hands.

'That is so hot,' Poppet sighed. She was obsessed with men holding women's faces in their hands when they kissed them after Matt Damon had done it with his love interest in *The Bourne Identity*.

Lizzy gave her a nudge. 'We can't sit round watching people kissing! We look like a pair of freaks!'

'Why do you have to turn a beautiful thing into something sordid? We watch people kiss in films and perfume adverts, don't we?'

Nic returned five minutes later in an ebullient mood. 'How are we doing?'

'We've got it down to two sites.'

'Great! Now all you have to do is write your profile.' She handed Lizzy the iPad.

'I have no idea what to put.'

'Big yourself up, baby!'

'I can't, I'm English.'

Poppet had a suggestion. 'Why don't you pretend you're writing a press release? Think of yourself as this amazing product that has just come on to the market and you have to convince *everyone* to try you out.'

Lizzy stared at the screen. 'Everything I think of makes me sound like a twat.'

'How about fun-loving and bubbly?'

Nic shook her head. 'Blokes read that as "fucking annoying and needy".'

'How about sociable?' Lizzy said. 'You can't go wrong with that.'

'You may as well write: "Thinks vodka for breakfast is taking it easy."'

'You write it then, Nicola! Actually, scrap that, you'll probably end up attracting me the next Josef Fritzl.'

Poppet went and bought another round of drinks to try and release Lizzy's writer's block. After fifteen minutes of writing and deleting, she decided to go for a list approach and keep it short and sweet.

Blonde hair, green eyes, penchant for the absurd. I like dark rum, Italian food, crime fiction, London, boisterous dogs that charge through people's picnics and good conversation. Lover of popular culture. Dangerous on a Boris Bike. Would like to meet a funny, easy-going chap, who knows his 'their' from his 'they're'. If you are proficient in large moth removal, this is also valued highly.

'Perfect,' Poppet said. 'Funny, but not too funny, remember men like being the funny ones. And you got the helpless damsel in distress bit in at the end.'

They chose a picture of Lizzy in the park from the previous summer, where Poppet said Lizzy's eyes looked nice, and in which Nic said she was showing off 'just the right amount of tit', and put it up. Afterwards Lizzy's brain hurt as if she'd just sat a major exam.

'Uh-oh, look,' Nic said. 'The Eyes are out.'

Across the table Poppet had taken on that euphoric drunken glaze that only meant one thing. 'Let's do shots!'

'It's a school night!' Lizzy protested.

'It's Friday tomorrow. Go on, live a little!'

Nic shrugged, as though it was a necessary evil she

had to go through. 'OK,' Lizzy sighed. 'But I'm only doing one. And no flaming sambucas!' She looked at her watch. 'I need to be home by midnight. I've got a busy day tomorrow.'

Chapter 10

Lizzy was woken up by the *beep beep* of a lorry reversing outside. Her whole body hurt, and it took a few moments to realize that instead of being tucked up in her pajamas in a warm bed, she was face-down on the sofa in her living room, still in her clothes.

She turned over and was hit by a wave of nausea. What had *happened* last night? She had very few recollections after leaving the cocktail club, except for ordering Jägerbombs in another bar, and Nic getting into an argument with a blue-haired transvestite about Whitney Houston . . .

Her mobile went off. It was probably Antonia wondering where the hell she was. Lizzy located her phone under the armchair. There was a sticky red smear on the screen that looked suspiciously like ketchup.

'Hello?' she croaked.

'Oh my God!' Poppet wailed. 'I've lost my bra!'

Lizzy sat up and winced. 'What?'

'I woke up this morning with my dress on but no

bra! Oh my God! I can't remember anything! What if someone took advantage of me in my drunken state?'

'Have you still got your knickers on?' Lizzy asked.

'Well, yes, but . . .'

'Do you *think* something might have happened?'

'I don't know, I can't remember!' Poppet gave a despairing moan. 'Oh God, what if I had sex I don't even remember and now I'm pregnant?'

'Pops, I'm sure no one took advantage of you and made you pregnant.' Lizzy felt the saliva rush into her mouth. 'I've got to go and be sick. Keep me posted on the bra.'

That morning was the longest of Lizzy's life. She had the kind of rancid hangover that hits you at a cellular level and makes you feel like your skin is about to peel off your face and your teeth are going to fall out. The one saving grace was that Antonia had phoned to say her daughter Christiana was sick and that she wouldn't be coming in. By 11 a.m. Lizzy had drained two litres of water and was sitting at her desk quietly wishing to die. Nic had been on an 8 a.m. flight out of Heathrow to New York. She'd sent Lizzy a picture of the massive fry-up she'd had for breakfast in the BA first-class lounge, which had nearly made Lizzy want to throw up again. The woman was a machine. How did she do it?

Just before lunch Lizzy went to have a hangover cry in the toilet and emerged feeling slightly better. When she got back to her desk there was an email from Poppet.

Found bra!!!!! It was in the side pocket of my bag. It's all coming back to me now, I took it off in the toilet because the underwiring was digging into my boob. PHEWZERS!! I'M NOT PREGNANT!!! Xx ☺ ☺ ☺

Lizzy wrote back:

I'm thrilled that you aren't carrying some random stranger's baby. Now can this day be over please?

Six o'clock couldn't come round quick enough. Lizzy slept the entire bus journey home and nearly missed her stop. She stopped off at her local Tesco Express: tomato soup was about the only thing she could face for dinner.

'Your card's been declined,' the man on the checkout said.

'I don't know why that is,' Lizzy said. 'Can you try again?'

The same thing happened. Lizzy paid for her shopping with her Visa card and left the shop with a very bad feeling. The ATM outside wouldn't let her withdraw cash either, so she immediately called up her bank. 'You're eight hundred pounds over your overdraft limit, Miss Spellman,' the woman told her.

Lizzy went cold. 'There has to be some mistake.'

'Let me just check . . . There was a cash withdrawal of five hundred pounds at 2.03 a.m. this morning.'

'Five . . . *hundred*?' Lizzy croaked.

'Were you out last night, Miss Spellman?'

'Yes, but . . . Oh my God! I must have only meant to draw out fifty pounds!'

'And you don't know where the money is now, Miss Spellman?' the bank woman asked.

Lizzy started to frantically search her bag in the middle of the street. All she found was a twenty-pence piece and one of those green charity tokens from Waitrose.

'It must be here somewhere . . .'

'Miss Spellman, I'm sure you're aware there's a twenty-five pound charge for every day you go over your overdraft limit?'

'Can't you move some money round from my other accounts?' Lizzy asked desperately.

'Let's have a quick look.' There was a short pause. 'You haven't got any money in your other accounts, Miss Spellman, and I see you've also reached the limit on your Visa card. Was there anything else I can help you with today?'

A frantic search at home didn't produce the missing money either. Lizzy sat down on the sofa and wanted to cry. Either someone had mugged her in Soho last night, or there was a cabbie driving round London right now with a very big smile on their face.

Even worse, she didn't get paid for another week, by which time her bank charges would probably have amounted to more than her pay packet. She groaned softly. This is what her parents had meant when they'd always banged on about saving for emergencies. She tried Nic's phone, but it went straight to voicemail. Poppet wasn't answering her phone either, and she'd just been moaning the other day how skint she was. Lizzy wanted to cry again. She was never, ever drinking again.

There was only one option left. Lizzy would have rather crawled on her hands and knees over hot coals than ask this person for money, but right now she didn't have much choice.

She dialled her sister's number. After what seemed like three terminally long rings, Lauren picked up. 'Can't talk, I'm at work.'

'I won't keep you. Er, can I borrow some money off you until next week?'

'How much?'

Lizzy swallowed. 'Five hundred pounds.'

'That's a lot. What do you need it for?'

'Um, I can't really tell you.' Lauren was incapable of keeping a secret. Before Lizzy knew it their mother would be on the phone giving her what for.

Lauren sighed heavily. 'Do you need money to go on holiday with Nic and Poppet again?'

'I only borrowed money for the flight to Costa Rica because Antonia was late paying my wages!' Lizzy took a deep breath. 'Trust me, it's not a high point in my life having to ask my little sister to bail me out.'

Lauren was silent for a moment. 'This is like the scene in *Dirty Dancing* where Baby borrows money off her dad to pay for Penny's abortion, isn't it?'

'I'm not having an abortion! You have to have sex to get pregnant for a start. I promise you, it's nothing like that.'

'You know *Dirty Dancing* is my favourite film,' Lauren said eventually.

'Yes, yes I do.' Lizzy picked a bit of dried ketchup off the arm of the sofa. How had it got there?

'You and I always used to watch it together,' Lauren told her. 'Do you remember when we recreated the lift scene in the paddling pool and I almost broke your arm when I fell on to you?'

'It's one of my favourite memories of us together,' Lizzy said dutifully.

'OK. I'll transfer the money over in the next hour. But if it does turn out to be for something dodgy you better tell Mum and Dad that I had nothing to do with it.'

Chapter 11

Lizzy walked down the long row of Victorian terraces and turned in at number 74. She rang the bell and heard it chime down the hallway. A few moments later the front door opened.

'Lizzy!' Karen Jones gave Lizzy a big hug. 'Good timing, I've just put the kettle on.'

Karen was Lizzy's favourite client. The single mum from Barnet was the founder of Night Night Baby, a range of bedtime products for children.

'Sorry about the mess,' Karen apologized as she led Lizzy down the cramped hallway. There were toys and boxes everywhere. Since she couldn't afford office overheads Karen was running her fledgling empire from her dining-room table.

They went into the kitchen, where there were more piles of paperwork covering every surface. Karen pushed a disgruntled tabby cat off the counter. 'Shoo, Trevor.'

Lizzy sat down at the table while Karen put the

kettle on and produced a plate of delicious chocolate brownies.

'I've got wine if you fancy it?' she asked. 'There's a bottle of white in the fridge.'

'I'm fine on tea.' Lizzy was still feeling slightly bilious from the Night of Carnage.

Karen sank gratefully into the chair opposite. 'When you work from home people always think you sit on your arse watching Jeremy Kyle all day.' She laughed. 'If only they knew!'

The inspiration for Night Night Baby had come from Karen's daughter, Molly, who had been a very bad sleeper when she was a baby. After ten straight nights of no sleep, Karen had been at her wits' end. Remembering an article she'd read about natural soothing remedies, she'd gone down to her garden and picked a concoction of herbs and lavender, which she'd hung in a muslin pouch above Molly's cot.

Amazingly, it had worked, and Karen had realized she might be on to something. What had started as a sideline had soon grown and Karen had left her job as an administrator in an electrical firm and remortgaged her house to put money into the new business. She was risking everything to go into a hugely competitive market, but she had a dream and Lizzy believed in her.

People like Karen Jones were the reason Lizzy did her job.

Karen showed Lizzy the latest product, a gentle oil to put into bath water. 'I've been trying it out on my friends' babies and the results have been amazing,' she said proudly.

It was these personal, homespun elements that were

integral to Night Night Baby. Karen Jones was the kind of woman you would trust with your child.

Unfortunately, it was proving hard to convince other people of that. A national baby magazine had promised them coverage in an article about sleeping patterns, but in the end it had gone with better-known brands.

'We've had some great reviews,' Lizzy told her client. 'We just have to keep persevering.'

'It's just a bit dispiriting when you put your heart and soul into it. Not to mention all your money.'

There were dark circles under Karen's eyes. 'You look tired,' Lizzy said gently. 'Are you taking care of yourself?'

'I get sleep when I can get it. That's about my only luxury these days.'

'Let me know if I can do anything.' Lizzy reached over and took her client's hand. 'We'll get there, Karen. You have to keep the faith.'

Karen gave a nervous laugh. 'I bloody hope so – I've got everything riding on it!'

Things had got off to a promising start with the online dating. One guy in particular called *Foxy698* had been messaging Lizzy quite a bit. She'd always had a thing for men in baseball caps, and there was a picture of him on the deck of a boat wearing one and looking really fit.

'He's asked me out for a drink, but I'm not sure,' Lizzy puffed. 'He keeps calling me "young lady", and his profile picture is of him holding a dead pheasant.'

Nic took a swig of her water. 'You say that like it's a bad thing.'

It was Monday night and they were power walking on the treadmills at the gym under Nic's apartment block. Lizzy was struggling to keep up, even though she was only on gradient three and Nic had hers hoiked up to Mount Everest levels.

'Would *you* ever do online dating?' Lizzy asked.

'I haven't got time to see you guys, let alone waste it going out with some random doofus.' Nic glanced cursorily at a man on a nearby chest press. 'Maybe I should start going to BMF again.'

Lizzy's legs and lungs felt like they were on fire. It was horrifying how unfit she was. She gazed at her wild hair and red face in the mirror. She would never meet her Mr Right in the gym, fact.

'By the way,' Nic said after a few minutes of focused concentration. 'Remember I've still got your five hundred quid. Let me know when you want it back.'

At first Lizzy thought she'd misheard her over the music. 'What did you say?'

Nic threw another jab at her reflection. 'The five hundred quid you drew out from the cash machine. It's lying on my kitchen worktop. I'll go up after this and get it for you.'

Lizzy slammed her hand on the emergency 'stop' button. The machine ground to a halt. 'I thought I'd lost it, or given it away to a homeless person! Why didn't you tell me?'

'I thought you knew. We had a conversation about it in the street.'

'Did we?'

'Yeah, you were trying to feed it back into the machine for ages and then some dodgy guys came over, and at that point I said I'd take it for safekeeping. Don't you remember?'

'No!' Lizzy cried. She'd got three white hairs from the trauma of all this!

A skinny blonde in top-to-toe Lululemon came over and stood in front of her treadmill. 'How much longer are you going to be?'

Lizzy was still recovering from the fact that she hadn't lost five hundred pounds of her hard-earned money after all. 'Um, not long.' She quickly pressed 'start' again.

'You're only allowed on for twenty-five minutes at peak times,' the blonde said haughtily.

Nic looked down from her gradient-fifteen vantage point. 'We'll be on for even longer if you keep inter-rupting us. If you don't mind, my friend and I were having a private conversation.'

Skinny Blonde's eyes narrowed. 'If you don't get off I'll tell the manager.'

'Do that and I'll key that nice little Mini of yours,' Nic said pleasantly. 'Apartment 42B, isn't it?'

Lizzy watched the girl stomp off. Being friends with Nic was like riding a thrilling and occasionally terrifying rollercoaster ride. Lizzy had once watched Nic take off her own lace-up brogue and throw it across a pub at a man who'd pushed Poppet out of the way at the bar. Nic's parents had split up when she was eleven and she had been sent to a counsellor by her mum, who was worried about the effect the divorce was having on her daughter. Once there, Nic had proceeded to run intellectual rings around the woman and had told her what she actually thought was that her dad was a lazy slob and that they were better off without him. Nic saw the world in black and white: people were either twats or they weren't. Cross her at your peril, but if you were her friend she was generous to a fault and had your back for life.

Money drama over, they got back to the matter in hand. 'So do you think I should go for a drink with him then?' Lizzy asked.

'With Foxface? Course you should.' Nic turned up the speed on her treadmill.

'Remember the penis thread!' she yelled as she started to sprint.

Chapter 12

Two nights later Lizzy found herself on her way to meet *Foxy698*. Toby – that was his real name – had chosen the venue, which turned out to be a bistro-cum-bar on the edge of Sloane Square. When she arrived there was a man sitting at one of the tables outside. He looked familiar, so Lizzy took her chance.

'Toby?'

She didn't know what blinded her first: the dazzling veneers or the bright red trousers. 'Hello darling,' he said, getting up and kissing Lizzy rather clammily on both cheeks.

'I'm Lizzy,' she said.

'Hope so, otherwise I've just kissed some random bird in the street, hahahahaha!'

Next door's table looked up at the foghorn laugh. 'I took the liberty of ordering you a G & T,' he told Lizzy.

She sat down. 'Fab, thank you.'

Toby flashed her another toothy smile. He looked a lot older than he did in his pictures, and his blond hair was alarmingly bouffant. Lizzy had a horrible suspicion he might have blow-dried it.

Toby crossed one red chino leg over the other. 'My workmates were quite impressed when I said I was going out with Headbutt Girl tonight. One of them said, "You'd better not be late, mate, or she'll break your nose as well, ha ha ha!"'

Lizzy managed a feeble smile. 'I don't normally go round doing that sort of thing. And technically I think it was more of a bang than an actual break.'

'It didn't scare me off, I like strong women.' He rested on his elbows and leant in. Lizzy got a faceful of pungent aftershave. 'What did you do to make Justin do a runner like that? There must be more to it than meets the eye.'

'Well um, I really don't know. I guess we weren't right for each other.'

'Whatever you say.' Toby shot her a knowing look. 'I bet you're a right handful.'

Lizzy changed the subject. 'Have you been on the site long?'

'A while,' he said breezily. 'You?'

'This is my first time.'

'A virgin, then! Don't worry, I'll be gentle with you.'

'Ha ha,' she said. He *was* joking, wasn't he?

Toby ran a hand through the bouncy hair. 'I don't want to sound boastful, but I've had a pretty good success rate.'

'Oh really?'

Lizzy's ironic tone was completely lost on him. 'You get a lot of lonely women on these kinds of sites.' He gave a wink. 'Let's just say they need plenty of love and attention.'

What a charmer! Lizzy was just wondering how soon she could leave without appearing rude when Toby grabbed her hand.

'You look like a woman of the world; can I be upfront with you?' He fixed her with what was clearly meant to be a penetrating gaze. 'Shall we just forget about the drinks and go and screw?'

Lizzy thought she'd misheard him. 'Sorry?'

'I'm bored wasting time on all this wining and dining bollocks. You and I have a strong sexual connection, Lizzy. Why don't we just cut the crap and get down to it? My place is only round the corner.'

Lizzy wrenched her hand away. 'I'm sorry, but you've got this all wrong. I'm sure deep down you're, er, a really nice guy, Toby, but you and I are definitely *not* having sex.'

'Really?' He looked crestfallen. 'But my apartment is really nice.'

'It's still a no, I'm afraid.' Lizzy picked up her handbag. 'Thanks for the drink but I'd better get going.'

'Was I too full-on with all the sex stuff?' he shouted after her. 'We can start again if you like. What's your star sign?'

Chapter 13

'Hello, Haven!'

'Lizzy, it's Tam.'

'Hey Tam!'

Tamzin was Lizzy's friend from another PR agency. 'Are you free tonight?' she asked Lizzy. 'We're doing this new photography exhibition on the Kings Road. It's bound to be full of pretentious dickheads, but we can catch up and have a few glasses of bubbles.'

Lizzy looked longingly out of the window. It was another gloriously sunny day. 'I'm meant to be going to hot yoga.'

'Oh don't give me that. There's free booze!'

Sod it, her exercise regime could start tomorrow. Lizzy reached for a pen.

'What's the address?'

'You do look funny,' Bianca chortled when she came off the phone. 'Like you've just come back from some mega-sick mash-up eighties rave.'

Lizzy was still wearing her Happy Halo round the office. She'd got used to the post boy and the man who came to refill the water cooler bursting into hysterics every time they saw her.

'How is your aura?' Antonia boomed across the office. Despite wafting round in Antonia Land most of the time, she had the ability to develop dog-like hearing when she wanted to.

Lizzy swivelled round in her chair. 'If you want the truth, I'm feeling slightly nauseous.'

'You're probably hungover again,' Antonia snapped.

The phone started ringing again. 'Hello, Halo! I mean hello, Haven!'

'Ken Dennings here!'

Ken was Lizzy's exuberant constipation client. The man behind A Helping Hand (suppositories, laxatives and organic fibre drinks), Ken's sole aim in life was to get a story about bowel movements on the front of the *Mail*.

'I see they didn't go with that feature idea we pitched them.'

'Did you see all the new stuff on Syria?' Lizzy said tactfully. 'I think that probably took precedence over coverage of the explosion of men over sixty-five suffering from haemorrhoids.'

'Ha ha, good laxative joke there, Lizzy!'

'Was there?'

'You said "explosion". Anyway, I see your point. Keep me posted.'

Lizzy said goodbye and hung up. She couldn't fault Ken for his blind optimism.

The exhibition was in an old lemonade factory. A group of tanned men in loafer/blazer combos and wafer-thin women in ankle boots and minidresses were standing outside smoking furiously. For one horrific moment Lizzy thought she'd spotted Toby, but thankfully it turned out to be a false alarm.

The gazelle-like creature on the door looked down her nose at Lizzy. 'Sorry,' she said, not sounding it at all. 'Your name's not on the list.'

'It's there, I can see it,' Lizzy said. 'Look – SPELL-MAN.'

'Oh yeah, Headbutt Girl. You'd better not be here to cause trouble.'

'Of course I'm not,' Lizzy said. Would they be issuing her with an ASBO next?

Snooty Door Girl begrudgingly stepped aside. 'Go on then.' She might as well have added, 'And don't steal anything.'

It became immediately evident why there was such a rigorous entrance policy. Lizzy was probably the only woman in the place who'd ever seen the wrong side of a size ten, and who wasn't dripping with thousands of pounds' worth of jewellery. Waitresses were wafting through the glamorous crowds with platters of perilously assembled canapés that no one was touching.

The photography exhibition was by someone called Jay Aziz, who presumably was the little man in a full-length black housecoat who everyone was fawning over. Lizzy didn't know much about art but she wasn't sure about the portraits of screaming faces, all with perfect teeth and hair. It was a bit like looking at the 'missing' list after a mass breakout from the Priory.

'Lizzy!' Tamzin came rushing up. The two women air-kissed in an OTT way, taking the piss.

'Sweetie! Mwah!'

'Mwah! Darling!'

Tamzin swiped two champagne flutes from a passing waiter and handed one to Lizzy. 'How are you, babes? I haven't seen you since, you know . . .'

'Since Justin dumped me on a karaoke stage and it went viral and I had journalists chasing me down the street, and *This Morning* devoted a whole show to what a psychotic nutter I am? Is that what you meant, Tam?'

Her friend frowned. 'No, I don't think it was that.'

They cracked up. 'What a knob!' Tamzin said. '*I* know you didn't want to marry him.'

'Thanks,' Lizzy sighed. 'You're one of the few people who do.'

One of Tamzin's colleagues came over and pulled her away, leaving Lizzy to wander round. No one paid her the slightest bit of attention. The women were dressed in various designer threads, Hermès bags slung over their shoulders and oversized Rolexes hanging off their skinny wrists. Lizzy's cat-print T-shirt from H&M was a poor show by comparison. At least she had bonded with the canapé waiter, who had quickly cottoned on to the fact that she was probably his only customer.

A group was fawning over another close-up of a screaming woman, which was bizarrely entitled 'The Ganges'.

'Jay has totally captured it, hasn't he? I totally had the same feeling of being unburdened from mass consumerism when I went to India in 04.'

The room filled up as more people poured in. Lizzy looked in vain for somewhere to put her empty flute. She should have gone to hot yoga.

Lizzy go her phone out and checked it, trying to look busy. No one had called or texted. As she stood there waiting for her Facebook page to reload a horrible smell crept into her nostrils. She sniffed and looked down to see a tiny chihuahua standing at her feet. How could such a small animal be responsible for such a stench?

By the disgusted looks Lizzy was getting, other people had noticed it too.

'It's not me!' She pointed down at the dog. 'Has anyone lost a dog?'

No one came to help, and Lizzy found herself standing in a space on her own. The chihuahua gazed up at her mournfully. It was wearing a pink T-shirt that said *J'adore Dior*.

Lizzy couldn't just leave it there. 'Are you lost?' she said, scooping the animal up. On closer inspection the poor thing didn't look very well. Holding the creature out in front of her, she started to make her way through the crowd.

'Um, hello! Has anyone lost a dog?'

Everyone studiously ignored her until a girl with mauve hair looked over. 'Yeah, she belongs to Muffy.'

'And can you tell me where Muffy is?' Lizzy asked politely.

'I don't know, try the toilets.'

Lizzy had no idea where the toilets were, so she headed back towards the exit. 'Lady with a small smelly dog coming through!' she called cheerily, just in case people thought the noxious vapours that seemed to be permanently emitting from the animal's nether regions were anything to do with her.

The dog shivered and Lizzy felt its stomach gurgle

ominously. 'Excuse me!' she said more urgently. 'We've got a bit of an emergency!'

At that point the chihuahua let out a small groan. In sheer panic, Lizzy shoved the dog into the hands of the nearest person to her. The man's eyes widened in shock as a spray of brown liquid fell out of the dog's bottom and splattered on to the floor and one of the man's tan loafers.

A nearby woman gave a shriek. 'Oh, that is gross!'

The man seemed to be in some sort of trance. He kept looking at the floor and then back up at the dog again.

'Bluey!' A skinny blonde rushed over. 'There you are!'

'I don't think she's very well,' Lizzy said apologetically.

'Does Bluey need a pooey?' the woman said in a baby voice. 'Let's take you outside, baby.'

She rushed off, holding the dog aloft like a winning trophy. Lizzy and the man were left looking at each other. 'I'm so sorry,' she started apologizing. 'I didn't mean to . . .'

She trailed off. He looked very familiar. Where had she seen him before?

Giving Lizzy a long, chilling stare, Elliot Anderson whipped a tissue out of his pocket and bent down to wipe the front of his shoe. He stood up again, his top lip curling with disgust.

Someone came over with a mop and bucket and Lizzy and Elliot were relegated to one side. All the other guests were giving them a wide berth.

'I'm Lizzy Spellman,' she said awkwardly. 'I think our paths have, er, crossed on email.'

Elliot Anderson continued to glare at her. He was taller and leaner than Lizzy had imagined, with a smattering of freckles on his nose that didn't exactly match the 'serious' journo persona. Up close the famous hair was more reddy-brown, like the colour of wet leaves on an autumn day. Not that now was the time to start waxing lyrical about the bloke's follicles.

Another member of the waiting staff came over and whipped the offending tissue out of Elliot's hand.

'I'm so sorry about your shoes,' Lizzy told him. 'I'll pay for any damages.'

'They're Italian leather,' he snapped. 'I doubt you could afford it.' With that, he turned on his heel and walked off in the direction of the toilets. Lizzy was left standing there like a lemon.

That went well. She sighed. What else could she do to make herself the most unpopular person here tonight?

Ten minutes later she still hadn't found Tamzin and was completely backed into a corner. A powerfully built man in a starched white shirt was blocking her exit. Lizzy tapped him on his considerable bicep.

He didn't seem to notice.

She tried again. 'Excuse me?'

He broke off his conversation and looked round irritably. 'What?'

'Can I just squeeze past?'

The man stared at Lizzy. He had a deep tan and the brightest blue eyes.

'I know who you are!' He pulled her into the middle of his circle. 'It's only bloody Headbutt Girl!' He put his

100

fists up in a jokey fashion. 'Come on then, do you fancy a fight?'

A brunette with her hair piled up in a casually elegant bun sniggered. 'Have you spoken to Jason recently?'

'Justin,' Lizzy said. 'And, er, no.'

'This is *hysterical*. So come on, Headbutt, what are you doing here?' The man crossed his arms. 'Found yourself a new chap yet?'

'Give the girl a break.' It was a male voice, directly behind Lizzy. Tan Man's features darkened.

'I don't think you're an authority on how to behave.'

Lizzy turned round and nearly fell over when she saw her rescuer. Elliot Anderson was staring at her tormenter over her head.

'I assumed you'd grown out of bullying when we left school.' Elliot's green eyes gleamed. 'What's the matter, Marcus? Not getting the chance to take it out on the minions at work these days?'

'Fuck off, Anderson.'

'Guys, play nicely!' the brunette said. She took hold of the big man's arm. 'Come on, darling, let's go and get some more 'poo.'

The group they were with evaporated like a puff of smoke. Lizzy and Elliot were left standing together again.

'Thanks,' she said awkwardly. 'That was nice of you.'

'I didn't do it out of chivalry,' he said stonily. 'Marcus is a wanker.'

'Elliot!' a husky voice wailed. 'Have you and Marcus been fighting again?'

Lizzy found herself gazing into the anguished face of Amber de la Haye. In the flesh the fashion designer was even more beautiful. The severe black trouser suit would have looked unforgiving on anyone else, but it was brought alive by Amber's tigerish eyes and the mane of hair that tumbled down her back like a waterfall. There was a half-moon scar on one alabaster cheek, an imperfection that only enhanced her smoky beauty.

Lizzy was entranced. It was like the woman had just run off the pages of an Emily Brontë novel.

'Cressie said you were winding Marcus up!'

Elliot shoved his hands in his pockets. 'Not really. He was being his normal prick-like self.'

Amber frowned. 'What's that smell?'

Elliot took hold of her arm and moved her away, but Lizzy could still hear the conversation.

'*Please* don't make any trouble tonight,' she heard Amber say. 'Can't you two even try and get along?'

'He's the one with the chip on his shoulder, not me.'

Amber put a placatory hand on Elliot's chest. Lizzy got a glimpse of the huge diamond on her engagement finger. 'I'm tired of fighting. Will you at least do me one favour and come and have a few shots taken with Jay?'

Lizzy watched Amber pull her glowering fiancé off. The guy was even more of a knob than Lizzy had thought. What the hell did Amber de la Haye see in him?

Within minutes Lizzy had found herself relegated back to the side of the room and contented herself with people-watching instead, swiping a canapé off her waiter mate whenever he came over. Once or twice she caught sight of Elliot loafing through the crowd, eyes guarded, not really bothering to engage with anyone. Even without doggy doo-doo on his precious loafers, Lizzy guessed he wasn't the life and soul of the party.

By eight-thirty the place had virtually emptied out and had taken on the rather sad feeling of a used-car showroom. The SW6 set had come to drink someone else's champagne and to be seen. There was no loyalty that required them to stay until the end.

Tamzin had promised she'd only be a few more minutes, so Lizzy amused herself by going round all the photographs again. She was definitely feeling a bit squiffy and carefree now. *Note to self: must not drink champagne on a Tuesday night!*

'Fancy one more?' a waitress asked. 'Might as well finish the bottle up.'

Lizzy looked at her empty glass. 'Be it on my head in the morning.'

They stood together and studied yet another screaming face of a man who also appeared to have a miniature shotgun floating in his open mouth.

'I'm going to have nightmares for weeks,' the waitress said. 'Is it bad to say I don't think it's very good?'

'Not at all. I'd go so far as to say it's a load of old bollocks.'

'And I've been talked to like a piece of crap all night! Some people are so rude.'

'Oh yes,' Lizzy agreed. 'Never before have so many who are so up themselves gathered together under one roof.' Her voice got louder. 'In fact, I wouldn't be surprised if we'd accidentally infiltrated the worldwide convention of people with their heads shoved up their own arses!'

There was a deliberate cough behind them. Elliot Anderson was standing under a nearby arch, his suit jacket over one shoulder. There was a strange look on his face.

'Elliot!' Amber was hovering impatiently by the entrance. 'Our dinner reservation is in five minutes!'

'Coming.' He turned and walked off.

'Shit, do you know him?' the waitress said.

Lizzy managed a weak smile. 'We're more email acquaintances.'

Chapter 14

Nic lived in a big block of modern flats by the Wandsworth roundabout. She was running late at work, so Lizzy and Poppet were let in by the nice concierge who kept a spare set of Nic's keys for when she drunkenly locked herself out. Pouring a glass of wine each, they went out on to the balcony. Nic's flat was on the edge of the building, so the view was three quarters the busy main road below and one quarter the River Thames.

'Do you think when Nic's got her penthouse suite in Mayfair she might employ us as her housekeepers?' Poppet asked. She was a surveyor for a large property company and spent most of her days tramping round building sites in her pink Hunter wellies.

'I hope so,' Lizzy sighed. She'd had Brian Baxter in her ear all afternoon; he was still going on about getting the bloody Red Arrows for a fly-by.

It was a drizzly summer's evening, so leaving the door open for a bit of air, the girls went back in. They hardly ever congregated at Nic's place because she was

hardly ever there. As usual it looked like a cross between a showhouse and a gym. The living room was
dominated by a giant sofa, a giant wooden coffee table
and an eighty-inch plasma TV. The set of kettle-bells in
the corner were the closest thing she had to ornaments.
When Lizzy had opened the hall cupboard to hang her
jacket up she'd nearly been crushed by the weight of
falling ski gear.

'Do you think we should buy Nic a few pictures or
a cushion to make it look a bit more homely?' Poppet's
own flat was a shrine to soft furnishings.

'I don't think there's much point, she probably
wouldn't notice,' Lizzy said. 'This place is only a stop-
gap for her.'

Nic had already owned two properties since they'd
been living in London, unlike Lizzy who'd rented the
same one-bedroom flat in Clapham since for ever.
Lizzy's landlord was a guy who lived in Sweden who
she heard from once in a blue moon. He hadn't put her
rent up since she'd moved in; she was kind of hoping
he'd forgotten she was living there.

They heard keys in the front door and moments later
Nic burst in in her suit, phone wedged under her chin.
She dumped her Mulberry and laptop bag on the floor.

'Yep, yep, we're doing the conference call with them
tomorrow at seven a.m. OK, see you then. I'll get the
coffees.'

'Do you ever sleep, or do you just hang upside down
in your bedroom like a vampire?' Lizzy asked her.

'Sleeping is for wimps. Is the wine open?'

They all sprawled over the sofa and Lizzy told them
about her run-in with Elliot Anderson.

'It was nice how he stuck up for you, though.' Poppet always tried to see the positives in any situation.

'Hardly, he was trying to get one over on this Marcus bloke. It was obvious they really hated each other.'

'Is Amber as beautiful in real life?' Poppet asked. 'She's one of my style icons. Her and Alexa Chung.'

'Poppet,' Nic groaned. '*No.*'

'What? I love Alexa Chung!'

'What does she actually *do,* apart from being thin?'

Poppet ignored her. 'What was the engagement ring like? Amber's, I mean. I read the wedding's in Italy, I bet it will be amazing.' She came over all dreamy. 'Maybe I'll end up getting married over there.'

Nic and Lizzy both feigned shock. 'I never knew you wanted to get married!' Nic exclaimed. 'You should have told us.'

'Oh, leave me alone. Just because you're a dried-up old cynic.'

Poppet had been planning her big day for years and was constantly updating her wedding dresses board on Pinterest. As Nic had remarked, all she had to do now was find her husband, although Poppet would get so carried away on the day with seating plans and flower arrangements she'd probably forget he was there.

'I like thinking about who I'd invite to my wedding when I'm on the toilet,' she sighed. 'It helps me go if I've got a stubborn poo that won't come out.'

'Charming.' Nic stuck her foot out and inspected it. 'I always wonder who would come to my funeral. Wakes are way more fun than receptions.'

'How many wakes have you been to?' Lizzy asked.

'A few. We die young up North, you know.'

'If you died, what song would your coffin be brought in to?'

'Lizzy!' Poppet wailed. 'That is really dark!'

'Don't tell me you never imagined your funeral play-list,' Nic told her. 'Come on, what song would you have playing when your coffin came in?'

Poppet hesitated. '"Breathe Again" by Toni Braxton.'

She couldn't understand why the other two fell about laughing. 'What? It's my favourite song!'

'I'd have "Toxic",' Nic declared. 'No question.'

'That figures,' Lizzy said. 'The thing is though, Nic, you wouldn't have any say in the matter because you'd be dead. If you go before me I'm going to make sure you come down the aisle to "Cotton Eye Joe".'

'You bitch. I'll rise out of my coffin and deck you.'

'Can we stop talking about our funerals?' Poppet wailed. 'It's making me feel really weird.'

'Well, it all smells lovely in the kitchen!' Lizzy said. 'What are we having for dinner?'

It was a joke. Nic's proudest achievement was never having once used the oven while living there. The instruction manual was still on the shelf inside.

She reached for her phone. 'San Marco take-out OK?'

'I wish Giuseppe wouldn't throw in free garlic bread.' Lizzy was so stuffed she could hardly move. 'Can someone pass me the Häagen-Dazs? I think it will help it go down.'

Poppet was curled up like a little cat on the end of the sofa. 'So guess who I got a text from,' she said casually.

'Matt Damon?' Lizzy asked.

'Ha ha. Sadly not.' She paused a fraction too long. 'Pete.'

Nic pulled a face. 'Pencil Dick Pete. What did *he* want?'

Poppet looked miffed. 'I wish you wouldn't call him that.'

Pencil Dick Pete was an ex of Poppet's, who had famously dumped her to allegedly concentrate on his accountancy exams. His nickname had come from a 'length versus girth' conversation the three girls had been having one night, when Poppet had let slip that Pete's willy reminded her of the HB pencils she used to use in school. Nic, who wasn't Pete's biggest fan anyway, had called him Pencil Dick Pete ever since.

'What did he want?' she asked Poppet.

'He just wanted to meet up for a drink. As friends,' she added.

This time Nic rolled her eyes. Pencil Dick Pete would resurface every few months or so. It was always the same: he would send Poppet a text out of the blue, asking if she wanted to meet for a drink. Poppet would always end up going along, whereupon Pencil Dick Pete would get her drunk on white wine and try to get her into bed. Poppet would refuse, because she was an old-fashioned girl with morals, and Pencil Dick Pete would say he respected her morals and would promise to take her out for dinner instead, which he never did. Poppet would be left hanging for ages, and then just when she'd got him out of her head the whole sorry saga would be repeated again.

'Are you going to meet up with him?' Lizzy asked.

'Of course not,' Poppet said, not very convincingly.

'Look, I know you two don't like him, but if you just got to know him . . .'

Nic interrupted her. 'I did get to know him. He's a complete tool.'

Poppet gave a winsome sigh. 'I just know how good we were together.'

'It's been *two years*,' Nic and Lizzy said in unison.

Poppet was wearing a wounded expression. 'We might not have been together that long but it was really special!'

'Pops,' Nic said patiently. 'We've been through all this.'

'He's just really busy with work . . .'

'He's always busy with work. Or has bad sinuses, or is away on family holidays, or whatever bullshit he feeds you.'

Poppet's eyes widened. 'You think he *lied* about spending last summer in Qatar with his uncle?'

'I'm saying if a man is genuinely interested in a woman, he will chase her to the ends of the earth to be with her. If Pencil Dick Pete wanted to be in a relationship with you, he'd be in a relationship with you.' Nic shook her head. 'He's just stringing you along, *chiquita!*'

'Nic's got a point, Pops,' Lizzy said more delicately. 'And he doesn't even really look that much like Matt Damon.'

Poppet looked dismayed. 'Do you not think?'

'Well, he's got hair,' Lizzy said. 'And a head and a mouth and a pair of eyes and a nose, so I suppose they've got those things in common.'

'Oh,' Poppet said faintly. 'Oh right.'

The other two studied her. 'Are you going to start crying?' Nic asked.

'No, it's just a bit of a . . . a bit of a shock.' She stared at the coffee table. 'So he definitely doesn't want to be with me?'

'I don't think you really want to be with him either,' Lizzy said, encouragingly. 'You just haven't met anyone you've really fancied since.'

'Well, screw him! And his pencil dick.' Poppet's chin had set determinedly. 'I'm not anyone's booty call.'

Nic gave her a wink. 'That's my girl.'

'Ooh good, I feel all empowered now.' She turned to Lizzy. 'What about you?'

Lizzy swallowed her mouthful of wine. 'What about me?'

'Have you had any more dating action?'

Lizzy hesitated. Despite her declaration that she was swearing off online dating after Toby, she'd found herself going back on for a nose around whenever her bus was delayed, which was pretty frequently. 'Actually there is this one who's just "liked" me,' she admitted.

She got her phone out and showed them *Blue_Skies'* profile. Poppet gave an excited squeak. 'He is total eye sex!'

Nic grabbed Lizzy's phone. 'He *is* hot. And us three never agree on men.'

'What are you waiting for?' Poppet squealed. '"Like" him back!'

'Hold on, hold on. I just don't get why he's "liked" me.'

'Get some self-esteem, woman!' Nic bellowed.

'I don't mean it like that,' Lizzy said, although she

did mean it like that a bit. 'It's just that he's way too hot to be on a dating website. What if he's a plant? You know, one of those good-looking people they pay to put up profiles to entice punters like me in.' She'd been giving it some serious thought. 'He could walk into any bar and girls would be all over him. There has to be a catch.'

'Maybe he's fed up with girls falling over him and wants to meet a more discerning type online,' Poppet said sensibly. Her face lit up. 'Imagine if you bumped into Justin when you were out with him!'

'But I won't bump into Justin, we live in a city of over eight million people.'

Nic yawned. 'I once bumped into the woman who used to do my Brazilian three times in one week.'

Poppet wrinkled her nose. 'TMI.'

OK, there was the minutest possibility of bumping into Justin, but it was a possibility all the same. 'Oh, what the hell!' Lizzy declared. 'I'll try and get a photo with this guy for posterity, even if he does do a runner afterwards.'

Chapter 15

Lizzy was startled into consciousness by her phone going off by her ear. *Antonia mob.* It wasn't even 6 a.m. Even for her boss this was a liberty.

'Antonia!' she tried to say brightly, but a phlegmy noise came out instead. Lizzy cleared her throat and tried again. 'Antonia?'

There was a silence and then suddenly someone squealed loudly down the phone. Lizzy sat bolt upright in bed. Was Antonia being *attacked*?

A voice boomed in the background. 'Christiana! Back on the potty! Bad girl!'

Loud crying erupted followed by a machine-gun round of hiccupping. 'Hello?' Lizzy shouted. 'Can anyone hear me?'

There was more muffled noise before Antonia came on the line. 'Who's this?'

'It's Lizzy. I think you might have called me by accident.'

'Christiana must have got hold of my phone again,

the little horror. NO, Christy! Potty!' She didn't bother apologizing. 'I'll see you in the office later.'

Christiana's screams were still ringing through Lizzy's head. There was fat chance of going back to sleep now, so she propped herself up on the pillows and checked her emails.

The fifth one down made her heart leap a little. It was an alert from the dating website. *Blue_Skies* had sent her a message!

She logged on. It was short and simple.

Hey Spellers29, you look like a nice person. How are things? Reuben.

Despite being woken at such an ungodly hour Lizzy was in a sprightly mood at work that day. She'd messaged Reuben back on the bus: short, pithy and with a smiley face on the end – even though Nic had specifically banned her from using emoticons – and it seemed to have worked because he'd replied straightaway. He really was so *hot*. Lizzy couldn't stop staring at one photo of him coming out of the sea, holding a huge surfboard. *Phwoar!* He had that sexy upper arm 'V' and a six-pack and everything!

She picked up the phone. 'Shaven Haven!'

'Lizzy?'

'Oh, hi Mum.' *Shit.* 'I thought you were Nic calling me back.'

'What's this shaven haven? Have they changed the company name?'

'Mum, I was just joking!' Lizzy exhaled. 'How are you?'

'Darling, you must stop drinking water!'

Lizzy glanced at the bottle of Evian on her desk. 'But then I'll die,' she said confusedly.

'Not *all* water, silly!' her mother cried. 'Tap water! Jacqui's sister's neighbour has read this horrendous thing about London tap water making you infertile! Apparently it's *infested* with oestrogen from the wee-wee of women on the pill. What's that, Michael? Oh, he's saying it apparently only affects men's fertility.' She gasped. 'I must phone Robbie! He goes up to London for meetings sometimes!'

The line went dead. As soon as Lizzy put it back on the hook it started ringing again.

'Mum, for God's sake . . .'

'It's Ken Dennings, Lizzy!'

'Sorry about that, Ken, I thought you were someone else. How are you?'

'I'm afraid I'm about to throw my toys out of the cot. I'm not sure about the direction A Helping Hand is going in.'

'Oh.' Lizzy sat up. 'In what way?'

'I've been thinking it would be a good idea to change the name back.'

This could be tricky. When Ken had first come to Haven PR his product had been in dire trouble. It had been a long and arduous process for Lizzy to convince him to rebrand.

'With all due respect, Ken, I think the reason A Clear Passage didn't take off was because it was a bit too literal. There's still a certain amount of embarrassment associated with buying constipation products. As yet most people unfortunately aren't as enlightened as you or I.'

'How about U Bend?'

'I think you'll probably run into the same issues.' Lizzy fervently hoped he wasn't going to suggest A Bum Deal again.

'OK, OK, I'll take your word for it. I've also had an idea for a new online campaign.'

'Great! What is it?'

'It's from this programme I saw the other night about the Alps.'

'Oh?' Lizzy said, wondering where he was going.

'There was this big avalanche, and it got me thinking. Isn't that a great analogy for A Helping Hand?'

'I'm not sure I follow . . .'

'Follow through, more like! Ha ha!'

'You were talking about avalanches.'

'Ah yes. What I mean is, all that compact ice just sitting there. One rock dislodges it and boom! The whole lot comes tumbling down. A Helping Hand could be that rock, Lizzy.'

'Wow!'

'I knew you'd like it. I was thinking we'd release it as a thirty-second clip on YouTube and watch it go viral. And you know all about that, Lizzy, ha ha!'

A new alert flashed up on her phone. It was another message from Reuben.

So when can I take you out for a drink? ☺ xx

Yes! She metaphorically punched the air.

'Lizzy? Are you still there?'

'Sorry, Ken, I was thinking it through. Can I sit on it and get back to you?'

'Be my guest. That's where I sit when I need inspiration.'

'Sorry?'
'The toilet! Ha ha ha!'

Avalanches of poo were far from Lizzy's mind as she went to meet Reuben two days later. They'd arranged to meet in a pub on the Strand but when Lizzy arrived five minutes fashionably late and walked through the bar, she almost walked straight out again. The dark, tousle-haired vision of gorgeousness sitting alone in the corner couldn't possibly be the man she was meeting for a blind date.

'Lizzy?' He got up from his chair. 'It is you, isn't it?'

She couldn't take him in fast enough. The soulful brown eyes, the dimples, the muscular body modestly nestling under a simple white T-shirt. Reuben was even better-looking in real life!

'Can I have my hand back?' he asked.

'What?' She let go. 'Oh, sorry!'

He grinned adorably. 'What can I get you to drink?'

'So what do you do?' he asked. They were sitting at the table with a half lager each.

'I work in PR.' Lizzy knew she was staring gormlessly, but it was beyond the realms of her control. People this good-looking just didn't go on dates with girls like her in real life.

There was a short silence. *Now you ask him what he does.* 'What do you do?' she asked.

'I'm a graphic designer.'

'Oh cool, who do you work for?'

'I'm freelance, I mainly work from home.' Reuben gave Lizzy a questioning smile. 'I hope you don't mind me asking, but it is you, isn't it? From YouTube I mean.'

She was yanked out of her lustful reverie. 'Yep, I guess you found me out.'

Reuben's handsome face was sympathetic. 'I didn't know whether you'd want to talk about it. Being jilted is a pretty traumatic thing to get over.'

'I wasn't jilted . . .' Lizzy gave up. It didn't matter how many times she said it, for the rest of her life she'd always be known as the girl who got the heave-ho by the man she wanted to marry. *Here lies the lonely grave of Lizzy Spellman. No one wanted to end up with her.*

'I think you're coping really well,' he told her.

Lizzy smiled bravely. 'Onwards and upwards!'

'If it was me I don't think I'd be able to leave the house. All those people looking at me, making judgements.'

'It's really not that bad,' she said. *Were* people looking at her and making judgements? 'Anyway, we don't want to talk about me all night. Do you come here often?'

He raised his eyebrow. They both started laughing. 'I can't believe I said that,' she said.

'It's my first time.' Reuben looked down at his hands. 'Actually, it's my first time out in a long time. I suffer from major depression.'

Lizzy had been admiring his shoulders. 'Oh,' she said awkwardly. 'I'm sorry to hear that.'

'None of my mates really understand.' Reuben gave her a devastating smile. 'You look like you're a good listener, Lizzy. Can I talk to you about it?'

*

'It basically turned into me giving him two hours of free therapy.' The next morning Lizzy was still feeling slightly drained from the experience. 'He suffers from clinical depression and low self-esteem. Apparently it comes from abandonment issues from when his dad walked out when he was a child.'

'How can anyone that hot have low self-esteem?' Poppet asked.

'An ex-girlfriend broke his heart.' Lizzy mouthed 'Thank you' at the girl behind the counter and walked out of Starbucks with her coffee. 'He thought after what I'd been through we'd connect on some deeper level.'

'Are you going to see him again?'

'He tried to take an overdose last year, Pops. I don't think I'm ready to take something like that on.'

'That is a bit heavy. How did you leave it?'

'This is the thing. I hailed a cab outside and I thought we'd just say bye and that would be it, but then he sort of kissed me on the lips and asked if he could see me again!'

'Was it nice? The kiss I mean?'

'It was only quick, but yes. Like when I have my mad sex dreams about David Beckham.' Lizzy had been left very confused by the experience. Reuben was extremely hot, but he clearly had loads of issues. Should she see him again or run for the hills?

Chapter 16

Work was even more hectic than normal. Antonia had taken herself off on a two-day retreat in West Sussex, where there was apparently no phone reception, so Lizzy was left to deal with Jocasta's Zen Ten hysterics as well as her own clients. She spent a whole hour on the phone to Brian Baxter one morning discussing whether an 'and' should be left in the press release for Santa's Little Helper. The Haven team was meant to take turns doing the company Twitter feed, but it was usually left to Lizzy to do. Having had no interest in social media until now, Antonia had ordered Lizzy to tweet 24/7. Coming up with new ways to talk about suppositories and man flu every thirty minutes was quite a challenge.

Reuben, or 'Hot Depressed Guy' as Nic was now calling him, had been WhatsApping her all week. He really was quite sweet and funny, and his spelling and punctuation were excellent. It was a shame, Lizzy reflected. It wasn't the poor bloke's fault he'd had his heart broken. Poppet, who was a sucker for trying to save a tortured soul, thought Lizzy should give him another chance.

Antonia breezed back in on Thursday lunchtime five pounds lighter and with reams of wooden beads round her neck. She dumped the latest *Vogue* on Lizzy's desk.

'Page one hundred and nine: article on healing crystals. Why aren't we in there?'

If Lizzy had problems managing her client expectations, managing her boss's expectations took it to a whole new level. The *Vogue* piece had insightful interviews with some of the most respected reiki masters in the world. Never in a million years would they have included quotes from some bloke with a dodgy moustache and beard calling himself Shaman Ron.

Lizzy carried on flicking through the magazine and got rather a shock when she suddenly saw the face of Amber de la Haye looking back at her. It was an exclusive interview with the fashion designer. Lizzy felt an unpleasant jolt in her stomach. Half of her was still expecting Elliot Anderson to make an official complaint to Antonia about Lizzy's seeming one-woman vendetta against him.

The photo shoot was of Amber floating around ethereally on a deserted beach. 'Ex model, animal-rights activist, darling of the fashion world,' the rapturous sell declared. 'Are there any more strings Amber de la Haye can add to her gilded bow?'

The journalist who had done the interview was clearly besotted:

Amber de la Haye greets me barefoot at the door

121

of her Chelsea townhouse looking exquisite in Donna Karan cashmere, her Italian rescue whippet Frieda hovering at her heels. Despite prior warning from Amber's PR that the designer was 'dead from exhaustion' from working round the clock on her new collection, there is no hint of tiredness etching the intoxicating features. 'Come in!' she says delightfully. 'I've got a batch of green tea biscuits cooling in the kitchen.'

There were a few paragraphs paying homage to Amber's stunning home and baking skills before Elliot's name was brought up.

There is no sign of Amber's fiancé, ITV *News at Ten* pin-up boy Elliot Anderson, and Amber is charmingly reticent about their relationship. 'Elliot's a very private person,' she says by way of apology. 'I don't think it's fair talking about him.' The pair are set to marry next summer and the location is tipped as the Italian Riviera. Surely it's a given that she'll be walking down the aisle in one of her own creations? There is a delightful peal of laughter. 'I haven't even thought about it yet!'

They make an unlikely pair, the radiant, eclectic designer who counts Cara Delevingne and Kate Moss as close friends and the serious, single-minded journalist who is being tipped by some as the next Jeremy Paxman. Dare we ask – what do they have in common?

Amber's brown eyes open wide as if the answer

were obvious. 'Elliot and I are soulmates. I couldn't imagine life without him.'

Hmm, Lizzy thought. They hadn't looked like soulmates when Lizzy had seen them. In fact, Amber had seemed sick to the back teeth of her moody fiancé.

'Have you finished?' Bianca asked. 'I want to see who I know in "Bystander".'

Ten minutes later Lizzy got another message from Reuben.

Hey. What are you up to? Isn't your boss back today? x

Lizzy smiled. He *was* good at remembering stuff.

She's just walked in, she wrote back. **So far no dramas! X**

A minute later her phone beeped again.

Short notice but do you fancy dinner tomorrow night? Xx

Antonia was advancing. Lizzy shoved her phone under a pile of newspapers. Her boss rested her huge bottom on the edge of Lizzy's desk.

'How did it go with chappy?'

Lizzy had made the mistake of telling Bianca about her date, and Bianca had promptly told Antonia. 'It was good,' she said cautiously. 'He's a nice guy.'

'Is there going to be a second date?' Bianca asked.

Antonia chortled loudly. 'Of course there's not! She'll have fucked it up somehow.'

'As a matter of fact,' Lizzy said huffily, 'I'm seeing him tomorrow night. He's just asked me out for dinner.'

After Antonia had waddled away, Lizzy messaged him back. **Love to x**

He came back almost immediately.

How about coming over to mine? Xx

Dinner at his? On a second date? With only a day's notice? Lizzy glanced across at Bianca, who was watching something with lots of sirens wailing on her phone. She got her Facebook page up. By some miracle Nic and Poppet were both online.

Eek! Reuben has just asked me to go over to his place for dinner tomorrow!! she typed.

Nic messaged back first.

And??

Lizzy: **It's a Friday night! Isn't it a bit weird he hasn't got plans?**

Nic: **His usual rendezvous with the dominatrix dwarf must have fallen through.**

Lizzy: **LOLZ. What if he's an axe murderer, though, or he's going to tie me up and throw me in his basement? Hold on, he's just sent me another message. It says: Don't worry. I live with a flat mate and he'll vouch I'm not an axe murderer ☺ x**

Nic: **He wants SEX off you.**

Poppet replied after a couple of minutes.

Sorry. Just been having a poo. It's only your second date!! Too soon for sex yet!!

Nic: **Pops, did you know these days people are allowed to sleep together before they get married?**

Hang on, Lizzy wrote back. **I might not have sex with him at all!! Xx**

Nic: **THREAD OF THE PENIS.**

Antonia swished past again on her mobile. 'Don't let work interrupt your social life,' she told Lizzy. 'Hello, yes? Can I make a reservation for dinner?'

Lizzy clicked back on to the press release she'd been writing about anal fissures and waited until Antonia

124

had gone. When she went back on Facebook there was another message from Poppet.

He IS hot! ☺ ☺ ☺

Make sure you give us the address, Nic had added. **And have a clear escape route to the front door.**

Poppet had the final word.

Don't forget condoms!!!!!!!! ☺ **xoxoxo**

Chapter 17

Lizzy was in a state of nervous excitement all day. The prospect of possibly having sex again – with a total hottie – had thrown her into a tizzy. Would she even remember how to do it? What if Justin's face popped into her mind at the crucial moment of entry and ruined it? Penis thread aside, there was also a more pressing issue at hand.

She called Nic at lunchtime. 'I'm not sure whether to get a bikini wax.'

'What kind of bush scenario are we talking here?'

'Well, I haven't had it done professionally since me and Justin split up, but I've been kind of keeping an eye on things.'

'I'll have the bacon cheeseburger, extra onions,' Nic said to someone.

'Where are you?' Lizzy asked.

'Having lunch with some work mates.'

'Nic!'

'What? You called me. Look, the best thing to do is send me a picture.'

'Of what?'

'What do you think?'

'You want me to send you a picture of my *bush*? Sorry,' Lizzy said to the woman behind the counter in Boots.

'What's the big deal? It's nothing I haven't seen before.'

Lizzy paid for her meal deal and walked out of the shop. 'I am not sending you a beaver shot!'

'I won't be able to tell without looking. Remember, Elizabeth, this could be a deal-breaker.'

Lizzy looked across the road at the Starbucks she got her coffee from in the mornings. 'If you put this up on Facebook I will hunt you down and kill you.'

She came out of the coffee-shop toilet five minutes later and sent Nic a photo.

Are you trying to put me off my lunch? came the reply.

It's not THAT big, Lizzy texted back, feeling rather affronted.

The reply pinged back immediately.

It's the size of a small planet.

Lizzy spent the afternoon calling round beauty salons.

Reuben lived in deepest darkest South East London, so Lizzy managed to leave work a bit early and set off. Her mother called just as they were pulling out of Waterloo.

'Hi Mum. I'm on the train.'

'Speak up, darling, I can't hear you.'

'I'm on the TRAIN,' Lizzy hissed. Her undercarriage was still stinging from a particularly vicious waxer that

Bianca had recommended. At least the redness had started to calm down.

'No need to shout. Are you going out tonight?'

Lizzy hesitated. Telling her mother she had a second date was the equivalent of inviting a vampire over the threshold. Her mum would come into Lizzy's love life wreaking chaos and terror and never, ever leave again.

The man sat opposite her was clearly eavesdropping. Lizzy turned her face to the window.

'I'm going for dinner with this guy I've met.' She didn't say it was at his house; her mother would have a blue fit and start going on about some article she'd read in the *Daily Mail* about date rape.

'This is an exciting development!' Mrs Spellman said. 'Michael, Lizzy's got a date!'

'Mum, can I call you back tomorrow?' Lizzy asked, uncomfortably aware it was rush hour and the whole carriage was now listening in.

'Dad wants to know who this chap banks with.'

'What's *that* got to do with anything?'

'You know he likes to know those sorts of things. Doorbell, Michael, that'll be the curry! Good luck, darling,' she told Lizzy. Her voice boomed out like a tannoy. 'Your father says: "Keep your hand on your ha'penny!"'

Chapter 18

Reuben's house looked a bit shabby from the outside in that way converted flats on a busy road often are. A scooter was parked by the bay window and there was a stained wheelie bin on a gravelled area that would be optimistically described by an estate agent as a front garden. Lizzy walked up the path, pressed the buzzer for flat B and waited nervously. A shadow appeared down the hallway and then Reuben appeared at the door, all tall and tousle-haired, bare brown feet poking out the bottom of his jeans. Lizzy felt another squeeze of desire.

'You look pretty.' He went to kiss her, but she got flustered and they sort of ended up banging noses.

'These are for you!' Lizzy thrust the Lindt chocolates at him. 'I bought rosé and white wine, I wasn't sure what you liked.'

'I like both.' He gave her his beautiful smile. 'Come on in.'

The flat was nicer inside, with pieces of modern art adorning the walls and a bare, utilitarian vibe going on. Reuben led Lizzy into the living room, where a guy in pink skinny jeans was standing expectantly, as if he were waiting for a bus.

'This is my housemate, Sven,' Reuben said. 'Sven, this is Lizzy.'

'Hi!' Sven grabbed her hand enthusiastically. He looked at Reuben. 'Seeing as your guest has arrived, I'll probably shoot off.'

He bounded from the room like a man who'd been granted a last-minute reprieve. Lizzy felt a bit nonplussed.

'Sven was keeping me company until you came.' Reuben gave her another slow, sexy smile. 'Right,' he said. 'Let me fix you a drink.'

Reuben sat down next to her on the small two-seater sofa and passed her a glass of rosé. He smelt of clean skin and Paul Smith aftershave. Lizzy's lust levels were climbing by the second.

'Cheers.'

'Cheers,' she said and they clinked glasses. The alcohol scored a direct hit in Lizzy's bloodstream, taking the edge off her nerves.

'You've got a really nice place,' she told him.

'Thanks. It could do with a lick of paint.'

'I like that.' Lizzy pointed to a print on the wall. It had loads of different bicycle wheels replicated over and over.

'That's one of mine.'

'Wow!' She was genuinely impressed. 'It's really, really good.'

'It's not really,' he said modestly.

'It totally is, Reuben!'

He shrugged, making his shoulders heave beautifully. 'Anyway. Tell me about your day. You must get to go to some really cool parties when you work in PR.'

'Some are quite fun,' Lizzy said, briefly fantasizing about walking into a launch party with Reuben on her arm. *That* would give all those snooty beauty journalists something to talk about.

Reuben was studying her intently. 'I can tell you're really good at your job.'

'I don't know about that. Although if you want to know anything about haemorrhoids and itching rectums, I'm your woman!'

Reuben's eyebrows shot up half an inch.

Why, Lizzy wondered, *did I say that?*

'I mean it,' he said. 'I can see why you work in PR. You're funny and confident and know how to put people at ease.'

Lizzy play-hit him on the knee. She was never good at taking compliments. 'You're not so bad yourself.'

'I am,' he sighed. 'I'm a really bad person.'

'You mean bad as in you're about to confess to murdering someone?'

'I'm not joking, Lizzy.'

She stopped smiling. 'Oh.'

'I'm sorry,' he said, staring fixedly at the carpet. 'I was really looking forward to you coming over tonight, but I'm feeling really low again suddenly.' He leant forward and put his head in his hands.

Their WhatsApp conversations had been so easy and fun all week it had almost been easy to forget he was suffering from clinical depression. She felt desperately sorry for him, but at the same time she hardly knew the bloke.

'Do you want me to go?' she asked awkwardly after a full thirty seconds of silence.

'No, stay.' He looked at her with his beautiful, sad eyes. 'Sorry. You didn't come over here to hear about my problems.'

Forty minutes later Lizzy had single-handedly drained the bottle of rosé and Reuben was still going.

'I just feel like there's no point,' he said gloomily. He'd been telling Lizzy about a new job he was applying for; apparently his therapist had told him he needed to get out of the house more. 'I won't get an interview.'

'Of course you'll get an interview. It sounds like a really great job.'

'That's exactly why I won't get it. It's my inner child, telling me I'm not good enough. I'll always be that little boy who was told he was too small and weak to play in the BMX park with the big boys.'

'Reuben, I'm sure you were a great BMX rider,' Lizzy said desperately. 'You just have to move on from that, er, bike and upgrade to a racer.'

'But *how*? *How* do I get to that racer, Lizzy?' Reuben turned to her imploringly. Once again her breath was taken away by how good-looking he was.

'Sorry, there I am going on about myself again.' He sighed heavily. 'Do you want to eat?'

What Lizzy actually wanted was the number for the nearest taxi firm, but she couldn't leave him like this. 'Sounds great! What are we having?'

*

Apparently Reuben had been planning to do a three-course meal, but he hadn't been able to cope with a major supermarket, so they ended up having filled pasta from the local Whistlestop.

'I think it's past the sell-by date.' He prodded a flabby, overcooked piece with his fork. 'God, this is awful. I'm so awful.' He put his head in his hands again.

Lizzy gazed at the beautiful dejected heap slumped across the table from her. It was like looking at a Michelangelo painting that had been left out in the rain.

She poured herself more wine and gazed at the TV, which had been left on in the background with the sound off. The ITN news had just come on. Oh God, was it only ten o'clock? She was exhausted. But seconds later she was wide awake. Elliot Anderson had suddenly appeared on the screen, a picture of a euro note in the background. Elliot was in a dark suit and looking very serious as he talked to the newsreader Mark Austin.

'My ex had a thing about that Anderson guy.' Reuben was gazing at the TV gloomily. 'I bet *he* doesn't have problems with self-actualization.'

The next moment Lizzy was taken aback as he sprang round the table and scooped her up in his arms.

'Oh Lizzy!' He started snogging her passionately.

She'd been halfway through a mouthful of pasta. 'Sorry!' she mumbled. 'I think you might have got a bit of my ricotta.'

'Will you take me to bed?' he whispered. 'I just want someone to hold me.'

Sex was a disaster. There was a lot of awkward

bashing of limbs and nothing seemed to fit together or go where it was meant to. At times Lizzy felt like they were playing a particularly invasive game of Twister. *I am having sex with a beautiful man*, she kept repeating to herself like a mantra.

After fifteen minutes of unsuccessful prodding and poking Reuben flopped down beside her. 'I'm sorry. I'm such a failure.'

'You've got nothing to be sorry about. Honestly.'

'It's my penis, isn't it? I've always hated it.'

'Of course not,' Lizzy said desperately. 'You've got a perfectly normal-sized penis.'

'You're saying it's not big enough? That I can't satisfy you? Oh God!' He rolled over into the fetal position and Lizzy watched in horror as he started hitting himself on the shaft of his willy. 'Stupid thing!' *Thwack.* 'Why don't you ever work properly?'

'Reuben!' She winced. 'What are you doing?'

'Just leave me alone!' There was another *thwack*.

Lizzy took the chance to grab her clothes and escape into the bathroom. She called Nic.

'I felt so sorry for him that I had sex with him! Now he's freaking out and beating up his own bell-end!'

Nic's voice brokered no discussion. 'This is a code-red situation! Get out of there!'

'I can't leave him when he's in this state!'

'Yes, you can. Tell him you've got an early appointment at the STD clinic.'

'OK, I'll try and think of something! I'll call you back.'

When she went back into the bedroom Reuben was sitting on the end of the bed in his boxer shorts. 'Who were you on the phone to?' he asked. 'You were telling your friends how awful I was, weren't you?'

'No!' she lied. 'Of course not!'

He put his head in his hands and stifled a sob. 'Oh God. I'm just so lonely. I miss her *so much*.'

Lizzy finally managed to extricate herself on the pretext of a sudden family emergency. The next day Reuben kept messaging to ask if she wanted to go over and get a takeaway and watch telly with him. Lizzy lay on the couch watching back-to-back episodes of *Murder, She Wrote* trying to block out the whole ordeal.

By 7 p.m. on Saturday, when she hadn't responded to his last three messages, his tone started to turn nasty.

You're obviously one of those girls who takes what she wants and leaves. I'm just glad I found out early.

At 9 p.m. another message came through.

You left your Elle Macpherson Intimates Dentelle thong here. I wonder how much Headbutt Girl's knickers would get on eBay?

I don't own any Elle Macpherson underwear, Lizzy wrote back.

There was a one-minute silence, then: **Sorry. It must be someone else's.**

Messages continued to arrive throughout the evening and into the next day. They ranged from Reuben apologizing for the size of his manhood, to him asking Lizzy if she fancied coming over and reading the Sunday papers with him. At three thirty she received one that made her blood run cold.

I filmed us having sex. If u keep ignoring me I'll put it up on YouTube. PS Antiques Roadshow – fan or not??? Xx

Poppet was at her parents' and wasn't picking up. In a blind panic Lizzy called Nic.

'Oh God, I shagged a complete psychopath!'

'Don't be stupid, Lizzy. Why would he put a video up of him being shit in bed?' Nic was in the middle of packing for a work trip to Beijing.

'I'm really worried!' Lizzy wailed. 'Should I call the police or something?'

'Don't do that. I'll be over in twenty minutes.'

Nineteen minutes later a cab screeched up. Nic was inside with her executive Samsonite suitcase.

'We're making a quick detour,' she told the cabbie, as Lizzy got in.

'What if he turns violent?' Lizzy said. 'I still think we should call the police!'

Nic looked dark. 'I'm worse than the police.'

Ten minutes later they were pulling up outside Reuben's. Lizzy watched from the back seat as Nic marched up the front path in the black M&S tracksuit she always flew in. She banged on the door and Reuben opened it a few moments later looking a bit confused. Lizzy couldn't hear what was being said but she saw Nic clench her fist and smash it into her other palm. Reuben went white and took a step back.

'What did you say to him?' Lizzy gasped when Nic got back in.

'It was more what I said I'd do to him. Let's just say the Dick-Hitter won't be bothering you again.' She checked her watch. 'Check-in closes in forty minutes. OK if we drop you at a bus stop on the way?'

Chapter 19

After the Reuben drama Lizzy was in need of some serious R & R, so she headed back to her parents' for the weekend. Her mother had wanted to know all about the date, but Lizzy had fobbed her off with something about there being no chemistry and escaped to sunbathe in the back garden.

It was a heavenly day in the London Borough of Bromley. Smells and sounds of neighbouring barbecues wafted lazily through the air. Lizzy lay back on the sunlounger and looked down at her belly. She definitely wouldn't be posting a selfie like Hayley-bloody-Bidwell who, according to her most recent Facebook status, was on Brighton beach at this very moment. Her smug hashtags read like a novel: *#suntanning #sun #tanning #suntan #bikini #saynotoicecream #lovinglife #loving #my #life #beach #Brighton #flatstomach #abs #toned #sixpack*.

Hayley was very proud of her flat stomach. She never failed to remind Lizzy that she worked hard for it, going to the gym four times a week and avoiding carbs Monday to Friday. In the summer she could still get away with wearing crop tops, and throughout December and January she wore bodycon dresses and things with belts as if to remind everyone of her amazing self-restraint. Lauren swore she'd once seen Hayley get full up on two Manzanilla olives.

Lizzy had always felt like a heifer next to Hayley-bloody-Bidwell, but now as she looked at her spare tyre cooking nicely in the August sunshine, she had the wonderful realization that she didn't *care* any more. Hayley had got her body by passing up on moments. What kind of life was that? Lizzy might never win a swimwear competition, but her wobbly bits were the physical manifestation of all the things that made her happy: the wine-fuelled evenings with Nic and Poppet, and Saturday nights at her parents' having cosy dinners on trays in front of the telly. It was about sunny afternoons whiled away in beer gardens, and cold winter days in the office warmed by Starbucks runs for pumpkin lattes. It turned out Lizzy's squashy stomach was a pretty good thing after all, because what was a person without human experiences and friendships and love and laughter?

'I'm sorry, old friend,' she said emotionally. 'I'll give you the respect you deserve from now on.'

'Uh oh, talking to yourself! First sign of madness!'

Lizzy almost jumped out of her skin. David from next door was poking his head over the fence. 'Sorry!' she said. 'I didn't see you there.'

'So I see. Were you talking to your tummy?'

'I was just, er, thinking out loud.'

'Jacqui talks to her bottom all the time. Calls it her

"Plumptious". I've heard her singing to it in the bathroom.'

'I think that's very nice,' Lizzy said decisively. 'More women should make friends with their body parts.'

'I've been on intimate terms with my todger for years, ha ha! Your dad around?'

Barf. 'He's inside. Do you want me to call him?'

'No need, just tell him I'm going to the tip tomorrow. He's got a couple of things he wants me to take down for him.' He nodded at Lizzy's chest. 'Tesco must be missing themselves a couple of melons, ha ha ha!'

The house was quiet when Lizzy came back indoors to get a drink. Wandering through into the hall she found her dad in his study. He was sat at the desk with two A4 files open, one saying 'DIANE' and the other saying 'BOILER'.

'Hullo Lizard.'

'Hi Dad, what you up to?'

'Just going through some admin.'

Lizzy's dad kept files for everything, including chronological records for each family member. 'LAUREN' was gargantuan and held all her sporting, musical and academic accolades, including a special achievement award for being Outstanding Air Cadet four years in a row. 'ROBBIE' was bulging with various skateboarding and cross-country certificates, and the letter from the BBC confirming he'd got on to *Junior Masterchef*. 'LIZZY' was woefully thin by comparison. Her crowning achievement was first prize in the 'Bromley Hawaiian Rollerdisco 1998', plus X-rays from all the bones she'd broken while growing up.

Lizzy pointed at 'DIANE'. 'Who's Mum run over now?'

Mrs Spellman was a law unto herself, but this was especially true when she got behind the wheel. One of Lizzy's earliest memories was getting pulled over on the school run by the police. Her mother's speeding tickets had been a constant source of amusement to the rest of the family over the years, especially Robbie who'd never failed to point out his mother's criminal history whenever she'd tried to bollock him about something.

'No one for once. She wants to know if she can get her bunions done on BUPA.'

The house phone started ringing. 'Can you get that, Lizard? Your mother's upstairs descaling the shower.'

Lizzy soon found out why her dad had been keen to avoid answering. 'Lizzy?' Lauren barked. 'Is that you?'

'Yes.' It was very noisy in the background. 'Where are you?'

'Gym. Did you get that link I emailed you?'

'The one about how the sugar in white wine causes premature ageing?' Lizzy said. 'I did, thank you. Very informative.'

'Think how much money you'd save on buying expensive wrinkle creams. Dad there?'

Lizzy looked at her father. He shook his head violently.

'He's just popped out to the shop,' she lied. 'Do you want me to give him a message?'

'Your sister keeps trying to reorganize my portfolio,' her father sighed after Lizzy had put the phone down.

'I've had the same financial advisor for years and I'm perfectly happy.'

Mrs Spellman came down the stairs in a pair of Marigolds. 'You look very pink,' she told Lizzy. 'Who was that on the phone?'

'Lauren. She sends her love; she was about to go into a spin class.'

Mrs Spellman snapped the gloves off. 'Did she mention she and Perry are coming over at the start of December?'

Perry was Lauren's trader boyfriend, who the family had yet to meet. Lizzy had seen pictures: Perry had very short hair and the same glaring look as Lauren. Apparently he'd been a star rower at college.

'They're staying here for a few days before they go skiing. Europe somewhere.' Lizzy's mum sighed wistfully. 'It would have been nice if they could've been here for Christmas Day, but Lauren's a busy girl.'

'Are you with us for Christmas, Lizard?' Lizzy's dad asked.

'Of course she is,' Mrs Spellman shouted as she went into the kitchen. 'Where else is she going to be?'

Chapter 20

Things were pretty slow at work. No one wanted to think about Christmas at the height of summer, and a lot of people were away on holiday. Bianca had gone to her dad's place in France – no one knew how long for because Antonia had forgotten to write the dates down in her diary. Antonia herself had been summoned by Jocasta to a two-day crisis summit at Babington House, although Lizzy suspected they were probably sitting round drinking chai tea all day and getting pedicures.

As usual it had been left to Lizzy to do everything, including the appraisal for a junior member of staff that Antonia had forgotten about. 'Just tell her she's not getting a salary increase!' she'd bellowed on a crackly line from Somerset.

In the afternoon Lizzy trekked out to Milton Keynes to see Brian and Debbie Baxter. They went to a Harvester for their business lunch (which Lizzy ended up paying for), where they took her through their five-year vision, which included Man Down and

Santa's Little Helper being included in Oscar goodie bags. By the time Lizzy got on the 17.51 back to London she felt like someone had reached inside her ear and pulled out her brain.

Nic was away with work, so Lizzy went to meet Poppet for a drink in Clapham. 'You look stressed,' Poppet told her. 'Bad day at work?'

'You could say that.' Lizzy ripped into a bag of crisps. 'I seem to be doing the job of three people but on only one person's salary.'

Halfway down a bottle of wine the creases had started to get ironed out of the day. 'Do you fancy getting something to eat?' Poppet asked. 'I'm not meant to be spending money this week, but I'll just load up on bread and only have a starter.'

There was a whole market garden sitting in the bottom of Lizzy's fridge, but after the day she'd had, she was in need of carbohydrates. 'I'll get up early tomorrow and make a vegetable soup instead,' she told Poppet. 'If I make up a big batch and freeze the rest, it will save me a fortune in buying lunch.'

'That's a good idea,' Poppet said encouragingly. She paused. 'Do you think anyone ever does that?'

Having decided to go to their favourite burger joint ('Men love their meat so you always get a good HMQ there,' Poppet pointed out), Lizzy went to the loo. When she returned Poppet was sitting there with a strange look on her face. Her iPhone was face-down on the table next to her.

'Are you all right?' Lizzy asked.

'Yes fine!' Poppet said brightly. 'Nothing to see here.'

She was acting very shiftily. 'Pops, what's going on?' Lizzy asked.

There was an ominous silence. 'Um, I've got something to tell you and I really don't think you're going to like it.'

Lizzy went cold. Had someone died? 'What's happened?' she whispered.

Poppet glanced down at her phone. 'I was just on Facebook while you were in the loo. Um, I don't know how to tell you this but . . .'

'Pops, you're scaring me! What is it?'

Poppet visibly swallowed. 'Justin's got a new girlfriend.'

Lizzy stared at her friend's face for a long moment. 'Oh, OK.'

'What are you feeling right now?' Poppet said. 'Tell me everything!'

'I'm not feeling anything.'

'Are you sure? You don't want to cry or throw something?'

Lizzy shrugged nonchalantly. 'Why would I get upset about someone who has shown such spectacular levels of twatdom? Justin means nothing to me.'

'It's still not nice finding out he's got a new girlfriend.'

'Honestly, Pops, she's welcome to him.'

'It's not anyone we know, if that makes you feel better.'

'Pops, you don't have to make me feel better. Like, who do I care who he goes out with?'

'Well, I think you're handling this amazingly.'

'Oh come on, it's not like he was never going to get

144

another girlfriend again!' Lizzy gave a smile. 'I wish him all the best. Truly.'

'Bravo you. I'll just get the bill then . . .'

'So who is she anyway?'

Poppet glanced up from her purse. 'I thought you didn't want to know?'

'I might as well. Just in case I ever run into her.'

'Um, she's called Natalie Chloe Dunn.'

'Is she pretty?' Lizzy asked pleasantly.

'I guess . . . if you like that sort of thing.'

'And what is "that sort of thing"?'

Poppet was starting to look very nervous again. 'Petite, brunette, er . . .'

Lizzy held her hand out. 'I want to see for myself.'

'Do you think that's a good idea?'

'Give me the phone!' Lizzy lowered her voice. 'Please.'

She watched Poppet type in her password and reluctantly hand it over. Sure enough, there it was. *Justin Thomas: In a relationship with Natalie Chloe Dunn.* His profile picture was him standing with a pretty brunette, their arms wrapped round each other.

'Are you OK?' Poppet asked anxiously.

A red mist started to build inside Lizzy. Did Justin not give even an iota of a shit about her feelings? They'd only been finished six weeks! And here he was, going out with a girl who looked at least a stone lighter than Lizzy *and* had nice, shiny hair. Meanwhile Lizzy was still single and reduced to terrible sex with manic depressives. Hot manic depressives, yes, but that wasn't the point. It wasn't fair!

'I don't think you should see any more.' Poppet made a grab for the phone.

'I want to see more! Get off!'

They began to wrestle over it. A waitress had started to come over with the card machine, but seeing what was going on, did a last-minute swerve.

'Ow! You just scratched me!'

'I didn't mean it! I've only got your best interests at heart!'

'THEN LET ME SEE THE STUPID BITCH!'

At that point the manager came over. 'Ladies, if you don't start behaving yourselves I'm going to have to ask you to leave.'

The two friends fell back, breathing heavily. Poppet had her iPhone clasped to her chest. 'You're allowed to ask three questions and that's it!' she told Lizzy.

Lizzy muttered something under her breath about the meaning of true friendship and ordered another bottle of wine.

The next day Lizzy woke up with a horrible hangover and the same sense of burning outrage. She was un-characteristically snappy at work, and even Antonia gave her a wide berth, choosing to terrorize one of the other account managers for a change.

Poppet had reluctantly gone off on a reconnaissance mission and called Lizzy at work to give her an update. 'They met through friends. It's only been going on for about three weeks.'

'Three weeks!' Lizzy seethed. 'Three whole *weeks*.'

'I bet it's only a rebound relationship, it won't last.'

'Yes it will! The rate they're going she'll have moved in by next week, and then they'll get married and live in a beautiful Victorian conversion and have a beautiful family, while I'll end up old and alone, reduced to pressing myself against hot schoolboys on the bus to get my sexual kicks!'

'Do you think there's a chance you're being a touch melodramatic?'

'Melodramatic?' Lizzy kicked a waste-paper bin across the office. 'Why would you say that?'

All afternoon she stewed. Her alloted questions to Poppet the night before – did Natalie look like the kind of girl who might get fat later in life, did Justin still have that giant blackhead on the side of his nose, and was there a tinge of regret and everlasting sadness on his face? – had hardly garnered her the information she wanted. She continued to bombard Poppet with more emails until Poppet put her foot down. 'You'll only torment yourself even more,' she told Lizzy. But Lizzy had to know more. It was like a festering wound that needed to be picked open.

The only way she could find out more information was if she had access to Justin's Facebook page herself. But there was a rather large problem in that she and Justin were no longer friends. An idea struck her. Suppose she set up a fake profile and sent him a friend request? Justin had over twelve hundred 'friends' so he wasn't exactly discerning.

Giving herself the moniker 'Heidi Milton', Lizzy downloaded a picture of a fit girl in gym shorts running along a beach. That was bound to get his attention.

'Lizzy, are there one or two Ls in "holistic"?' Bianca asked.

'You're meant to be the one with the expensive education,' Lizzy snarled. 'Look it up.'

For the next hour Lizzy checked Facebook like a nervous twitch. Just before 4 p.m. she struck gold. *Justin Thomas has accepted your friend request.* Steeling herself, Lizzy went on to his wall.

'Feeling happy ☺,' he'd written at 8.03 p.m. the night before, tagging a 'Natalie Chloe Dunn'. There were photos of him and Natalie at the pub together, him and Natalie sitting by the Thames with plastic glasses of Pimms together, a filtered Instagram shot of two lattes with hearts swirled into the froth with the hashtag *#sundays*. It was like they'd been together for three years, not three weeks! Another post said *Justin was at Sophie's Steakhouse with Natalie Chloe Dunn and two others.* Lizzy clicked on to see the other names. Helen Naylor! The same Helen Naylor who Lizzy had shared a tent with at Glastonbury! Helen Naylor, who still had Lizzy's seventy-five pound All Saints top Lizzy had generously lent her two years ago!

'Treacherous *bitch*,' she muttered.

One of Lizzy's colleagues came over to her desk. 'I'm doing a Frappuccino run to Starbucks. My treat.'

'Leave me alone!' Lizzy howled. 'Can't you see I'm in the middle of a meltdown?'

Chapter 21

Lizzy's fug had showed no sign of abating. Normally such a positive person, it was like dark forces had crept into her body and taken over. At work she took to hunching over her computer on Justin's Facebook page, reading out his status updates in a horrible baby voice. '"Justin was at Café Boheme with Natalie Chloe Dunn." That's the third time they've eaten out this week! Oh my God, that's *sick*. He's posted a picture of two spoons coming out of an ice-cream sundae!'

Everyone in the office avoided her as if she had the Ebola virus. Lizzy's desk became a quarantined pit of misery as work piled up and her inbox threatened to explode under the weight of unanswered emails. In the street she had pavement rage every ten seconds and hissed at *Big Issue* sellers who got in her path, even if they had cute dogs with neckerchiefs. On the bus she took to muttering 'Get a room' loudly if a couple even dared to look at each other.

*

By the end of the week Poppet and Nic had staged a crisis intervention, and forced Lizzy to come to a free music concert in Hyde Park.

'You have got to get a grip,' Nic told her. 'When did you last shave your legs?'

Lizzy swigged wine straight from the bottle. 'What does it matter?' she snarled. 'Like anyone's going to ever run their hands over them again.'

'Can we have our old Lizzy back please?' Poppet pleaded. 'I don't like being scared when I pick up the phone to you.'

The two factions eyeballed each other across the picnic rug. Lizzy on one side, Nic and Poppet on the other. East versus West, a Berlin wall of Tesco canapés and bottles of two-for-one Zinfandel between them.

In the end Nic gave it to Lizzy straight. 'Look, we all know what Lemar said about if there was any justice in the world, and at the moment you're feeling pretty hard done by because Justin has got a new girlfriend already. But you have to snap out of this because you're in danger of turning into a giant twat. Are you receiving me?'

Lizzy opened her mouth to retaliate before the realization finally hit. Nic was right. She *had* been acting like a complete idiot.

'I'm sorry,' she said meekly. 'Will you forgive me?'

Poppet grinned. 'Of course we forgive you, silly!'

'Does that mean you're going to stop cutting and pasting me all Justin's status updates with the word DIE after them?' Nic asked.

They made Lizzy – or rather 'Heidi Milton' – immediately defriend Justin on Facebook and had a toast to her re-found sanity. 'I've been really worried,' Poppet told her. 'You were so brave about the break-up. I thought you were having some kind of delayed reaction.'

'Maybe I was.' Lizzy watched a jet streak across the evening sky. 'I guess I just believed that I'd be the one who'd meet someone first, and Justin would stay a single universal woman-repellent after what he'd done. Or, even if he *did* meet someone, she would be fatter and uglier than me, and he'd live the rest of his days in regret.' Lizzy shook her head. 'I was pissed off he got in there first. I was pissed off I was replaced so quickly – with someone hot. I was REALLY pissed off that he got away with this whole thing without a mark on him. How is that fair?'

That was the nub of the matter really. Good things didn't always happen to good people. People did bad things and got away with it. Karma wasn't always your friend. Nic was right. You just had to suck it up.

'Life's a long game,' Poppet said wisely. 'You never know how it will pan out. It's just annoying how it always seems to be the men who move on first. Remember Anthony Fraser from uni, who got engaged to three different girls in our first year? Men can just turn their feelings on and off like that. I don't get it.'

'Because men are one-dimensional numpties with only enough room in their emotional bank for what's going on directly in front of them.' Nic threw a salted cashew at a loitering pigeon. 'Women are far more whimsical and sentimental. They spend months self-flagellating themselves about the: "What if's" and the: "If I'd done that/hadn't done that we'd still be togethers". Whereas men are already thinking: "Clare from accounts is pretty hot. How do I get to bang her?"'

'*You're* a woman,' Poppet pointed out.

'And I think like a man. You have to stay one step ahead in this game, Pops.'

A couple on a picnic rug near them had been getting more and more amorous. The girls watched as the man rolled on top of his companion and started dry humping her.

'You see?' Nic said to Lizzy. 'Do you really miss that?'

'It's so unseemly!' Poppet lamented. 'There are no standards of decorum these days. Next thing you know it will be legal to have sex in the street!'

Someone threw a condom packet at the couple and everyone around them cheered. '*You* can talk,' Nic told her. 'You gave Pencil Dick Pete a blow job in a churchyard!'

'Don't say that!' Poppet squealed. 'I thought it had been deconsecrated!'

Time with your friends was all a girl needed to feel that all was right with the world again. The next day the girls hired a pedalo on the Serpentine and then went to sit in a pub beer garden where they drank so much Pimms that Poppet was overcome by a bladder emergency on the bus home and semi-wet herself, just like old times. Back at her flat they carried on drinking until they all passed out in Poppet's king-size bed.

Even after vast amounts of alcohol, Nic was unable

to lie in. At some ungodly hour she went off to get the Sunday papers and left the other two sleeping off their hangovers. Lizzy was in the middle of a dream about quenching her thirst in a sparkling mountain stream when she felt a dead weight land on the bed.

'Guess who's split up?' Nic held up the tabloid.

Lizzy prised her eyes apart. It was hard to make out what was going on in the grainy pictures. 'News at Ten: You're Dumped! Amber calls off engagement to Elliot after row in the street!'

'Oh my God!' Poppet sat up and immediately went green. 'I think I'm going to be sick.'

While Poppet hyperventilated into a wet flannel Nic read out the story in her best newsreader voice: 'In dramatic scenes captured outside the Royal Albert Hall on Friday, Amber de la Haye finished with ITN hunk Elliot Anderson. In the astonishing exchange the fashion designer, thirty-one, was overheard emotionally telling her 32-year-old fiancé: "I can't DO this any more."'

Lizzy sat up to take a better look at the pictures. Elliot (in a black tuxedo) and Amber (in a white dress) were standing on the pavement in front of the Albert Hall, in the middle of what appeared to be a flaming row. In one shot Amber was gesticulating angrily with her hands, while Elliot had his arm out as if trying to pacify her. The montage finished with her storming off down the street, her long hair flying out behind her. Elliot was gazing after her looking utterly bereft. The paper had zoomed in on his face with the word *ANGUISH* underneath it, in case the reader was in any doubt.

'Sheesh,' Nic said. 'To be in the public eye, eh?'

Lizzy felt physically sick. It was like watching herself back on that karaoke stage again. She wouldn't be in Elliot's expensive Italian leather shoes for all the money in the world.

Chapter 22

The next day the split was being updated hourly on the *MailOnline*. Apparently the couple had been having problems for some time. 'Amber tried hard to make it work,' a 'friend' of the fashion designer was quoted as saying, 'but sometimes loving someone isn't enough.'

According to reports, Amber had fled to a bolt-hole in France. A long-lens paparazzi had captured her looking gaunt and beautiful behind a pair of her own-label sunglasses as she boarded a friend's private jet. Next to it there was a picture of Elliot looking grim-faced as he arrived at work that morning.

Amber's spokesperson had asked for her client 'to be left alone during this difficult time'. Elliot had also refused to comment.

The Haven office was alive with speculation about the latest celebrity split. 'I always thought Amber was way too cool for him,' Bianca said. 'She should be going out with Pharrell Williams or someone like that.'

'She can go out with whoever she wants now.' Lizzy answered her phone. 'Hello, Haven?'

It was a small wobbly voice. 'L-Lizzy?'

'Karen? What's wrong?' Lizzy rushed into the meeting room to take the call and shut the door behind her. 'Whatever's the matter?'

'I've been up all weekend trying to make the sums add up.' Her client suppressed another sob. 'I can't afford to pay all my suppliers, Andy's being a complete shit . . .'

Andy was Karen's obnoxious ex-husband. 'What's he done now?' Lizzy asked.

'Just the usual mind games. I normally rise above it, but I'm on the edge at the moment. I feel like jacking it all in but they've given my old job away and there's nothing else out there. I'm going to lose the house and me and Molly will end up homeless—'

'You're not going to end up homeless,' Lizzy said firmly. 'We just have to hang on in there. I believe in you, Karen.'

'You're about the only person who does. And I can't even afford to pay you any more.' She started crying again.

'Karen, listen to me. Everything will be OK.'

'How will it be OK?' Karen sobbed. 'I've run out of money.'

Lizzy bit her lip. If Karen couldn't afford to pay Haven PR they would have to part ways. Unless . . .

'How about if you pay a reduced rate for the time being? Would that help?'

'W-w-what do you mean?' Karen gulped.

'How about if you only pay half of your monthly retainer until the end of the year? Things always pick up in the run-up to Christmas. You can pay back what you owe then.'

'But what will Antonia say?'

Lizzy looked through the window. Her boss had her feet up on her desk as she laughed uproariously down the phone. 'Antonia will be fine,' Lizzy lied. 'Besides, she hardly ever looks at the accounts. She won't even notice.'

'Things will pick up! It's just been a bad few months.' Karen sounded like she'd been given a last-minute reprieve from death row. 'Oh Lizzy! You're an angel!'

Lizzy hung up and immediately felt anxious. What had she just done?

'We need to make this quick, people,' Antonia barked a second later. 'I've got a Skype session with my shamanic guru at 1 p.m.' The morning meeting was meant to take place at 10 a.m., but it never happened until at least midday because Antonia was never ready on time.

There was a nerve-stripping screech from the other side of the office. 'MINE!' a child shouted. Antonia was having childcare issues so she'd brought Christiana into work with her. A makeshift crèche had been set up in a corner and the poor intern was saddled with baby-sitting duties while the rest of them crowded around Antonia's desk.

Lizzy gave a quick update of where they were with the Santa's Little Helper launch, which was happening that weekend in Aylesbury.

'I'll be coming along to that,' Antonia announced. 'Brian and Debbie will feel a lot better if I'm there to keep an eye on things.'

Hmm, Lizzy thought. More like stand around on her phone all day and take credit if the event's a success.

'And Karen?'

Lizzy flushed guiltily. 'What about Karen?'

Her boss looked up from her iPad. 'Oh I don't know, where's she going this year on holiday? Can she recommend any good box sets? What have we got coverage-wise, you dingbat?'

There was a *thud* followed by a loud scream. The intern was kneeling on the floor with her hands over her nose. Christiana was standing over her with a staple gun in her hand.

'Christy! Play nicely!' Antonia bellowed. 'Mummy won't be long!'

Luckily Antonia had the attention span of a gnat with ADHD, so Karen was quickly forgotten. 'I had a great idea in the bath last night for a cross-brand promotion,' she told the team. 'I've been reading this a*maz*ing book about how we all store all this negative energy from our ancestors in our gut, and I was thinking it would be a*maz*ing to team up the Happy Halo with A Helping Hand and call it A Helping Halo. The one-stop cleansing combo for every woman's needs! What was the strapline I thought of?' She looked heaven-wards. 'Fight off the demons of the past and become the warrior goddess you are destined to be!'

From the blank faces around her she might as well have been speaking in Mandarin. 'If you could make that happen,' she told Lizzy. 'Set up meetings with the heads of Boots, Space NK, etc. Oh, and let's get a date with Gwyneth Paltrow's people in the diary, she'd be a great brand ambassador.' She broke off. 'No, Christy! Not the phone! Play nicely!'

Everyone watched as three-year-old Christiana

wrestled the intern's iPhone out of her hand and smashed it into smithereens against the wall.

Lizzy arrived at San Marco first that evening. 'Lee-zee!' Giuseppe bounded up like a pre-neutered cocker spaniel. 'Haven't seen you on the telly lately.'

'Ha ha, very funny.'

'My nephew, he meet someone now. But I always keep eye out for you. Come! I give you best table.'

Poppet and Nic arrived together ten minutes later. Nic was sporting a new, shorter haircut that made her look like she hurt people for a living.

Poppet was in a twitchy mood. 'Did you see on Facebook that Emma Summers has got engaged?'

Nic looked up from her phone. 'To that weird hairy guy with the squint?'

'I think he's had corrective surgery. That's the fifth person I know who's got engaged this year! They're dropping like flies and I can't even meet a man who wants to take me to the cinema and for a meal at Waga-mamas afterwards! I'm going to be left on the shelf, I just know it.'

'Don't be ridiculous,' Lizzy told her. 'You'll have to push me off first to get a space.'

Poppet wasn't listening. 'There was this thing on Mumsnet the other day about how twenty-nine is the prime biological window! Even if my Mr Right is out there, what if I don't meet him until I'm forty? It will be too late to have children and even if we do manage to have one miracle IVF baby and get to be in *Bella* magazine, I'll be chasing it round the park in my wheelchair!'

'All the interesting women have children over forty.' Nic was still furiously typing away on her phone. 'Look at Meryl Streep, Emma Thompson, Julianne Moore . . .'

'It's all right for you two, you're career women! I wish female emancipation had never been invented. All I want to do is marry a nice man who will look after me and we can move to the country, and I'll stay at home looking after our children.'

'I'm going to pretend you didn't say that,' Nic told her.

'But I did say it!' Poppet cried. 'It's what I want! Why are women made to feel our worth is only measured by salary zeros and how many glass ceilings we have to smash at work? Dammit, why did Matt Damon go and have kids with that Italian bitch!'

'Pops, I don't think it's healthy to spend so much time on Mumsnet,' Lizzy said. 'Look how it winds you up.'

'I can't help it! Everyone is settling down except me! Have I done something terrible in a previous life and this is God's way of punishing me?' She looked on the verge of tears. 'I want that conversation about whether it's still the done thing to have favours so much it actually hurts.'

'Really? Is that what you really want?' Nic finally put her phone down. 'You think ending up with six crystal wine goblets in your cupboard and a Jamie Oliver chef's knife is a sign that you've made it?'

'I'm not sure I'd have crystal goblets, but—'

'Poppet,' Nic interrupted. 'It's all a load of bollocks. Do you really think Emma Summers and every other stupid cow who's got engaged this year has really done it because they've found "The One"?'

Poppet opened her mouth but Nic put a hand up and silenced her.

'People like Emma Summers aren't getting married because they're in *love*! Do you think that when Emma Summers was a little girl she dreamed of marrying a guy with a facial tic and beard dandruff? Everyone's in such a panic about this stupid self-imposed deadline that they're grabbing anyone and anything they can. Someone needs to blow a bloody great whistle and shout: "Will everyone just STOP? Bridezilla over there! Do you *really* want to live out your days with a guy who wears utility clothing at the weekend like he's some sort of suburban Bear Grylls? And you in the corner! Rattling round with all that folic acid inside you! Do you actually want kids, or are you just going along with it because you think you have to? Are you too scared to admit that – shock horror – there might be other options out there?"' Breathlessly defiant, Nic sat back. 'You see it every day across the land: dead-eyed couples in restaurants and traffic jams with bugger all to say to each other. These fools aren't settling down, they're just *settling*!'

'Is there a heart that beats in there, Nic?' Poppet said stiffly. 'Only sometimes I do wonder.' Then she went off to sulk in the loo.

Nic slumped against the banquette. Even for her it had been quite a diatribe.

'Are you OK, hun?' Lizzy asked.

Nic sighed. 'I know I was harsh on Pops but some-times I just want to shake her. She doesn't need to worry. As if someone isn't going to snap her up.'

Her friend was looking really tired. 'Is Simon giving you loads of hassle?' Lizzy said.

'Nothing I can't handle.' Nic pulled her hand over her face. 'Maybe I just need to drink less.'

Poppet came back from the loo wearing the wounded expression of a puppy whose tail had just been accidentally shut in the door by its owner.

'I'm sorry, Pops,' Nic told her. 'I didn't mean to go off on one.'

'Other people are allowed to have points of view. You can't always shout them down just because they don't agree with you.'

'I know. Will you forgive me? I promise to be meek and amenable from now on. I'll even send Emma Summers a congratulatory helium balloon if it will make you love me again.'

Poppet couldn't stay cross if she tried. 'Of course I still love you,' she told Nic. 'And I was thinking when I was on the toilet, maybe you *have* got a point about the beard dandruff!'

Chapter 23

It was Saturday and the day of the Santa's Little Helper launch. Lizzy had planned to leave London by 8 a.m. at the latest, but with various Christiana issues and Antonia's Abel & Cole delivery turning up late, it was nearly ten by the time they got on the road. Lizzy had already had five irate calls from Brian Baxter, and was starting to sweat profusely.

'You handle stress really badly,' Antonia told her. 'Have you thought about transcendental meditation?'

Lizzy thought about punching her boss's lights out, then lurched forward as the Range Rover screeched to a halt at a set of red traffic lights. There was a playing field on the left, where two teams of men were playing five-a-side football.

'Aren't they revolting?'

'Who?' Lizzy sighed.

'Men! Look at them with their skinny little legs and fat bellies, chasing a ball around. Emotionally, they never progress beyond the age of fourteen. Women don't even start channelling their inner goddess until the age of forty.' Antonia drummed her fingernails on the steering wheel. 'And the tragedy is that we have to endure those cretins for the rest of our lives just because we needed to get sperm out of them.'

'I don't know if that's true about *all* men.' Not that Lizzy was feeling that hopeful about the other sex right now.

'Ha! You wait until you have kids.' Antonia rammed the car into first gear. 'Not that future generations will suffer the same hardships that we have. In evolutionary terms women are becoming by far the stronger species.' She dangerously overtook a minibus with 'Sunset Care Home' written on it. 'You mark my words. In a hundred years' time the modern male will have died out and we'll all be getting our babies from Scandinavian sperm banks!'

Fortunately Antonia drove like the secret lovechild of Jenson Button and The Roadrunner. With the Range Rover bulldozing everything out of its path they reached the outskirts of the Buckinghamshire town in barely an hour. Antonia had spent most of the journey on the hands-free to her husband telling him where he could find various things for Christiana and discussing intimate healthcare issues. Lizzy now knew more about Erik's ingrown hair problem to ever feel comfortable looking him in the eye again.

At least it was a lovely day for the launch; the sun beating down and blue skies stretching out like a giant smear of paint. They should get a good turnout, especially with the mince-pie ice cream that Lizzy had persuaded a local dairy to make for the occasion. Even Antonia had agreed it had been a masterstroke.

The local radio had been on since they'd left the motorway. An advert for 'Carl Pitter master carpet-fitter' seemed to be on a thirty-second loop.

'Why are we listening to this shit?' Antonia asked. 'It's giving me a migraine.'

'They've promised to give us a trail.' Lizzy looked at the clock on the dashboard. 'It should be on any moment . . .'

The music faded out. 'That was a slice of the sultry Shania Twain for a sultry day! In local news, it's the Shane Castle summer festival today, with fun for kids and parents alike, so get yourself down there. And tomorrow local entrepreneurs Bernard and Deirdre Baxter are launching their new herbal drink Satan's Little Helper in the market square.'

'It's SANTA'S Little Helper and it's TODAY!' Lizzy howled. 'I can't believe this!' How many times had she emailed over the details?

'Well, there's clearly been a cock-up somewhere,' Antonia huffed. 'You're on your own when we see Brian and Debbie.'

Sure enough, Brian was waiting for them looking like a scowling, hairy-chested relation of the Mario Brothers. 'Did you just hear the radio? They didn't get anything right. Did you send them the wrong press release or what? And they made me and Debs sound like a pair of dozy amateurs!'

'Lizzy is doing her best to rectify the situation,'

Antonia breathed. 'I can only offer my sincerest apologies, you know this would have never happened under my watch.'

Lizzy had been on hold to the radio station for the past fifteen minutes. 'Yes! Hello?' A loud *beeeeep* pierced her ear as she was cut off.

Antonia conveniently swanned off to say hello to Debbie, and Brian crossed his arms. 'This is not what I pay you for.'

'I'm sorry,' Lizzy said. 'I'm just as annoyed as you are.'

'I doubt that. And what time do you call this? Me and Debs have been here since 8 a.m. She's had to bring her mum along and the old dear is about to conk out with dehydration.'

Lizzy looked at the grey-haired lady dozing on a folding chair under one of the Santa's Little Helper themed umbrellas. She didn't look that well.

'I have to say, it's all looking brilliant!' she said heartily.

It was the exaggeration of the century. The stall with its mistletoe bunting and flashing Christmas tree looked completely incongruous on a swelteringly hot August day. Trays of sweaty mince pies sat between carefully assembled pyramids of Santa's Little Helper bottles. A vat of mulled wine was bubbling away ferociously in the background.

'Where's the ice-cream man?' Lizzy asked.

'He's just called,' Brian said gloomily. 'Their generator has broken down in the heat and all the ice cream has melted.'

'What? Why has no one rung me?'

'Probably because you've been on the bloody phone to the radio station.' Brian shook his head. 'Not what I pay you for, Lizzy, you're meant to be on call twenty-four/seven.'

They gazed across the deserted square. 'Where are all the press?' he asked plaintively. 'I thought you said you had loads of interviews lined up.'

'I've just left them all another voicemail.' Lizzy was starting to get a terrible feeling about the whole thing.

Antonia had disappeared on the pretext of making an urgent phone call, so Lizzy had been left to man the stall with Debbie Baxter. Instead of the green elf hat and sash that Lizzy was wearing, Debbie had gone off-plan with fish-net tights and a satin minidress trimmed with white fur. She'd already been called a prostitute by a young mum pushing a Bugaboo past. So much for catering to the female market.

A group of youths had been loitering for a while, spitting on to the cobbles and making derogatory comments about Debbie's chest. One of them sidled up to Lizzy.

'How much?'

'It's retailing at £9.99 but we're giving away free samples today. It's packed with a blend of seven different herbal ingredients . . .' Lizzy reeled off the sales pitch.

'So what does it do for you?'

His accent was a bizarre hybrid of Home Counties meets ghetto Brooklyn. '*Do* for you?' Lizzy asked confusedly.

The boy sucked his teeth at her. 'It's a new legal high,

right? This place is well boring, we need something to liven it up.'

'Sod off, you little druggie!' Debbie hissed. 'Or I'll call your mum!'

Ten minutes later a police car wailed into the square. Two officers who looked like they should have been sitting their A levels sprang importantly out of the car.

'We've had a tip-off someone is selling controlled substances,' the shorter one announced. 'Can you tell me what's going on?'

It took a further fifteen minutes of explanation, plus a rigorous testing session by the officers, to determine that Santa's Little Helper was legitimate.

'We've just been up the summer festival at Shane Castle, the place is packed,' the taller one told Lizzy. 'Not a very good turnout here, is it? You should have got the local radio to give it a mention.'

An hour later their only customers had been the police officers, a couple of elderly women and a bored traffic warden who'd wandered over to see what was going on.

'This is a fucking disaster!' Antonia hissed. 'Do something!'

'I am trying!' Lizzy was attempting to get hold of all the press who were meant to be turning up, but she was still getting a barrage of voicemails. The one journalist she had managed to get through to had clearly been pissed and had told Lizzy that he'd forgotten that it was his parents' silver wedding anniversary. It was a blatant lie. The truth was no one in their right mind wanted to spend a scorching hot weekend at the end of August standing round a town centre drinking mulled wine.

'Tweet about it!' Antonia instructed Lizzy.

'I have already!'

'Do another one then! Say there's free food and booze for the next thirty minutes and that people had better get their arses down here!'

Lizzy did as she was told, in a slightly less rude manner. 'We've had a retweet already! And another one.'

'You see?' Antonia said smugly. 'All it needed was a little lateral thinking.'

Not long after a camper van rolled into the square, followed by more camper vans and what looked like a 1960s school bus painted in various shades of the rainbow.

The convoy drew up next to the stall. A young guy with dreadlocks stuck his head out of the window. 'Is this the free festival?' he asked Lizzy.

'Free festival?' What was he talking about?

The man waved his phone at her. 'People have been tweeting about a party with free food and drink.'

More vehicles poured in. The market square started to resemble a summer solstice at Glastonbury. Lithe, suntanned men wandered round in the sun with plastic glasses of mulled wine. Rugs had been laid out on the ground, off which people were selling jewellery and incense candles. Someone else had set up a yoga flash mob outside Caffè Nero. Groups of local children were staring goggle-eyed at the exotic, tattooed creatures in front of them.

Brian Baxter had just been asked if he wanted his astrological chart doing and was about to blow a gasket.

'We're not running a "Hippies Reunited" convention here! Do something!'

'These people are fucking disgusting!' Antonia whispered violently. 'Get rid of them, Lizzy!'

So much for them all being children of the universe. Lizzy went up to a young woman who was sitting on the kerb playing with an adorable baby. She smiled at Lizzy.

'Are you one of the organizers? It's such a lovely idea to bring us all together.'

Lizzy shut her mouth and bid a hasty retreat. Antonia could do her own dirty work.

To make matters even worse, the local press then decided to turn up, probably after hearing something untoward was going down on the market square. A local reporter cornered Lizzy on the cobbles.

'Three young people have died in the last year after overdosing on these so-called new legal highs,' the reporter informed her. 'Don't you think you're being irresponsible? What kind of message is this sending out to kids?'

'Santa's Little Helper is completely natural and safe,' Lizzy said desperately, searching for Antonia to come and rescue her. 'It's just to help stressed-out mums when they need a little pick-me-up.'

'I think you'll find there's another product that's cornered that market already,' the reporter quipped. 'It's called white wine.'

At least the products were going like hot cakes now. All the local kids had lined up at the Santa's Little Helper stall and were bulk-buying.

'Let's go and get wasted,' Lizzy heard one of them say to their friends.

This was a disaster! Bloody Antonia was nowhere to be seen. An incandescent Brian Baxter dragged Lizzy to one side.

'You couldn't have made more of a pig's ear of this if you'd tried!'

'I understand, Brian, but I'm trying my hardest.' She tried to look on the bright side. 'At least the product is selling.'

'Yeah, to a bunch of drug-crazed school kids!' He shook his head. 'Well done, Lizzy, you've just ruined three years of my and Deb's hard work in one afternoon!'

Lizzy miserably watched him stomp off. This was a complete and unmitigated disaster.

A few minutes later the same police car that had come past earlier wailed into the square. The two young officers jumped out. 'All right, we're shutting this down!' one of them cried.

'You can't!' Lizzy wailed. 'I've been working for months on this! You've already tested them – you know they're fine!'

'We can't be seen to be condoning drug use,' one of them told Lizzy, 'even if we know they're legit. It's all about public perception these days . . . All right everyone, move along! If you go peacefully no arrests will be made.' The officer snatched a bottle of Santa's Little Helper off a small boy standing nearby. 'Does your dad know you're down here?'

Half an hour later the square was empty again,

debris and litter strewn across the ground. The Santa's Little Helper stall looked like it had been ravaged by wild animals: someone had even stolen the themed umbrellas.

Debbie Baxter's mum had suffered a sugar overdose from eating too many mince pies, and had been carted off home. Brian Baxter was striding round the square doing a good impression of the Incredible Hulk.

'It's a bloody great shower of shit!' he was shouting at Antonia, who had miraculously reappeared from somewhere now everyone had gone.

'I know, I know,' she gusted sympathetically. 'I will be having *strong* words with Lizzy about her strategy for press launches in the future.'

'Bit late for this one, though, isn't it?' He jabbed a finger. 'I'll tell you something for nothing, Antonia, Debbie and I will be reviewing our relationship with Haven PR *very* closely in the morning.'

Lizzy escaped her boss's death stare and went to cry in the toilet of Caffè Nero. If she still had a job on Monday morning it would be a miracle.

Chapter 24

It was obviously a quiet news day, because the launch, with the added bonus of Lizzy's stardom, swiftly went up on the *MailOnline*. The next day the *Sunday Mirror* went with the headline: 'Headbutt Girl in Legal High Scandal' and *#santaslittlehelper* was trending on Twitter. Lizzy turned her phone off and spent the day hiding in her flat updating her CV. It was almost like 'Girl Who Gets Jilted . . .' all over again.

Antonia had been ominously quiet the whole way back to London, and had said they would 'review the situation' on Monday. Fearing the worst, Lizzy got into the office early. Her boss was already at her desk, which was definitely a bad sign.

'There you are,' Antonia said unsmilingly. 'Let's go into the meeting room.'

Feeling increasingly sick, Lizzy followed Antonia in. Her boss shut the door. 'I've just got off the phone to Brian Baxter.'

Lizzy swallowed. 'Oh?'

Antonia sat down heavily in her usual chair. 'It

would . . . *appear* that pre-order sales of Santa's Little Helper have shot through the roof.'

'Oh?'

'In fact so much so, that Brian and Debbie are talking about taking on extra staff to meet demand.'

'Oh?'

'Will you stop sounding like a complete moron?' Antonia snapped. 'What I'm trying to tell you, Lizzy, is that despite the *adverse* conditions, the launch has been deemed a raging success and the Baxters are delighted.'

'Right,' Lizzy said faintly.

At that point Antonia actually smiled. 'Which just goes to show, there's really no such thing as bad press.'

'So I'm not sacked?' Lizzy asked.

'I won't pretend I wasn't cross. You put Haven PR's reputation – and my reputation – on the line.' Antonia sighed, as if she had to make the world's most difficult decision. 'But seeing how everything has turned out, I'm willing to give you another chance. But if you do have any maverick ideas for launches in the future, *do* try and share them with me first.'

Lizzy walked out feeling completely stunned but relieved to still have a job. That was the thing about PR: you slogged your guts out all year trying to get someone to write about your product, and then just when it looked like your job was on the line, you un-intentionally pulled off the coup of the year.

She received a standing ovation as she walked into San Marco that evening.

'Here she is!' Nic announced. 'The woman responsible for the new designer drug sweeping Britain!'

'Don't.' Lizzy sat down and poured herself out a huge glass of wine. 'I've already had my mum in my ear about bringing the family name into disrepute.'

'You did look really cute in your elf costume,' Poppet told her. 'I think you should wear hats more often.'

'See, every cloud?' Nic said. 'Now you know you suit hats.'

What would she do without her friends? 'And how were *your* weekends?'

Poppet crossed her arms and looked at her lap. 'What's wrong?' Lizzy asked Nic.

'While you were caught up in the Santa's Little Helper drama, Poppet had her own little drama.'

'What happened?' Lizzy put her glass down. 'Pops, are you all right?'

'Do you want to tell Lizzy, or do you want me to?'

'You can.' Poppet put her napkin over her head. 'I don't want Lizzy to see my shame,' she whispered.

Nic shot Lizzy a look. 'She slept with Pencil Dick Pete on Saturday night. She's been wallowing in a pit of self-loathing ever since. I've told her it doesn't matter and we all make mistakes, but she isn't having any of it.'

There was a load moan from under the napkin. 'I hate myself!'

'Oh dear,' Lizzy said. 'How did this happen?'

Nic explained quickly. 'Pencil Dick Pete asked Poppet to meet up for a drink, but it turned out he was upset about splitting up with this girl and needed someone to talk to.'

'And I was fine with that!' The napkin blew in and

175

out. 'I'd completely convinced myself I could do the whole female friend thing! But then he bought another round and I hadn't had anything to eat, and before I knew it we were in bed together! And *then* I sent him a text afterwards, not because I want to get back with him or anything, but because it's just polite to check in with someone after you've had sexual relations with them – and he hasn't even had the courtesy to text me back!'

Nic pulled the napkin off Poppet's head, but she still wouldn't look at Lizzy.

'Poppet, darling,' Lizzy said. 'You've got nothing to be ashamed of. So what if Pencil Dick didn't text you back? It just proves what a douchebag he is.'

Nic nodded. 'And at least he didn't threaten to put a video of you having sex on the Internet.'

Poppet gasped. 'How do I *know* he didn't film it? There was a suspicious tin on the bedside table that he didn't want to open in front of me. Oh God, it could have had a secret camera in it! *And* my hair was looking awful because we'd just had sex in the shower!' She flopped face-first on the table. 'My parents will never live this down. And even worse, Pencil Dick Pete has now got one over me.'

'Who gives a shit about him?' Nic told her. 'Look, you obviously needed a shag. He was there to be used and abused. It's not what he got out of you. It's what *you* got out of *him*.'

Poppet's eyes widened. 'I didn't think of it like that.'

'Start thinking of it like that.' Nic put a hand on Poppet's shoulder. 'Stop beating yourself up about it. *You* used *him*.'

'You're right. I used him.'

'Say it like you mean it.'

'I used him! I used him and I abused him and I left him there like a bit of discarded meat!'

'Jesus, Pops,' Nic said. 'What did you guys *do* together?'

'Oh God,' she said after they'd all laughed for about five minutes. 'I needed that.'

Lizzy looked at her friends. Nic had dark circles under her eyes and Poppet even had a spot on her chin, which was a first in all the years Lizzy had known her.

'You know what we need?' she told them. 'A weekend away.'

Poppet lit up like a Christmas tree. 'Ooh, that's a great idea!'

'Nicholas?' Lizzy asked. 'I know your aversion to leaving London when you're not working, but how about it?'

'I suppose I do need a break,' Nic sighed. 'I've been having these really disturbing dreams about Zac Efron.'

'Zac *Efron*?' Lizzy and Poppet said in unison.

Nic shook her head violently. 'I don't want to talk about it. So where are we going?'

Chapter 25

'Pops, where do you think you left your car?' Lizzy said. 'Are there any landmarks that might help?'

The three were stood in a myriad of backstreets on the Clapham/Brixton border. As Nic couldn't drive and Lizzy didn't have a car, Poppet was the designated driver for the trip down to Dorset. Unfortunately she had no idea where she'd last parked.

'*Think,*' she muttered to herself. 'I only used it to go to IKEA last week!'

Nic stared down the line of bumper-to-bumper cars. 'I fought to get a half day off for this.'

Twenty minutes later they finally located Poppet's Peugeot down a side street she swore she'd never even seen before. It took a further five minutes of back-and-forth Austin Powers-style nudging before they were finally on their way.

It was fair to say Poppet wasn't the most confident of drivers. She always got passers-by to parallel-park for her, and then there was the time she'd infamously driven down Kensington High Street on the wrong side of the road. As Nic had pointed out, someone who shut their eyes when they were going around roundabouts was not best equipped to deal with London traffic. Especially London traffic at rush hour on a Friday. By the time they'd eventually pulled out on to the M3 towards Dorset, Lizzy and Nic had seen off a bottle of Banrock Station between them to calm their rising heart rates.

Nic had managed to get them into a boutique hotel that had been recommended to her by a colleague who'd stayed there. Sweetbriar House was located in a hamlet just outside the historic town of Shaftesbury. As long as there were no hold-ups they should be down there in two hours.

Lizzy was in the back seat with a bag of Pick 'n' Mix and a can of Gordon's gin and tonic. In the front Nic and Poppet were having a discussion about Zac Efron. 'There must be some deep-rooted attraction there,' Poppet was telling her. 'Otherwise why would you be dreaming about him?'

'He's just so goddamn perky.' Nic gazed out of her window. 'I don't even know who I am any more.'

A coach with King's School Blandford written down the side started to overtake them. Spotting Lizzy and her friends, all the boys ran to the back and started pulling remedial faces.

'They're probably going to be running the country in twenty years' time,' Nic sighed. 'How depressing is that?'

One of the boys gave her the V-sign. Nic gave him the V-sign back.

'Don't encourage him!' Poppet scolded.

'He started it.'

The boy gave Nic the bird. She gave him the bird back. The boy made an aggressive wanking gesture. Nic waggled her little finger back. The boy's face faltered for a moment, before he stuck his fingers down his throat and pretended to be sick.

'Oh you *amateur*.' Undoing her seat belt, Nic pulled her top up and flashed him.

'Nicola!' Poppet screeched. 'You can get done for that!'

The bus pulled past. The last thing Lizzy saw were fifty shocked, pimply faces as the bus sailed off into the middle lane.

The girls collapsed into hysterics. 'Oh my God!' Poppet squealed. 'We've just passed a speed camera! What if we get reported?'

'They'll have to identify us by Nic's baps then.' Lizzy's stomach muscles were aching from laughing.

Nic wiped a tear from her cheek. 'I haven't had such a good release for ages. Who needs Boxercise?'

Poppet did a very unladylike snort. 'Did you see their *faces*?'

It sent them all off again. 'Mercy,' Nic groaned. 'My stomach muscles can't take any more.'

They drove on for a few moments in an exhausted, happy silence.

'Isn't this great?' Poppet said.

Lizzy leant between the seats. 'Do you mean Nic setting a bunch of twelve-year-old boys up for a lifetime of therapy?'

'I mean *this*. The fact that we can just jump in the car and go off on this big adventure. We can do what

180

we want, when we want. If I was going on a romantic weekend away with somebody I'd be worrying if I'd packed matching underwear, and eating too much at dinner so I'd be too full to go on top later.' Poppet sighed happily. 'I'm not wearing any make-up all weekend! Well, maybe a tiny bit of Touche Eclat.'

The engine shrieked horribly. 'Pops,' Lizzy said. 'Do you think it's time to move into third gear?'

It was nearing 7 p.m. by the time they approached the hamlet. 'I am dying for a wee,' Nic groaned. 'I've got about two litres of white wine sloshing round inside me.'

They drove past another row of pretty little cottages. 'It can't be that far now,' Poppet said.

'Keep going.' Nic had the AA printout on her lap. 'It's half a mile more on the left.'

Poppet wriggled round in her seat. 'I've got butterflies I'm so excited! I'm going to have a lovely long soak in the bath and then sit in the garden with a nice drink and watch the sunset.'

Lizzy had been thinking the same. Sweetbriar House conjured up visions of flagstone floors and calming neutral decor. And Nic had said something about there being a hot tub.

'I wonder who else is staying there?' Poppet steered the car round a bend. 'Maybe we can have a big murder mystery-style dinner party tomorrow.'

'I haven't come all the way down here to speak to a load of randoms,' Nic grumbled. 'I get enough of that with my job. Left here.'

Two minutes later they pulled up outside a handsome

stone lodge with white shutters on every window. The gardens were sprawling and beautiful. Lizzy instantly relaxed. It was just what they needed.

The car park adjacent to the lodge was full, so they left the car by the side of the road. Poppet had brought so much stuff with her that the other two had to help carry it in.

'What have you *got* in here?' Lizzy asked, as she precariously wheeled one of Poppet's giant suitcases up the path. 'It's more than I'd take for a two-week holiday.'

'Oh you know, just stuff!'

The entrance hall was deserted when they walked in. It had a very boutique feel: there was a large sitting room on the left with big sofas and a beautiful Victorian fireplace. Lizzy imagined herself chilling out in there later with a gin and tonic. Or maybe they'd push the boat out and get some champagne.

'Where is everyone?' Nic said. 'If they worked for us, I can tell you now they'd get sacked.'

'Can I help you?'

The girls turned round. A woman was standing behind them wiping her hand on a tea towel. She was wearing a flour-stained Cath Kidston apron.

'Er yes!' Lizzy said. 'We're booked in for two nights? Name of Cartwright?'

The woman frowned ominously. 'Are you sure?'

'Perfectly sure.' Nic gave her the booking confirmation email she'd printed out. The woman studied it.

'I hate to tell you this, but you've booked for this date next year.'

'What?' Nic snatched the paper back.

The woman smiled apologetically at Lizzy and Poppet. 'I remember the name now. You're our only booking for that far ahead.'

Nic was utterly horrified. 'I can't believe what a massive dick I am. I should have "Mega Twat" tattooed on my forehead. How could I have booked the wrong year?'

Poppet gave the owner an apologetic look. 'It's not your fault, you've been under a lot of strain at work,' she told Nic.

'I should have *known* it was too good to be true when I booked it at such short notice.' Nic pulled her gold Barclaycard out of her wallet. 'Can we just book in now? I'll pay extra for any inconvenience.'

'I'm afraid all our rooms are occupied.'

The girls exchanged a look. 'Are you sure you can't find us somewhere?' Poppet begged the woman. 'I won't take up much space, I'm really small.'

The woman looked dubiously at Poppet's luggage. 'I'm really sorry, we've been booked out for months.'

Lizzy couldn't quite believe it. She'd heard those horror stories of people getting the wrong date, or turning up to places that had double-booked, but it had never happened to her. It had to be the worst feeling in the whole world.

'Can you recommend anywhere else we could stay?' she asked.

'It's the Great Dorset Steam Fair this weekend, you'll have a hell of a job to find somewhere.' The woman looked at the gutted faces in front of her. 'I'll go and ask my husband, he might know a place.'

*

The owner's prediction had turned out to be ominously true. Every hotel and gastro pub for miles was booked up. They had eventually managed to get in a Travelodge on the side of a busy roundabout, and had ended up having a room-picnic of Ginsters pasties and going to bed at 9 p.m.

The following day Nic was still apologizing and wouldn't let Lizzy or Poppet pay for the room. 'I've ruined everything,' she said as they sat in the car park, pondering their next plan of action. 'I'm going to punish myself so bad at the gym next week.'

'Will you stop beating yourself up?' Lizzy told her. 'It's one of those things.' Although she did have to admit, waking up to the sounds of the A348 wasn't quite the same as being lulled awake by chattering birdsong.

'What now?' Poppet was sitting gloomily behind the wheel. 'Do we just go back to London?'

'It seems a shame, now we're all the way down here,' Lizzy said. 'There has to be a vacancy somewhere that doesn't have a sanitary hand wipe in the room.'

Nic had her phone out. 'And I'm going to bloody well find it.'

Using her contacts, a bit of bribery and sheer determination, she eventually managed to book them into a B & B that had had a last-minute cancellation. It was on the other side of the county, but it was a place to stay.

'Hurrah for Queen Nicola!' Poppet cried. 'Now we've got the whole day to explore! What does everyone want to do?'

*

A very pleasant morning was spent driving past fields of cows and pointing at stately homes in the distance. At lunchtime they stopped at a little tea-shop for doorstep cheese sandwiches and delicious homemade carrot cake.

Poppet looked out of the window. 'I suppose we should go for a walk. Or does driving round count as a walk? I do feel like we've seen a lot.'

Nic was outside, stomping round the car park as she tried to find reception. The other two watched her wave her phone in the air; apparently Simon had sent an email that needed replying to immediately. 'I wish she'd switch off from work for once,' Poppet said. 'He can give her one weekend off, can't he?'

Lizzy watched Nic karate kick a dog-waste bin. 'You know what she's like, she thrives on stress.'

They paid the bill and plunged back into the lanes. 'Isn't it amazing how people live in such remote places?' Poppet said. 'Where do they go to get takeaway coffees? Or a manicure? And what if someone needs an emergency bikini wax?'

Nic sat up in the front passenger seat. 'What the hell is that?'

A horrible scraping noise was coming from under the car. 'Oh my God!' Poppet squealed. 'I've hit something!'

The car shuddered to a halt. 'I can't look!' Poppet had her hands over her face. 'What if it's a baby deer and its mummy is standing up the road and saw the whole thing?'

Nic turned round. 'You go,' she told Lizzy. 'I hate blood.'

'So do I!'

'I hate it more. I got us the rooms for tonight, remember.'

'Please, Lizzy!' Poppet pleaded. 'What if it's still alive under there?'

Oh God. Lizzy reluctantly got out, bracing herself for a little hoof sticking up from under the car.

'What is it?' Poppet cried. 'Just give it to me straight!'

Lizzy stood up again. 'I think your exhaust pipe has fallen off.'

The other two got out and had a look. 'Crumbs!' Poppet said. 'It *is* the exhaust pipe. What do we do now?'

'Ring for a Dominos?' Nic suggested. 'Failing that you could always try the AA.'

'Oh, my parents bought me AA membership for Christmas! I was furious because I'd been dropping hints about that nice black handbag from Reiss with the gold buckle on the front.' Poppet gazed across the rolling rural landscape. 'I suppose a Reiss handbag wouldn't save us now.'

She disappeared off down the lane waving her phone in the air. Nic plopped down on the grassy verge. 'I knew we should have gone on a city break.'

Lizzy walked across to the other side of the road. Beyond the fence were green fields as far as she could see. Someone would come along sooner or later, wouldn't they?

When she turned round Nic was flat on her back on the verge with her eyes closed. The car had its hazard lights on. A piece of broken-off exhaust pipe lay further up the lane.

It *was* a pretty funny scene. *Ooh look! One bar of reception!*

'What are you smiling about?' Nic asked a few moments later.

'I just tweeted about us being broken down in the wilds of Dorset.'

Nic stared at her. 'You get the only bit of reception for miles and you send a tweet rather than call someone for help?'

Lizzy clapped a hand over her mouth. 'I didn't think of it like that. It was just the perfect tweet material!'

Twenty minutes later the country lane was still empty. 'Great,' Nic said gloomily. 'We might not be found for days, by which time the crows will have picked our carcasses dry and they'll have to identify us by our dental records.'

'Ssh!' Poppet said. 'I think I can hear something!'

They all strained their ears. Sure enough it was the sound of an engine in the far distance. And unless Lizzy was mistaken, it was coming their way.

'We're saved!' Poppet shouted. 'Ooh, what if it's a load of fit farmers like the ones off the Yeo Valley ad?'

The next moment a battered old Jeep zoomed round the corner. A man was behind the wheel. He pulled up behind their car.

'Is he going to get out or just stare at us?' Nic asked.

'He looks familiar.' Poppet gave a gasp as the driver's door opened. 'Is that who I think it is?'

Lizzy watched in disbelief as a pair of battered old wellies appeared, followed by a distinctive crop of dark-red hair.

'Hi,' Elliot Anderson said, looking like he'd just run into his worst enemy.

Chapter 26

'Do you think we should say how sorry we are about him and Amber?' Poppet whispered.

The three girls were standing on the side of the road while Elliot Anderson from the ITN *News at Ten* crawled round under Poppet's Sahara-yellow Peugeot.

'Does he look like a man who wants to receive commiserations?' Nic said. 'Just stand there looking helpless and pretty, he's our ticket out of here.'

Elliot stood up and brushed his hands off.

'What's the prognosis, Doctor?' Nic asked.

He didn't smile. 'It's not going anywhere. Do you want a lift to the garage?'

It looked like it was the last thing he wanted to do in the world.

'Only if you don't mind,' Poppet said.

'I'm hardly going to leave you out here, am I?' he muttered, before stomping back to his car.

Elliot didn't take his coat off the front passenger seat, and no one wanted to sit with him anyway, so the girls crammed in the back with their bags on their laps. Lizzy found herself wedged so close behind Elliot she could count the freckles on his neck, and see what looked like a bit of dried grass in the crown of his hair. Was this really happening?

Poppet was making a valiant effort to make conversation. 'I don't know what we'd have done if you hadn't come along. Are you on a weekend break like us?'

'My mother lives round here.' He turned up 6 Music, and they didn't speak for the rest of the way.

The garage was a twenty-minute drive away. '206, is it?' the owner said. 'Earliest I can get you an exhaust is Tuesday.'

'I'm meant to be on a 7 a.m. flight to Brussels on Monday,' Nic told him. 'Can't you get one sooner?'

The man wiped his hands on a piece of greasy cloth. 'I'll see what I can do. It's not so often I get such pretty ladies turning up on my doorstep. In the meantime I've got a car round the back you can use to get round in.'

'Thanks.' Nic batted her eyelashes coquettishly. 'You're our knight in shining overalls.'

Elliot had stayed outside. For the past couple of minutes he'd been having an intense conversation with someone on his mobile. There had been a lot of hand-waving and eye-rolling.

'We've obviously caught him at a bad time,' Poppet whispered.

They watched him walk back across the forecourt towards them. He held the phone out to Lizzy. 'It's for you.'

'For me?' she said confusedly.

Elliot looked pained. 'Just take it, will you?'

She cautiously put the phone to her ear. 'Hello?'

'Is that one of Elliot's friends?' It was a woman with an American accent.

'We're more acquaintances,' Lizzy said diplomatically. 'Our car broke down and Elliot was, er, kind enough to give us a lift to the garage.'

'Then you must come for afternoon tea!' the woman cried.

Lizzy could feel Elliot's eyes boring into her. 'That's very kind, but . . .'

The phone was practically snatched off her. 'What have you said?' Elliot snapped.

He listened for a few moments. 'For God's *sake* . . .' He gazed out over the fields for a moment and visibly collected himself, before turning back round.

'My mother and I would be delighted if you'd come round for a cup of tea this afternoon,' he said, looking anything but.

It was hard to know who looked more awkward. Lizzy opened her mouth to decline, but Poppet got in there first.

'We'd love to! Thank you.'

Elliot's face dropped. 'Right. Well, it's Beeston Lodge,' he said reluctantly. 'Just off the B4589.'

The girls watched him walk back towards the Jeep. 'What time do you want us to come?' Poppet called.

He didn't turn round. 'Come when you want.'

'Tell me again, why did you think it was a good idea to say yes?' Nic asked.

They were driving along in a Volkswagen Polo with

cobwebs stuck in the windscreen wipers. The owner had produced it from somewhere round the back of the garage. Lizzy wasn't sure if it was technically a hire car, especially with the SpongeBob SquarePants air freshener hanging from the rear-view mirror.

'It would have been rude to say no!' Poppet wailed. 'I just panicked!'

All Lizzy could think about was the footage of Elliot gazing after Amber like a broken man. He'd obviously come to his mum's to get away from everything, and here they were, gatecrashing his grief. This was going to be so awkward!

'Left at the eagle,' Nic instructed.

'What eagle?'

'The eagle!' Nic pointed at a gatepost with a stone eagle on the top of it. 'That bloke from the garage said to turn left at the eagle!'

The Polo did a sharp swerve, nearly taking out the other gatepost in the process. There was a large shiny new FOR SALE sign stuck in the ground.

'Beeston Hall,' Poppet read out. 'But Elliot said they lived at Beeston Lodge, didn't he?'

Nic peered up the long drive. 'We haven't seen another house for miles. Let's try our luck.'

They started down the long drive. 'It's just like *Downton Abbey*!' Poppet said excitedly.

Lizzy looked out of the window at the rolling parkland. Elliot's mother had sounded very grand on the phone. She could just imagine some snooty aristocratic blonde.

A full five minutes later the house came into view. Actually, 'came into view' was an understatement. The magnificent building rose out of the ground like the *Titanic.*

Nic gave a low whistle. 'It *is* like *Downton* bloody *Abbey.'*

Poppet was so overcome that she stalled twice. The car finally pulled up on the huge gravel turning circle. They gazed up at the building. 'Something tells me this isn't Beeston Lodge,' Nic said as she unbuckled her seat belt.

The lodge turned out to be a ramshackle cottage off to the right of the main house. The unkempt garden would have given Alan Titchmarsh nightmares. Whoever lived there had obviously let nature take its course. Six giant head sculptures sat around the perimeter of the overgrown lawn, as if standing sentry over the property. They were an incongruous sight amongst all the weeds and wild flowers.

Elliot's car was nowhere to be seen, nor indeed were any other vehicles. 'Where is everybody?' Poppet asked. 'It's a bit spooky.'

'Let's go back to the hall,' Lizzy said, but she didn't hold much hope. The stately home had looked as deserted as the rest of the place.

Up close it was clear that Beeston Hall was in need of serious repair. The stonework was covered in green moss and several bits looked like they were crumbling dangerously. In every window they looked through there were rooms covered with dust sheets. The odd gilt-framed painting over a fireplace or a chandelier hanging in an empty room were the only remains of grand lifetimes that had been long lost. One room was filled entirely with what looked like easels, all stacked up in long rows against each other.

They skirted round the perimeter of the house and came back to the front. 'No one's in,' Nic said. 'Let's get the hell out of here.'

She started violently as an unearthly screech sliced through the air.

Poppet pointed into the distance. 'Someone's coming!'

A figure with a walking stick was moving across the lawn, followed by a boggle-eyed chihuahua, two waddling ducks and a mangy peacock. As the extraordinary menagerie got closer the huge bird let out another blood-curdling shriek.

The woman waved. 'I'm sorry if Leonardo startled you, but he makes a damn good guard dog.'

Lizzy couldn't stop staring. Everything about the woman was . . . red. Wild, curly, hennaed hair escaping from a polka-dot red headscarf, a T-shirt with a red lipstick pattern, a long red leather coat that flapped around her ankles. The outfit was finished off with a pair of battered red suede knee-length boots. A pair of sparkly red glasses sat perched atop the mound of hair, and what appeared to be miniature tomato soup cans dangled from each ear.

'We're looking for Mrs, er, Anderson?' Lizzy called. The woman had to be some sort of eccentric housekeeper.

She arrived in front of them breathlessly. 'I'm so delighted you could make it! I'm Cassandra Beeston, Elliot's mother.'

Chapter 27

'It's so nice to have visitors. When my husband was alive we did a lot of entertaining, but it's pretty quiet these days.'

They were in the kitchen of the ramshackle cottage. Cassandra was moving around in the background boiling kettles and hunting out cups and saucers.

She came back to the table. 'I'm afraid it's not the good china.' When she put the tray down Lizzy noticed the puffy, arthritic hands.

'Shall I pour? How does everyone take it?'

They sat in silence, politely sipping their tea. 'It's so fortunate that you were in the area,' Cassandra said eventually. 'Have you known Elliot long?'

Lizzy felt Nic kick her under the table. 'We're more email acquaintances.'

'Elliot isn't the most communicative of people at the best of times, but he's barely said a word since the split. I suppose he's finding it hard to open up to people.' Cassandra peered hopefully at Poppet. 'Has he said anything to you?'

A look of panic crossed Poppet's face. 'Um, only that he's, er, hurting and he's feeling really . . . sad?'

Cassandra sighed. 'I just wish I could reach out to him, but he won't let me in.' She looked at the clock again. 'I don't know where Elliot could have got to. He knew you were coming.'

Nic put her cup down. 'We should think about making a move.'

'Already?' Cassandra asked anxiously. 'But you've come all the way up here. At least let me show you round.'

She took them next door to Beeston Hall. Apparently Cassandra had moved into the cottage when the stately home had got too difficult to maintain.

'After all, there's only me now.' She looked round wistfully. 'I feel dreadfully guilty when I come in here. It feels like we've abandoned an old friend.'

It was easy to see what she meant. The hall's interior was even worse than the outside. The opulent wallpaper was peeling and mouldy velvet curtains hung at the windows. A clammy smell of damp was unmistakable.

Cassandra's pets had accompanied them into the Hall. Leonardo the peacock seemed to have taken a particular shine to Nic.

'If that motherfucker doesn't stop eyeballing me I'm going to kick its beak off!' she hissed to Lizzy.

'Try not to show your fear. It's probably picking up on it.'

'Nic's got a phobia of giant birds,' Poppet told Cassandra. 'Her mum used to leave her in front of the Rod Hull and Emu show when she was little.'

The peacock came even closer. Nic shrieked and leapt behind Lizzy.

'Don't mind Leonardo, my dear,' Cassandra told her. 'His bark is worse than his bite.'

Despite the decay it was obvious the building had once been breathtaking. A mahogany staircase as wide as the deck of a ship dominated the cavernous entrance hall. It flowed up into a landing bigger than the upstairs of Lizzy's parents' house.

'That's Elliot's great grandfather, Radcliffe.' Cassandra pointed to an oil painting on the wall. A man with giant white whiskers gazed jauntily off into the distance. 'He's the black sheep of the family, gambled away all the money.' She chuckled. 'The Beestons are very much a dynasty of two halves. Elliot definitely hails from the more serious side. I think he used to despair at his father and me.'

Poppet loved nothing more than a stately house tour. 'What's down there, Cassandra?' She pointed down a dark passageway.

'There goes the path to my secret lair! Come along, Popsy, I'll show you.'

'It's Poppet actually.'

'What a lovely name.' Cassandra linked arms with her. 'Where did it come from?'

Nic pulled Lizzy back as they strolled off. 'Why didn't you tell her we're not friends with her son? This is totally weird!'

'I couldn't! You saw how excited she was to think Elliot had some friends!' Lizzy watched the chihuahua cock its leg against a curtain.

'Half an hour more and we're out of here. It's going

to be obvious when Elliot comes back that we don't know each other!'

A few minutes later even Nic had stopped moaning. Cassandra had taken them into a vast conservatory with a glass roof that arched upwards like a chapel. Sunlight poured in through the huge windows. It was as if there was no separation between them and the open countryside.

The room was in a state of creative chaos, with dripping paint pots and unfinished canvases everywhere. The only bit of furniture was a sagging chaise longue in the corner with a large tabby cat asleep on it.

'What used to be the orangery,' Cassandra told them. 'Now it's my humble studio.'

One of the windows had a random pane of green glass. Cassandra walked over to it. 'That was from when Elliot shot his catapult through the window,' she told them. 'I was in here working and suddenly I heard the glass shatter and this thing flew straight in and knocked the easel over! I'd been working on a sunset and red paint went everywhere, me included!' She laughed. 'Elliot came running in, thought it was blood and was inconsolable! The poor boy thought he'd maimed me!'

'Did you go mental?' Poppet asked. 'My mum would have chopped my head off!'

'Not at all, we thought it was funny. His sister was normally the naughty one, it was very un-Elliot, showing a bit of rebellion!' Cassandra sighed. 'It didn't last long.'

There was an easel by the window, facing out on to the view. Lizzy went over to have a look.

'Cassandra, this is amazing!' Lizzy was the first to admit that she knew nothing about art, but even she could see Elliot's mum had a real talent. There was something Van-Gogh-like about the way the bold brush strokes had elevated the landscape.

'You like it?' Cassandra looked down at her swollen knuckles. 'These damn things don't help much these days.'

There were canvases stacked up around the room. 'Do you sell your work?' Poppet asked.

'I sure do, although there's not so much of a market for artists like me these days. We're considered a bit twee and old-fashioned. What I'd really love to do is turn this place into an artists' retreat, or start up an academy for kids with talent.' Cassandra smiled ruefully. 'Elliot is dead set on selling the place off. Thinks I'm a silly old woman with my head in the clouds. We're kinda in a stand-off about it.'

They continued the tour outside. Cassandra had a mobility buggy that she used to get around on longer walks, and she took off across the grass at a terrific pace with the girls in hot pursuit. With each passing minute Lizzy became more enchanted with the place as Cassandra showed them the lake, the private stretch of river, the woodlands and the yard that had once housed top racehorses.

'It must have been an amazing place for Elliot to grow up,' Poppet said. 'Like being in your own enchanted kingdom!'

'That's what Max and I thought. We didn't impose many rules and regulations on the kids. We both grew up with strict parents, so we wanted our kids to have the freedom to find their own way in the world.'

Lizzy looked across at the derelict stables. It was so sad that the place had been left to fall into such disrepair, but even she could see what a colossal – and costly – task it would be to restore Beeston Hall to its former glory. She couldn't blame Elliot for wanting to take the money and run.

As they made their way back to the cottage, Cassandra told them more about her life.

'My father was a big Bible man, but the meanest son of a bitch you could ever meet. My mother died when I was a little girl, so for years it was just me and him. I used to lie in bed at night and plan the day I got outta there.' She laughed. 'I don't know what I thought was going to happen, maybe Elvis himself was going to come through town and sweep me up in his arms and save me, but in the end I ran away from home when I was fifteen and became a wing walker.'

'What's a wing walker?' Poppet asked.

'You know, girls who stand on the wings of planes.' Cassandra deftly swerved the mobility buggy to avoid a clod of earth.

'You used to do that?!'

'I did, Popsy. It was the most thrilling time of my life, when everything really began for me. We were part of a travelling troupe called The Jets, and we used to go all over the country performing at air shows. There were four of us girls, and we had the most outrageous pink flying suits with our stage names written across the front.' Cassandra laughed again. 'I was Scarlett Sue, on account of my hair.'

Lizzy was fascinated. Why wasn't her mum this cool? 'How long were you a wing walker for?'

'Three years. I saw and did things I didn't think were possible – and not all of them to do with aerobatics! It was the best education life could have given me, but then the head pilot went and got himself killed by flying into a tree.' Cassandra sighed. 'I think he'd smoked a bit too much marijuana that day. After that the troupe broke up, and I decided to head to New York to try and make my fortune. To tell you the truth, I was kinda over it by then anyway. They didn't have waterproof mascara back in those days, and your face just looked a *state* half the time.'

By the time they got back to the lodge the Jeep was parked outside. Lizzy's heart sank.

'The prodigal son finally returns!' Cassandra exclaimed a little too brightly.

Elliot was leaning against the counter in the kitchen, morosely drinking tea from a floral mug.

'There you are,' his mother said. 'I was wondering where you'd got to.'

'I've been mending the fencing up by the lake.'

Cassandra smiled at the others. 'My son is quite the handyman when he comes home. Only this morning he was on my roof fixing a leaky tile before the bad weather sets in. He risks life and limb to keep us all together!'

'I wouldn't have to if we sold the bloody place.'

The silence seemed to stretch on for ever.

'Will you excuse me?' Cassandra said. 'I just have to go and take my tablets. I get all these stupid pains if I stand up for too long.' She left the room rather stiffly.

Elliot remained where he was, staring at a fascinating spot on the worn flagstone floor. *How can someone who has a career on TV be so socially inept in real life?* Lizzy wondered. Then again, he probably hadn't been anticipating having to entertain a bunch of random girls in his kitchen, especially when one of them had insulted him on two separate occasions, as well as being responsible for him getting covered in dog diarrhoea.

'Do you come home a lot?' Poppet asked Elliot.

His green eyes briefly flickered on to her. 'When I want to get away from everything.' It couldn't have been more pointed.

It seemed like an age until Cassandra came back. 'Look at you all still standing there! Elliot, why haven't you offered our guests a seat?'

'We *really* should think about going,' Nic said. 'We've got to check into our B & B.'

'Oh, but you must stay here!' Cassandra exclaimed. 'Mustn't they, Elliot?'

Elliot gazed at his mother in open horror. 'They've just said they've got to go.'

'We've imposed enough,' Lizzy said hastily.

'I insist!' she said. 'We can't have you staying in a B & B when there's a perfectly good spare room here.' She looked at Lizzy hopefully. *Don't leave me*, her expression seemed to be saying.

Lizzy didn't dare look at Nic. 'That's really kind of you. We'd love to stay.'

Chapter 28

Despite the obvious spectre at the feast everyone else made a real effort at dinner.

'I've never had pheasant before,' Poppet told Cassandra. 'It's really nice.'

'Shot on the estate this morning! There's a wonderful man in the village who comes up and keeps the game down for us, he can take a bird out through the heart from half a mile away.'

Poppet went pale and put her fork down.

Lizzy was trying to ignore the brooding figure slumped to her left. 'How long have you owned the Hall for?'

'The Beestons have been here for seven generations. Beeston Hall was built after the Restoration by Lord Selwyn Beeston, Elliot's great-great-great...' Cassandra let out a peal of laughter. 'Forget it, we could be here all night!'

'How come your surname is Anderson?' Poppet asked Elliot.

'It's my maiden name.' Cassandra gave her son an

anxious smile when he didn't reply. 'Working in the financial world, Elliot didn't want to draw special attention to himself.'

Elliot gave a strange bark of laughter.

'Did you say something, darling?' Cassandra asked.

'No,' he muttered.

Lizzy swiftly changed the subject. 'How did you meet your husband?' she asked Cassandra.

Cassandra looked relieved at the intervention. 'You want to know how a small-town girl from Missouri ended up as lady of the manor? I was a penniless student at Rhode Island School of Design, singing in the bars at night to earn myself some money. One night this young man came in by himself and sat at the bar. He was very well-dressed but that wasn't why I noticed him. He was drinking pina coladas with all these pink flamingos and umbrellas. I thought he was gay!' She let out a delightful peal of laughter. 'Turns out he wasn't gay, because he asked me out later that night and six weeks later we were married!'

She stopped. There was a strange groaning noise from the end of the table. Nic had fallen asleep in her seat and was snoring softly.

'Does she often do that?' Cassandra asked.

'She works really hard.' Poppet prodded her. 'Nic!'

She woke up with a jump. 'What? Is the peacock in here?'

Poppet shot Nic a look. 'Carry on, Cassandra. It sounds like a real love story.'

'It really was. Max brought me back here and we didn't have a day apart until he died eleven years ago.' Cassandra suddenly looked terribly sad. 'There's not a day that goes past I don't miss him. We never had much money, but we had each other, and our art and our music and our beautiful children, of course. There was always love and laughter around the place.'

Elliot made the same strange sardonic sound. Lizzy was starting to wonder if he had a pheasant bone stuck in his throat.

'So you've got one other child?' Poppet asked Cassandra.

'Yes, Elliot's older sister Skyla lives in America now.' Cassandra said wistfully. 'I'd like to see more of her of course, but she's living a wonderful life out there. And I still have my lovely son.'

They all watched Elliot morosely push a carrot round his plate.

'Anyway!' Cassandra said. 'You don't want to hear tales of our family all night.' She gave Lizzy a smile. 'What do you do for a living, my dear?'

'I work in PR.'

'Public relations! How wonderful! I'd imagine it's very glamorous.'

'Ha! Hardly!' Elliot was wearing an expression of complete contempt.

'He's only joking,' Cassandra hastily told Lizzy.

'It's all right,' Lizzy said nicely. 'It's just a bit of friendly rivalry between journalists and PRs, isn't it? They pretend to look down on us, and we pretend to think they're rude and objectionable, and everyone just gets on with it.'

'You're not really trying to imagine you're on the same level as us, are you?'

'Elliot, be a little more hospitable to our guests,' Cassandra said sharply.

'Our guests? *You're* the one who invited them.'

'Elliot!'

He chucked his fork down. 'I *told* you that all I wanted was to be left alone this weekend. So what do you do?' He jerked his head at Lizzy and her friends. 'Invite Wilson friggin' Phillips round! Genius idea, Mother, one of your best yet!'

'Oi, I'd better not be the fat one,' Nic said, trying to make a joke.

Elliot jumped up. 'I've had enough of this.' He stormed out of the room.

Cassandra had gone white. 'Elliot's right. I shouldn't have dragged you girls into this. I just thought if he had some company, someone his own age . . .'

Her poor hands were trembling. 'There, there,' Poppet said. 'I'll get you a glass of water.'

Nic had a suggestion. 'Do you want me to go and have it out with him, man to man?'

'Thank you, Nic, but I think it will only make matters worse. Oh God!' Cassandra looked distraught. 'Now he really never will talk to me again. I just felt I had to do *something*. I've never seen him like this before. Amber was the love of his life.'

'Do you know why they split up?' Poppet asked.

She shook her head. 'All he told me was that he'd messed it up. It's just so sad. They've known each other since they were sixteen. Everyone always said they were perfect for each other. Amber was so sweet and so beautiful. She was the only person who could bring the best out in Elliot.' Cassandra shook her head again. 'I don't think he will ever get over this.'

'Do you want one of us to go and talk to him?' Poppet suggested reluctantly.

'Maybe it would help.' A glimmer of hope crept into Cassandra's eyes. 'You're in PR, Lizzy; you're good with people! Maybe you can say something and bring him round. Please, Lizzy, I'm at the end of my tether. Will you do it, for my sake?'

There was a light under the last door down the hallway. Lizzy stood outside for a moment before lifting her hand and knocking softly.

'What?' a voice snapped.

'It's Lizzy,' she said self-consciously. 'Can I come in?'

There was a long pause. 'The door's open.'

She pushed it open and went in. It was a single bedroom, in the same shabby-chic style as the rest of the cottage. A glowing MacBook Air stood on an old wooden desk in the far corner.

Elliot was standing in his socked feet looking out of the open window. Beyond, the night sky was bright with stars.

'I'm guessing my mother sent you,' he said without looking at Lizzy.

'She's worried about you, Elliot.'

He gave a derisive snort. 'Oh really?'

Lizzy took a deep breath. 'I don't want to shove my oar in, but I have kind of been there as well. You know, with the dumping thing and the ensuing public humiliation.' She laughed weakly. 'In fact, contrary to popular opinion, I didn't think my ex was going to ask me to marry him, but that's another story.'

'Girl Who Gets Jilted at 30th Birthday and Headbutts Boyfriend Who Didn't Actually Get Jilted At All,' he said moodily. 'Not quite so catchy, is it?'

Lizzy managed a wry smile. 'I do know what it's like to have your private life splashed all over the papers and there's absolutely nothing you can do about it.'

There was no response. Something large swooped past the window. Lizzy took a deep breath.

'Look, I'm really sorry about you and Amber. But it doesn't help if you lock yourself away and refuse to talk to anyone. You need to be around your friends and family, Elliot.'

He swung round, green eyes bristling with hostility. 'Oh I'm sorry, I didn't realize you dabbled in therapy as a sideline. Thank you for your comprehensive analysis of my emotional welfare. Be sure to let me know where to send the bill.'

He stomped across the room and sat down at the computer. 'If you don't mind, I've got work to do.'

He might be heartbroken but there was no need to be so bloody rude! 'You need to get over yourself!' Lizzy retorted. 'You're not the first person in the world to get dumped!'

He ignored her and started typing furiously. Lizzy stared at his rigid back and shoulders. At least she could tell Cassandra she'd tried. Pulling the door shut, she left Elliot alone.

Lizzy woke with a jump. Everything was too dark. It took a few seconds to work out why the bed was lumpy and it was so unnaturally quiet outside. She was in a bedroom at the home of a woman she'd only just met, in the middle of deepest darkest Dorset.

Her mouth felt drier than a shepherd's sandal. Cassandra had ended up bringing out some home-made sloe gin which had made even Nic's eyes water. Lizzy had a vague recollection of doing the Macarena across the kitchen with a tea towel on her head. Would she ever be trusted to behave when alcohol was put in front of her?

She tried to move her legs, but a heavy weight was pressing against them. Panicking slightly, she grasped her phone and shone the light down the bed, expecting to find some wild animal that had crept in uninvited, or even worse, Leonardo the peacock, but instead she was greeted by the sight of Poppet curled up across her feet, dead to the world.

Lizzy breathed a sigh of relief. It wasn't the first time Poppet had gone walkabout and ended up in an unfamiliar bed. Apparently she always instinctively ended up facing the same way her bed was at home, but Poppet's sense of direction was so terrible that Lizzy privately had her doubts.

'Pops!' she whispered. There was a little sigh. Lizzy tried to lift one foot to shake her. 'Poppet!'

Her friend gave a dreamy smile. 'Bananas?'

With some difficulty Lizzy slid out of bed, leaving Poppet slumbering happily. Nic was across the room in a narrow put-up bed. She was sleeping how she always did: on her back with her arms folded, as if she were about to be buried. Lizzy glanced over briefly and did a double take. Nic's eyes were wide open and staring upwards.

'Are you awake?' Lizzy whispered.

No reaction. Lizzy crept over and waved her hand over Nic's face. Nic's gaze remained fixed on the ceiling unblinkingly. It was really creepy. Was Lizzy the only one amongst her friends with normal nocturnal habits?

She crept out of the room in her polka-dot pajamas. At the end of the hallway Elliot's door was shut. She prayed she wasn't about to have an excruciating corridor run-in with him in his underpants. That was one confrontation she would *not* be able to handle.

Mercifully his door stayed closed. Padding along the unfamiliar corridor, Lizzy reached the kitchen doorway and came to a halt.

Cassandra was standing by the window. She was wearing a patterned kimono, her curly hair sitting on her shoulders. The moonlight was streaming in, softening Cassandra's face and giving Lizzy a glimpse of the rare beauty she had once been.

She was looking towards the hall, a wistful expression on her face as if she was remembering happier times, memories filled with love and life and laughter. Lizzy suddenly felt desperately sorry for this vivacious, arthritic woman, living all by herself in this cottage with its bits of worn, too-big furniture.

'Cassandra?'

She looked round distractedly. 'Oh, it's you, Lizzy. Did I wake you?'

'No, I needed a drink.'

Cassandra chuckled softly. 'Yeah, the sloe gin can do that to you.'

She got Lizzy a glass of water and they both sat down at the table. 'You couldn't sleep either?' Lizzy asked.

'I don't sleep much these days. It must be my age.'

'He'll be OK you know,' Lizzy said softly after a short silence.

'I'm not so sure. I know it doesn't look like it, but Elliot feels things very deeply. Not that he'd ever admit it to me.' She shot Lizzy a sidelong look. 'My son pushes me away. Thinks I'm a terrible mother.'

'Why on earth would he think that?'

There was a wry smile. 'Probably because I wasn't like all the other mothers. You may have noticed we're not exactly conventional up here.'

'Who wants to be conventional? It's totally boring.'

'You do say the sweetest things.' Cassandra's face fell serious again. 'I don't know, Lizzy. I feel like I lost him a long time ago.'

She looked so sad again. Lizzy didn't know what to say. 'Shall I put the kettle on?' she suggested.

'Would you mind? It's just that I'm feeling a little weary.'

'Leave it with me,' Lizzy said.

She set about making a pot of tea with Cassandra watching. 'He used to be such a thoughtful boy, you know. Elliot I mean,' she told Lizzy. 'He would pick wild flowers from the garden and make the most beautiful bouquets for me.'

'Really?' Lizzy said in astonishment. She couldn't imagine Elliot doing anything so sweet and sensitive.

Cassandra nodded. 'Still waters run deep with Elliot. He was always the sensible one in the family, really quite straight-laced at times if you want the honest truth, but there was always this sensitivity about him. It broke my heart when he went away to boarding school, but it's always been the tradition with the men in this family.' She sighed. 'The first time he came home there was already this . . . distance between us. I feel like I've been losing him ever since.'

Lizzy brought the mugs over to the table. 'I'm sure he'll come round, don't worry.'

Cassandra sighed again. 'I don't know about that. If he can't reach out to me now, when will he ever?'

They sat drinking their tea in a companionable silence until the first streaks of sunrise appeared in the sky. Then Lizzy stumbled off to bed, kissing Cassandra good night on the cheek.

When the girls got up the next morning Elliot was already packed and gone.

Chapter 29

Lizzy was having a casual loaf through Facebook while Antonia was out of the office. Recently her timeline had become infested with adverts for rapid weight loss, spiritual retreats and yoga pants that held you in. A psychoanalyst would have a field day: *Single. Poor self-image. Feelings of disillusionment. Possible early mid-life crisis.*

She was reading another post that promised to zap her belly fat in five days when the phone started ringing. Lizzy picked it up, one eye still on the screen. The 'after' picture was so doctored the woman's belly button was headbutting her nipples.

'Hello . . .' *Where am I?* 'Er, hello, Haven.'

'Ken Dennings here!'

'Ken! How are you?'

'Pretty good, pretty good! I've had some more thoughts on changing the name. I still think we can make constipation sound a bit more *fun*, Lizzy.'

It had become like a little game between them. 'Go on then,' she said.

'Bum and Dad?'

'It's inventive, Ken, I'll give you that.'

'How about this then: A Sense of Release. Do you get it? It's a play on "a sense of relief", combines the two elements.'

'You're nearly there, Ken. Keep 'em coming.'

Lizzy put the phone down and looked at the card on her desk. After they'd finally made it back from Dorset on Sunday evening Lizzy had sent Cassandra a thank-you note for their impromptu stay. She hadn't expected a reply back, but this morning a beautifully hand-painted card had arrived in the post. She re-read the message for the umpteenth time.

Dear Lizzy

It was so lovely to meet you and your friends. Thank you for trying to talk to Elliot. I'm still desperately worried about him. I know it's a big ask, but could you try to keep an eye on him? I'm sure you must run around in the same circles in London. It would really help put my mind at rest.

Do come and visit me any time you like.

Best wishes,

Cassie Beeston

She'd added her email address, asking Lizzy to keep in touch.

Lizzy groaned inwardly. How was she meant to keep an eye on someone who she barely knew and who'd already told her in no uncertain terms he didn't want her help? As much as she felt for his mother,

Lizzy wasn't the patron saint of the dumped and heart-broken. Elliot Anderson was not her problem.

Two days later something unexpected happened. Lizzy got an email from the man himself. It was short and to the point.

If it's not too late, I'd like to take you up on your offer. I'll come to you. E.

Lizzy was about to send a non-committal reply with a link to the Samaritans when Cassandra's face flashed into her mind.

I know it's a big ask, but could you try to keep an eye on him? It would really help put my mind at rest.

'This better earn me brownie points in heaven,' she muttered and pressed 'reply'.

That's fine. When do you want to meet up?

Two hours went past. Lizzy was starting to think Elliot had had second thoughts when she got a reply.

Tomorrow? I've got a meeting near your office.

Lizzy quickly checked her work diary.

There's a place round the corner from me called Café Crème. See you there at 12?

Fine. See you then.

There was no thank you.

When she got to the café the next day Elliot was already there, his tall frame wedged uncomfortably under one of the low tables. He looked completely out of place amongst the yummy mummies trying to calm their squalling babies.

He got up awkwardly. 'What can I get you?'

'Latte please.'

'Skinny or full-fat?'

'Skinny, please.'

'Oh. You look like the kind of person who drinks full-fat milk.'

Lizzy stared at him. Elliot's cheeks turned ever so slightly pink.

'I'll go and order,' he muttered.

She took her jacket off and asked herself again what the hell she was doing.

'Thank you for seeing me,' he said stiffly when he sat down again.

The woman at the next table kept giving them curious glances. She probably thought they'd formed some kind of Z-list Lonely Hearts Club.

'How are you doing?' Lizzy asked.

Elliot shot her an irritated look. 'What do you mean, how am I doing?'

'You emailed saying you wanted to meet up,' Lizzy flashed back. 'So I'm asking you how you are.'

'Sorry,' he muttered. 'I didn't mean it like that.'

Five minutes later they were both still sitting there staring into space. Despite the premise of meeting to talk, Elliot had said only three sentences since she'd got here.

She decided to try one last time. 'Have you heard anything from Amber?'

He muttered something under his breath.

'Sorry, I didn't catch that,' she said.

Elliot looked at her hotly. 'I said this was a ridiculous idea.' He threw a load of coins down on the table and stood up. 'Sorry I wasted your time.'

Lizzy was left watching open-mouthed as he strode

215

out. The woman on the next table smiled sympathetically.

'Hard dating them when they're on the rebound, isn't it? If I were you, I'd get out now.'

Chapter 30

The next day Lizzy had booked the afternoon off and went to meet her mother for their annual lunch in Selfridges.

'Your father's started going to Pilates,' Mrs Spellman announced over a glass of fizzing Prosecco. 'He's worried about his expanding waistband.'

She reached into her handbag for her diary. 'Do you know what time you'll be coming home on Christmas Eve?'

They were barely into September. 'Mum, I don't know what time I'll be getting home tonight yet, let alone in three months' time.'

Her mother tutted. 'You sound just like your brother. Speaking of which, have you heard from him recently?'

'Not for a while.' Robbie had always been notoriously rubbish at keeping in touch. These days Lizzy would have to send five text messages before she got one back from him.

'It's like getting blood out of a stone trying to get

an invitation over there. Apparently Hayley is very,' Mrs Spellman made quote marks with her fingers, "territorial".'

'She's certainly territorial over Robbie,' Lizzy sighed.

'I suppose I should be thankful that at least he's with someone.' Her mother had that look she got whenever she was about to start interrogating Lizzy about her love life. 'What's going on with you? Are there any nice boys on the scene?'

'I don't like it when you use the word "boys", Mum. It feels a bit weird.'

'All right then, chaps, beaus, studs, shag-buddies, whatever you young people call them these days.'

'Mum! Eww!'

The waiter arrived with their food. Lizzy waited until he'd gone. 'At this current time, Mother, there is no one on the scene.'

'You live in London! There are men everywhere!' Mrs Spellman waved her hand round the restaurant. 'Look at all of them!'

'It's not that easy. You don't just walk out of your front door and bump into the love of your life.'

'Have you thought about becoming a lesbian?'

Lizzy nearly choked on her Prosecco. 'Mum!'

'Don't look so wide-eyed, darling, it's perfectly acceptable these days. Carol-from-down-the-road's-sister's-daughter has just "come out".' Her mother made quote marks again. 'Set up a "love nest" in Brighton with her girlfriend.' She squeezed a slice of lemon over her smoked salmon. 'You know, I thought about becoming a lesbian once.'

'What?!'

'It was only briefly. Your father was really annoying me at the time.'

It took a few moments for Lizzy to recover from *that* bombshell. 'Mum, I'm not about to turn gay.'

'How do you know until you try?' Her mother shrugged. 'Maybe it's the reason you've never been able to find lasting happiness with a man. Your father and I often wonder.'

'Oh great!' Lizzy lowered her voice as a waiter walked past. 'So you spend hours round the dinner table discussing my sexuality?'

'We don't just discuss that, darling. I know it's hard to fathom, but Dad and I have got a life outside you and your brother and sister.' Her mother forked up a mouthful of rocket. 'Anyway, I think you'd make a very nice lesbian. I've always liked you with shorter hair.'

'Not all lesbians have short hair, Mum. Look at Portia de Rossi.'

'Who? All I'm saying, darling, is that if you do want to "come out"' – at this point there were more quote marks – 'you've got nothing to feel ashamed or worried about. Your father and I are very open-minded. I think we'd even let you share a bed with your girlfriend when you came to stay.'

'Mum! No one is sharing my bed when I bring them home! For the last time – I'm not gay!'

'Shame.' Mrs Spellman picked up her glass. 'It would give those bitches down at the tennis club something to choke on their cappuccinos about.'

*

After their disastrous meet-up Lizzy hadn't expected to hear from Elliot again, but two days later there was another email. It was as friendly as ever.

Free tomorrow?

'You know your problem?' Nic said when Lizzy rang her to ask what she should do. 'You're suffering from a severe case of "Lame Duck Syndrome". Any creature that's suffering or in distress, you want to help.'

'Would you go?'

'No, I'd have had him put down by now.'

It sounded very tinny wherever she was. 'Are you in a lift?' Lizzy asked.

'No, I'm in Tokyo.' There was another voice in the background. 'Simon's here. I've got to go.'

Post-breakup, people often feel sad, lost, empty, alone, and angry. Having an outlet to express the pain, discomfort, fears, and sadness, such as a therapist's office, can reduce the sense of guilt and shame a person may feel for not 'getting over' it yet.

'What are you doing?'

Antonia was doing one of her unnerving walkabouts round the office. For someone with such a large bottom she could move with the stealth of a cat. Sometimes she'd be standing over Lizzy's shoulder for five minutes before Lizzy realized she was there.

'Nothing.' Lizzy quickly closed down the Google page on 'How to deal with a person suffering from heartbreak.'

'You haven't been dumped AGAIN?' Antonia announced.

Everyone looked up. 'Oh Lizzy!' one of the other account managers cried. 'You poor thing.'

'Sweets, I am sorry,' Bianca told her. 'I'm going to this party tonight, do you want to come along? You'll be a lot older than everyone else, but it might take your mind off things.'

'I haven't been dumped!' Lizzy protested. 'I'm looking for a friend,' she told Antonia.

'Course you are. My heart bleeds and all that, but would you mind doing it on your own time, darling? We are trying to run a business here.'

Chapter 31

Lizzy walked into Café Crème full of dread. Elliot was there before her again at the same table they'd sat at last time.

'Hi.' He did the same awkward hovering thing. 'What can I get you to drink?'

At least he was slightly more welcoming than last time. 'I'll have a double gin and tonic please. And maybe a flaming sambuca to start.'

Elliot stared at her uncomprehendingly. 'I don't think they've got an alcohol licence here.'

'I was joking,' Lizzy said feebly. 'Coffee would be great.'

You could have cut the atmosphere round the table with a cake knife. 'Skinny latte?' the waitress asked.

Lizzy seized on it gratefully. 'Here thank you.'

The girl gave Lizzy a sympathetic look and walked off.

'Thanks again for the coffee,' she said.

Elliot gave a non-committal nod and picked up his

phone again. He must have checked it ten times in the last five minutes.

'What did you want to talk about?' Lizzy asked him.

He gazed at the tablecloth, avoiding her gaze. 'I don't know. What do you want to talk about?'

Lizzy heard her BlackBerry buzz with another email. She really had better things to be doing than this.

'If you don't actually talk about how you're feeling, then there's absolutely no point me being here.'

'I don't know how I'm feeling,' he snapped. 'I'm sorry if I can't just open my heart on request.'

'I'll tell you how I'm feeling!' she snapped back. 'Pissed off with being spoken to like a piece of shit!'

They sat there in a furious silence, looking anywhere but at each other. 'Look, I'm sorry,' he said eventually.

Lizzy nearly fell out of her seat. Was that an actual apology?

Elliot put his hands on the table and then took them off again. 'I just find this kind of . . . stuff really difficult.'

That was an understatement. 'Look, let's have one last go,' Lizzy said. 'Why don't I ask questions and you just answer them? If you want to, that is.'

He shrugged reluctantly. 'Go on then.'

Lizzy crossed her arms and sat back. 'Elliot, on the happiness index, where are you today on a scale of one to ten?'

'Are you being serious?'

'Don't push your luck, mate,' she warned him. 'I'm about a nanosecond from walking.'

'I just don't see the point in validating your feelings against a hypothetical index. One person's idea of happiness could be completely different from another's.'

'It was just an idea,' she sighed. 'OK. When did you and Amber first meet?'

'Why do you want to know that?' he said suspiciously.

'I don't know, because it might be cathartic? And right now I'm pretty much running out of other options.'

They stared each other out across the table.

'Look, this isn't working,' Lizzy told him. She started to get her things together. 'I'm not really qualified for this. I think you need to speak to a professional.'

'She came to our school in the lower sixth,' Elliot suddenly blurted out. 'I was sixteen and I thought she was the most beautiful girl I'd ever seen.'

Lizzy looked up from her handbag. Elliot was smiling desperately at her. 'Five hundred boys stuck at boarding school in the middle of a windswept moor. You can imagine the reaction when Amber turned up.'

Lizzy sat back. She remembered Cassandra's comment about Elliot falling in love with Amber from the off. 'Did you start going out together then?'

He shook his head. 'We were best friends for years. We both had our own things going on romantically, but I guess there was always this unspoken agreement that we'd get together in the end.'

'The old: "If we haven't met anyone else by the age of thirty, we might as well end up together,"' Lizzy said dryly.

'It wasn't quite like that,' Elliot said, equally dryly.

'Amber is an incredible woman, the kind of person every man dreams of ending up with. I would have been a fool not to want to be with her.'

'So when did you, you know, realize that you wanted to be with her?'

'Eighteen months ago she'd just come out of a serious relationship and I knew if I didn't make my move, I'd probably lose her for ever. Like I said, girls like her don't stay single very long. We got together and I asked her to marry me last Christmas.' There was a ghost of a smile. 'What was the beautifully romantic thing she said? "Jesus, Anderson, what took you so long?"'

Something cataclysmic must have happened to make Amber call off the engagement. 'Do you mind me asking what happened?' Lizzy said.

There was a long silence. 'Let's just say I wasn't the man she thought I was.'

What does he mean by that? Lizzy wondered. The next moment the anguish had crept back into Elliot's face. 'I just miss her. I miss her company. It's so weird, we were part of each other's lives for so long and now there's just this . . . *silence.*'

'Are you sure you can't work it out?' Lizzy asked.

There was another pause. 'Yes. Now do you mind if we talk about something else?'

Lizzy met up that night with her friends at YO! Sushi. Nic had her own theory about why Elliot and Amber had broken up.

'Bet she caught him shagging someone else.'

'They were engaged, Nic!' Poppet said.

'That gives him even more reason. Once men get

225

that ring on the girl's finger it's an insurance policy to act how the hell they want.'

'I dunno, he seems a bit rigid and principled to be the cheating type.' Lizzy watched the conveyor belt go past. Could she fit another Californian Roll in?

'It's obvious, isn't it?' Poppet said. 'They waited all these years before getting together and then Amber must have realized Elliot wasn't "The One" for her after all. Poor bloke. What a kick in the stomach.'

'And now he's using Lizzy as a drop-in therapy session,' Nic said.

Poppet shook her head. 'Men are so weird. They either want to have meaningless sex with us, or cry on our shoulders. Why is there no middle ground? Why can't we be their friends *and* their lovers?' She sighed. 'All I want to do is go for romantic walks down the Embankment with someone and throw up handfuls of autumn leaves.'

'Send, you effing thing!'

Lizzy and Poppet looked at Nic. Nic was simultaneously emailing on her BlackBerry, shovelling Spicy Seafood Udon into her mouth and drinking wine. There were so many different coloured plates around her it looked like the aftermath of a children's party.

'How many of those have you had now?' Lizzy asked.

'Leave me alone,' Nic mumbled. 'Can't you see I'm stress eating?'

Chapter 32

'You're late,' Elliot announced, still tapping away on his iPad as Lizzy rushed into the café.

Antonia had been having another Zen Ten/Jocasta meltdown and Lizzy had rushed out on the pretence of having to go and buy some tampons. Still slightly breathless, she took her coat off and sat down.

'Why do girls do that?' he asked.

'Do what?' she asked confusedly.

He had a combative gleam in his eye, quite different to any expression she'd seen him wear before. 'Wear so much animal print.'

She looked down at her jumper, which had the face of a roaring tiger on it. 'What's wrong with animal print?'

'You think it's cute and sexy, but it just makes you all look mad. No wonder you're—' He shut up.

'Oh my God! Were you going to say, "No wonder you're single"?'

Elliot had the grace to look slightly contrite. 'It just doesn't send out a good impression. As if you live on your own with six hundred cats or something.'

'Yeah well, at least I don't walk round in the same boring navy and grey suits all the time.'

He looked mortally offended. 'This is Armani.'

'Still boring. A nice sparkly cat brooch would liven it up.'

'Oh yeah, that would look *great* on the news tonight.'

'Don't knock it until you've tried it. Why can't the news be more fun? I'm sure you'd get more viewers.'

'Thanks for that. I'll be sure to bring it up with ITV's chief executive next time I see him.'

Lizzy picked up her coffee.

He narrowed his eyes. 'What are you smiling at?'

'Nothing. I didn't realize you took such a keen interest in my wardrobe.'

'It's not exactly easy to ignore it.' He shot another look at Lizzy's jumper. '*Tigers.*'

That was the start of a bizarre friendship. Or the 'Bloodbath Coffee Club' as Nic was calling it. Over the following weeks Lizzy and Elliot would meet at Café Crème and basically argue for an hour. It was understandable that Elliot would be in a bad place after losing Amber. Lizzy just didn't realize how dark. The man was so cynical he made Jack Dee look like Mary Berry.

'How can people print this rubbish?' He was reading one of the women's magazines from the rack on the wall. 'Fate Found Our Mate!'

Lizzy put her bag down. 'What's wrong with that?'

He shot her a look. 'Listen to this:

'A chocolate torte brought us together!' says Sue from Holyhead: 'I'd only popped out to the shop because I'd bought the wrong butter. Kevin and I met eyes over the self-service tills and I knew he'd be the man I'd spend the rest of my life with. I made the same chocolate torte for our wedding cake!'

'I think that's really sweet,' Lizzy said.

Elliot snorted horribly. 'Or how about this one: "Driven Together – we met in a car crash!" Good God.' He chucked the magazine down. 'Common interests and goals in life get people together, not some other-worldly set of forces conspiring. All this stuff does is put pressure on other women because they haven't bumped into their own Mr Right buying sink un-blocker in Halfords.'

'I never saw you as down with the sisterhood.'

He didn't appear to be listening. 'And even if you *do* end up meeting the person of your dreams in the frozen-food aisle at the supermarket, you only pile unrealistic expectations on them and vice versa, and everyone ends up getting let down.' He gazed blackly round the café. 'Fate. What a load of *bollocks*.'

It was becoming clear that Elliot thought quite a few things were bollocks. He trusted nobody and everybody had an agenda. Some of them Lizzy could understand – politicians, banks, big corporations and Christopher Biggins – but others: *Big Issue* sellers, the National Trust, guide dogs, mental health charities – were just ridiculous. Elliot even harboured a bizarre suspicion of *Countryfile*'s Kate Humble ('Too cheerful, she's hiding something'), who Lizzy had always privately liked because they shared the same hair.

It wasn't just their opposing outlooks. They inhabited completely different worlds. Lizzy spent her weekends catching up on sleep and seeing her friends. As far as she could make out Elliot chilled out by visiting obscure art galleries and attending global finance summits in Washington. She liked Agatha Raisin and Jojo Moyes; Elliot considered *The Economist* and Jonathan Franzen to be light reading material. When Lizzy had tried to argue the cultural significance of *Miss Congeniality* 2, an Amazon delivery containing a box set of the Coen brothers' films had arrived at her office the next morning. Lizzy had never met anyone who thrived so much on confrontation. It was exhausting, infuriating and at the same time, strangely invigorating.

She'd tried to bring up the subject of Amber a few times but Elliot would just shut down and revert to his previous monosyllabic self. She hadn't pushed it any further. If he wanted to talk about it he would.

Meanwhile she and Cassandra had been emailing on a regular basis.

Is he always this argumentative? Lizzy wrote after one particularly exhausting debate about *Made in Chelsea* and popular culture.

Oh yes! Cassandra had emailed back. Sounds like he's getting better!

Nic couldn't get her head around it. 'Do you want to bang each other or what?'

'No way!' Lizzy genuinely meant it. 'He's the most objectionable arse I've ever come across. I'm surprised

Amber put up with him that long, quite frankly.'

'Then what? You're doing all this out of some weird promise to his mother?'

'Maybe.' There was something about Elliot that for some reason touched Lizzy. He was like an angry wounded animal. 'I suppose I feel a bit *sorry* for him,' she said.

Poppet nodded wisely. 'He's had his heart broken and he's like a lone raft, cast adrift in the sea of humanity. You're his lighthouse, Lizzy, guiding him safely back to shore again.'

'What the hell are you going on about?' Nic turned back to Lizzy. 'I don't get what *you* get out of it. You sit there and he shouts at you for an hour? People get paid good money to do that, it's called a career in counselling.'

'Nicola, Lizzy is helping someone in their hour of need!'

She shook her head. 'Be it on your head, Mother Teresa.'

Lizzy didn't want to say it, but in a way Nic was right. There was another deeper, more poignant reason she'd started to look forward to their exchanges. Her friends wouldn't understand: Nic was an only child and Poppet had an older sister. The ripostes flying back and forth between her and Elliot, the one-upmanship and point-scoring, the way Lizzy wanted to give him a dead arm within ten seconds of meeting him – they reminded her of the relationship she'd had with her brother before Hayley-bloody-Bidwell had come along and driven a wedge between them.

Chapter 33

Lizzy had just ordered when Elliot came striding down the street on his phone. Spotting Lizzy through the window, he gave her an imperious forefinger.

'Something important?' she asked sarcastically when he came in.

'Another call from a developer about the Hall.' Elliot sat down and looked round for the waitress. 'I suppose my mother's told you all about her grand vision of turning it into an art school.'

'I think it sounds like a great idea.'

He looked at Lizzy as if she were an idiot. 'It's a terrible idea. The sooner we sell it the better.'

'Your mum doesn't want to go.'

'Of course she doesn't want to go. My mother floats round with her rose-tinted glasses on thinking everything is going to be all right. Unfortunately a fairy godmother isn't going to sweep in and wave her magic wand and turn Beeston Hall into the art world's version of *Fame.*'

'Your mum's got her dreams. What's wrong with that?'

'There's nothing romantic about running a stately home. My dad tried every hare-brained scheme there was to keep the place going, poor bugger, and in the end the stress finished him off.' He shook his head. 'I have no intention of letting the same thing happen to me.'

That evening Lizzy was lying on the sofa mindlessly watching an E! special about Kim and Kanye when she got a text from her brother Robbie.

Yo DJ. Hayley's away this weekend. Fancy coming to hang with the yokels?

It was typical Robbie. While Lizzy couldn't function without her diary and had palpitations about double-bookings and leaving it too long between friend rotations, Robbie just went with the flow. Which normally meant going where Hayley told him to and spending his Saturday nights at couples-only dinner parties.

Along with the gym and Topshop, Hayley lived for her dinner parties. Once, when Lizzy's plans had fallen through, Robbie had asked her if they could invite Lizzy along with them to someone's house that evening.

'I think it's a bit rude to ask if we can bring someone else at this late stage. Sorry, Lizzy.'

'But there's only four of us. They've got a massive dining-room table.'

Hayley's smile had turned rictus. 'I think Michelle's

already done the stuffed chicken breasts. And I know she's only bought two packs of the Gu cheesecakes.'

'We can't just rock up with your singleton sister!' Lizzy had overheard her hiss at Robbie later. 'What would everyone talk to her about?'

Lizzy had already made plans for the following weekend, but she hadn't seen her brother since the barbecue. Getting time alone with Robbie was as rare as hen's teeth. She'd better make the most of it.

Autumn finally kicked in and a band of cold weather descended on Britain. The windows of Café Crème were steamed up that day as Lizzy ran in with her umbrella.

Elliot strode in a few minutes later. His thick wet hair and rangy body reminded Lizzy of a red setter. She half-expected him to shake his coat out before he sat down opposite her.

'You're late,' she said pointedly.

He was bristling with energy. 'Some of us have got deadlines to meet. The news doesn't write itself, you know.'

'Anything exciting? Have they decided to change the pound coin for chocolate buttons?'

He looked round for the waitress. 'As if I'd tell you. You're the enemy.'

'Like I care anyway. You journos are way too far down the pecking order of things for us PRs to worry about.'

'Ah yes, I forgot how important your work is. How are you getting on with the Hungry Halo? Has it succeeded in single-handedly curing first-world depression?'

'*Happy* Halo. So you did read the press release?'

'I got halfway through the first paragraph before the superlatives started making my eyes bleed.'

'You try writing five hundred words about the wondrous effects of cleansing dirty auras,' Lizzy grumbled.

'Who the hell is Shaman Ron anyway? He looked like Operation Yewtree's next arrest. I wouldn't let him anywhere near my aura.' Elliot shuddered. 'Seriously, though, don't you ever question what you're doing?'

'What do you mean?'

He sat back and appraised Lizzy in his annoying superior way. 'Don't you want to do something else with your life other than trying to promote a load of twaddle that no one is interested in? Why don't you get a proper job?'

'PR is a proper job.'

'PR is not a proper job,' he said loftily.

'Excuse me, mate, just because we're not all breaking financial *world exclusives* and going on the telly to talk about whatever baseline the Bank of England has set.'

'You mean the base rate. Which, in case you were interested, is still at a record low of 0.5 per cent.'

'Whatever.' Lizzy was getting increasingly annoyed. 'OK, I admit the Happy Halo is a low point, but by and large I enjoy what I do. You can't sit there and dismiss what I do for a living just because it doesn't match up to your idea of what is "important" work.' Oh God, she'd just made air quote marks at him like her mother!

'And what would you say "important"' – he did them back at her – 'work is?'

'Why does it have to be "important"? Why can't

235

people just go to work and have a laugh? Be nice to each other? Get along as a team? We're not all on the hunt for solo glory.' Lizzy sat back and crossed her arms. 'Slagging off other people's jobs is just rude, and rudeness is actually a sign of ignorance, so who's the stupid one now?'

Elliot's eyes had a sparkle in them. 'I am sorry. I didn't realize I was in the company of such brilliance. Please forgive me if I demeaned your esteemed profession in any way.'

'Don't worry, I'm used to it,' she said. 'You journalists may look down on the work we do as trivial and meaningless, but actually . . .'

She stopped. Her stomach was making really weird gurgling noises.

'Are you all right?' Elliot asked.

Oh God. Antonia had deposited a suspicious brown bottle on Lizzy's desk that morning. 'Try this out, will you?' she'd boomed. 'A friend of mine has just started a new business up.' Lizzy had been feeling pretty lethargic, so she'd taken a good gulp of the so-called 'cleansing tonic'. Now it felt like a hand had reached in and was viciously squeezing Lizzy's bowels. Surely Antonia wouldn't have let her try anything dangerous?

She stood up. 'Would you excuse me for a moment?'

Ten minutes later she was still locked in the café's only toilet. An angry queue was forming outside.

'How much longer are you going to be?' a woman shouted. 'I need to change my daughter's nappy!'

Lizzy was going to need a nappy at this rate. There was a knock at the door. 'I'll be out in a minute,' she groaned.

'Lizzy, it's me.' Elliot lowered his voice. 'Are you all right?'

'Yes, just got my zip stuck! *Aaah!*' she moaned.

'Are you sure you're all right?'

'Perfectly,' she panted.

A baby had started crying in the corridor.

'What's going on in there?' It was a new voice. 'This is the manager. I won't tolerate you doing drugs in there.'

'I'm not doing drugs!' Lizzy shouted hysterically.

'Then what the hell are you doing in there?'

At that moment the most enormous fart she'd ever heard erupted from Lizzy's back end. It seemed to go on for ever, as if a balloon had deflated and was wailing round the room. When her nether regions finally shuddered into silence you could hear a pin drop.

Lizzy put her head between her legs and quietly wished to die. There was a cough from outside.

'I really have to go,' Elliot said through the door. 'I'm interviewing Bill Gates at three.'

'Say hi from me!' Lizzy cried. '*Ow!*' She was nearly ejected off the toilet as another violent spasm ripped through her body. What the hell had Antonia *given* her?

Chapter 34

'I can't believe you had laxatives meant for a dog!' Antonia chortled. 'That is so bloody funny.'

Lizzy was only just back at work after an entire twenty-four hours on the toilet. She'd had to call a taxi to take her home from the café and ask the driver if he had a plastic bag she could sit on. It had turned out that Antonia's friend, who was married to a vet, had given Antonia a bottle of high-strength lactulose that had been meant for a constipated dog, instead of the new product she was working on. Apparently Lizzy had taken enough to clear the bowels of an elephant.

'You would have probably been all right with a Yorkshire terrier, but it was a prescription for a Rhodesian ridgeback.'

Antonia didn't stop laughing all morning.

Lizzy felt delicate for the rest of the week. It was only on Saturday morning when she was off to see her brother that she felt truly confident about not being within ten yards of a bathroom.

Robbie met her at the train station in a new Audi 4x4.

'When did you get this?' Lizzy asked. It was neat as a pin inside, as if it was the first time anyone had driven it. Having witnessed the swamp-like conditions of her brother's bedroom growing up, she couldn't believe he was in possession of such a mature car.

'A few months ago.' He put his arm round the back of Lizzy's seat and started reversing. 'Hayley wanted something bigger.'

Lizzy opened the glove compartment. 'Oh my God, you've even got a road atlas.'

'Wait until you see my leather driving gloves.' He gave his sister a horrible leer.

Robbie and Hayley lived on an estate on the edge of a large village. The houses were so identikit that Lizzy could never remember which one they lived in. Last summer there had been a particularly embarrassing incident when she'd farted through next-door's letter-box as a practical joke on Robbie. Luckily the neighbours had been out.

The house was as immaculate as the car. There was a big baroque mirror in the hallway, and, above it, the word HOME was spelt out in decorative wooden letters.

'Do you want to take your bag up?' Robbie said. 'I'll go and stick the kettle on.'

Lizzy went into the smaller spare room. BE OUR GUEST had been stencilled in silver on the wall and a pillow on the bed had SWEET DREAMS embroidered on it. Even when Hayley wasn't there she exerted her control-freak presence.

Lizzy went to use the bathroom, which had a helpful

TOILETTE sign on the door. Inside there was another instruction on the wall to SOAK, RELAX, ENJOY. When she went back downstairs to the kitchen – sorry, the PANTRY – Robbie was making tea under a poster that said BON APPÉTIT.

'Extra milky, one and a half sugars.' He handed her a mug that said DOMESTIC GODDESS.

The work surfaces were empty apart from a set of red TEA, COFFEE and SUGAR canisters. WINE was spelt out in metallic letters above the bottle rack on the wall.

Lizzy pointed at the kettle. 'You haven't got a sign for it. How do you know what it is?'

Robbie looked at her. For a moment Lizzy wondered if she'd gone too far.

He pointed solemnly at the oven. 'OVEN.'

It was her turn. 'FLOOR.'

'WINDOW.'

'FRIDGE MAGNET.'

'POT OF CORIANDER.'

'AIR.'

They carried on the game until they were both in fits of laughter. 'Hayley's the one in charge of interior design,' Robbie told Lizzy. 'As long as I've got a sofa and a flat screen I'm happy.'

They went back into the living room. Lizzy sat down on a cushion that said LOVE. 'Where is Hayley again?'

'She's gone to a spa with her friends. Champions?'

'I think you mean Champneys.'

'That's the one. She said to say "hi" by the way, and to make yourself at home.'

They exchanged a look. Hayley's idea of 'making people feel at home' was something of a contradiction. She had once made Lizzy drink red wine in the garden in December because they'd just had new cream carpets put down.

'What do you fancy doing, kiddo?' Robbie asked. 'Hayley said we could go for a nice walk, or we could watch a film, or go to the garden centre . . . Oh, hold on.'

He put a coaster under Lizzy's mug. 'Hayley'll go mental if we leave rings.'

Lizzy watched her brother sit back down. It was like looking at a shell of his former self. He was wearing slippers for God's sake.

'What do *you* want to do?' she asked.

Robbie blinked, as if free thought was an alien concept. 'I dunno. We could go for a walk?'

'Do you want to go for a walk?'

A smile tugged on the corner of Robbie's mouth, the smile he'd always got when he'd been about to convince Lizzy to do something naughty. 'What I really want to do is get pissed.'

After six hours of solid drinking at the nearly deserted pub in the village, Lizzy and Robbie staggered home. When she'd fallen asleep on the pool table while lining up to take a shot they'd decided to call it a night.

Lizzy belched in a very unladylike fashion. 'Have you got any sambuca at home?'

'Don't think so. We've got Baileys.' Robbie suddenly sprang into the middle of the road. 'DJ Lizard in da house!'

'MC Robster on da decks!'

They both did the running man before chest-bumping each other. Lizzy lost her balance and fell into the verge. Robbie was cracking up as he pulled his sister up. 'Come here, you muppet.'

They continued to weave down the dark country road, arms wrapped round each other. 'I love you, DJ,' Robbie slurred.

'I love you too, MC.'

'This is nice, just the two of us hanging out. Bruv and sis together!'

'For-eva!'

'I know! Let's phone Lauren.' Robbie fumbled for his phone and promptly dropped it on the road. 'Oh bollocks, the screen's smashed.'

'Use mine.'

It took six *beeps* before Lauren picked up. 'Hello?'

'All right, Squirt! It's your big sis and bruv!'

'Are you drunk?'

'Completely smashed.' Lizzy put her other hand over one eye. If she did that she could see. 'Where you, babes?'

'Having dinner with Perry and his parents,' Lauren hissed.

'Send a high five from the Bromley massive!'

'Yeah right, I don't want them knowing my family are complete piss-heads.'

'We love you, Squirt,' Robbie bellowed down the phone.

'I told you, don't call me that! You two are so immature.'

'We love you, Squirt!' Lizzy shouted.

'All right, I get it. Can I go now? The petits fours are here.'

The lane lit up as a set of headlights pulled up beside them.

'Rob?' A blonde girl was sitting behind the wheel of a huge silver 4x4.

He peered in the window. 'It's Michelle! Hi Michelle. You all right, mate?' he said to the guy in the passenger seat. 'This is my sister.' Robbie put his arm around her. 'DJ Lizard, Michelle and Rich.'

'Hello,' Michelle said suspiciously.

'Where have you guys been?' Robbie asked them.

'Dinner party,' Rich said. His eyes were dead.

'What are you doing out here, Rob?' Michelle asked pointedly.

'We've just been to the pub and got totally pished.'

Michelle gave Lizzy an unfriendly look. 'Does Hayley know?'

'Probably not, I should tell her really.' He slapped his forehead. 'My phone's dead.'

Rich leaned across. 'Do you guys want a lift?'

Michelle looked like the last thing she wanted was a pair of drunkards in her pristine car. 'We're all right thanks, mate,' Robbie told him. 'The fresh air will do us good.'

They watched the car drive off. 'Uh-oh,' Robbie sighed. 'That's me in the doghouse.'

Back at home Robbie put The Stone Roses on at top volume and they danced round the living room with their shoes rebelliously on.

'Do you think Hayley will mind us drinking the Moët?' Lizzy slurred.

He looked up from fiddling with the Sony system. 'It

was only a present for being Michelle's bridesmaid, I'm sure she won't mind.'

By the time the pizza turned up they were both too drunk to eat. Robbie produced a dog-eared spliff from somewhere and they took the alpaca rug off the sofa and went to smoke in the garden.

They sat on the picnic bench under the rug and looked at the moon as they passed the joint between them. 'How are the Two Amigos?' Robbie asked.

'Pretty good. Nic's working her arse off these days, she'll probably end up running the country by the time she's forty.'

'How about Poppet?'

'Still the same. On the eternal hunt for the perfect man and/or matching sofa throw.'

Robbie stretched his legs out. 'That guy still on the scene? What was his name, Pepperoni Pete?'

'Pencil Dick Pete. And no, thank God. Why?' Lizzy joked. 'Are you interested?'

'Don't be daft.' He gazed upwards. 'I am *wasted*.'

'Not as wasted as me.' She could swear she'd just seen something that looked like a flying saucer.

'Still, it's been good hey? Just you and me, hanging out.' Robbie had the wistful tone of a man on his last reprieve.

'We can do it again you know. I'm sure Hayley won't mind.'

'If she gets another good Groupon deal on Champneys, maybe.'

Lizzy turned to look at her brother. His profile was in shadow, making his expression hard to read. Robbie had always been like a meandering river, ambling along at the same pace without any hiccups or interruptions. What was really going on under there?

'Rob?'

'Yeah?'

'You are happy, aren't you?'

He blew out a thick cloud of smoke. 'What do you mean?'

'With Hayley?'

'Course I'm happy with Hayley. Why wouldn't I be?'

Lizzy tried to assemble her words. 'I just want to make sure that you're with Hayley because, you know, you're definitely sure that you want to spend the rest of your life with her. And not just because she's got nice boobs and was the prettiest girl at school. Not that I spend much time looking at your girlfriend's boobs,' she added hurriedly.

'You're bonkers, Liz,' he said affectionately.

'Bonkers I may be,' she said, 'but you're my big bruv and I care about you.' She gave him a jovial nudge. 'I just want to make sure that, you know, Hayley is "The One"! Whatever that may be!'

What she really wanted to do was shake her brother by the shoulders and shout, 'DON'T YOU WORRY THAT YOU'VE JUST SETTLED?'

'You don't like her much, do you?'

'Of course I do! She's your girlfriend, Rob. If you're happy then I'm happy.'

'You don't have to worry about me and Hayley.'

'So you're a hundred per cent sure? That she's the one for you?'

'How can anyone be a hundred per cent sure about anything?' He was starting to sound a bit exasperated.

'But I do know that Hayley's good for me and I wouldn't want to be without her.'

There was a moment's silence. 'Sorry, Robbo, I didn't mean to go off on one. I'm just drunk and emotional.'

He stubbed the joint out on the patio and sat up. 'People who are single have this idealized view of romance. It's probably why they're still single. Being in love isn't all about red roses and high passion and drama. Sometimes you just find someone and knock along together. Me and Hayley, we're a team.' He waved his arm round. 'We've bought a house together. I've got a two-grand barbecue with infrared sizzle burners. Isn't that the sign of a man who's in it for the long haul?'

Lizzy gazed round the small pristine garden and suddenly sobered up. Had she got it all wrong? Forget meeting Mr Right and having that thunderbolt moment. Was owning a posh barbie and 'knocking along together' what it was really all about?

Chapter 35

'One latte, one Americano,' their waitress said.

'Americano here.'

'*Please*,' Lizzy added. 'I'm sorry,' she told the waitress. 'He doesn't get out very often.'

Elliot ignored her. As usual he was absorbed with his iPad. Conversations – apart from disagreeing with Lizzy or holding her to ransom over an innocent comment she may have made about, say, the weather – were frequently punctuated by him breaking off to reply to texts and emails. Apparently being a high-profile financial journalist was a very important and time-consuming job.

She watched him frown intently at the screen. 'What shampoo did you go for in the end?'

He glanced up. 'What are you talking about?'

Lizzy got her copy of *heat* out. 'You're in their "Spotted" section. "News at Ten *hunk Elliot Anderson in Boots at Charing Cross looking confused as he tried to decide between Toni & Guy Volumising Shampoo and L'Oréal Elvive for Men*."' She put the magazine down. '*Do* you use volumising shampoo? You have got a lovely bounce.'

'I'm not even going to dignify that with a response.'

She chortled and for the next few minutes contented herself with people watching until Elliot finally put his iPad away. 'How was your weekend with your brother?'

It was Lizzy's turn to look surprised. 'How did you know I was with my brother?'

'You tweeted a picture at 4 a.m. of you both with flowerpots on your head.'

Lizzy had absolutely no recollection of the incident. She'd woken up at midday to find the house in disarray and Robbie passed out face-down on the sofa. Hayley had been due back at 2 p.m. The brother and sister had done an emergency clear-up before Lizzie had scarpered, but despite texting and calling she hadn't heard from Robbie since.

There was a more immediate issue than Robbie doing his usual AWOL act. 'You follow me on Twitter?' Lizzy rarely checked her new followers these days. After 'Girl Who Gets Jilted . . .' she had been horrified at the amount of people clustering like vultures waiting for her subsequent breakdown.

'Quite a few people I know followed you after your YouTube debut. It's hard to believe, I know, but you were quite big news at the time.'

'You mean people like Mary Nightingale from the *News at Ten* follow me?'

'I'm not sure if Mary does.' Elliot arched an eyebrow. 'She might have been put off by your incessant photos of cats in elf outfits.'

'You still follow me.'

'I follow hundreds of people, it's my job. Don't think you're anything special.'

'Elliot, if you really want the latest news on constipation products all you have to do is pick up the phone and call,' she told him.

He did his ignoring thing again. 'It's the reason I found you when you broke down.' He nodded at Lizzy's phone. 'Your tweet, and then I saw you were near because of location services on Twitter.'

'And here I was thinking it was a random act of kindness.' She gave him a quizzical smile. 'Seriously, you came out to find us?'

He shrugged. 'I was in the area.'

'I want to know your service provider. We barely had a bar of reception between us the whole time we were there.'

'You just have to know the right spots.' He picked up the iPad again. 'So was it a good weekend with your brother?'

'Really good. I hope he's not in too much trouble with his girlfriend, though.'

'The bad sister leading him astray?'

'That's how Hayley sees it.' Lizzy sighed.

Elliot gave her a keen look. Instead of his normal variation of dark suits he was wearing a moss-green jumper that matched his eyes. Lizzy wondered if it was deliberate. He was always well turned out and although Lizzy could never spot a label, it was obvious everything was top-end. Being engaged to a fashion designer had obviously rubbed off on him.

'You've got a younger sister as well, haven't you?' he asked.

'Yeah, Lauren. She lives in New York.' Lizzy paused. 'Your sister lives in America, doesn't she?'

'Colorado.' He didn't volunteer any more information.

'What's she doing out there?'

'Living in a famous hippy commune making wooden jewellery. Let's say she took more after our mother.' He gave Lizzy's fox-print scarf a disparaging look. 'I think you'd get on.'

A little boy on the next table had been staring at Elliot for some time now. 'You're like me.' He pointed at his red hair.

'Charlie!' the boy's mother admonished.

Unexpectedly, Elliot smiled and leant across towards them. 'How old are you, Charlie?'

'Four.'

'Do you like having red hair?'

The boy shook his head. 'Sometimes people call me names.'

'Don't you listen to them. They're just jealous. Red-headed people have special powers, OK?'

'Like a superhero?' His little face lit up.

Elliot gave him a wink. 'Like a superhero. We're better than everyone else. Remember that, OK?'

Lizzy had been surprised and rather touched by the exchange. 'Were you bullied at school?'

'Of course I wasn't bullied,' he said irritably. 'And I know it's hard to believe but a person's hair colour isn't their one defining characteristic. We're not all like Kim Kardashian.'

'Oh, so you do know who she is. I thought all things celebrity were beneath you.'

'Is this the way this conversation is going to go? I have got better things to be doing with my time.'

'Temper, temper,' she chided. 'You don't want to be living up to that red-headed cliché.'

'Ditto with the ditzy blonde thing.'

Lizzy didn't rise. Really, she could almost tune him out now if she wanted to. 'So what did you do at the weekend?'

'Went home.'

'How's your mum?' she asked nonchalantly.

'Fine. Why are you asking?'

'Don't look so suspicious. It's not a rude question.'

'My mother is fine. Still floating around on Planet Cassandra with no concept of what actually goes on in the real world.'

Lizzy put her coffee cup down. 'Why do you hate your mum?'

She watched his eyes widen in shock. 'I don't hate my mum, what are you talking about?'

'Then why are you so dismissive of her?'

'I'm not dismissive of her.'

'Yes, you are. All she wants to do is be part of your life. She's up there at that Hall all by herself. Don't you think she must be really lonely?'

'If she sold the bloody place and got herself a cottage in a village somewhere, she wouldn't have to be lonely.'

'You're her son. She needs you.'

'My mother knows I'm there for her,' he said gruffly.

'Then why don't you talk to her? She's been really worried about you since you and Amber broke up.'

Elliot frowned. 'How do you know?'

'Um. Your mum kind of asked me to keep an eye on you . . .'

'She did what?' He looked appalled.

'She meant well,' Lizzy said hastily. 'Don't have a go at her about it.'

There was a long silence. 'You don't understand,' he said finally. 'My mother comes across as this larger-than-life character, but you wouldn't say that if she was your mother. My parents meant well, but they were bloody useless. Our home life was utterly shambolic. I used to have to buy and wrap everyone's presents at Christmas, mine included. I was the one, aged eleven years old, who had to deal with the electricity board when we were about to be cut off, and somehow find the money for wages when the estate staff hadn't been paid. My mum and dad's idea of good parenting was leaving Skyla and I to do whatever we wanted, and thinking it was OK to turn up at my school with whatever was left of the family silver to pay the fees for that term.' He shook his head. 'And then there was the time they thought it would be a good idea to do a duet guitar recital at the end-of-term assembly. That wasn't embarrassing *at* all.'

'I'm sure they were only doing their best.'

'So now she wants to take an interest in my life at the age of thirty-two?' he asked tartly. 'I've managed perfectly well without her until now.'

'Have you ever thought that she might need *you*?'

'I needed her when I was growing up! Everyone thought I had these cool, bohemian parents but I used to get so jealous when all the other kids would come back to school after being at home for the weekend and they'd have all sat down with their families for a Sunday roast. Meal times didn't exist in our house; Skyla and I just ate when and what we wanted.' He gave Lizzy a sideways glance. 'You know, I ran away from home once in protest when I was eight. I went and camped out in the woods overnight, but then the next morning I felt bad about upsetting my parents, so I went home. You know what they said when I got back?'

'I imagine they were pretty pissed off.'

'They hadn't even noticed I'd gone.'

'Oh Elliot,' Lizzy said softly.

'My mum thinks she gave me this wonderful uncon-strained upbringing, but all *I* wanted was someone to tell me what to do once in a while. Look, I'm not say-ing I had an abused childhood by any means, but now maybe you understand why I wouldn't put my mother up for Mum of The Year. And I know I'm a grumpy git,' he went on, 'but when you're the only grown-up in your family at age seven, you don't exactly end up being a devil-may-care kind of person.'

'Why don't you tell your mum how you feel?'

Elliot rolled the dregs of his coffee around in the bottom of his cup. 'It's too late. There's nothing she can do about it now.'

'It's never too late. If you told your mother how you really felt, she'd at least understand why you're so angry with her.'

'Maybe,' he admitted after a long pause.

'I do get where you're coming from,' Lizzy told him. 'But you have to let go of things, there's no point letting them sit inside you and fester. Everyone needs their family,' she sighed. 'If I held a grudge against *my* mum for some of the stuff she's said and done, we'd have stopped speaking years ago.'

'I can't imagine your mother inviting a bunch of naturalists to stay for a whole summer.'

'Maybe not,' Lizzy laughed. 'But I'm sure Cassandra was only doing her best. And you know she's always loved you. Isn't that enough?'

'You think I'm being pig-headed, don't you?'

She looked at him amusedly. 'I just think you need to lighten up.'

There was a wistful smile. 'Amber used to say that.'

There it was again. That look of such deep sadness and *regret*. Lizzy had almost started to forget the reason they'd started meeting in the first place. As she looked at his stricken face it was obvious that Elliot was still finding it hard to move on.

She wasn't sure what to say. 'Have you spoken to her?'

'No.' He stood abruptly and started to gather his things up. 'Shall we get the bill?'

Chapter 36

The girls were spending the evening at Poppet's. Despite the fact Christmas was still over two months away, there was a home-made wreath on the mantelpiece and pinecones on the hearth.

Going round to Poppet's flat was like stepping back in time. An aroma of lavender and rose petal hit you as soon as you walked through the front door, while the hallway was lined with framed sepia photographs. In the living room there was an old-school TV that Nic complained gave her migraines because the screen was so small, and an antique display unit Poppet had got off eBay to house her vintage teacup collection. She was the only person Lizzy had ever met who took her own embroidered napkin to eat in Pret A Manger.

The hostess came back into the living room carrying a tray. 'Gingerbread cake,' she announced. 'It's still warm from the oven.'

'Mmm,' Lizzy and Nic said. They were both on their phones.

'I swear you're a ninety-year-old woman trapped

in a young person's body.' Nic was sitting on Poppet's Laura Ashley love seat, her legs splayed out like a bloke's. 'You'd be happy in a bygone era where women rode round on penny farthings and had gentlemen walkers.'

Poppet started to cut slices. 'You may scoff but I'll have you know I'm part of a revolution.'

'Are you, Pops?' Lizzy was still scrolling through Twitter.

'I was reading about it the other day. People like me are part of this thing called "The Home-grown Revolution". More and more young women are rejecting modern consumerism and going out every Saturday night and are choosing to stay in instead to knit and make their own jam and stuff. It's all about getting back to the simple things.' She looked excited. 'I was thinking about going foraging on Clapham Common for my dinner tomorrow.'

'That's nice, Pops.' Lizzy had started following Elliot, but he wasn't very interesting and was always going on about stuff to do with decimal points and indexes. She reread the tweet about something called: 'QE3'. What did banking have to do with cruise ships?

'For God's sake!' Poppet suddenly cried.

Lizzy nearly jumped out of her seat. 'Whatever's the matter?'

'Look at you both! I invite you round and make you nice things and all you do is sit there on your phones ignoring me. I may as well not be here!'

Chastened, Lizzy put the phone down. 'Sorry, Pops.'

'Sorry isn't enough! No one talks any more! What would our ancestors think if they were to look at us now? We're supposedly living in this enlightened age and all we're doing is regressing as human beings! No one *listens* to anyone any more.'

'I think that's a bit harsh . . .'

'Be quiet, I'm talking! At this rate we'll be giving birth to children with monstrously sized index fingers who can only communicate through the power of emoticons! Forget type two diabetes, "Scrollitis" will be the thing that takes down the NHS!' Poppet punched an embroidered cushion. 'I'm part of a revolution! And I'm rising up and taking back the lost art of conversation!'

She sat back and looked pointedly at Nic.

'What's that?' Nic asked. 'I've just got to send this email.'

'From now on I'm banning phone usage in this house!' Poppet announced. 'Lizzy and I are waiting for you, so the three of us can have a proper conversation.'

'Go ahead and start without me.'

'Put the phone down, Nicola.' Poppet's voice took on the dangerous edge of a stressed-out mum giving a child their final warning. '*Nicola! Put the phone down.*'

'Oh, for fuck's sake.' Nic threw it on the carpet. 'I'm going for a slash.'

'Don't you think Nic's really aggro at the moment?' Poppet said after Nic had stropped off to the toilet.

'Nic's always aggro.'

'I mean *really* aggro. I'm worried she's working too hard.'

Lizzy thought about it. Nic had threatened to brain an entire girl gang on the train on the way there be-cause they'd refused to take their feet off the two spare seats, but these random acts of violence were nothing new. Nic had always been like Mount Vesuvius: a fiery, spitting pit of lava that was liable to blow at any second.

Nic's BlackBerry was lying on the sofa where she'd thrown it. Lizzy and Poppet both looked over as it started ringing.

'Don't answer it,' Poppet warned. 'We are not slaves to these contraptions!'

Lizzy was incapable of ignoring a ringing phone. 'Sorry, Pops, it's the PR in me.' She looked at the screen. 'Ha! Guess who?'

'Simon?'

'I hope Nic's getting overtime.' Lizzy answered. 'Hello, Nic Cartwright's personal answering service!'

'Nicola?'

'No, it's Lizzy. I'm a friend of Nicola's.'

'Oh, hello Lizzy!' Nic's boss sounded very jolly. 'I haven't interrupted anything, have I?'

'No, we were just about to have some cake. Nic's away from her phone at the moment, shall I get her to call you back?'

'Don't worry, I've just nipped out from parents' evening. Can you just tell her I'll send the new proposals for Beijing through later?' He paused. 'What kind of cake is it?'

'Gingerbread.'

'My favourite! Well, don't let me disturb you any more. You girls have a nice evening.'

'Simon called,' Lizzy said when Nic returned from the loo. 'He wasn't quite the ogre you make him out to be.'

'You spoke to him?'

'Don't worry, I didn't tell him what a depraved monster you really are. He says he's sending the Beijing proposal over and he'll catch up with you first thing.'

Nic threw herself back down on the sofa and closed her eyes. Poppet was right, Lizzy thought. She really did look knackered.

Thursday was a big day for Lizzy. She and her team were doing a pitch for a new client. The super-stylish team and elegant offices weren't what Lizzy had been expecting at all. Especially as she'd turned up dressed as a giant tomato, complete with a green cap on her head for the stalk. It was only when she was five minutes into her presentation that it started to dawn that something was horribly wrong.

'Sorry, I just don't get what a vegetable has to do with the long-term vision for Bellafinique,' the company director said. A shiny spot was glinting off her frozen forehead, a sure sign of Botox.

'Bellafinique?' Lizzy looked to Antonia nervously. Her boss gazed back at her as if they'd never met. 'I thought we were pitching for Veggie Vibe.'

'This is a pitch for Bellafinique?' the director said irritably. 'The revolutionary new skincare range for women?'

Lizzy looked round vainly for help. Bianca was slouched against the wall in her runner bean outfit, texting.

'Oh,' she said feebly. 'I thought we were here pitching for a new vegetable juice.'

There was a slow tumbleweed moment across the grandiose boardroom. The director looked down her retroussé nose at Lizzy. 'Do we look like the sort of people who work in the world of *vegetable* juicing?'

One of her colleagues sniffed. 'And any idiot knows a tomato is actually a fruit.'

On the way out Lizzy got stuck in the revolving door and had to be pulled free by the doorman. They trudged back to Antonia's Range Rover, which she'd left brazenly in a disabled parking bay in the shadow of St Paul's Cathedral.

It turned out that Antonia had got her dates wrong and the Veggie Vibe pitch had been last week. 'I get sent so many briefs. How am I meant to keep up with everything?'

'I've been working on this for *six* weeks,' Lizzy wailed.

'And even then you can't even get your bloody fruit and veg right.'

'Why didn't you say something before, then?'

'I thought you were being abstract.' Antonia dumped her bag on the bonnet and started searching for the car keys. 'I don't know why *you're* so moody. I'm the one who has to try and keep this business going! I'm the one with a husband who lies round the house doing sweet FA all day when he's meant to be taking care of our daughter!' She shook the bag. 'Come on, you fuckers, where are you?

'It's not easy existing on three hours sleep a night, when everyone is pulling you in every-which-way direction!' she continued. 'The last thing I need is you throwing your toys out the cot. I get enough of that at home.'

'I'm sorry,' Lizzy said guiltily. 'I'm sure you're under a lot of pressure.'

'You have *no* idea.' Antonia finally located her keys. 'I'm meeting the girls for lunch at Soho House. I'll have to drop you at a tube station on the way.'

'Can we get changed first?'

'If you have to,' Antonia sighed, as if Lizzy had demanded something completely unreasonable.

Bianca was now leaning against a nearby bollard continuing her text conversation. She hadn't broken her concentration once since they'd left the pitch.

'Bianca!' Lizzy managed to get her attention for a second. The sooner they got out of these stupid costumes, the better. She was *never* going to humiliate herself like this again.

'Oh shit, traffic warden!' Antonia shouted. The car suddenly roared off with the boot still open and the girls' clothes and bags in the back.

'Quick, ring her and tell her to come back!' Lizzy said.

Bianca tried. 'She's not picking up. What do we do now?'

They had no money, no travel cards, no nothing. 'There's only one thing we can do,' Lizzy said gloomily. 'Start walking.'

They began trudging through the sea of grey suits. It was lunchtime and the streets were rammed. Despite the autumnal temperatures, Lizzy started to sweat profusely. Then she caught sight of herself in a shop window. It was hard to tell where her face ended and the outfit started.

The outfit was also bringing back uncomfortable

memories of being dressed up as Henry VIII. 'I'm terribly sorry,' she said to a handsome man in a smart black overcoat who was trying to get past her without spilling his coffee.

'Your stomach's in the way,' he said irritably. 'Can you move it?'

To make matters worse, even dressed as a summer vegetable, Bianca looked stunning. She was attracting admiring looks from the male City workers and someone had mistaken her for Cara Delevingne in post-club fancy dress.

There was a man on the corner of the street dressed as a pizza slice handing out leaflets. He gave them a commiserative look.

'This way!' Lizzy shouted gallantly.

'Sweets, can't we get a cab?'

'We haven't got any money!'

'I don't mind begging. I'm sure I can get someone to give us the money.'

'We are *not* begging.' Bianca had already swanned ahead. She seemed to have some inbuilt ability that allowed her to dart like a fish through the crowds without looking up from her phone.

A few minutes later they found themselves in a big square flanked by imposing white buildings with Coliseum-style pillars.

'Look.' Lizzy pointed. 'That's the Bank of England.'

'Cool,' Bianca yawned. 'Is that a new club?'

Lizzy walked towards it, seeing an empty bench she could collapse on. The famous building was a bit grimy close up. You'd think with all their money they could at least hire somebody to give it a good clean.

She plonked down dispiritedly and pulled her cap off. Her bladder was reaching critical point.

'Sweets, we can't walk all the way back to Fulham,' Bianca said. 'What are we going to do?'

A sleek black car pulled up in front of them with two granite-jawed men sitting in the front. At the same time a small wooden door to the left of the Bank of England's main frontage opened and a group of people came out. Lizzy's mouth dropped open as she saw Elliot walking slightly ahead, deep in conversation with someone she was pretty sure was the Chancellor of the Exchequer.

They were heading straight for her. Lizzy thought about running to hide behind a nearby statue, but she wasn't exactly wearing the right outfit for a fifty-metre sprint. Maybe if she stood *really* still Elliot wouldn't notice her.

The two men reached the car. As one of the minder guys leapt out to open the rear passenger door Elliot glanced over at Lizzy. His eyes widened first in astonishment, and then horror, before settling for acute embarrassment.

'Hello!' she said brightly. 'Fancy seeing you here!'

Chapter 37

As Lizzy walked up to Café Crème Elliot was sat outside, wrapped up in an expensive-looking grey suit and matching dark-grey scarf.

'No tables inside,' he announced. 'Can you brave al fresco?'

'Fine with me.' Lizzy put her bag down and took the seat opposite. 'Whose is this?'

'Whose do you think?' Elliot tucked his phone away. 'I got you a bran muffin.'

'Thanks.' Lizzy looked over at his plate. 'What have you got?'

'Chocolate truffle cake.'

Lizzy gazed back at her muffin. It was rather bland and boring by comparison.

'Don't you want it?' He looked rather crestfallen. 'I thought that was the sort of thing girls like. You're all watching your weight, aren't you?'

'Are you saying I need to diet?'

'No!' His eyebrows shot up in alarm.

Lizzy smiled. 'Elliot, I'm joking.' Although that was

the second comment he'd made about her weight. Amber was as thin as a rake, maybe he thought that anyone over a size twelve was classified as obese.

The waitress came out. 'Usual, is it?'

'Yes please,' Lizzy said.

Elliot sat back in his chair. 'I'm probably going to regret asking, but why *were* you in the heart of the financial district dressed as a giant tomato yesterday?'

Running into him had turned out to be their saving grace. He'd lent Lizzy the money for a taxi no questions asked, clearly not wanting to be seen with her in public for a moment longer. Antonia hadn't got back from lunch until after five, so Lizzy and Bianca had had to sit around in their costumes all afternoon. Lizzy could now confirm: going to the loo in a giant spherical red suit *definitely* had the edge over the Henry VIII costume.

Elliot winced after she'd finished relaying the whole debacle.

'Your boss sounds like a muppet.'

'I could think of a stronger word.'

'Although I thought a tomato was a fruit and not a vegetable?'

'I realize that by now, thank you,' Lizzy sighed.

A man selling roses had been moving down the cafés on the street. He approached Lizzy and Elliot's table.

'Red rose for your pretty lady?'

'No!' they said in unison. 'We're not together!'

The flower seller shrugged and moved on.

'I'm not saying, you know, I find you *repulsive* or anything,' Elliot added awkwardly.

'Thanks,' Lizzy said sardonically. 'I'll take it as a compliment.'

The waitress came back with their order. 'So, come on then!' Elliot said afterwards. 'What's going on with your love life?'

'Why are you speaking like that?'

'Speaking like what?' he asked confusedly.

'Asking me about my love life in the manner of a hearty uncle. I get plenty of that from David, my parents' next-door neighbour.'

'I have no idea what you're talking about. Now answer the question.'

Lizzy wasn't comfortable with the conversational swerve. 'Can we talk about something else, please?'

'Come on, I want to know. You're always asking me; now it's your turn.' He was like a terrier on a scent. Lizzy was beginning to understand what his interview subjects must feel like.

'You sound like my mum. There isn't an abundance of single, hot men who aren't secret psychopaths on every street corner. Believe me, I've been looking.'

'Well, you're hardly going to meet one staying in and watching *The Housemaids of Atlantic City* every night.'

Lizzy flushed guiltily. 'It's *The Real Housewives of Orange County* and I don't watch it *every* night.'

'You're not trying hard enough,' he told her. 'There must be some bloke who will take you out.'

'I don't want "some bloke" to take me out. I want to meet my Mr Right.' Lizzy corrected herself. 'Or, my Mr-You're-Not-Quite-Right-But-You're-Perfect-To-Me-Anyway.'

Elliot looked cynically amused. 'Do you really believe in all that stuff?'

'Yeah, I do actually. Just because it didn't work out for you.'

The words were out before she could think. 'I'm sorry,' she said quickly. 'I didn't mean it.'

Elliot's face had shut down again. 'You're right,' he muttered. 'Who am I to sit here and cast judgement?'

There was another long silence. Lizzy looked down at Elliot's half-eaten cake. It was glistening at her invitingly. Picking up her fork, she sliced a bit off.

'Don't take the icing!' he said in outrage. 'That's the best bit!'

'So why aren't you eating it?' She popped it in her mouth.

'I was saving it until the end!'

'Don't be so stingy.' Lizzy went in for another mouthful. 'Ow! What are you doing?'

A man reading his paper on the next table gave them an odd look. Lizzy retreated to her side of the table, rubbing her knuckles.

'I can't believe you just hit me with your fork!'

Elliot had a mildly triumphant look about him. 'When you've been to boarding school you get territorial about your food.'

After retreating on to more familiar ground and arguing about their top five cultural destinations in London ('I can't *believe* you wouldn't have M&M's World in there,' Lizzy told him facetiously), they paid up and left.

'This is a first,' she commented. Elliot had set such a pace she practically had to sprint to keep up.

'What's a first?' he asked.

'You, deigning to walk down the street with me.

Usually you up and leave me to pay while you go off in pursuit of some world exclusive.'

'I don't leave you to pay!'

'I was *joking*.' Elliot was actually very gentlemanly and always picked up the bill. 'You're very easy to wind up,' Lizzy told him. 'At least try and give me something to work against.'

She saw the look on his face. 'I said it was a joke!'

Elliot was staring down the street. Lizzy followed his gaze and saw a tall, well-built man striding towards them. The piercing blue eyes looked very familiar. Hang on, it was that bloke Marcus from the art exhibition!

He stopped dead in their path. 'Anderson,' he said coldly. 'I didn't expect to see you in these parts.'

'Yeah well, it's turned out to be your lucky day.'

Lizzy stared up at the two men. Why were they speaking like they were in a fifties Western?

'What brings you round here?' Marcus enquired. 'I can't imagine it's a house-hunting expedition, you couldn't even afford to buy a doorbell round here.'

Lizzy watched Elliot's jaw clench. They weren't actually going to start fighting, were they?

'Spoken to Amber lately?' Marcus enquired.

Elliot's glare faltered. 'No.' He swallowed. 'Have you?'

'Quite a bit, as it happens.'

'How is she?'

'Brilliant, mate. Hardly mentions your name at all.' The smug smile widened. 'In fact, she's been leaning on me quite a lot.'

Elliot took a step forward. Lizzy put her hand on his arm.

'Oh, look who it is,' Marcus said. 'Headbutt Girl. Don't tell me you're scraping the bottom of the barrel with *him*.'

'You twat,' Elliot said furiously.

Marcus smirked. 'Now, now. I know you're fond of rows in the street, but that's not my style at all.'

He leaned in, his eyes as flat and cold as a shark's. 'Just stay away from her, all right, Anderson? If you know what's good for you.'

Brushing unnecessarily past Elliot's shoulder, he strode off.

Lizzy glanced nervously at Elliot. His face was tight with fury. 'What was all that about?'

He didn't reply for a moment. 'Amber was engaged to that . . . Marcus before we got together.'

So that's why they can't stand each other! 'Oh,' Lizzy said inadequately. 'That's a bit awkward.'

Elliot was staring off stonily into the distance. 'Do you want to talk about it?' she asked.

He shot her a look. 'No I bloody don't. What are you, my counsellor? Actually, don't answer that.'

A woman and a small girl on a scooter were coming towards them. Elliot stepped back and waited until they'd gone past. 'Sorry,' he sighed. 'I just wasn't expecting to see that . . . him.' He checked his watch. 'I've got to go.'

'Are you sure you're all right . . .?' Lizzy started to say, but Elliot had already turned on his heel and was striding away down the street.

269

Chapter 38

Lizzy tried Karen's number again. 'Hello,' the cheery voice said. 'You have reached the voicemail of Karen Jones at Night Night Baby.'

Lizzy left another message and hung up. It was very unlike her client not to return her calls. Lizzy was starting to get a bad feeling about this whole thing. The Christmas deadline to start paying the money back was only eight weeks away.

She was staring gloomily out of the window, wondering if she'd committed some kind of fraud when her email alert beeped. It was from Elliot.

I've been thinking. I don't buy it you can't find a man. Have you tried online dating?

Of course I have, she wrote back. It wasn't a great success.

What about a singles night?

Why the sudden fascination with her love life?

Why? Are you going to come along and be my wingman?

Lizzy smiled to herself and pressed send. That would shut him up.

Go on then.

He had to be winding her up.

Are you being serious?

Yes.

Lizzy sat back. Was this the weirdest thing that had ever happened, or what? The next moment it hit her – Elliot was using her as cover because he wanted to go himself!

She shook her head. He was such a proud, prickly little thing. Why didn't he just come out and say it was that?

OK, you're on, she wrote. She'd take pity on him – after all, this was a significant step.

Let me know the venue. I'm not exactly an expert on these things.

Lizzy went back through her inbox. One of the dating websites she had joined was always sending her newsletters about various events. She and Poppet kept meaning to go to one, but when it came round they ended up staying in the pub or going home to share an M&S meal deal and watch crap telly. No wonder they were both still single.

She found the latest email and opened the link. Sure enough, there was one that Thursday at a pub in East London. She emailed the details over to Elliot, fully expecting him to back out now the deal was on the table, but he came back straight away.

Fine. As long as I don't have to talk to anyone.

Er, that's kind of the idea of these nights? she wrote back.

I'm coming along as your wingman. That's it.

Fine, if that was the game he wanted to play.

*

Two nights later they met outside the tube. Elliot was already there, waiting impatiently next to an *Evening Standard* seller. He was wearing another suit Lizzy hadn't seen before – the guy had more suits than she had shoes – and an expensive-looking navy coat.

'You look nice,' she told him, trying to be encouraging.

Elliot gazed at her oddly. 'I've just come from work.'

'OK then, how do *I* look?' It was a low point when you had to ask Elliot Anderson for a sartorial compliment.

He peered at Lizzy's Topshop tunic, which she'd teamed with thick tights and ankle boots. 'You're not wearing animal print. I suppose that's a start.'

When they reached the pub Elliot started to get twitchy. 'I'm not sure this is a good idea after all,' he muttered. 'What if someone recognizes me?' He shrank into the shadows as a group of people walked past them.

Lizzy didn't need him to start dithering, she was nervous enough! 'What are you complaining about? I'm the one who had 2.5 million hits on YouTube after my boyfriend dumped me!'

He stared at her, aghast. 'Was it really that many?'

'You've been on the *MailOnline*'s Sidebar of Shame as well, you know!'

Elliot looked pained. 'Don't remind me.'

Lizzy had to practically frogmarch him to the front door. There was a girl there with a clipboard, waiting to tick people off as they came in. 'Hello,' she said to them. 'Are you here for the event?'

'Yes,' Lizzy said, at the same time as Elliot said: 'No.'

Lizzy nudged him. 'Lizzy Spellman and Elliot Anderson,' she said with as much confidence as she could muster.

'You gave them my real name?' Elliot muttered.

The door girl's eyebrows had shot up. 'You're really Lizzy Spellman? Me and my colleagues all thought it was a joke name! Who'd actually have thought it, "Girl Who Gets Jilted" turning up at a singles night . . .' She trailed off.

'Well here I am, in person,' Lizzy said stiffly.

'Great! You know how it works, right? You get a red straw if you're single and available, or a green straw if you're not.'

'Two red ones please,' Lizzy said, before Elliot had the chance to object.

A dozen pairs of eyes swivelled on them as they walked through the front door. Elliot dropped his straw on the floor as if it had burnt his fingers.

'You'll need that,' she told him. 'Or are you just going to rely on your looks and devastating charm?'

Elliot didn't want to go to the bar, so he shoved a twenty-pound note in Lizzy's hand and retreated to the nearest wall. Anyone would think he was expecting John Wayne to kick through the saloon doors any minute and let off a round of shots.

To her pleasant surprise, it was all rather relaxed. Groups of friends stood round having conversations instead of staring boggle-eyed at anyone who walked past. It almost felt like a normal night at the pub. Almost.

'I was beginning to think you'd gone,' Elliot grumbled when Lizzy got back from the bar.

'I had to wait ages to get served, I think it's the

barman's first shift.' She handed Elliot a beer and watched his eyes skitter nervously around the room. It was astonishing. Here was a man who interviewed famous bigwigs and politicians for a living, reduced to skulking in the corner like a teenager at the school disco.

'I knew it was a bad idea to come,' he muttered.

Lizzy rolled her eyes. 'It was your idea to go to a singles night in the first place!'

Trying to ignore the Grinch at her side, Lizzy took a sip of her vodka and looked round the room. She ended up catching the eye of a rather attractive bearded man who was rather comically drinking his pint through his red straw. He tentatively raised his eyebrows at her. Lizzy tentatively raised hers back. This could be easier than she'd thought.

The next moment Lizzy was blindsided as a girl with a huge lipsticked mouth and long blonde hair rushed up and threw herself at them.

'Elliot! Oh my God! I thought it was you!' She released him from her hold. 'I didn't expect to see you at one of these things.'

'I'm with a friend,' Elliot said quickly. 'Moral support.'

'We all say that, right?' The blonde girl gave Lizzy a smile and turned back. 'I was sorry to hear about you and Amber,' she told him. 'It's good to see you getting back out there.'

'Who was that?' Lizzy asked after the girl had rushed off to greet someone else.

'A friend of my sister's.' Elliot looked like he couldn't quite believe what had just happened.

*

With a few drinks inside her Lizzy had the confidence to start circulating. Annoyingly, the hot bearded guy from before had vanished. She had chatted to a divorcee with raging garlic breath, and a man who'd talked to her chest during an entire conversation about the over-gentrification of Hackney. Despite her best intentions, she was starting to flag.

Now she was talking to a guy who'd spent the last five minutes telling her about his job in IT.

'How nice,' she said absently.

'How nice that my firm has just announced two hundred redundancies?'

Lizzy blinked. 'What I mean is, how nice you've managed to keep your job!'

At that moment the crowd parted like the Red Sea. Lizzy saw Elliot still in the same spot she'd left him, clutching his pint protectively. He was wedged in between two separate groups of girls, all trying to make eye contact with him. He looked so out of his comfort zone that her heart went out to him.

'Would you excuse me?' she said. 'I must go and save my friend.'

She went over to him. 'You don't look like you're enjoying yourself.'

'Aside from my father dying, I'd put this up there as one of the worst nights of my life.'

'Why don't you go and start chatting to some girls?' Lizzy suggested. 'I can introduce you if you want.'

'I don't want to talk to any girls.'

'Then why are you here?'

'I told you,' he said sulkily. 'I'm meant to be your wingman.'

'Elliot, I thought you were just using me as an excuse because you wanted to meet some girls.'

He looked distinctly horrified. 'What? I'm not that desperate.'

'Oh thanks a lot!'

'I didn't . . . You know what I mean,' he sighed.

Lizzy looked at the cross, awkward figure hunched against the wall. 'You really came out tonight just to give me support?'

'That's what friends do, isn't it?' he muttered.

'Lizzy? It is you, isn't it?'

She turned round to see a dark-haired guy standing there. 'Lizzy from Haven, right?' he asked.

It took a moment to compute. 'Greg! Oh my God!' It was Greg! Cute Greg with the puppy-dog eyes who she'd flirted with heavily at the PR Awards! 'Fancy seeing you here!'

Greg looked uncertainly between her and Elliot. 'Are you two . . .?'

'We're not together,' they both said in unison.

'Oh, right.' Greg looked back at Lizzy. 'How's it going? I mean after the whole . . .'

'Getting myself back out there, as you can see,' she said dryly. 'What about you? Have you had any luck?'

Greg looked down at his red straw.

'I've chatted to a few girls, but it's all getting a bit feral.'

The understated decorum of earlier had gone, thanks to two hours of heavy drinking. The three of them watched a couple shake hands to introduce each other and then start snogging each other's faces off.

Lizzy glanced at Elliot; he was gazing at them with the look of someone who'd just had something unpleasant wafted under their nose.

'Do you fancy going on somewhere else and getting a drink?' Greg asked her.

'Sure!' Lizzy looked back at Elliot. 'I take it you don't mind getting out of here?'

'I know this cool bar about five minutes away,' Greg said once they were outside.

'Sounds great.' Lizzy smiled back at him. He really *did* have lovely eyes.

'What about your, er, friend?'

Elliot had gone to stand pointedly a couple of metres away. Lizzy felt like a teenager on her first date being chaperoned by an over-protective father.

She went over to him. 'We're going for a drink. Do you fancy coming?'

'Sorry, the last time I checked in the mirror I wasn't bright green and covered in prickles.'

'Fine,' she sighed. 'I was just checking.'

Elliot stopped her as she turned to go. 'Email me to let me know you got home safely.'

'I'm a grown woman, I think I can get home by my-self.'

He shot Greg a suspicious look. 'You barely know the guy. How do you know what he's planning?'

'He's a really nice guy, I know him through my job, and I'm sure he's not planning anything!' Greg glanced over at her raised voice. *Sorry*, Lizzy mouthed apologetically. *One minute.*

'Are you sure you don't mind?' she asked Elliot. 'I feel bad about leaving you.'

He sighed. 'It's a singles night, isn't it? You're supposed to go home with someone.'

'I'm not going home with him.'

'You might. Anything could happen.'

'Nothing will happen! I'm not that kind of girl.'

Elliot shrugged. 'It's no business of mine if you are.'

'Well, I'm not! I don't do that kind of stuff on the first night.'

The right eyebrow went up. 'Stuff?'

'Oh shut up!' God, he was so annoying!

'Lizzy!' Greg called. 'They start charging after eleven to get in.'

'Coming!'

They started walking off together. 'You're going to love this place, they do great cocktails,' Greg told her.

'Sounds great.' Lizzy looked back over her shoulder. Elliot was trudging away in the drizzle with his hands in his pockets. He looked so dejected and . . . *alone*. And after that run-in with Marcus he must be feeling crappy. What was it about the miserable sod that pulled at her heartstrings?

She stopped suddenly. 'You know what, I might go and find my friend after all.'

Greg's face fell. 'Really?'

'He's been through a bad break-up and I'm a bit worried about him. I'm really sorry, Greg.'

She started running back over the uneven cobbles. 'Elliot!'

The third time she called his name he turned round. A look of astonishment crossed his face. 'What are you doing?'

'I changed my mind,' she panted as she caught up with him.

Elliot's brow furrowed confusedly. 'I thought you were in there.'

'He wasn't really my type after all,' Lizzy lied.

He gave her a look as if to say *girls*.

'Fancy another drink?' she asked.

'Are you hungry?'

Lizzy hadn't eaten since lunch. 'Starving.'

As if by magic, a cab was sailing towards them with the orange light on. Elliot stuck out his arm to flag it down. 'Chinatown please,' he told the driver.

The West End was jumping. Their taxi driver wove expertly through the packed streets and deposited them at the entrance to Chinatown.

'The place doesn't look much,' Elliot said as they walked up to a modest restaurant, 'but the food is spectacular.'

Judging by the owner's rapturous welcome, Elliot was obviously a regular. The place was rammed, but after greeting Elliot like a long-lost son, the little man managed to find them a table next to the kitchen.

'Where did you learn to speak Chinese?' Lizzy asked in disbelief.

He tried to look modest and failed. 'I just know a little bit.'

The kitchen was open, so they sat and watched the chefs hard at work amongst the sizzle and the steam. It was quite a show. Elliot ordered a bottle of wine and set about recommending things to Lizzy.

279

'You have to try the squid. And the belly of pork is something else.'

He'd taken his coat off and rolled up his shirtsleeves, revealing well-shaped forearms with a dusting of freckles. His thick hair had gone slightly crinkled from the rain, making him look more approachable and human. Lizzy watched as he called the owner back over and they conversed animatedly about something. The brooding wallflower of an hour ago had gone.

'So I take it you won't be going to any more singles nights then?' she asked him when the owner had gone.

'Put it this way, I would rather gouge my eyeballs out with red-hot teaspoons.' Elliot snapped the menu shut and put it down on the table. 'But tonight has merely proved my point.'

'Which is?'

'You're not trying hard enough,' he said triumphantly. 'You were in there with Greggy Boy and you wimped out at the last minute.'

'I did nothing of the sort. I told you, I didn't fancy him,' she added. She was hardly going to tell Elliot that she'd felt sorry for him. The god of dating had better have someone else lined up after her act of self-sacrifice. Or maybe she could get in touch with Greg and apologize and see if he'd go out with her another time. Lizzy picked up her drink. 'At least I made an effort to speak to people, instead of skulking by the jukebox like Billy No Mates all night.'

'We weren't there for me,' he reminded her. He picked up his own glass. 'Shall we make a toast?'

'To what?'

'How about to you not being able to close the deal, and me making a terrible wingman?'

'I'll drink to the second one.'

They clinked glasses. 'What are you smiling at?' Elliot asked her.

'You,' Lizzy said. '*This.* Who would have thought we'd ever get to a point where we were sat having a civil meal together?'

'You see, I'm not a complete ogre.'

'What was it you said in your first email?' she reminded him. 'Something about me spending my life peddling meaningless drivel?'

'I recall you telling me to cheer up.'

'Damn right. Miserable git.'

They grinned across the table at each other.

'Was I really that bad?' he asked her.

'Put it this way,' Lizzy said. 'If you were to ask me what was the more appealing prospect: hanging out with Hitler during his final hours in his underground bunker or meeting up with you for coffee, I would have gone with Hitler every time.'

Elliot had the grace to look contrite. 'I wasn't in the best place back then. I'm sorry if I upset you.'

'It's all right,' she told him. 'I didn't let your darkness infect me. It was like water off a duck's back.'

'Have you always been this relentlessly sunny?' he asked. 'You're like the girl in *Enchanted*. I'm surprised a flock of sparrows hasn't burst in yet and started circling round our table.'

'A-ha!' Lizzy crowed. 'You've seen *Enchanted*! That's hardly your normal highbrow fare.'

'It was on a flight and I'd seen everything else. I

like Amy Adams. Oh shut up,' he muttered. 'You're so annoying.'

Glowing with delight, Lizzy retreated to her side of the table. They should make winding Elliot Anderson up into a national pastime.

Bits and pieces of food began to arrive. 'Tuck in,' he announced. 'Otherwise I'll probably end up eating everything.'

They concentrated on their plates for the next few minutes. 'You're right, the squid is unbelievable,' Lizzy mumbled. 'How come I've never been here before?'

'Contrary to your opinion that I'm a boring old fart I do actually know some good places to go.'

Lizzy pulled a face at him and then forked up another mouthful of noodles. 'So, you and Marcus,' she said after she'd swallowed.

'What about me and Marcus?'

She'd been dying to ask him more about it. 'So did you steal Amber off Marcus? Is that why he hates you so much?'

'Of course I didn't *steal* Amber from him,' he retorted. 'It was only a matter of time before she worked out what an arse he is for herself.'

'You mentioned at the café you were at school together.'

'Yes, unfortunately. He was a thuggish twat even back then. We didn't get on from the start.'

'Too similar?' Lizzy suggested.

Elliot looked affronted. 'Certainly not! I have a brain for a start.'

Lizzy poured them out more wine. 'And then Amber came along and you became *love* rivals.'

'If you want to call it that. Luckily she was far too mature to take any notice of the pathetic one-upmanship of testosterone-fuelled schoolboys. And anyway, it ended up that she and I became friends.' There it was again. That wistful face Elliot got whenever he talked about her. 'Marcus wasn't so subtle. He kept on relentlessly chasing her over the years. God knows how he persuaded her to get engaged to him. I always told Amber she must have been going through some kind of temporary madness.' He gazed blackly past Lizzy's shoulder.

Shit. They'd been having a good time until then, and Lizzy had made the classic mistake of bringing up The Ex. But just as quickly, Elliot seemed to snap out of it. 'Come on, back to the job in hand. This place operates a clean-plate policy.'

Ten minutes later Lizzy had eaten so much her stomach was in danger of exploding. 'Mercy,' she said. 'Take it away from me.'

Elliot was still going. She watched him finish not only his share, but all the stuff she couldn't manage. The man wasn't carrying an inch of spare fat. Where did it all go?

They bypassed dessert and asked for the bill. When it came back Elliot picked it up before Lizzy could get in there. 'I'll get this.'

'You really don't have to.'

'I'll put it through on expenses. I'll just say I took a contact out for dinner.'

'Happy Halos *are* trending on the stock market, you know.'

'That doesn't even make sense.' Elliot's lips twitched. 'You are an idiot on so many levels.'

The bill had come with two fortune cookies. 'After you,' Lizzy said. 'Let's see what our futures hold.'

'You first. After all, you're the one who believes in this crap.'

They ended up both going for a cookie at the same time. As their fingers brushed, from out of absolutely nowhere, Lizzy felt a weird crackle of static between them.

In that moment the world narrowed to a pinprick. She stopped being aware of the table of rowdy men next to them and the clatter and shouts of the staff in the kitchen. All that mattered was her and Elliot. His greeny-hazel eyes held hers, steady and questioning. Deep in the pit of her stomach, Lizzy felt the unmistakable ache of desire.

One of the drunken men stood up and banged into Lizzy's chair, severing the moment. Elliot blinked and gave Lizzy a slightly puzzled look.

'Go on then.'

'Go on what?' Lizzy felt stunned by what had just happened. Or had she totally imagined it?

Elliot was acting as if he'd felt nothing. He nodded at Lizzy's fortune cookie. 'What does the message say?'

She had to concentrate to get the wrapping off. 'Bread today is better than cake tomorrow,' she read out. Was that something to do with all the crap she ate?

He cracked his own cookie in half and frowned. 'The cleverer you think you are, the dumber you look.'

Lizzy burst out laughing. It was a welcome relief from the tension. 'I'd say that was spot on.'

Back outside even the hectic streets of Chinatown were starting to settle down for the night. There was a lone black cab on the other side of the road, the engine chugging expectantly.

Elliot looked at his watch. 'Last tube has gone. You'd better get that.'

Lizzy waved at the driver to indicate she was coming. 'Thanks for dinner,' she said awkwardly. 'And for being my wingman tonight.'

'I wasn't exactly very good at it.' He was fixated on an old drunk who was staggering down the street. 'You'll have to ask someone else next time.'

'Yeah, I guess I will,' she said, wondering why that made her feel disappointed.

'Night then,' he said.

'Night,' she said. He seemed to be waiting for her to go out of politeness, so Lizzy hurried over the road and got into the cab. As they pulled off she dared herself to look through the back window. Elliot had already disappeared into the night.

Chapter 39

The next day at work Lizzy couldn't concentrate. The more she thought about the moment of bristling chemistry, the more she started to doubt it. They had never had anything like that before. Elliot was good-looking if you liked that pompous, arrogant thing, but Lizzy didn't.

Stop being ridiculous, she told herself furiously. *This is Elliot we're talking about. Moody, infuriating, objectionable Elliot. Moody, infuriating, objectionable Elliot who is heartbroken after splitting up with his fiancée.* She half-expected a flashing red light to appear in front of her and an automated voice to start going off. *Warning. This man is heartbroken. Warning. Keep clear.*

She was unusually distracted all morning. It was only when Antonia threw a green teabag at her head that Lizzy realized her boss was talking to her.

'Sorry, I was just thinking about something else.'

'Hungover more like,' Antonia said disapprovingly, despite the fact that she'd gone for a 'business lunch' at Highroad House and not appeared again until nearly home-time, with champagne-flushed cheeks.

All day Lizzy kept an eye on her emails. Elliot didn't message her. She certainly wasn't going to contact him. *Is this a game I'm playing all by myself?* she wondered more than once.

That evening Nic had managed to get them a table at a new restaurant in Covent Garden. There had been the usual dramas at the office, so Lizzy was running a bit late. When she got out of the tube she texted Nic to say she was two minutes away.

There was also a missed call from Robbie. Lizzy called him back as she walked down the street, but it rang out to voicemail.

'Robbo, it's me. What's up? Call me back.'

The celebrity-owned steakhouse had such a discreet entrance that Lizzy walked past it twice. Poppet and Nic were already there and halfway down two Kir Royales.

'Ooh, what's the occasion?' Lizzy asked.

'Just because we're us.' Poppet caught the eye of a waiter. 'Another one of these please!'

Nic was hunched over her drink like someone in severe pain. Apparently she was jet-lagged and also constipated, because her bowels had crossed three different time zones in the last seven days.

'If I'd known I'd have brought some Helping Hand with me,' Lizzy told her. 'I'll pop a few products in the post to you first thing tomorrow.'

'Thanks, but I always use alcohol as a laxative. It's much more enjoyable.'

'She'd already had half a bottle of Pinot before we met,' Poppet whispered worriedly to Lizzy.

The girls ordered more wine and then the waiter asked them how they liked their steaks done.

'Red raw,' Nic told him. 'Beating, pulsating, still dripping with blood as if you'd just dragged that cow in now and killed it with your bare hands.'

The young man looked slightly alarmed. 'I'll see what the kitchen can do.'

Alone again, the girls settled back with their fresh drinks.

'Seen Elliot lately?'

Nic was looking at Lizzy, with that penetrative, interrogative look she got sometimes. Lizzy flushed. 'Last night, as a matter of fact.' She took a sip of her drink. 'We, er, went to a singles night together.'

Poppet sat upright. 'You went to a singles night with Elliot Anderson? How did *that* happen?'

Lizzy told them about the mission to find her a man. Afterwards Nic screwed her nose up.

'Why would Ginger Bollocks care what happens in your love life?'

'Maybe he's trying to live vicariously through Lizzy,' Poppet said.

Nic gave a not entirely pleasant snort. 'So did you pull this Greg or what?'

'No.' Lizzy hesitated. 'I ended up going out with Elliot for dinner. I just felt a bit sorry for him, you know. The poor bloke's clearly still gutted. I couldn't let him just walk off . . .'

'Yes you could.'

Lizzy stared at Nic. 'I suppose I *could* have, but I didn't think it was a very nice thing to do.' She looked pointedly at Poppet. 'I didn't really fancy Greg anyway. So it was a lucky escape.'

'Oh, come on, Lizzy! Is this the same Greg you went on about for a *month* after you met, who you were practically crying about because he took five days to accept your friend request on Facebook?'

'Nic,' Poppet said uncomfortably.

'What's your point?' Lizzy asked defensively.

'My point *is* that you've fallen for Elliot.'

'No I haven't!'

'Oh my God! He's all you talk about when we meet up these days. How annoying Elliot is, how funny Elliot is, how he did this, how he said that. We've both noticed it, haven't we, Poppet?'

Poppet stared awkwardly into her wine glass.

'I don't know what you're talking about,' Lizzy said.

'Er, hello, newsflash? He's using you, Lizzy! He's using you as a shoulder to cry on, until he finds someone new. You're either in major denial, or you're being fucking naïve.'

Lizzy felt a surge of white-hot anger. 'Fuck you, Nic.'

The best friends glared at each other.

'What is it with you?' Lizzy continued. 'Why do you have to drag everything down to some weird, dark level?'

'I'm not bringing anything down, sweetheart, I'm giving you a few home truths. If you don't like them, it's not my problem.'

'Girls,' Poppet said pleadingly.

She was totally ignored. 'You know sometimes,' Lizzy told Nic, 'you can be a real bitch.'

'No, it's called being a realist.' She pointed a finger at Lizzy. 'You should take your head out of the fucking clouds and try it some day!'

'If that's what being a realist is, I'll take my head in the clouds any day!'

Nic's eyes had gone completely black. For a second Lizzy seriously wondered if she was going to lean across the table and punch her.

'Screw this. I haven't got much of an appetite anyway. This should cover it, Poppet.'

She threw down a couple of twenties and walked out. The other two were left open-mouthed.

'What just *happened*?' Lizzy asked. She felt physically sick.

'I don't know!' Poppet shook her head. 'She's been on the edge for weeks.'

'*Have* you been talking about me?'

Poppet's cheeks went pink. 'We were just looking out for you. It seems a bit weird, your relationship, I mean.' She gave a tentative smile. 'You said the same stuff when you warned me about Pencil Dick Pete.'

'It's nothing like that,' Lizzy said stiffly. 'I told you, Elliot and I are just friends.'

Lizzy had spent the rest of the night stewing, but by the morning she'd calmed down. A part of her, the part she didn't want to own up to, knew the reason she'd reacted in the way she had was because Nic's words had struck a raw nerve. What *was* going on between her and Elliot? Lizzy didn't want to think about it, but was he just using her as an emotional stopgap like Pencil Dick Pete? And even if he was, why did she care?

She had called Nic up first thing and left a concili-
atory voicemail. Her best friend's temper was like
someone striking a match: it flared up and died down
almost immediately. Whatever beef Nic had with someone, she always got over it.

But by Monday, when Nic still hadn't returned any of
her calls or texts, Lizzy started to get worried. Poppet
hadn't heard much either, other than a text from Nic
saying she had a busy week and was staying in all
weekend to get some rest. This was from the woman
who had once come third in an Ironman competition
she'd hardly trained for after working a sixty-hour
week.

Do you think she's still constipated? Poppet emailed Lizzy.
I know how angry I get when I haven't been for a couple of days.

To make matters worse, Lizzy was now facing radio
silence from Elliot. They normally emailed at the start
of the week about meeting up, and Lizzy had sent him
a couple of messages on the Tuesday morning, but
nothing had come back. Before, she would have just
assumed he was busy and wouldn't have given it much
thought, but Nic's words had struck a raw nerve. The
longer time went by and there was still no reply, the
more Lizzy started to get wound up. So he had time to
tweet every five minutes about the bloody Eurozone,
but he didn't have ten seconds to reply to her email? It
was just rude!

November was always busy in the Christmas run-
up. Work was more hectic than normal, which at
least helped keep Lizzy's mind off things. On the

Wednesday morning she was knee-deep in writing a press release when Antonia came over.

'Can you tell me what the fuck is going on?' She handed Lizzy a sheet of paper.

Lizzy went cold as she saw the printed bank statement.

'Do you know why the hell Karen Jones has only been paying half her monthly retainer since September?'

'I've got no idea,' Lizzy said. 'It's probably just a mess-up with her bank. I'll get right on to it.'

She spent the next ten minutes in the loo panicking. When she came out she went straight over to Antonia.

'I've called Karen, it *was* a mess-up with the bank. She's promised to have it sorted out in the next twenty-four hours.'

'Good. The last thing we need is clients trying to shaft us, especially the ones who aren't making us any money.'

'Have you been looking through the accounts recently then?' Lizzy asked casually.

There was a smudge of hummus on Antonia's chin from the crispbread she'd been snacking on. 'Well I *am* the owner of the company,' she said ultra-sarcastically.

'I'm happy to still keep an eye on them,' Lizzy said. 'It's one less thing for you to worry about.'

Antonia's bulbous blue eyes were like searchlights into her soul. Lizzy started to sweat profusely. 'Just make sure it doesn't happen again, OK?' Antonia turned back to her crispbread.

Lizzy went back to her desk and tried to calm her jangled nerves. *You'd better start praying for a miracle from the PR gods.* Otherwise they were up shit creek without a paddle in sight.

The next day she got an email from Elliot's mum. Cassandra was her normal chatty self, telling Lizzy about a painting she was working on and how she hoped the stonework on the Hall would make it through another winter. It was almost as an aside at the end that she mentioned Elliot.

He's been calling me a lot more recently, which has been lovely. Call it a mother's intuition but I think he might even have met someone new! I rang him the other night when he was at a restaurant opening and I could hear a girl's voice in the background. When he rang me back the next day he was so happy and upbeat, it was like speaking to a different person. I don't suppose he's mentioned anything to you? We're getting on so well at the moment I don't want to rock the boat and scare him off with questions! Lizzy, I can only thank you for being such a kind friend to him through this difficult time. You know the offer to come to Beeston Hall is always here.
Love and best wishes, Cassie xx

It felt like someone had crept up behind Lizzy and poured a bucket of cold water over her.

'Off out, sweets?' Bianca asked as she stood up.

'I just need to get some air.'

'Are you all right? Sweets, your coat!' she called after Lizzy. 'You'll freeze to death out there!'

Lizzy didn't need a coat. The initial feeling of shock had been replaced by a rising anger. She left the office and crossed over the road to the ornamental park where she often ate her lunch in the summer. Mind buzzing, she started pacing round the small perimeter.

What restaurant opening? Elliot hadn't mentioned anything to Lizzy about it. And who was this girl he'd met? Lizzy realized that aside from an hour or two a week when they met up for coffee, she knew nothing about what he got up to. She didn't even know where he lived, other than it was some apartment on the river. He'd always had his own place, some fishy excuse about him and Amber keeping different hours and her being a bad sleeper. He could have started a whole new relationship and Lizzy wouldn't have even known. Then again, why *would* she have known? It's not like there was anything official between them, was there?

She sat down on a damp bench. She should never have gone along with this stupid thing in the first place. Cassandra had been looking for anyone to help and Lizzy had willingly stepped in. Nic was right: she'd been a naïve idiot. Cassandra and Elliot had both used her in their own ways. Lizzy watched a sparrow land on the ground in front of her and start pecking for non-existent crumbs. The worst thing of all was that she'd let them.

Chapter 40

Saturday was a foul day, cold and windy. Poppet and Lizzy hibernated at Lizzy's, drinking tea and watching the *Murder, She Wrote* omnibus. Apparently Nic was on some team bonding day with work. Not that Lizzy knew this first-hand, since Nic still hadn't returned any of her calls.

Poppet had assumed Lizzy's preoccupied mood was to do with Nic, which in part it was. 'I'm sure she'll come round soon. Give her time.'

'The ball's in her court now. I'm not going to beg.' Lizzy stared moodily at the TV screen.

Beside her, Poppet sighed unhappily. 'Oh, dark times.'

An hour later they were on their third episode. Jessica Fletcher had lured the killer to a museum in Cairo and the police had just turned up to arrest him.

'She knows a lot of dodgy people, doesn't she?' Poppet was busy putting her hair up in a bun for the umpteenth time. 'Her lifelong friends always seem to turn out to be master criminals. I wonder if there's going to be some sort of big finale, where it's revealed she's been hiding in plain sight the whole time, like a female Dr Evil.'

Outside it had started to rain heavily. Only 3 p.m., and it was getting dark already. Lizzy got up. 'Another cuppa?'

'Ooh, yes please. Out of my special mug.' Poppet snuggled into the sofa. 'I'm so happy we're not going out later.'

Lizzy went out to the kitchen. It would be her fifth cup of tea that day, but she still couldn't shake the cold, hollow feeling inside.

She stared out of the window at the scrubby bit of grass that counted as a communal garden as she waited for the kettle to boil. At least they had *Strictly* and *X Factor* to look forward to, and an M&S meal deal for two.

'Your phone beeped!' Poppet said when Lizzy came back in the living room. It was another email from Elliot; after his disappearing act a flurry of messages had started to arrive, asking to meet up. Lizzy hadn't replied. Two could play at that game.

She chucked the BlackBerry on the sofa.

About forty-five minutes later the doorbell rang. The two girls exchanged a look. 'Who's that?' Lizzy said fearfully.

'I don't know, it's your flat!'

No one knocked on your door in London unless they were the police or religious fanatics. Lizzy went over and peered out of the window. The front porch jutted out, so you could never see who was there.

The doorbell rang again. 'Do you want me to get it?' Poppet asked.

'I'll go.' If it was Jehovah's Witnesses Lizzy didn't want them invited in for the evening.

She walked down the hallway, picking her knickers out of her bum. If it *was* Jehovah's Witnesses, hopefully they'd be scared off by Lizzy's scarecrow hair and zebra-print onesie.

Lizzy pulled open the door, ready to issue a polite 'bugger off'. Her mouth fell open. Instead of a man and woman with smart suits and hopeful smiles, Elliot was standing there holding a rather bedraggled umbrella.

'Hiya,' he said awkwardly.

Lizzy was in shock. 'How did you know where I lived?'

Elliot dragged his gaze away from her zebraprint onesie. 'You've told me the name of your street before and that you live in a block of flats. The rest was down to journalistic deduction.' He nodded at the windowsill, at the figurine of Moominpappa Lizzy had bought off eBay.

She started to recover from the fact that Elliot Anderson was standing on her doorstep. 'You're very presumptuous, rocking up like this.'

He tried a grin. 'I looked up *Murder, She Wrote* on the TV listings.'

'You've been very quiet lately,' she said. 'If it wasn't for your tweets I'd have thought you'd fallen off a cliff.'

He looked semi-contrite. 'I've had a pretty full-on week.'

'How come? Have you been out meeting lots of women?'

Elliot's eyebrows shot up. 'What are you talking about?'

'You tell me.' She crossed her arms and then uncrossed them, in case it looked like she was overreacting. 'You've been presenting this heartbroken front, but who knows what you really get up to?'

He started to look distinctly uncomfortable. 'I'm not sure where this has come from, I have no idea what you're talking about.'

'How was the restaurant opening?'

'The what?'

'Didn't you go to a restaurant opening this week?'

He frowned. 'How do you know that?'

'Someone I know saw you there,' Lizzy said quickly.

'Right,' he said after a moment. 'Yes, I went to a restaurant opening. I'm sorry I didn't mention it . . .'

'Why would you?' she said blithely. 'I'm just a shoulder to cry on.'

'What the hell are you talking about?' he said angrily.

Lizzy kept a pointed silence. Eventually Elliot sighed. 'I'm not sure what I've done wrong here. One minute everything was fine between us, the next minute you're treating me like I'm Harold Shipman. I'm sorry if I went off radar. Like I said, things have been pretty hectic.'

To give him some credit, he did look knackered. 'It's just rude when someone emails you three times in a row and you don't get back to them,' she informed him.

'I know. I wanted to wait and see you in person.'

So he just ignored her in the meantime? Was his life so important that he couldn't take ten seconds to fire off a quick one-liner to acknowledge Lizzy's existence? Men! They needed to get over themselves!

The black cat from next-door materialized from the undergrowth. Lizzy watched it slink down the path. 'Why are you here, Elliot?'

'To see you,' he said simply.

A gust of wind blew through the front door. Lizzy noticed the front of Elliot's jeans were soaked. 'Fine,' she sighed. 'You'd better come in.'

To Poppet's credit she didn't freak out when Lizzy presented a rather soggy Elliot in the living room. 'You're very tall,' was all she said, gazing up at him with huge Poppet eyes.

There was the matter of drying Elliot's wet clothes. The only thing Lizzy had to offer him in the meantime was a Primark onesie with yellow ducks that she'd accidentally bought in size large.

'This is technically animal print,' he said when she presented him with it.

'It's this or risk dying of pneumonia. I'll leave you to get changed,' Lizzy said, fleeing the room.

She and Poppet were whispering violently when a figure in head-to-toe duck-print appeared in the doorway. 'How do I look?' Elliot asked awkwardly.

Lizzy gave him the once-over. 'Mad.'

Poppet was more encouraging. 'With your height you can carry off anything,' she told him.

Considering the bizarre circumstances, the three of them settled down in their onesies to watch TV in a surprisingly companionable silence. Poppet kept shooting Elliot incredulous little looks, as if she couldn't quite believe he was sitting on the sofa next to her. 'Do you colour your hair, or is it natural?' she asked him.

'All mine, I'm afraid.'

'It's very unusual. I mean, it's not *ginger* ginger, is it? You should think about doing a Grecian 2000 advert. I reckon it would be really popular.'

Elliot looked blank. 'It's a hair dye for men,' Lizzy told him, trying not to laugh. God bless Poppet, she could bring a person down to size without even trying!

A few minutes later Lizzy got up to make another round of tea. Elliot's jeans were drying on the radiator in the hallway and his expensive brogues were on her boiler stuffed with loo roll. It was all too weird. *What the hell are you doing here?*

She quickly shot into the bathroom and put a bit of mascara on. Not for Elliot's benefit of course. She just looked a bit washed out.

When she returned to the living room he and Poppet were discussing their favourite TV detective shows.

'I was always a big fan of *Dempsey and Makepeace*,' he was telling her. 'Makepeace actually. I had a poster of her on my wall at school.'

'Do you ever watch *Rosemary and Thyme*? It's definitely in my top three.'

Elliot adopted a tactful expression. 'I can't say I'm that familiar with their work.'

Lizzy plonked their mugs down. 'Elliot's more of a fan of film noir, Pops.'

Poppet looked a bit confused. 'Are we talking about coffee now?'

By the time they'd watched another hour of Jessica

Fletcher sleuthing and an episode of *Total Wipeout*, Elliot started to make signs of going.

'Are you sure?' Poppet asked. '*Strictly*'s on in a minute.'

'No, no, I don't want to intrude.' He was adamant.

Elliot went off to change and came back in his normal clothes. He shot a look at Lizzy. 'I left the, ah, onesie in the bathroom.'

'This has been nice, we must do it again. Normally there's three of us, but Nic and Lizzy have fallen out.' Poppet clapped her hand over her mouth. 'I mean—'

'What have you fallen out over?' Elliot asked Lizzy.

'It's nothing,' she said, quickly ushering him out of the living room.

The windows of the house across the street were lit up by fairy lights. 'I can't believe Christmas is next month,' Elliot said.

'What are your plans?'

'I'll be back at the Hall for the day itself and then I was thinking of going skiing. Haven't booked anywhere yet.' He glanced at her. 'You?'

'I'll be at home with my family.'

'In Bromley?'

'Yeah.'

They exchanged polite smiles.

'Lizzy,' he said quietly.

Her heart started to thump slowly. 'Yes?'

Elliot turned to face her. Under the porch light Lizzy could see strands of gold amongst the rich dark-red hair.

'I was w-wondering,' he stuttered on the word. 'I was wondering if I could take you out for dinner?'

'What about the girl you met?'

'Girl? What girl?'

'Your mum thinks you've met someone. She heard a girl in the background when she spoke to you at the restaurant opening.'

'I thought you said your friend saw me?'

Lizzy flushed. 'It doesn't matter.'

'I'm sure my mother heard lots of voices; I was in a crowded room with a hundred other people. Lizzy, don't look at me like that. Don't you get it? *You're* the girl I've met, you bloody idiot.'

Lizzy was so taken aback that all she could think to do was go on the attack. 'I can't work you out, Elliot. One minute you're demanding we go out on the pull to find me a bloke, then you go AWOL for a week, and now you track me down at home using your powers of investigative sleuthing and ask me out for dinner. What's going on? Why did you come along to a singles night if you're interested in me?'

'I thought we could spend some time together.' He looked at his feet. 'You know, away from the coffee shop.'

'At a *singles* night? Why didn't you just ask me out for a drink?'

'As mad as it sounds, it seemed liked the best option at the time. I didn't want to end up with egg on my face if you turned me down.'

'You were worried about *me* turning *you* down? The high and mighty Elliot Anderson worrying about a lowly PR?'

'Of course I was worried!' Elliot was starting to sound

exasperated. 'You're funny and sexy and sparky and opinionated and vivacious, and you always light up the room whenever you walk in. Why would you want to go out with an old grump like me?' He went bright red.

'Say something,' he said nervously after a minute. 'You're starting to freak me out.'

'I don't know *what* to say,' Lizzy admitted.

He grabbed her hand, taking her by surprise. 'I know you felt it in the restaurant as well,' he said urgently. 'Don't tell me you didn't.'

They stood on the doorstep looking at each other. The opening credits of the *Strictly* theme tune floated down the hallway.

'I felt it too,' she said eventually.

Elliot breathed out slowly and released Lizzy's hand. 'So come out for dinner with me.'

'No.'

'Why?'

'Because I'm not a substitute for Amber, or some other emotional void in your life.'

'You're not—' He stopped. 'I'm not asking you because I'm on the rebound or anything like that.'

'Aren't you?' she asked suspiciously.

'No!' He hesitated for a moment. 'Look, I know my situation isn't . . . ideal. If it were the other way round I'd be equally wary. But Amber and I are in the past. I want to move on, and with you.' He gave Lizzy a tentative smile. 'Unless I've got it totally wrong and I'm about to make a spectacular arse of myself, I like you and I think you like me. So will you please let me take you out to dinner?' There was a wry eyebrow. 'Do I have to get down on my knees and beg?'

'Begging would be nice.'

'Lizzy, please say you'll go out for dinner with me?'

'Stop it, you idiot, the neighbours will see!'

He got up again, grinning. 'One dinner is all I'm asking. If it doesn't work out we can go back to shouting at each other over coffee. Deal?'

'Deal,' she said. For a startling moment she thought Elliot was going to kiss her, but his head jerked away at the last moment and his mouth ended up clumsily grazing her cheek.

'I'll be in touch then,' he muttered. Lizzy watched him hurry down the path and disappear into the night.

'Are you OK out there?' Poppet's voice drifted out of the open door.

'Yeah, coming!' Lizzy put her hand to her cheek. She could still actually feel where Elliot had kissed her, as if his fingers were playfully tickling her skin.

'What am I *doing*?' she said out loud.

Chapter 41

This time Elliot was quick to get back to Lizzy, and they agreed to go out for dinner that Friday – somewhere he had chosen.

There had been a few texts back and forth between them, although they had been mainly formal. Arranging what time and where, did Lizzy have any allergies, etc. Somehow it felt safer and more manageable that way.

Only Poppet knew, and she was keeping her usual positive outlook on things. 'He was a lot nicer than I'd expected. More human. And he must be keen if he came to find you.'

'But what, Pops?' Lizzy knew her friend too well.

'Just be careful, Lizzy. I don't want you to get hurt.'

The week dragged and hurtled past in equal measure. By the time Friday arrived Lizzy was a nervous wreck. Antonia had left the office early as she was going to Norfolk for the weekend. Everyone else pretended to work for another hour and then decided to head down to the pub.

'Sweets, are you coming?' Bianca asked.

'I've got a few more things to do,' Lizzy lied. 'Have a good weekend.'

Bianca pulled on her Alice Temperley parka that had cost more than Lizzy's last summer holiday. 'Don't work too hard, darl. Ciao!'

Ten minutes later Lizzy was at the bus stop. The roads were jammed with red buses, none of which were hers. From nowhere she felt that lurch in her belly again, like a washing machine that had jammed half-way round the spin cycle. It was quite a good analogy, she reflected. Her stomach had been doing strange things all week.

'Get a grip,' she muttered. 'You're a grown woman of twenty-eight. It's not like you've never been on a date before!'

The woman standing next to Lizzy shot her an odd look. Luckily at that point Lizzy's bus decided to make an appearance. *It's just dinner,* she told herself as she climbed up to the top deck. *I'll go along and be funny and vivacious and yet slightly aloof, which will only add an air of beguiling mystery. And if it doesn't work out, it doesn't work out. As Elliot said, we'll just go back to trading insults over weekly coffee.*

Lizzy found a seat and sat down. Who was she kidding? She was at the point of no return. Whatever happened tonight would change things between them for ever.

*

At home Lizzy showered and shaved, waxed and plucked. Her eyeliner had to be reapplied three times because her hand was shaking so much. Choosing which red lipstick to wear had become a Herculean task. Ninety minutes and an emergency change of tights later, she was finally ready.

She'd only worn the dress once, at a winter wedding last year. A black number with long lace sleeves from Warehouse, there was nothing particularly showy about it, but it fitted Lizzy as if it had been made for her, and she liked the way the sweetheart neckline showed off just the amount right of décolletage. She'd teamed it with her black heels from Zara, the ones with the delicate ankle-straps. Lizzy sucked her stomach in and turned sideways. Was the lipstick too much?

Too late to do anything now. The cab was here. Lizzy gave herself a final once-over in the mirror. Her reflection looked back, like an old friend wishing her well in battle. 'It's dinner, that's all,' she said loudly. It had become like a mantra.

Lizzy was too nervous to say much on the journey. 'You look familiar,' the cab driver told her. 'Where have I seen you before?'

'I've just got that face.' She gripped her clutch bag.

They were meeting at a new restaurant on the River Thames at Bankside. The place had recently opened and was booked up for months. Elliot must have pulled some strings to get them in there. It only increased Lizzy's trepidation: she'd give anything to be in Nando's with Nic and Poppet right now.

Nic. Lizzy's hand instinctively strayed to her phone,

to call or send a text because it was *weird* doing this and Nic not knowing about it. But then Nic's words came into her mind: *He's using you, Lizzy.*

Lizzy stared grimly ahead. Screw Nicola Cartwright. She'd show her that she wasn't always bloody right.

Lizzy's resolve wavered when they reached their destination.

'Have a great night, love,' the cabbie told her. 'Lucky bloke, going out for dinner with a girl like you.'

'Thanks,' Lizzy said gratefully. 'You've no idea how much I needed to hear that.'

It was a short walk to the towering Art Deco building. Feeling hideously self-conscious Lizzy tottered into the lobby. A couple were waiting for the lift. The woman gave Lizzy a friendly smile – or maybe she was just relieved that she wasn't the one walking in by herself.

The doors pinged open on the tenth floor on to an impressive lobby. Lizzy waited for the couple to step out before following them over to the shiny black reception desk that looked like a giant onyx stone. Four model-esque young people dressed in black were sat behind it. Atmospheric lighting glowed on the walls. The place felt more like a luxury spa in Thailand than a restaurant a stone's throw from the Tate Modern.

Beyond, in the main restaurant area, Lizzy could see the London skyline glittering back at her from the vast windows. The tinkle of a piano was coming from somewhere. It was all too sleek, too perfect, too intimidating. Lizzy started to edge away. She couldn't do this. She'd just have to text Elliot and say she'd suddenly been struck down with a life-threatening virus . . .

'Can I help?'

Lizzy's finger hovered over the lift button. The girl on the far end of the desk was looking at her.

'Have you got a dinner reservation?' she asked.

'Er yes.' Lizzy walked back up again. 'It's under the name of Anderson?'

The girl didn't even check. 'Mr Anderson is waiting in the bar. Would you like to go through?'

The room was already buzzing with Friday-night diners. Elliot was sitting by himself at the bar, staring off into an unseen place beyond the spirit bottles. The tense body language was more indicative of someone about to face the electric chair than have an intimate tête-à-tête.

Lizzy walked up behind him. 'Hello,' she said awkwardly.

It seemed to take him a second to realize who she was. 'Hi. You found it OK?'

'Yes, no probs.' She clambered up on the stool next to him, a perilous exercise in her heels and dress. By contrast, Elliot was dressed in jeans and a sober navy blazer. Lizzy felt like a Christmas decoration that had accidentally blown into January.

'What can I get you to drink?' he asked.

The sweet, funny, nervous Elliot that Lizzy had last seen standing on her doorstep was gone. Stiff, formal Elliot was back in his place. Lizzy's heart began to sink. Had he been having second thoughts?

'Glass of white wine please.' Lizzy was about to commit the cardinal sin – drink white wine on a first date and on an empty stomach – but she needed the Dutch courage.

At least there was the spectacular view to get distracted by. Thousands of lit-up windows looked back at Lizzy, twinkling like a starry night. Dominating it all was St Paul's Cathedral, pushing up out of the sharp metallic landscape like a giant mushroom. The Shard was off in the far distance. How Lizzy wished she was over there right now instead of this slow-motion car crash she was a front-seat passenger in.

'It's amazing here, how did you get us in?'

Elliot drained his beer. 'I know one of the guys who owns it.' He gestured to the barman. 'Can I get another one of these?'

Things didn't improve when they sat down.

'How's work?' she asked.

'Fine,' he muttered. 'For the third time.'

Lizzy gazed desperately round the restaurant. Everyone else was getting on like a house on fire. They might as well have employed a band of travelling minstrels to dance round their own table singing: 'Look away now! Awkward first date!' Or, even worse: 'These two should have stayed as mates!'

A merciful intervention was provided in the form of their waiter. Handing Lizzy and Elliot a menu he started to reel off their specials. Unable to remember the specials at the best of times, Lizzy didn't take a single word in.

Elliot seemed to be suffering from the same predicament. 'What did you say the cod loin came with?'

The waiter looked down at his pad. 'Pancetta, puy lentils and sun-dried tomatoes.'

'Would you say the tomato is a fruit or a vegetable?' Elliot asked him.

The man looked rather surprised. 'It's a vegetable, isn't it?'

'You see!' Lizzy said triumphantly. 'I'm not the only one in the world!'

'My friend here gets a bit mixed up with her fruit and vegetables.' Elliot had a familiar gleam in his eyes.

'*Technically* a tomato may be a fruit,' Lizzy said loftily (she'd since Googled it), 'but that's just semantics. You don't get pear and tomato tart, do you? Or a tomato crumble and custard?'

Elliot crossed his arms. 'It's a fruit, give it up.'

'It's a bloody vegetable!'

The waiter arched an eyebrow. 'Tell you what, I'll leave you two to fight it out and I'll come back when you're finished?'

It was like someone had suddenly taken a bottle stopper out of the evening and released all the tension.

'You're so annoying,' she told Elliot. 'I'm going to make you a tomato crumble now and force you to eat it.'

The waiter came back and took their orders. Elliot was the wine expert, so Lizzy let him choose. After extensive deliberation he decided on something unpronounceable from the Rhône Valley.

Wine poured, they sat back and faced each other again. 'I have to say, you don't scrub up that badly.' He was back to his normal bullish self.

'I don't normally wear dresses. You're very lucky.'

Lizzy took a sip of her wine. It was deliciously heady.

'Black suits you. It makes you look very . . .'

'Elegant?' she prompted.

Amusement flashed in the green eyes. 'I'll give you elegant. Although I'm still expecting you to pull out a clutch bag in the shape of a frog or a parasol with poodles on it.'

'You can talk. I'm not the one with the duck-print onesie.'

'*Your* duck-print onesie,' he corrected her. 'And it was an emergency. An emergency that you took great pleasure exploiting, might I add.'

'You didn't seem to mind being exploited. I don't think I've ever seen a male over the age of five look so comfortable in an avian-themed romper suit.'

They pulled childish faces at each other. Lizzy felt a familiar glow of warm delight. *This is more like it!*

'Well, you could have made more of an effort,' she said.

'What's wrong with what I'm wearing?'

'You look like you're going boating.'

Elliot picked up his wine glass. 'This from a woman who bases her sartorial style on Doctor Doolittle.' He looked down his nose at her. 'On second thoughts I don't think I do like you in a cocktail dress. You're even more full of yourself.'

Starters and main courses came and went. The food was utterly delicious and for some reason, instantly forgettable. All Lizzy could concentrate on was the infuriating, tousle-haired, freckle-nosed man sitting opposite her.

They shared a salted-caramel chocolate tart for

dessert. Elliot was being surprisingly agreeable, although Lizzy didn't suppose hitting your companion over the knuckles with your fork was de rigueur in a five-star restaurant.

Their waiter came back. 'Can I get you coffees, any liqueurs?'

Lizzy glanced round. To her surprise most of the other tables were empty. They must have been there for hours.

'Coffee?' Elliot asked her.

Coffee = coffee breath. 'I'm fine thank you.'

He looked back at the waiter. 'Can we just get the bill?'

When it came Elliot insisted on paying again. 'The owner owes me a favour.' The gleam in his eye hinted they might have got the table through the means of blackmail.

They made their way through the restaurant. Lizzy was in front and she suddenly felt rather exposed and self-conscious. Was Elliot checking out her bum and legs?

The door back out to reception was wide enough for them both to get through, but Elliot stepped aside. There was no reason to touch her, but as Lizzy went through the door she felt Elliot momentarily put his hand on the small of her back. A shock surged up her spine and splintered off into the rest of her body. *This is crazy!* the rational part of her brain thought. *How can Elliot suddenly have this effect on me?*

There was only one girl left at the reception desk. 'I'll just get your coats.' She disappeared off through a discreet doorway.

Alone for the first time that evening, the easy camaraderie drained away. The subtext that had been hovering on the sidelines all evening finally forced its way to the front. *Hello! It's me! Sexual tension! You might as well acknowledge me because I'm not going anywhere!*

Lizzy had suddenly become acutely aware of every detail of Elliot's physicality: his height, the broadness of his shoulders, the way he always stood slightly back on his heels as if he were assessing something. There was a triangle of smooth pale chest behind the undone top button of his shirt. She had an insane desire to reach out and stroke it.

They stood looking at each other. 'What do you want to do?' he asked.

The sentence was so loaded it could have started firing off rounds.

'I d-don't mind,' she stuttered. 'We could go to a bar . . .'

The words caught in her throat as Elliot took one of her hands and held it in both of his. His warm firm fingers encircled her wrist.

Lizzy's heart rate accelerated from first gear straight into fifth. Elliot's thumb moved up a fraction to lightly stroke the fleshy bit of her palm. A chain reaction went off inside Lizzy's body.

'What do you want to do?' she whispered.

His gaze was electric. 'Take you back to mine.'

Chapter 42

They'd left their hot, stolen moment in the reception on the tenth floor of the building. Now they were back into fresh air and real life again.

Somehow Elliot had managed to regain his normal composure. 'Are you going to be OK?' he said, looking at Lizzy's heels. 'It's a bit of a walk, but the river is stunning this time of night.'

Lizzy was fine to walk. All normal feeling had vacated her body. She was electric. She felt as light as a feather. She could have danced all the way to Timbuktu in these bad boys.

Other couples were walking past, arms wrapped round each other. Elliot kept his hands in his pockets as he walked alongside, but still close enough to brush against Lizzy's arm every now and again. She snuck a look at his profile. Was he feeling the same as her?

'Are you cold?' he asked suddenly. 'I can give you my jacket.'

'No, I'm fine.' Lizzy didn't feel cold. She couldn't feel anything except the slow *dur-dur dur-dur dur-dur* drumming of her heart.

They made their way through Southbank with its street buskers and food stalls, past the Royal Festival Hall and on to the London Eye. Elliot pointed out various historical and architectural facts to Lizzy along the way, but it felt like a charade they were both going through. London was so beautiful that night, under an almost clear moonlit sky, but all she was aware of was the energy between them and the shower of invisible sparks that went off every time she and Elliot made physical contact.

Even at that late hour the river was busy. Taxi boats chugged past with their last passengers for the night, and a police speedboat swooshed through the dark waters, leaving a tide in its wake. On the other side were Big Ben and the Houses of Parliament. It made Lizzy suddenly think of Justin and the infamous thirtieth birthday party. How weird that the worst thing that had ever happened to her had brought her and Elliot together.

They stopped to look at the view. 'That's the roof of the Savoy,' Elliot told her. 'Did you know it's where The Queen and Prince Philip went public for the first time as a couple?'

'I didn't know. I thought I was supposed to be the one who was up on celebrity gossip.'

'Do you think they'll stand in front of the restaurant and say that about us in years to come?' He gazed down at her and the lights from the river seemed to be shining in his eyes. 'That was the first official date for

Headbutt Girl and that grumpy ginger arse from off the telly?'

Then it happened again. Just like that strange moment at the restaurant in Chinatown where everything around them had stilled. The Thames shrivelled into a thin trickle and the iconic buildings seemed to flatten and dissolve. It was like Lizzy and Elliot were the only people who had ever been in the world.

'Lizzy,' he said simply. Cupping her face in his hands, he leant in and kissed her.

A moment later he pulled away. 'Are you all right?' he said uncertainly. 'You seem a little . . . distracted.'

'I'm fine,' she gasped, still reeling from the revelation. Elliot did the holding-a-girl's-face-thing! Wait until she told Poppet! Lizzy took a breath to collect herself. 'As you were.'

He gave a relieved grin. 'Come here, you nutter.'

With that, he grabbed Lizzy by her coat collar and kissed her right out of her shoes.

Elliot lived in a spectacular glass-fronted block over-looking the Thames. His two-bedroom apartment had been designed with sharp minimalist lines and had a view straight out on to the river.

Lizzy had dived straight into the bathroom as soon as they'd arrived and was horrified by the clown-like apparition that looked back at her. Her red lipstick was now smeared all round her mouth. It was Elliot's fault for being such a good kisser. Who *knew*? she thought in wonder. Who knew that mouth, the same bad-tempered mouth that hurled out insults and general all-round grouchiness,

317

was also capable of such softness and . . . *sexiness*?

Lizzy pressed her forehead against the mirror. The cool glass was a respite against the burning thoughts that were whirling round her mind. *Oh God*. They were probably about to get naked in front of each other for the first time. What if her body repulsed him? What if he had something hideously wrong with his willy? Would the sex be the disaster zone it had been with Reuben?

'You don't have to sleep with him,' she said to her feverish, glittery-eyed reflection, knowing at the same time that she really, really wanted to.

There was a soft tap on the door. 'Are you all right in there?' Elliot called.

'Coming!' Lizzy stood up and snapped her clutch bag shut. It was too late to back out now.

When she returned to the living room Elliot was standing by the window. He'd only switched one lamp on, creating a more intimate feel. There was a bottle of red wine and two glasses on the coffee table. Lizzy felt another prickle of anticipation.

It was a beautiful apartment and yet, Lizzy had already noticed, also a very masculine apartment. There hadn't been any expensive shampoos or eye-creams in the bathroom, and there weren't candles or fashion magazines lying under the glass coffee table, or any other little signs a woman's touch might once have been around the place. If there had ever been any evidence of Amber's existence it certainly wasn't here now.

It was *weird* how they'd been engaged and hadn't

lived together. At a time when they should have been gleefully feathering the marital nest, Elliot and Amber had been living miles apart, in separate areas of London. Had Amber deliberately kept her fiancé at arm's length because she'd known something wasn't right between them?

She realized Elliot was studying her. 'You've got that pensive look about you again,' he told her.

'I'm fine. Really.' Lizzy had kicked her heels off by the front door and now Elliot seemed even taller than ever. His eyes glowed in the half-light, the dark shadows accentuating his high cheekbones. Lizzy felt another lurch deep in the pit of her stomach.

He came towards her and they started kissing, this time more urgently. 'Oh Lizzy,' he murmured. 'You don't know how many times I've wanted to do this.'

At that moment Lizzy realized how many times she'd wanted to do this as well. To run her hands through Elliot's thick hair, feel his lean, energetic body pressed against hers, inhale the scent of his subtle, woody aftershave. How many times had she looked at the freckle on the right of his bottom lip and secretly wondered what it would be like to kiss it?

Elliot scooped her up and, without pausing for breath, started to carry her across the living room. Suddenly all Lizzy could think was how heavy she must feel compared to Amber.

He must have sensed something was wrong. 'Are you all right? It feels like you've gone into rigor mortis.'

Lizzy didn't say anything. Elliot gently tipped her back on to her feet. 'Are you all right?' he repeated.

'Hey.' He tipped Lizzy's chin up with his finger so she had to look at him. 'What's wrong?' There was a pucker between his eyebrows.

'Are you sure you're over Amber?'

He stared at her for a moment. 'Of course I'm over Amber. I've already told you that. I wouldn't lie to you.'

Wouldn't you? she thought.

'I mean it,' he whispered. 'You've got *nothing* to worry about.'

Very slowly he started to unzip the side of Lizzy's dress. She felt his warm hand slide in and cup the soft flesh of her waist. His hand moved up to her ribcage, his fingers tantalizingly stroking the wired underside of her bra cup. This time a seismic eruption went off in Lizzy's body. Without further ado she let Elliot sweep her back up into his arms and take her through to the bedroom.

Chapter 43

Lizzy woke up facing an unfamiliar white wall. *Where am I?* was her immediate thought, followed by the more alarming *Why am I naked?* She always slept with her pajamas on, even when she was really drunk. The realization hit her a second later. She was in bed at Elliot's!

Snapshots of last night flashed through her mind. Elliot on top of her, Elliot underneath her, Elliot doing amazing things with his hands, his tongue, his . . .

The bedroom was too quiet. There was no warm body behind Lizzy spooning her, nor the sound of someone breathing gently. Instinctively she knew she was in bed alone.

A quick roll over confirmed there was indeed a big Elliot-sized hole in the bed. She sat up and pulled the duvet round her. 'Hello?'

There was no answer. Putting a pillow in front of her for modesty's sake (like she had any of *that* left), Lizzy got out of bed and went over to the door.

'Hello? Anybody here?'

Elliot wasn't making breakfast in the sleek modern kitchen, nor was he reading the papers in the airy open-plan living room. Lizzy was utterly mortified. He'd done a runner! From his own apartment!

In the cold light of day he'd obviously taken one look at Lizzy – had she been snoring? With her mouth open? – and had decided that it had been a big mistake. Lizzy hugged the pillow to herself miserably. He hadn't even stayed around for a bit of morning jiggery-pokery. Had she been *that* bad in bed?

The winter sun was streaming in through the windows, making Lizzy feel even more exposed and humiliated. Oh God, she shouldn't have slept with him on the first night! This was exactly what happened with Poppet and Pencil Dick Pete! You gave men the magic key into your lady-garden and then they climbed over the wall and buggered off!

The next moment she was nearly ejected out of her own skin as someone burst through the front door. 'Lizzy?'

Thank God! she thought ecstatically. *You came back!*

Elliot came into the living room with a large brown-paper bag and two takeaway coffees. 'Nice outfit,' he said dryly. 'Are pillows the new lingerie?'

'Dressing gowns are old hat these days you know.'

He put the drinks down on the coffee table. 'Sorry, I should have left a note that I'd gone to get breakfast. Were you worried?'

She made a nonchalant noise. 'Hardly. I've only just woken up.'

Elliot had a smirk on his face. 'Not that I'm complaining about seeing your bare bottom, quite the opposite in fact, but there are a few hundred people walking past. I'm not sure all the young children are quite ready for that sort of sideshow.'

'Oh my God!' She jumped away from the window like a scalded cat.

The next moment Elliot had chucked the pillow on the sofa and was wrapping his arms round her.

'You're freezing!' she protested.

His cold hands moved round on to Lizzy's buttocks. 'I was rather hoping you'd warm me up.'

The coffee had gone cold by the time they came to drink it. Lizzy sat by the window in one of Elliot's shirts eating a fresh croissant. It took all of her will-power not to take a picture and put it up on Face-book. *#saturdays #croissant #london #riverview #winter #nofilter #IHADHOTSEXLASTNIGHT #hot #sex #last #night #lovingmylife.*

Elliot came back over with two home-made espressos. 'What are your plans for today?'

'I'm meant to be going Christmas shopping,' Lizzy sighed. She watched a stream of fluorescent cyclists whizz past. 'I promised myself I'd have it all sewn up by the middle of November this year.' She glanced at Elliot. 'What are you doing?'

'I'm meant to be preparing for an interview on Mon-day.'

'Your old mate the Chancellor of the Exchequer?'

'Actually it's the business secretary this time.' He muttered something she didn't hear.

'What was that?' Lizzy asked.

'I said if I do any more research it will be coming

323

out of my ears. Unless he decides to do something controversial before then like eloping with a cross-dressing troglodyte.'

Was that his subtle way of saying he was free? 'Well,' Lizzy said uncertainly. 'I suppose the shops aren't going anywhere.'

Elliot tugged on his ear, looking adorably bashful. 'Do you fancy spending the day together?'

Firstly Lizzy had to address the issue of clothes. Thankfully she'd had the foresight to pack a pair of ballet pumps in case of an emergency blister situation and rather disgustingly, she'd found a pair of black leggings from yoga balled up in a side pocket of her bag. Put together with a sweatshirt of Elliot's, a pair of his Arran socks and her black dress coat, Lizzy emerged from the bedroom wearing an ensemble that would have been described in certain parts of London as 'eclectic'. Unfortunately just not the part that she was in.

'Do I look totally mad?' she asked as she came into the kitchen.

Elliot was standing by the espresso machine going through some post. 'No more than normal.' He opened his arms. 'I think I'm starting to like mad.'

They emerged hand in hand into the crisp winter's day. Lizzy was suddenly conscious of her ruffled appearance. Elliot had just been raking his hands through her hair in the lift in a most passionate manner. Annoyingly he was looking his usual smooth self. You'd never know such a wanton sex beast lurked within.

'There's something I've always wanted to do,' he told her.

'Are you taking me to see an art installation?'

He pinged one of her curls. 'Don't be such a philistine.'

'I'm not! I'd love you to introduce me to more art.' Lizzy crossed her eyes. 'Expand my mind,' she intoned in a silly voice.

'Idiot.' He pulled her off down the path.

'You want to go *rollerblading*?'

They were at a hire place in a back street behind the Southbank. It would have been less of a surprise if he'd taken her to a Soho sex show.

'I've always thought it looked fun, but I never had anyone to go with.' Elliot looked like he was having second thoughts. 'We can do something else if you want.'

'Rollerblading is great.' She hadn't done it for years. Lizzy smiled at the guy behind the counter. 'Have you got a size six?'

As Elliot seemed to be Master of the Universe in every other aspect, Lizzy was fully expecting him to be a natural. It turned out that he was absolutely dreadful.

'Have you never done this before?' she asked. They'd been going for ten minutes and they'd only gone a hundred yards down the riverbank.

Elliot was still gripping on to the railing for dear life. 'I went rollerskating once when I was a kid.'

'Only once?'

'Funnily enough there weren't many skate parks growing up in rural Dorset.' He scowled at her. 'Would you mind not skating backwards as you talk? It's making me feel even more inferior.'

'Sorry.' Lizzy turned round and zoomed off again. This was fun! She was definitely going to bring her rollerblades up from home next summer.

'Oi, Torvill, wait up!'

She swung round in an arc and waited for Elliot to catch up. 'Remind me why you're the bloody Roadrunner on wheels again?' he panted.

'You're looking at Bromley Hawaiian Rollerdisco Queen, 1998.' Lizzy waggled her eyebrows suggestively. 'You should have seen me in my hula skirt.'

'I'd rather have not, thanks. You've shown me a picture of you as a teenager.'

'Now, now,' Lizzy chided. 'You're really not in a position to mock me, are you?'

Elliot muttered something under his breath that didn't sound particularly endearing.

'Come on.' She held her hand out.

'Come on what?'

'You and I are going rollerblading.'

He looked horrified. 'This railing is the only thing between me and certain death.'

'Don't be silly. You just need to relax. You've done lots of skiing before, haven't you?'

Elliot gazed down the crowded Saturday riverbank. 'A black run is a walk in the park compared to this.'

Lizzy prised his whitened fingers off the rail. 'Easy,' she told him. 'I've got you.'

They started to proceed along at a snail's pace. Elliot wobbled along beside her, emitting frightened little squeaks.

'You're doing really well,' Lizzy said encouragingly, as an old lady on a mobility scooter overtook them.

He dragged his eyes away from the path to give her an evil. 'You're loving this, aren't you? Holding all the power.'

'I don't know what you're talking about,' she said innocently.

'Elliot?'

A smartly dressed woman stopped in their path, nearly causing Elliot to crash into her.

'Didn't have you down as a rollerblading man,' she said amusedly.

Elliot gave a pained smile. 'This is, er . . .' He seemed unsure how to introduce Lizzy. To be fair, he did have other things on his mind at that moment.

'Hello, I'm Lizzy,' she said.

They both jumped as Elliot lurched backwards. Luckily he managed to grab on to Lizzy, nearly pulling her arm out of its socket.

The woman raised an amused eyebrow. 'Are you all right there, Elliot?'

'Perfectly fine,' he gasped. 'Just having a few teething issues.'

'Well, don't let me interrupt you.' She smiled at Lizzy. 'Nice to meet you.'

'Who was that?' she asked after the woman had walked off.

'My editor.' Elliot looked like he couldn't quite believe what had just happened. 'I am never going to live this down in the office.'

*

She had to hand it to Elliot for bloody-minded persistence. After forty minutes of sweat, toil and a lot of swear words, he had finally mastered it. He wouldn't be topping the leader board for style any time soon, but at least she'd got him off that bloody handrail.

There was a clear stretch ahead of them. 'Go, Elliot!' Lizzy yelled as he pushed off ahead of her. He glided along and did a miraculous impression of someone who actually knew what they were doing, before coming to a rather ungainly stop at the top of a path.

'You see!' she called. 'You can skate!'

Elliot's wind-flushed face was triumphant. 'Take *that* and shove it up your bloody Bolero!'

Really, did he have to be so ungracious in victory? The next moment Lizzy saw his eyes widen as he started to roll backwards down the path.

'Put your brakes on!' she shouted.

It was too late. Elliot started to pick up speed, arms flailing like a windmill. A mother with a pushchair had to leap out of the way.

Lizzy could only watch helplessly as he flew down the path and crashed into a low wall. His body did a slow-motion flip over the top of it and disappeared.

'Elliot!' She raced down the slope. He was lying in a crumpled heap on the ground, rollerblades still spinning.

'Have you hurt anything?' she gasped.

He sat up wincing. 'Only my pride.'

They walked back to the hire shop in their socks, Lizzy doing it out of solidarity. 'Are you sure, mate?'

the Australian guy behind the counter asked Elliot. 'You've got another two hours.'

Elliot handed the boots back to him. 'I think I'd better quit while I'm ahead.'

The rest of the day was spent doing less strenuous activities. They wandered down to Borough Market and ate gourmet burgers for lunch. Afterwards they walked along the river, past the Globe Theatre and the ugly grey *Financial Times* building at Southwark Bridge where Elliot worked. From there they walked all the way to the Isle of Dogs where Lizzy thought it would be funny to tweet a picture of the shiny new dockside with the hashtag *#gonedogging*.

'You're hilarious,' Elliot told her. 'If you tag me in that you're going straight in the river.'

Saturday slipped seamlessly into Sunday and Elliot took Lizzy on a tour of the nearby City. London was cold and deserted and impossibly romantic, and they went to the most magical place Lizzy had ever been, a beautiful garden in a ruined churchyard that looked like something out of Arthurian legend. They ended up sharing a bottle of red in a cosy wine bar before Lizzy looked at her watch and realized it was nearly eleven o'clock. They had spent over forty-eight hours together. It felt like it had been forty-eight minutes.

Back on the street, Elliot put his arms round Lizzy's shoulders.

'I'm glad this happened.' His eyes searched hers. 'Us, I mean.'

'I'm glad it happened too.'

They smiled at each other goofily. Elliot swept Lizzy

up in another kiss. It was only a loitering cab's yellow light that made him pull away.

'You'd better get in that.'

'Are you trying to get rid of me?' she said jokingly.

'If only you knew.' They pressed their mouths against each other's, eking out the final moments.

'Text me to let me know when you've got home,' he told her as she climbed in.

'I promise.'

He winked and gave her a little salute. The cab pulled off, taking Lizzy away from him.

'Clapham is it, love?' the driver asked.

'Yes please.' She sat back in the seat. *I miss you already.*

Chapter 44

Despite having had virtually no sleep all weekend, Lizzy floated into work the next morning. Was there such a thing as cloud ten? Because she definitely felt she'd just rocked up on it.

'Sweets, you look amazing!' Bianca exclaimed. 'Have you been on a spa break?'

'You could say that,' Lizzy said smugly, as her text alert went off again. She picked her phone up, expecting another message from Elliot, but it was from Robbie. Lizzy read it and the smile dropped off her face.

I've broken up with Hayley. Can I crash on your sofa for a couple of nights?

'It wasn't anything I said, was it?'

Robbie looked at his sister. 'What do you mean?'

'When I came to stay. All that stuff about Hayley being "The One".' Lizzy gave him a rueful grin. 'I hope I didn't set the cat amongst the pigeons.'

They were on opposite ends of her couch, their feet tangled up in the middle. The remains of the

Thai takeaway Lizzy had got in were on the floor. Unusually for brother and sister, neither had much appetite.

Robbie tucked his hands under his armpits, the way he always did when he was being thoughtful. 'Not really. I guess you had just articulated what I'd been in denial about. Things started to go really wrong after Hay came back from her spa break. I thought we'd done a pretty good job clearing up, but she went mental about the state the house was in. I mean *really* mental.'

'Ouch. Drinking her champagne probably didn't help.'

'Uh-uh. She started going off on one about our family and said some pretty harsh things . . .' Robbie changed the subject diplomatically. 'I always thought Hayley was a really caring person who liked looking after me, but now I've started to realize that she just liked controlling me.'

No shit, Sherlock. 'How did Hayley react when you told her you were ending it?'

'At first she cried and cried.' Her brother looked really upset. 'Then she got really *cross*, like I'd ruined everything. She kept saying about what people were going to think, and all the Christmas parties we'd been invited to. And our summer holiday to St Lucia in May, she'd booked that months ago. Obviously I said I'd pay for anything so she's not left out of pocket.' Robbie sighed. 'I did think about holding out until May so at least Hayley would have got her holiday, but she would have booked skiing by then. It would have gone on and on.'

'What are you going to do about the house?'

He rubbed his eyes. 'I need to get on to a solicitor. I just haven't been able to face anything like that.'

'Let me know if I can do anything,' Lizzy told him. 'And you're welcome to stay here as long as you want.'

She picked up the wine bottle and refilled their glasses. 'Are you going to be OK, Robbo?' she asked. 'You and Hayley were together a pretty long time.'

'I think so.'

'What about Hayley?'

'Hayley will be all right. In fact,' he added wryly, 'I think she's more upset about having no one to do the Waitrose shop with on a Saturday morning, than she is about losing me.'

'I'm sure that's not true,' Lizzy said tactfully.

'It is. She just wants some bloke who will go along with whatever she says. I'm not knocking her; I was happy to go along with it.' He plucked at Lizzy's cushion with the print of the black and white bull dog on it. 'I'm thirty-two not fifty-two. Turns out I'm not ready for that bad-boy barbecue after all.'

The penny had finally dropped. Lizzy did an inward *Yes!* 'What have Mum and Dad said?'

'I haven't told them yet.' Robbie gave her his big-eyed smile and Lizzy knew what was coming. 'I was hoping you'd do it for me.'

'Don't you think it's better coming from you?'

'Please Lizzo, Mum will only go off on one about money and the house.' Her brother suddenly looked exhausted. 'I just can't face her at the moment.'

There were still five weeks to go until the big day but the Spellman house had gone into Christmas

333

lockdown. The kitchen had become a forbidden-food zone.

'Not those cashew nuts, they're for Christmas,' her mother told Lizzy when she went into the cupboard for a snack.

'A stollen finger?'

'No, they're for Lauren's visit.'

'At least allow me a cracker.'

'Not the nice ones, I'm saving them for Christmas.' Mrs Spellman was sluicing out the coffee percolator. 'Have the Jacobs if you must.'

Lizzy looked at the sell-by date. 'They expired in March!'

'They need eating up then. No, not that pickle.' Her mother whipped the jar out of her daughter's hand. 'That's for Boxing Day.'

The stuffed olives were out of bounds, as were the Baileys and the amaretto, when Mrs Spellman discovered Lizzy in the drinks cupboard about to have a pre-dinner snifter. The woman was like a tracker dog. Defeated on her quest for contraband, Lizzy wandered through to her dad's study to find him doing the *Telegraph* sudoku.

'Mum's gone mental. I'm not allowed to eat or drink anything!'

'Try living with her. She's banned me using any of the quilted toilet roll until Christmas Eve.' Her dad shifted uncomfortably in his seat.

'I'm going to get a drink of squash instead,' Lizzy said. 'Do you want one?'

'Careful.' Mr Spellman looked up from his sudoku.

'You'd better make sure your mother's not saving the tap water for Christmas.'

Lizzy had only rung at lunchtime to say she was popping home for dinner, so she joined her parents for heated-up picky bits in the dining room. Mini samosas jostled for attention with cooked sausages and stuffed vine leaves. There was even a pot of Rowntree's jelly for afters. No wonder her dad was always complaining he had indigestion.

Lizzy was gazing at the schizophrenic selection in front of her when she realized she was being watched. 'Is everything all right, Lizard?' her dad asked.

'Yes, why shouldn't it be?'

'It's just that we don't often get a midweek visit from you.' Mr Spellman hesitated. 'Is everything all right at work?'

Aside from me fiddling the books and being in danger of being sacked for misconduct? 'Work's fine,' she lied.

Her parents exchanged A Look. 'If you've come home to ask for money, I'm afraid the family finances are a bit stretched at the moment,' her mother said. 'What with the new boiler and our Holy Land cruise in March.'

'I haven't come home to ask for money.' Lizzy thought about Karen Jones again and felt a bit sick.

There was another heavy silence. Mrs Spellman's right eyebrow was hovering expectantly.

'No, Mum,' Lizzy sighed. 'I'm not about to come out.'

'Then what on earth is it? Because as much as we love you, darling, I know you haven't come all the way out here just out of the goodness of your heart.'

Lizzy took a deep breath. 'It's Robbie.'

Her mother's hand flew to her throat. 'Is he in trouble?'

'Yes. And no, depending on how you look at things. He's finished with Hayley.'

She waited for her parents' reaction.

'When was this?' her mother cried.

'Last week.'

'Last week? Why didn't he say anything?' Mrs Spellman's head was swivelling between her daughter and husband like a meerkat's. 'He could have at least waited until after Christmas, I've only just wrapped up Hayley's See by Chloé perfume! Thank heavens I kept the receipt.'

Mr Spellman shot his wife a warning look.

'What *happened*?' she fretted. 'He seemed perfectly happy the last time we spoke; they'd just had the new curtains put up in the living room.'

'I think that's part of the problem.' Lizzy looked to her dad for backup. 'Rob's not sure he wants to settle down yet.'

'He should have thought about that before he bought a house with her! Oh Michael, all that money they've wasted on that place. I bet that bitch goes for all of it. That's your grandad's inheritance money!'

'Robbie and Hayley are both adults,' Mr Spellman said reasonably. 'I'm sure they can sort this out amicably.' Even so, he did look a bit worried. 'Poor old Rob, what a blow.'

'Why didn't he tell us himself?' Lizzy's mum demanded.

'He probably didn't want you to start worrying about the house and money,' her husband told her.

'Of *course* I'm going to be worried. It's what mothers do! I've got three grown-up children, two of whom are now single!' Mrs Spellman slumped back in her chair. 'People are going to think the fault lies with me and your father, that there's something wrong with our relationship!'

'Now hang on—' Mr Spellman started to say.

Lizzy stepped in before her mum totally went off on one. 'Mum, you don't want him to stay with Hayley if he's unhappy, do you?'

'Of course not.' Mrs Spellman sighed heavily, as if the weight of the world was on her shoulders. 'It's just that life is one big game to your brother. He bowls through everything without thinking about the consequences.' She looked a bit cross. 'I can't believe he got you to tell us he'd split up with Hayley, he's bloody useless.'

'He is useless,' Lizzy agreed. 'But if you come down all heavy-handed you'll only drive him away.'

They sat there in silence for a few moments while her parents digested the news.

'You may as well eat up, you two,' her mother told Lizzy and her dad. 'Before the picky bits get cold.'

'I might try and give Rob a quick call first.' Mr Spellman got up and left the table.

'Robbie will be OK,' Lizzy told her mum. 'He always falls on his feet.'

'I just want you all to be settled and happy.' She shot Lizzy a look. 'You never stop worrying about your

337

children, you know. Not even when they've grown up and left home.'

Lizzy wisely kept her mouth shut. Announcing that she'd started seeing someone who'd been jilted by his fiancée would just about finish her mother off.

Chapter 45

'So where's your brother now?'

They were in a tiny restaurant off a cobbled back-street in Soho. It was impossibly romantic: low ceilings and flickering candlelight and feel-good British grub. Elliot was certainly pulling them out of the bag.

'He's staying with a mate for a while, until he and Hayley sort the house out. I think her dad is going to buy Rob out.' Lizzy gazed out of the window at a bill-board poster opposite advertising a club night. 'I hope it doesn't drag on for months.'

Elliot refilled their glasses. 'These things take as long as they take.'

'How poetic. Did they teach you that at Cambridge?'

Their waiter came over. 'Is everything all right?'

'Yes, lovely.' Lizzy smiled. 'Couldn't be better.'

He went away again and left them in peace.

'Can I ask you something?' Lizzy said. 'You have to be honest.'

'That sounds ominous. No, I wasn't called Ellie in a previous life.'

'Well, that's my first question answered.' Lizzy folded up her napkin and put it on the table. 'When was the first time, you know, that you felt something? For me, I mean. Was it in the Chinese restaurant?'

'Earlier,' he said simply. 'Obviously we had, er, our run-in over email but when I saw you at the art gallery I sort of fancied you then. Your comment about everyone having their heads up their arses made me smile. I thought to myself: *Here's a girl who's got something about her.*'

'You were still with Amber then,' Lizzy said pointedly.

Elliot went red. 'Of course I wouldn't have acted on anything. Amber and I were already in trouble . . . not that I'm trying to make excuses . . .' He blinked. 'Perhaps we should move on.'

'Perhaps we should,' Lizzy said dryly. She studied Elliot's face in the candlelight. 'But you were so *horrible* to me back then. And when we stayed at your mum's! Bin Laden would have received a warmer welcome.'

'I behaved appallingly,' he admitted. 'I was upset about Amber and angry at myself about the way things had turned out, and then you rocked up out of the blue at the Hall. It totally threw me. I was so embarrassed for you to see me in such a mess, and the house and everything . . .'

'You're telling me. I'm surprised you didn't chase us off with a shotgun.'

'That's because everyone kept bringing Amber up and I didn't want to talk about it! You all just saw me as this sad charity case, and I couldn't stand it. I thought the best thing to do was keep out of the way.

After you came to talk to me and I'd bitten your head off I sat there for hours plucking up the courage to come and say sorry, but then I heard you all getting drunk in the kitchen. It was probably a good thing,' he added. 'Every time I opened my mouth the wrong thing seemed to come out.' There was a wry smile. 'In fact, pretty much everything I said to you back then made me want to bang my head against the wall afterwards.'

Would you believe it? All the time Elliot had been acting like a giant arse towards Lizzy, he was now saying was because he'd had feelings for her. Men were so weird. It was like the boy in the playground who pulled the girl's pigtails and made her cry because he secretly fancied her.

'When you tweeted about breaking down nearby I thought it must be fate,' he admitted.

'Fate?' Lizzy feigned shock. 'I thought you didn't believe in all that stupid stuff.'

Elliot grinned boyishly. 'Yeah, well, maybe I do now.'

A warm glow spread through Lizzy that had nothing to do with the sticky toffee pudding they'd just shared for dessert.

London had turned into a winter wonderland, a shiny, happy place of jollity and goodwill. Leicester Square was unrecognizable as Lizzy and Elliot walked through the Christmas fairground that had been put up there.

Lizzy gazed around her. 'I do love this time of year.'

Elliot neatly pulled her round a pile of orange-coloured vomit. 'You mean a month of forced merriment and hangovers culminating in major organ failure on Christmas Day?'

'No, Ebenezer Scrooge.' Lizzy watched a woman in a sparkly party dress hugging a *Big Issue* seller's dog. The animal was wearing a knitted red Santa Claus hat. 'I mean that everyone stops being so *London*.'

'Hark at the beacon of eternal hope and joy.'

'Listen mate, one of us in this outfit has to be.'

Elliot chuckled. His hand skimmed across Lizzy's bottom. 'Are you staying at mine tonight?'

'If you play your cards right.' Who was she kidding? She was putty in his hands. *Not literally I hope*, Lizzy thought, clenching her buttocks.

Piccadilly was lit up in an avenue of arctic-blue lights. Something on the right caught Lizzy's eye. 'I know where we should go!'

She started to drag Elliot towards the entrance to M&M's World.

'Are you being serious?' He ground to a halt. 'I am *not* going in there.'

'I'm telling you, you're missing out.'

'I doubt it. Funnily enough M&M's World wasn't in my "Ten Things I Must Do" when I moved to London.'

'Come on.' She tugged at his hand. 'All the culture vultures come here.'

Despite the late hour the place was packed with tourists. Lizzy quickly lost Elliot in the crowds and blinding glare of primary colours. She thought he'd walked straight back out again, but a quick look outside proved fruitless. He wasn't answering his phone either. Had he gone and locked himself in the toilet in protest?

She eventually found him on Level Three in the

Pick 'n' Mix section. He was standing in the corner on the phone, talking intently. Judging by the serious expression on his face, it was a heavy conversation. He spotted Lizzy and did his imperious pointy finger thing to say, *I'll be with you in a minute.*

Charming, she thought as he turned his back on her. She wandered round the Pick 'n' Mix section, her eyes straying back on Elliot every thirty seconds or so. Who was he on the phone to? 'Sorry about that,' he said a few minutes later, tucking his phone back in his pocket.

'Everything all right?' Lizzy asked him. 'I'm not keeping you from breaking another financial world exclusive?'

'Not this time.' He gazed at the wall of different coloured M&Ms. 'Jesus. Willy Wonka has nothing on this place.'

Twenty minutes later they staggered back out into the fresh air. Elliot was looking faintly nauseous. 'I can't believe I've just spent fifteen quid on Pick 'n' Mix.' He gazed at the bulging bag in disbelief.

Lizzy was feeling mildly sick herself from the confectionery fumes. 'Here, I got you something.' She gave him the personalized 'Elliot' sticker book. 'It's a present, so you have to pretend to like it.'

'I got you something as well.' He pulled the notepad out of his back pocket. '"Libby" was the nearest they had.'

'Aw sweet, thank you!'

'You're welcome,' he grumbled. 'Now can we get out of here?'

*

Luckily a brisk walk in the fresh air seemed to perk him up, and Elliot performed to new heights in the bedroom. Afterwards Lizzy lay in his arms, feeling blissfully content.

'Have you had any new offers on the Hall?' she asked. The bedroom blinds were still open, casting a pinky-mauve hue into the room.

'Why do you ask?'

'I was just wondering.'

Elliot stopped tracing circles on her back. 'That tone makes me suspicious. Have you and my mother been conspiring again?'

Lizzy pushed herself up on one elbow. 'I've been doing a bit of research into stately homes. There's loads of stuff you can do, like hiring the land out for shooting and fishing. You could convert the stable blocks into holiday lets and your mum could have her artists' retreat. There's even this place in Northumberland that hires its land out for battlefield re-enactments.'

'Sounds like you've been giving it a lot of thought.'

'All I'm saying is, is selling the only option? I really think Beeston Hall could be turned into a profitable business.'

'That takes time and money. Neither of which we have any of.'

'If you did a proper business plan, I'm sure you could get financial backing. You must have loads of contacts,' Lizzy persisted. 'I could do the PR. I really think you could make a go of the place.'

'Are you sure my mother hasn't put you up to this?' he said amusedly.

'I promise. This is all me, a hundred per cent.'

Elliot gave her a long appraising look. 'You're really serious, aren't you?'

'Deadly.'

'We wouldn't have a hope in hell. Do you know how many places like Beeston Hall go under every year?'

'Will you just think about it?'

'I'll think about it but that's it. And don't go off putting ideas in my mother's head and giving her false hope.'

Lizzy made a *zip* motion. 'My lips are sealed.'

'Battle re-enactments.' He shook his head.

'They look *amazing*. We could all take part.'

'Er, no thanks. M&M's World is as far down as I'm letting you drag me. Over my dead body are we ever going back to that place.'

'I have the photographic evidence from that; I could blackmail you into wearing chain mail.'

'After the rollerblading I think I've done enough damage to my reputation,' he sighed.

They grinned goofily at each other.

'Lizzy Spellman, you mad woman.' Elliot twisted his finger round one of her curls. 'You've come into my life wreaking your havoc. What am I meant to do with you?'

'Someone's got to pull you down from that pedestal you've put yourself on.'

'Right, you've asked for it.' He went for her ribs.

'Elliot!' she screamed. 'Stop it!'

Lizzy was no amateur in the tickling stakes but Elliot played dirty. 'Mercy!' she panted, as she ended up dangling head first over the bed. 'I'll do anything!'

His eyes glinted. 'Anything?'

'Not *anything*. A girl has to have some standards . . .'

Elliot pulled her on top of him. 'Unfortunately I'm not quite so saintly.'

Chapter 46

Something strange was happening to Lizzy. She found herself standing by the radio waiting for it to boil in the mornings, and had tried on several occasions to tune in the kettle. She was walking round with a permanent smile, despite the fact that she couldn't remember the last time she'd got eight hours' uninterrupted sleep. For the first time in living memory the chocolate in her advent calendar held no appeal. Technically she was running on empty, but Lizzy had never felt more full of energy. A magic had entered her life that had nothing to do with Christmas.

Things were happening so fast between her and Elliot that Lizzy felt helpless – and unwilling – to stop it. Ever since they'd kissed by the riverbank she'd been like a helium balloon, floating along unanchored and out of control, powerless to control her destiny. She'd started subscribing to the *ft.com* and would read Elliot's articles word for word, even though most of the time she hadn't got a clue what he was talking about. Along with her regular TV shows, Lizzy had series-linked the

News at Ten and would sit at home endlessly replaying clips of Elliot talking about the Eurozone debt crisis and tax thresholds, her heart swelling with lust and pride. 'You know that good-looking chap Elliot Anderson off the news?' she felt like announcing to people in the morning queue at Starbucks. 'He's only my bloody boyfriend!'

Bianca had asked her several times why she was in such a good mood, but Lizzy didn't feel like sharing it with people yet. Things were so happy and uncomplicated between her and Elliot at the moment, and as soon as she told people the scrutiny and inevitable gossip would begin. Lizzy could just see the *MailOnline* headline now: 'From Designer to Bargain Basement. Jilted Elliot Moves on with HeadButt Girl.'

It would have to come out at some point, of course, but hopefully by then people would have lost interest in them and wouldn't care. For now, Lizzy was perfectly content to float around in her bubble of pheromone-fuelled euphoria.

There was one dark spot in Lizzy's current state of bliss. Nic. Knowing there was bad blood between them made Lizzy feel lopsided and weird, like she was a triangle with one side missing. Poppet hadn't seen or heard much from Nic either – apparently they were launching a new hotel in Beijing and Nic had barely been in London. 'She just bites my head off whenever I bring your name up,' Poppet lamented to Lizzy. 'I don't know what's got into her.'

The more it went on, the more Lizzy started to fear that Nic had cut her out of her life for good. The worst thing of all was that she had no idea why.

After work Lizzy went to meet her mother for a coffee in a packed Caffè Nero just off Regent Street.

'That place is like a zoo.' Her mother was laden down with M&S bags from the superstore at Marble Arch. 'There were no checked shirts left with a sixteen-inch collar, and the only black leather gloves I could find had tassels on the front of them. I thought they were a bit much for your father. I've been to five Marks' now and they've all sold out of decent plain ones. I got stuck in traffic for *two hours* coming out of Bluewater.'

'Why don't you do your Christmas shopping on-line?' Lizzy suggested.

'Oh, I don't want to bother with all that. It's far too much stress and bother.'

The subject soon turned to Robbie. 'He told your father the other night he's thinking about going off travelling.' Mrs Spellman indignantly stirred a sachet of Canderel into her filter coffee. 'And your father's not exactly discouraging him.'

'What's wrong with that?' Lizzy asked.

'What's the point in him sitting all those accountancy exams only to throw it all away and go off backpacking around Australia a couple of years later? Jacqui's sister's cousin's boy did exactly the same thing, gave up a really good job with Admiral and when he came back he couldn't find a job for love nor money. Even McDonald's wouldn't have him.' Mrs Spellman shook her head. 'He ended up working at a mobile aquarium selling fish food until he'd saved enough money to go off gadding round the world again.'

'I'm sure Robbie will think through anything he does properly,' Lizzy said reassuringly.

'Humph.' Her mother didn't sound convinced. 'I suppose I can be thankful that your sister has a good job that she takes seriously.'

'I do too, Mum.'

'I meant you as well, darling.' Mrs Spellman got her diary out of her handbag. 'What time did you say you'd be coming home on Saturday?'

That weekend Lauren and her boyfriend Perry were arriving for the pre-Christmas get-together. More planning had gone into it than a state visit.

'We're having Christmas drinks at midday and sitting down to lunch at one o'clock. Can you be home by ten?'

Lizzy's immediate thought was that it would eat into cosy sex time with Elliot. 'That early?'

'I need you to help me with stuff,' Mrs Spellman said. 'I can hardly ask your sister to start hoovering after she's flown in from America, and I can't rely on your brother.'

'I'll be there, Mother, don't worry.'

'Good girl.' Her Mother put her diary away. 'You're looking well,' she told Lizzy.

'Is that another way of saying I've put on weight?'

'Quite the opposite.' Mrs Spellman inspected her daughter with an expert eye. 'You've got a real glow about you.'

Lizzy decided to take the plunge. 'I've met someone.'

Her mother instantly went on to red alert. 'Have you?'

'Yeah.' Lizzy toyed with her coffee.

'And?'

'And what?'

'I can't read your mind, darling! Has he got a name? What does he do for a living?'

'His name's Elliot and he's a journalist for the *Financial Times.*'

'A financial *journalist.*' Mrs Spellman looked very impressed.

'*And* he's also an economics correspondent on the *News at Ten*,' Lizzy said proudly.

Her mother looked impressed. 'You're dating a television personality! Has he been on *I'm a Celebrity . . . Get Me Out of Here!*?'

'Mum, he's a serious news journalist, not a reality TV star!'

'When are we going to meet him?'

'Whoa, there. I'm not thinking about things like that yet.' The thought of letting her mother loose on Elliot filled Lizzy with a cold horror.

'Don't be so silly. Your father and I don't bite.'

That was debatable, on her mother's side at least. 'Er, there is something else.'

Mrs Spellman looked up sharply. 'Oh?'

'He was – Elliot, I mean . . .' Lizzy braced herself, 'he was engaged before we met.'

Her mother's eyebrows moved up precisely half an inch, before settling back down again. 'Oh right,' she said.

'Is that all you've got to say? I thought you'd go mad.'

Mrs Spellman brushed some crumbs off the table. 'I was engaged when I met your father.'

'What? I didn't know this. Who to?!'

'It doesn't matter,' she said casually, as if the fact that Lizzy would never have been born if she'd gone ahead with the first engagement was entirely inconsequential. 'What I mean is, these things happen sometimes. I'm not saying don't be careful, darling, but we're all allowed to make mistakes. Sometimes people get engaged for the wrong reasons.'

Her mother never ceased to amaze her. 'Thanks Mum. That means a lot.'

'Well, you're not getting any younger, darling, are you? Beggars can't be choosers.'

'Mum!'

'Is that the time? I need to get a move on.' Mrs Spellman started putting her coat on. 'I assume you'll be bringing him along with you to Lauren's Christmas lunch?'

'No way! It's far too early for stuff like that.'

'No arguments, Elizabeth.' A steely glint entered her mother's eye. 'I want to meet this Elliot for myself.'

Chapter 47

Lizzy took a deep breath and rang the bell. Karen Jones came to the door after what seemed like an age.

'Lizzy, hi.' She sounded resigned rather than welcoming. 'You'd better come in.'

The narrow house seemed even more chaotic than normal. An overdressed Christmas tree was wedged in the corner of the small sitting room.

'It looks fab,' Lizzy said enthusiastically.

'I put it up for Molly's sake more than mine.' Karen gazed at it. 'I don't feel much like celebrating this year.'

Karen had always been a big woman and proud of her curves, but she'd visibly lost weight. It didn't suit Lizzy's Night Night Baby client. All of Karen's bounce and energy had gone.

In the kitchen Lizzy made the tea while Karen walked round listlessly picking up things and putting them down again. She was moving like an old woman. 'Me and Molly have had this bug. It's really hit me for six.'

They sat down at the table with their mugs of tea.

'I'm sorry, Lizzy, I haven't got anything to offer you.'

'Don't be silly.' Lizzy watched Karen distractedly scratch at the patch of eczema on her neck. 'How are you?'

'Sorry I haven't been in touch,' Karen said as if she hadn't heard. 'Things have been pretty difficult recently.'

'I've been really worried,' Lizzy said gently. 'Is Andy still giving you hassle?'

'Arsehole ex-husbands are the least of my troubles.' Karen gave her a tired smile. 'I had a meeting with the bank.'

It clearly hadn't gone well. 'Oh?'

'Unless I start turning a profit in like, the next five minutes, I'm going to go bankrupt. Which means I won't be able to afford to pay my mortgage, which means Molly and I are going to lose our home.' It was said in a matter-of-fact way but a nerve was flickering under Karen's right eye.

'There has to be a way,' Lizzy told her. 'You've come so far. We can't give up now.'

'That's exactly why we should give up,' Karen said dully. 'You put your heart and soul into something and it still doesn't work out.'

Lizzy got her work iPad out of her bag. 'Let's see where we're at. I'm chasing up a few things that sound really promising.'

'I'm sick of promises that never lead to anything!' Karen exhaled shakily. 'You don't have to whitewash it any more, Lizzy. We're fighting a losing battle.' She sat back in defeat. 'I've got nothing left, Lizzy, nothing. I can't even afford to pay you back the money.'

'Let's keep going through December,' Lizzy said desperately. 'I'll step up on the tweeting and I've got some favours to call in from a couple of journalists. Let me see what I can do.'

'Lizzy, you're not listening,' Karen said angrily. '*I can't pay you back!*' The next moment her eyes welled up with tears. She slumped down on the weather-beaten table. 'Oh Lizzy. What's the point?'

They spent two hours going through every conceivable plan they could think of, but in the end it always came back to the same thing. Night Night Baby wasn't making money. It was absolutely heartbreaking to see Karen in such a state.

Lizzy left Karen's house with an impending sense of doom. If only she could get people to see what a great product Night Night Baby was! She felt terrible, as if she'd let Karen down. The worst feeling of all was that Lizzy felt like she'd lulled Karen into a false sense of security. Had she encouraged Karen to go down a path that had no pot of gold at the end of it? Believing in dreams didn't mean you were going to end up being successful in reality.

'*Shit,*' Lizzy muttered to herself. She had got them into a bloody big hole. How the hell was she going to get them out of it?

'Are you all right?' Elliot asked her. 'You seem a little preoccupied.'

He took the menu out of Lizzy's hand and turned it back up the right way, before giving it back to her.

'Sorry,' she sighed. 'It's just work stuff.'

Elliot looked sympathetic. 'You want to talk about it?'

355

Lizzy shook her head. She was too embarrassed to tell Elliot what she'd done. To make matters even worse Jocasta Reynolds-Johnson was kicking off again and Antonia was about to have a level-ten meltdown. When Lizzy had left the office that evening you could have cut the atmosphere with a knife.

'I don't want to bore you with it. I'm sure it will work out.' *Starting with me getting fired,* she thought glumly.

Giuseppe came back to take their order. 'Just the tricolore salad for me please,' Lizzy said.

'Is that all you want?' Elliot asked.

'I had a big lunch,' Lizzy lied. She didn't have much of an appetite.

'It must be love,' Giuseppe told Elliot. 'Normally she's a real piggy.' He winked at Lizzy. *'Oink oink.'*

'What do you think of the place?' Lizzy asked once she'd got rid of Giuseppe. 'Not quite up to the normal Michelin-starred places you must go to?'

Elliot gazed at the plastic grapevine on the wall with silver tinsel wrapped around it. When they'd walked in there had been a five-foot statue of a glowing Jesus by the front door. 'It's got a certain charm, I like it.'

'Liar.' Lizzy smiled at him. 'Are you sure you don't mind coming to my parents' on Saturday?'

'For the fifth time, no. Weirdly, I'm rather looking forward to it.' He reached across and touched the end of Lizzy's nose. 'I'm looking forward to meeting the two people who created a lunatic like you.'

'Charming. You might change your mind when you meet my mother.'

'Well, mine's not exactly normal.'

They exchanged another grin. 'Stop stressing,' Elliot told Lizzy. 'It will be fine.'

Giuseppe came back and dumped their orders on the table. 'I'm happy to see someone is prepared to take Lizzy on,' he told Elliot. 'She had a bad time after the YouTube.' He lowered his voice. 'I worry for a while no one would go near her. You know, damaged goods. For time she would come in here and eat and drink too much, nothing else in her life. I say to her: "No one wants to dance with Cinderella at the ball if she like a baby elephant!"'

'Yeah, thanks for that, Giuseppe,' Lizzy mumbled.

He gave her a fond look. 'But now I see her happy again. You think you'll marry her?' he added conversationally to Elliot.

'Giuseppe!'

'Sorry about him.' Lizzy was still blushing two minutes later. 'He gets a bit carried away sometimes.'

'Don't worry about it.' Thankfully Elliot had looked highly amused by the whole thing. Unless he was putting a front on and was planning to escape out of the men's toilet window any minute. *If my mother doesn't manage to sabotage my love life,* Lizzy thought, *at least I know I've got Giuseppe.*

'I spoke to my mum earlier, she was asking about you,' Elliot told her.

'Oh cool. Is she OK?'

Elliot put his fork down. Even he seemed to have been defeated by the four seasons pizza. 'She wanted to know what was going on with us.'

'Have you told her then?'

'Is it so much of a secret?'

'No! I just wondered what she'd think after, er . . .' Lizzy shut up. 'What did you tell her?'

'Why?' he said carefully. 'What would you have liked me to say?'

'I don't know,' she mumbled. 'You're the one who had the conversation.'

Elliot looked distinctly amused. 'I don't think I've seen you look so coy before.'

'I'm not being coy, I'm just not very good at this part.'

'What part?'

'You know.' Lizzy started shredding her napkin. 'The "Are we or aren't we?" conversation.'

'Are we or aren't we what?' he asked innocently.

The twisted sod was actually enjoying this. 'I mean, have we got an exclusive thing going on? Are we just casually seeing each other, or are we girl . . .' Lizzy couldn't bring herself to say the words. 'You know what I mean. Are we officially *together*?'

'Why are you whispering? No one can hear.'

'Elliot!'

The corners of his mouth tugged up. 'I'd say so, wouldn't you?'

'Nicola come in here the other night getting take out,' Giuseppe announced when they came to pay the bill.

Lizzy came down from the cloud of happiness she'd been floating on with a bang. 'Was she OK?'

'You tell me.' He shook his head. 'She not look so good. I say to her: "Uncle Giuseppe is worried. You look like you have the weight of the world on your shoulders!"'

Lizzy could feel Elliot's eyes on her. 'And what did she say?'

'She say she having hard time at work. That's all you girls do. Work, work, work! No time for fun or love!' Giuseppe nudged Elliot. 'You don't want to put your career before this one, Lizzy. I can tell this one a *real* man.'

They departed into the cold night air. 'Are you going to tell me what you and Nic have fallen out about?' Elliot asked.

'Just something silly,' Lizzy said quickly.

Elliot gave her one of his looks that said *girls*.

They started walking down a long street of huge white semi-detached houses. Opulent wreaths hung on polished front doors, while plush Christmas trees twinkled out of bay windows.

'Banker land round here,' Elliot commented.

'Would you ever like to live here?'

He shook his head. 'Too claustrophobic, in more ways than one. And I like being near water.'

A tall, thin figure was hurrying along on the other side of the street. Lizzy's immediate thought was how late it was to be out with a baby. Blood-curdling wails were coming from the buggy the person was pushing. It was hard to tell from the long padded coat if they were a man or a woman, but as the figure stopped and stooped to look into the pram a swathe of blonde hair fell out.

'Oh sweetie, what can Mummy do?'

The woman pushed her hood off her face and Lizzy found herself gazing at a face that looked weirdly familiar. A second later she realized why: it was Tiana

Dawson – a famous Australian supermodel who now lived in London with her financier husband. She'd made headlines in the *MailOnline* earlier in the year when she'd been pictured on a beach, only a week after giving birth to her daughter, with a completely flat stomach.

Tiana was crouching down by her crying child, desperately trying to calm her. It was a world away from the ice-cool Amazonian who was the face of several major fashion houses.

'Wait here a minute,' Lizzy told Elliot.

Crossing over the road, she tentatively approached the celebrity. The supermodel's eyes flickered towards Lizzy and she pulled her hood back up.

'Excuse me,' Lizzy said.

'Now really isn't a good time. Aurelia darling, please . . .'

'I just wanted to—'

'What?' Tiana snapped. 'Take my picture and post it on Twitter, so everyone can see what an irresponsible mother I am walking the streets with my baby at eleven o'clock at night?'

Lizzy glanced across the road at Elliot. He shook his head.

'Actually, I just wanted to know if you'd like to try these,' she said.

Tiana looked at Lizzy's hand suspiciously. 'What are they?'

Lizzy held out the selection of Night Night Baby products that had been buried for ages in the bottom of her bag. 'I'm a PR and one of my clients has this amazing range of products for babies who can't sleep.

I've only got a few bits and pieces on me, but you're welcome to take them.'

'I'm not going to endorse anything, if that's what your game is,' Tiana said frostily.

'I'm not playing any game. I just thought you might need some help.' Lizzy tried a smile. 'Believe me, this stuff works.'

'I'm paying four thousand pounds an hour for a baby whisperer.' The supermodel gave a humourless laugh. 'Thanks and all that, but I don't think a lavender pillow spray is going to help.'

Chapter 48

Lizzy walked into the heady fug of festive pot-pourri and the smell of roasting turkey.

The family home was strangely quiet. 'Hello?' she called. 'Anyone in?'

There were voices coming from the direction of the kitchen. Lizzy walked through to find her sister standing in her running kit gulping down an isotonic sports drink. A strapping young man with a crew cut was stretching his hamstrings by the counter. As he stood up Lizzy got an eyeful of the bulge in his cycling shorts.

'Hi guys!' she said.

Lauren put her drink down and opened her arms. 'Come here.'

It felt like hugging a lump of granite. Her little sister had developed even more muscles since the last time Lizzy had seen her.

'You smell of booze,' Lauren said chidingly.

'Do I? Must be the bottle of Baileys I had on the train over here.'

Lauren's companion gave her a blank stare. 'I'm

joking,' Lizzy said hastily. 'It was only a chocolate liqueur I found in my coat pocket. The centre went all over my fingers . . .'

Lauren shot her a warning look. 'Perry, this is my older sister Lizzy.'

'Not *that* much older!' Lizzy said brightly. 'It's lovely to meet you, Perry. Lauren's told us so much about you.'

It was hard to know where to look. Perry's packet wasn't so much the elephant in the room as a whole herd of them thundering through. He gave Lizzy a formal handshake, obviously keen to keep the mad older sister at bay.

'Nice to meet you, ma'am.'

No one spoke for a moment. 'Well,' Lizzy said heartily. 'You two have obviously been out in the fresh air.'

Compared to Lizzy, who'd woken up still in yesterday's make-up, Lauren and her boyfriend were basking in a pink, athletic glow. It was all Elliot's fault, Lizzy reflected. She'd only gone to lie down next to him last night for a cuddle and ended up not leaving the bed for the next twelve hours. Although it was probably more accurate to say they hadn't left the bedroom. Elliot certainly had more than just the missionary position in his repertoire . . .

'Have you been out far?' she asked, secretly smiling at the memory.

'Just a twelve miler.' Lauren rolled her head from side to side to iron out the kinks. 'Best thing for getting rid of jet lag.'

'Mum and Dad not around?'

'Mum's upstairs. Dad's gone to B&Q to get some more fairy lights.'

Lizzy put her bag back on the floor and ended up eye-to-eye with The Packet. 'Mum said you're bringing some guy for lunch,' Lauren said when she stood up. 'Edward?'

'He's called Elliot.'

'I told you what happened to Lizzy,' Lauren told her boyfriend.

'Yeah, the whole Headbutt Girl thing. That was kind of a big deal for a while.'

'Thankfully it's all blown over now,' Lizzy said quickly. 'Oh, hi Mum!'

Mrs Spellman burst into the kitchen dressed in her lounge tracksuit and with three hair rollers on the crown of her head. Her eyes fastened for a second on Perry's groin. 'Lizzy! I wasn't expecting you for a couple of hours.'

Lizzy stared at her mother. 'You said to come at ten.'

'Did I?' Mrs Spellman said indifferently, as if she hadn't threatened her daughter with pain of death if she didn't come over early to help.

She went over to the cooker and lifted the lid of a saucepan up. 'Seeing as you're here I'm sure I can find you a few little things to do.' She beamed at Perry. 'I'm proud to say the Spellman family Christmas runs like clockwork.'

'I don't want Perry thinking we're some shambolic bunch of English eccentrics,' she hissed to Lizzy in the hallway. 'You know how controlling the Americans get about national holidays.'

By quarter to one Lizzy had hoovered the entire house, peeled a mountain of carrots, spray-painted some fir cones and helped her dad rearrange the furniture in the living room so everyone had somewhere to sit. She'd lost one of her rocking-horse earrings somewhere and had sweated less in a spin class. She was running upstairs to slap some more make-up on when the doorbell went.

'Can someone get that?'

She was met by a resounding silence. 'Fine, Cinderella will get it!' she shouted and went back down the stairs.

The first thing she saw was the beautiful bunch of flowers.

'Don't get too excited, they're for your mum.' Elliot looked annoyingly perky considering how little sleep they'd had.

He gazed at Lizzy's wild hair. 'You look like Sideshow Bob from *The Simpsons*.'

Lizzy's dad appeared in the hallway. 'You must be Elliot!'

'Nice to meet you, Mr Spellman.'

'Please, call me Michael,' he said, as the two men shook hands.

Elliot produced a good bottle of red from his shoulder bag. 'This is for you, Michael. Lizzy mentioned that you were a fellow Pinot Noir fan.'

'I certainly am!' Mr Spellman examined the label. 'That's really very good of you, Elliot.'

'Elliot!' Mrs Spellman was advancing down the stairs in her Christmas best. 'We're so delighted you could make it.'

'Thank you for inviting me.' He gave Lizzy's mum the bouquet. 'The florist said that winter roses should last all the way up until Christmas.'

'They're beautiful! Oh Elliot, you shouldn't have!

Oh, look, Lizzy! Look, Michael! Aren't they incredible!'

Her mother looked like she was about to give birth with the excitement. Lizzy shot her boyfriend a look. *Bloody smoothie.*

'Lauren and Perry are on their way back, she's been showing him round Bromley,' Mrs Spellman explained. 'And Lizzy's brother should be here any minute now.'

She said it with an air of irritation. Robbie's phone had been going straight to voicemail all morning. God only knew where he'd got to.

'I'll try him again,' Lizzy said. 'His battery's probably gone dead.'

'If you wouldn't mind.' Mrs Spellman frowned at her daughter. 'You're looking a bit bedraggled, darling, why don't you nip upstairs and tidy yourself up?'

At three minutes to one Lizzy was putting the finishing touches to the smoked salmon when she heard the doorbell go. She carried the tray of canapés through to the living room and found her brother like the conquering hero with everyone around him.

'All right, DJ?' Robbie had grown a beard since the last time Lizzy had seen him.

Lauren had her arm around her big brother's waist as she gazed up at him adoringly. 'What time did you get in last night, Rob?'

He pulled a face. 'About three hours ago.'

'Amazing!'

In Lauren's eyes, her big brother could do no wrong. Robbie could have told them he'd been shooting up heroin all night and Lauren would still have giggled girlishly.

Mr Spellman opened the Moët Elliot had also brought with him. 'Who's first? Don't be shy, Perry, you'll get trampled to death in this house if you don't fight your way to the front!'

They sat down an hour later in the dining room to a table groaning with festive fare.

'Diane, stop fussing. We've got enough to feed the five thousand,' Mr Spellman told his wife.

'I'll just get the other cranberry sauce.' She rushed back into the kitchen.

They pulled crackers and read out the rubbish jokes. Mr Spellman made a toast. 'Here's to a happy early Christmas! Perry, it's lovely to have you here.'

'And it's lovely to have you here, Elliot,' Mrs Spellman said coquettishly. She was actually blushing. 'Please everyone, tuck in!'

Lizzy had ended up sitting next to Robbie and Perry. At least Perry had swapped the cycling shorts for chinos and a navy sports jacket, which he was still wearing despite repeated offers from Mr Spellman to hang it up.

Elliot was on the other side of the table next to Mrs Spellman. He was looking rather adorable in a cream cable-knit cardigan and a green paper hat. Teamed with the dark-red hair he looked like a little festive elf. Lizzy made a mental note to tell him later.

'Another potato, Elliot?' she heard her mother ask.

He gazed down at the giant mound of food on his plate. 'I might come back for one later.'

'A man who knows his limits.' Mrs Spellman nodded approvingly. 'Unlike Michael, who keeps going until there's nothing left, and then has to spend the rest of the day on the toilet with tummy trouble!' She shook her head. 'Lizzy's just the same.'

Was her mother deliberately trying to sabotage her love life? Lizzy picked up the bottle of Oyster Bay and turned to Perry. His paper hat was valiantly trying to cling on to the shiny crew cut.

'Red or white?' she asked.

'I'm all right with the soda water.' He put his hand over the glass, just in case Lizzy was about to try any funny business.

OMG, she thought. *It's Hayley in the form of a six-foot-four American footballer player.*

'So you guys have just had Thanksgiving?' Elliot was saying to Lauren.

She nodded. 'We went to Perry's parents' place in the Hamptons.' She looked at Mrs Spellman. 'Mum, they have got the most amazing house on the beach. How big was the Christmas tree in the entrance hall again, Pez?'

'Fifty foot.'

'Golly!' Mr Spellman said. 'I bet your father had a job getting that home in the car!'

Perry gazed at Lizzy's father. 'We got it delivered.'

'How many people did your mother have for lunch, Perry?' Mrs Spellman asked.

He glanced up from the mountain of turkey.

'Thirty. It was kinda a small affair this year.'

'Perry's brothers are away climbing the Himalayas,' Lauren said proudly. 'Isn't that right, babe?'

Her boyfriend shrugged his massive shoulders. 'It's kinda a warm-up for Everest next year.'

Everyone looked very impressed. Robbie gave Lizzy a nudge. 'You have enough trouble climbing to the top of the stairs, don't you?'

The conversation turned to jobs. Apparently Perry had just been poached from the bank Lauren worked for to go and trade for a rival company.

'Perry's hoping to be a managing director by this time next year.'

Her boyfriend's face split into a big grin. 'Yeah baby!'

They high fived loudly across the table. It was the most animation anyone had seen from him all day.

'Elliot's a financial journalist!' Mrs Spellman had nearly spilt her wine during Perry's sudden burst of activity. 'And he's a presenter on the *News at Ten!*'

'I'm not one of the *presenters*, Diane . . .'

'Oh shush.' She waved her hand at him. 'You're on the television, aren't you?'

'Who do ya work for?' Perry asked Elliot disinterestedly.

'The *FT.*'

'Ah OK.' Perry shot Lauren a lofty look. 'We don't pay much attention to you guys.'

There was a short silence. Robbie raised his eyebrows amusedly at Elliot.

'It is funny how out of all the people in the world, Lizzy's ended up with a financial journalist,' Mrs Spellman mused.

'Why is that funny?' Mr Spellman asked.

'She's always been so useless with money!' Mrs Spellman laughed gaily. 'Do you remember when she spent an entire week's pocket money on a rock from that gipsy woman who used to come round?'

'She told me it had mystic powers,' Lizzy said feebly.

'Jacqui watched her pick it out of number seventy-four's skip!' Mrs Spellman chortled.

'I was only eight, Mum!' Lauren was eyeballing her sister over the glazed parsnips. 'I'm not *that* bad with money,' Lizzy said uncomfortably.

'You're not bad at all. In fact, you were making some pretty pertinent points the other day about MMP.'

Lizzy looked at Elliot. 'I was?'

He nodded. 'I think you're totally spot on about them looking after their bondholders at the expense of shareholders.'

Lauren frowned. 'I still own a load of MMP stock.'

'Hmm,' Lizzy said knowledgably. 'You might want to think about selling that.'

Elliot gave her a little wink.

Two hours later they tumbled down from the table full of food and booze.

'Where do you want these dishes, Diane?' Elliot asked.

'Just put them by the sink. Michael can do them later.'

'Where *is* Dad?' Lizzy asked. He'd muttered something about checking the fire and hadn't come back.

'Where do you think? In the bathroom.' Mrs Spellman rolled her eyes. 'I'm going to have to fit him with a gastric band for Christmas.'

Back in the hallway Lizzy and Elliot stole a kiss under the mistletoe. 'Are you having a nice time?' she whispered.

'I'm having a really nice time. You sold your family to me as a bunch of lunatics.'

'They *are* lunatics.'

He nuzzled her neck. 'And I told you, I'm embracing all things mad these days.'

They sprang apart as Mrs Spellman popped her head out of the kitchen doorway. She smiled at them indulgently. 'Elliot, would you be a dear and come and help me open the pickled walnuts?'

'Sure, no problem.'

Mrs Spellman gave Lizzy an approving look. 'I must say, it's nice to have a *real* man around the house.'

Much to his mother's disgust Robbie had taken up smoking again. Lizzy found him on the back porch constructing a roll-up.

'Yo DJ.'

'Yo MC.'

Lizzy pulled the door shut behind her. 'Nice to have the troops together again.'

'For sure. Lauren's on good form.'

They looked through the window into the living room, where Perry was still staring at a basketball game on the TV.

'Perry is . . .'

'Very Lauren,' Lizzy finished for him.

They exchanged a smile. 'Elliot's a nice guy,' Robbie said. 'Mum's his number one fan.'

'I know.' Lizzy still couldn't believe how well he'd fitted in. Would the man ever stop surprising her?

Her brother lit up and took his first drag. 'Mum also mentioned he'd been engaged before.'

Lizzy hesitated. 'Yeah.'

Robbie picked a bit of tobacco off his lip and looked

at her through squinted eyes. 'Does it bother you?'

'It did,' Lizzy admitted. 'But I think I'm over it.'

'Just be careful.'

'Why?' She felt a stab of paranoia. 'Do you think there's something I need to be careful about?'

'Chill out, DJ.' Robbie landed a gentle play-punch on Lizzy's arm. 'I'm just looking out for you. That's what big brothers are for.'

Chapter 49

An hour later Mr Spellman had emerged from the bathroom and was watching the sports channel with Perry, an enforced cup of mint tea from Lizzy's mother on the table in front of him. Elliot and Robbie had gone for some male bonding at the pub. Mrs Spellman was on the sofa marking all the films in the *Radio Times* she wanted to watch with Post-its. Lizzy was sneaking a mouthful of brandy butter from the fridge when Lauren charged into the kitchen and rugby-tackled her to the floor in a hug.

'Love you, Lizzo!'

Lauren's eyes were glassier than a pair of Christmas baubles. Lizzy got nervous on the rare occasions that her sister got drunk these days. Lauren always started challenging people to arm-wrestling competitions and demanding to know how much their yearly bonuses were.

'I'm a bit pished,' she said in a sotto whisper. 'Don't tell Perry!'

Lizzy spat out a piece of Lauren's hair from her mouth. 'Of course I won't.'

'I love you, Lizzy!' It was like being in the death grip of a famished boa constrictor.

'And I love you.' It was a novelty being the sober, sensible one.

Lauren sprang up and grabbed the red cooking wine off the kitchen counter. She took a swig straight from the bottle. 'You never did tell me what that five hundred pounds was for.'

'I've paid it back, does it matter?' Lizzy joked nervously. 'Are you going to tell me you forgot to charge me interest on it?'

Lauren looked a bit hurt. 'I know you think I'm a total money bore but I've got your best interests at heart.'

'I was only teasing. I'm sorry. It was really good of you to loan me the money. I promise it won't happen again.'

'It probably will, though. It's all right, I'm not having a go. I've come to realize that we can't be good at everything.' She crossed her muscular arms. 'You're rubbish with money, the same way I'm crap at making friends.'

'Lauren, that's not true,' Lizzy said gently. 'I'm sure you make a lovely friend. Look how, er, supportive you are as a sister.'

'I can make friends, but I can't seem to keep them. Girls don't seem to like honesty. If Elliot was sending *your* old sorority sister naked photos of himself and had invited her to his family cabin in Vermont and everyone was talking about it, you'd want to know, wouldn't you?'

Lizzy blinked. 'Er, I guess I would.'

'There are all these stupid rules,' Lauren said despondently. 'I always end up saying the wrong thing to the wrong person.'

Lizzy gave her little sister a hug. 'You can only be yourself, and *your* self is great,' she told her. 'If people don't like it, sod them.'

They stood there with their arms round each other. '*Did* you need that money for an abortion?' Lauren said in Lizzy's ear.

Lizzy pulled away. 'No! I've paid it back, can't we just forget about it?'

'I wouldn't judge you if it was,' Lauren told her. 'It still makes me sick about all the prejudice that Penny had to go through.'

'Lauren, *Dirty Dancing* was set in a sixties American holiday camp. You can't compare it to how things are now.'

Her sister shrugged. 'This is Bromley in the noughties. What's the difference?'

By 10 p.m. Lizzy and Elliot were back on the train to London, weighed down with full bellies and Mrs Spellman's turkey sandwiches. They were sharing the carriage with festive revellers heading into the capital for a Saturday night out. Lizzy had a headache from the amaretto shots Lauren had made her do at the front door. She was starting to feel like she'd done Christmas and New Year's Eve in one fell swoop.

'You were a big hit with the Spellmans,' she told Elliot. 'I think my dad might have some serious competition for my mum's affections.'

'Your parents are lovely people. I can see a lot of you in your mum.'

'Don't say that!'

Elliot laughed at the look of horror on Lizzy's face. 'It's a good thing. You've both got this amazing zest for life, and the ability to connect with anyone.' He brushed her cheekbone with the tip of his finger. 'What I want to know is, where did the animal-print fetish come from?'

'A-ha. You haven't seen Mum's famous sequinned flamingo jumper. She only gets it out for special occasions.'

He groaned. 'Is that what I've got to look forward to in the future?'

The future. A wonderful tingling spread through Lizzy. *He thinks we've got a future!*

The next minute she was nearly ejected out of her seat by the most almighty shriek. Even the rowdy partygoers stopped playing their drinking games and looked round.

Elliot's eyes were watering. 'Don't suppose you've got a tissue?'

Lizzy dug round in her handbag and found him one. 'Do you always make that sound when you sneeze?'

He looked nonplussed. 'Turkey always irritates my nose for some reason.'

There was another extraordinary explosion. Lizzy started to giggle.

'What's so funny?' Elliot sniffed.

'You! You make a really weird squealing sound when you sneeze!'

'I do not!' He did it again. 'Stop laughing at me!'

Lizzy couldn't stop. The revelation that gruff, pompous, award-winning journalist Elliot Anderson made a noise like a piglet when he sneezed was the funniest thing she'd heard in a long time. As she looked at him – indignant and red-eyed as he held the novelty 'Xmas Squirrel' tissue over his nose – Lizzy was hit by the startling and wonderful realization that she was head over heels in love with him.

Chapter 50

The next day Elliot had to go into the office for a few hours. Lizzy woke to a note on the pillow next to her. *Should be back by 2 p.m. Make yourself at home. E x*

The bed already felt empty without him. Finding an old T-shirt of his in his workout gear drawer, Lizzy wandered through to the kitchen. The apartment was filled with a shimmery bright light that matched Lizzy's mood. It took a few minutes to work the espresso machine, but she finally succeeded and took her prize through to the living room, feeling very cosmopolitan.

The river was like a giant silver snake ambling past. Lizzy sat in the window seat and gazed at the darts of sunlight hitting the water. Even though neither of them had said anything about how they'd felt on the train, there had been a new intensity to the sex last night. Everything had suddenly felt more deep and meaningful, as if an unspoken pact had developed between them. Was that how it worked? When the moment happened, you both just knew?

The river path was busy with Sunday traffic. A man

in a green parka coat was standing underneath the window talking on his phone. Lizzy felt like throwing open the window and shouting down to him. *I'm in love with a beautiful man! And I think he might feel the same way!*

Lizzy stared dreamily out over the rooftops as she drank the rest of her coffee. She had a few hours before Elliot got back. She might head into Covent Garden and do a bit of Christmas shopping. What should she get him? It was probably still too early to get anything too expensive, but she didn't want to go down the novelty present route either. *Then again,* she thought wryly, *when you realized you were on hundred percent, bang-to-rights in love with someone, what was the point in holding back?*

When should she tell Elliot that she loved him? She'd almost said it last night in bed, but had chickened out at the last minute. The circumstances had to be right: declarations of love required you to have a sober head. Maybe she could drop the bombshell over a delicious but healthy salmon dinner lovingly prepared by herself. Or was that too much? It might be better to whisper it in Elliot's ear on one of their romantic late-night walks. But the age-old dilemma – what if *she* said it and horror of horrors, he didn't say it back? Lizzy watched a pigeon swoop on to next-door's window ledge and swiftly defecate. Maybe she should wait for him to say it first.

She got up and started to wander round the living room, picking up things and putting them down again, and going over to gaze at Elliot's intellectual-looking bookcase. There was no doubt that he had good taste, but the place could do with a bunch of flowers or two to liven things up. Maybe she'd get him one of those nodding Japanese cats as a stocking filler, just to annoy him.

At the end of the room was a large cabinet, in the same dark wood as the other bits of furniture in the apartment. It was simple and unobtrusive: *nothing to see here, thank you very much.* Lizzy pressed on a corner of the biggest door and watched as it quietly popped open.

She found herself looking at a wall of A4 black box files. Everything was neat and labelled meticulously. Lizzy knew she shouldn't have been surprised. What did they say about people's cupboards being a true reflection of what a person was really like? Her own flat was rammed full of crap that she never used. Cupboard doors would burst open of their own accord and spit random things out like a scattergun. She wasn't sure what that said about her.

It felt wrong, standing here looking at Elliot's private affairs. What if he walked in now and found her? *Just shut the door and go and get in the shower,* she told herself. *You're doing the mad snooping thing!*

Except that Elliot was at work and would never be any the wiser. Her hands seemed to be beyond her control. Lizzy went on opening more cupboards and drawers, feeling an increasing sense of relief and guilt that nothing was out of the ordinary. *Why?* said the same annoying little voice. *What are you expecting to find?*

She was just about to shut the cabinet door when something on the bottom shelf caught her eye. It was an old cardboard box, looking rather out of place amongst the meticulously filed paperwork and shiny box files. Lizzy pulled it out and sat down cross-legged on the floor next to it.

A musty smell wafted out as she opened the flaps. Inside was a big pile of photographs, all chucked in together. Elliot obviously didn't apply his ordered filing system to old photographs. On the top of the pile was an official picture of a school rugby team. Fifteen teenage boys standing together in formation with their arms folded. A wiry Elliot was on the front row, sporting nineties-style Hugh Grant hair as he gazed solemnly into the camera. And was that Marcus at the back with a horrible crew cut? Even then he'd had the same smug expression.

Underneath there were more team photos, all with Elliot in different school years with a variety of dreadful haircuts. There were also a few family photos, but unlike the official school portraits these were loose and a bit dog-eared, as if they'd fallen out of an album. One was of Elliot as a small boy, standing in front of Beeston Hall. He had his arms round a taller, tangle-haired blonde girl who Lizzy assumed was Elliot's sister Skyla. They were standing in-between a tall, jolly man who was the spitting image of Elliot and a much younger, glamorous-looking Cassandra. Elliot and his sister were both holding old-fashioned fishing nets. Despite Elliot's serious expression, he looked adorable in a pirate's hat and an Orville T-shirt that said, *I Wish I Could Fly.*

Lizzy began to relax. This was just a box of childhood memories like everybody else had. She was about to put the lid back on when she saw a flash of gold at the bottom of the box. Carefully lifting the pictures on top of it, she pulled the photo album out.

The cover was beautiful and ornate, and it felt fat with content. Lizzy opened it and her heart shot up into her mouth. On the very first page was a picture of a fresh-faced Elliot and Amber crouching by a stream, grinning as they looked into the camera. The dedication was dated Elliot's twenty-first birthday. *To my darling E, my one and only! Here's to the next twenty-one years. All my love now and forever, A.*

Even with a dodgy perm Amber had been stunning. With a growing feeling of sickness Lizzy turned the page. For the next twenty pages Elliot and Amber's history was played out in glorious, excruciating detail. Amber in a long stripy scarf cheering a muddy Elliot on at the side of a rugby pitch, Amber and Elliot at their upper sixth dance together, both looking gawky and self-conscious in black tie. Them on a saggy floral sofa, bare legs tangled up together. On stage in a play, Elliot in a comical floppy hat while Amber looked ravishing as a Lolita-esque peasant girl. Them at another ball, this time older and more self-confident and poised. A close-up of a bare-chested Elliot asleep with a cute black Labrador puppy, Amber and Elliot sunbathing on a jetty on a lake, her looking like a supermodel in a black string bikini . . .

If that hadn't stuck the knife in enough, Amber had annotated each picture with lovely flowing handwriting: times, dates, locations and exuberant captions. *Bel-Air baby! White Russians – never again!!* A secret, indecipherable language that Lizzy would never be able to understand. The last photo in the album was

Elliot and Amber standing in front of the famous Trevi Fountain in Rome. Elliot had his arm round Amber and was smiling into the camera as she gazed up at him adoringly. *Ciao bella! We'll always have Roma!*

Lizzy closed the album with a snap. The sound matched how she was feeling inside, like something had broken. She put the box back and slumped against the cabinet. For some reason, a memory from her own schooldays swam into her mind. Her GCSE art exam: a seaside scene that Lizzy had poured her heart and soul into. She really thought she'd created a masterpiece, but when her results had come back from the exam board, she'd been devastated to have only been awarded a D. 'I'm sorry, Lizzy,' her art teacher had told her. 'Sometimes things aren't quite as good as we think they are.'

Lizzy had the same feeling now, that she'd been labouring under the illusion that she'd got something special, only to find out it wasn't that special at all. Amber and Elliot had such a rich history together and a love that had endured across the decades. How could she ever compete?

Chapter 51

The next day she met Poppet for an emergency summit at Pret and told her what had happened. There was a long silence afterwards. 'Have you asked him about it?' Poppet asked.

'I'm hardly going to tell him I was poking round in his cupboards, am I? Can you imagine how that would go down?'

The hollow feeling of dismay she'd had in her stomach since yesterday just wouldn't go away. Elliot had come back from work with a beautiful bunch of flowers for her and had been extra lovely, insisting on cooking dinner for Lizzy and paying for a cab to get her home early the next morning. It had only made Lizzy paranoid. Did he have a guilty conscience?

'Everyone has pictures of their ex tucked away,' Poppet reasoned. 'I wouldn't read too much into it.'

'Oh, come on, Pops. If you were going out with a bloke who'd been dumped by his fiancée and you'd found a photographic tribute of their amazing life together hidden away on a shelf, would *you* be happy about it?'

'No,' she admitted. 'I guess not.'

Lizzy stared gloomily into the street. Why the hell had she opened the box? It had been better not knowing.

The next day was Haven's Christmas lunch. Antonia had announced that there were no funds for frivolity in the company pot, so everyone was paying for it themselves. There had been a bit of a hoo-ha in certain factions when Bianca had suggested going to Nobu followed by the notorious Box nightclub, but in the end Antonia had stepped in and announced that they were going to a restaurant on the Kings Road. It was owned by an old friend of Antonia's, apparently, who would do them some kind of deal. It would probably still end up costing more than what most Haven employees earned in a week, but no one had dared protest.

In the run-up to Christmas Antonia had turned into the anti-Christ and had banned sugar from the office because she thought it was affecting everyone's performance, so Lizzy and her colleagues had been reduced to sneakily eating mince pies and advent calendar chocolates under their desks. Antonia had been in a foul mood for weeks, and because she conducted all her affairs on her mobile in the middle of the office, everyone knew she was 'fucking stressed' about not getting any new business. They'd lost out on two pitches recently, because Antonia never gave her team enough time to prepare and they always went in on the back foot. Without Lizzy's more established clients and Jocasta Reynolds-Johnson's sizable retainer, things would be looking very bleak indeed.

Added to which, Lizzy was dangling on permanent tenterhooks. Every time Antonia came over to her desk or her name flashed up in Lizzy's inbox, Lizzy's heart would leap into her mouth. It was only a matter of time before her boss found out about Karen Jones. All Lizzy could do was wait for the axe to fall and hope – no, *pray* – that Antonia would show leniency and not sack her on the spot.

At five to twelve they downed tools and went to catch a bus to the nearby Kings Road, all dressed up in their Christmas finery. Antonia had already gone ahead in a cab, muttering something about an important meeting, but Bianca had overheard her in the corridor changing the time of her pedicure.

Someone had brought along a bottle of Jägermeister for the journey, but Lizzy just couldn't get in a festive mood. Elliot kept asking if she was all right, but Lizzy could hardly tell him the truth and own up that she'd been through his private possessions.

To make matters even worse, she'd woken up that day really missing Nic. It just felt so *weird* that she wasn't in Lizzy's life. It was always there on the periphery of Lizzy's vision, no matter what direction she looked in. The fact that it was Christmas made Nic's absence even more apparent and horrible. Lizzy had bought her presents months ago: a gift voucher to the Go Ape theme park and the *Ragga Dancefloor Anthems 1992* album Lizzy had found on eBay. (Nic was stuck in a musical time warp.) The gifts were gathering dust on Lizzy's sideboard at home, destined to never get opened.

Lizzy still had no idea what she'd done wrong.

Sometimes friends just fell out, but there had been no bubbling tension under the surface, or a feeling of drifting apart. Not that Lizzy was aware of anyway, but then again, since when was she the best person to judge what was really going on with someone? *Oh Nic!* she thought miserably. *I need you.* Her friend had always been able to cut through the crap and see things for how they were.

The restaurant was at the unfashionable end of the Kings Road and was decked out like a retro alpine ski lodge with an eighties menu to match. The owner was a woman called Saskia, who looked like she weighed about the same amount as one of Antonia's calves, and who was dressed entirely in maroon velvet. Judging from the rapturous welcome they'd received from Saskia and the calamitous shouting coming from the kitchen, Lizzy got the impression they weren't used to a glut of customers. They were the only party there, which was lucky as the place was tiny.

Lizzy found herself between Bianca and the work-experience girl, who'd ended up getting a last-minute invite. The girl was scarily ambitious and by the time the first course had turned up – a choice of melon balls or a sickly-looking prawn cocktail – Lizzy had been asked twice about when she was thinking about moving on.

Antonia had turned up in a pair of flip-flops with newly pink toenails and a Heal's bag full of Happy Halos, which she'd promptly handed round. 'I want you all to go into at least five bars on the way home with these on and spread the Halo love,' she had ordered. 'Somebody has to get this bugger promoted.' She had shot Lizzy a dirty look.

'Have you thought about ringing round a few journalists and asking them to do a review on it?' the workie suggested. 'I'm sure they wouldn't mind.'

Lizzy smiled through gritted teeth. 'I'll bear that in mind, thanks.'

The restaurant was BYO – Saskia had blithely mentioned something about a police raid and losing their alcohol licence, so everyone kept traipsing out to the nearest off-licence. By the time dessert came round, most people were absolutely trollied.

'So why are you so happy at the moment?' Antonia boomed at Lizzy. Her cheeks were even redder than normal. She'd been quite happy to sit there all afternoon and drink other people's wine.

'What do you mean?' Lizzy gazed at the rather plastic-looking rum baba on her plate and had a disturbing flashback of *This Morning*.

'You're walking round with a smile like the Cheshire cat at the moment. You've got a new fella, haven't you?'

Lizzy glanced round. The rest of the table was playing a game of 'I Have Never'.

'I might have,' she said cagily.

'I *knew* it!' Bianca declared. 'It's so obvs!'

'Is it?' Lizzy thought she had been playing it all discreet and knowingly, the way Frenchwomen always did in films when they were having a liaison with a rich and powerful man.

'Totes!' Bianca chortled. 'You've been coming into work with your hair all mussed up at the back and you're always ten minutes late these days.'

'You filthy little shagger,' Antonia said with relish.

'Antonia!'

'I'm not saying it like it's a bad thing.' She stuck a spoon into her tiramisu. 'Somebody's got to be having it these days.'

'Spill the beans!' Bianca said excitedly. 'Who's the hottie?'

'It's just this guy.'

'Sweets, I need deets!'

'She's probably embarrassed about him,' Antonia boomed. 'Is he a litter-picker or something?'

'No, actually,' Lizzy said coldly.

'Who is he then?' she demanded. 'I don't know what the big secret is, it's not like I'm going to have heard of him.'

Lizzy gazed at her boss across the table. Pink lipstick was smeared across Antonia's horse-like front teeth. *Rise above it*, Lizzy told herself. *Rise above it and change the subject. Antonia doesn't need to know anything about your private life.*

'Actually I think you might know him. Elliot Anderson?'

Antonia looked up from her pudding. 'Elliot Anderson from the *FT*? *News at Ten* Elliot Anderson who was engaged to Amber de la Haye?'

'Is he the guy who looks a bit like Eddie Redmayne?' Bianca squealed. 'He is totally hot!'

'You?' Antonia was looking incredulous. 'And him?'

'What's so weird about that?' Lizzy said defensively.

'Nothing, except that I happened to have dinner with Tils last week at Highroad House and Elliot and Amber were at the table next to us.'

Lizzy went cold. 'What?'

'When was it now?' Antonia gazed at the ceiling. 'It must have been a Wednesday because I'd just been to see my kinesiology woman.'

Lizzy was frantically rewinding in her head. *Wednesday. Wednesday. Wednesday.* Elliot had told her he'd gone to meet a work contact!

'They looked *very* cosy together,' Antonia continued. 'They had the table in the corner by the fireplace, the one you always ask for if you don't want to be disturbed. I'm sure it was only because the place was pretty busy that night,' she added innocently.

'Sweets, are you OK?' Bianca asked.

'Oh, *Wednesday*! Sorry, I'd just got my dates mixed up,' Lizzy told her boss, gulping back the panic. 'I thought they were meeting Tuesday night.'

Antonia's face fell. 'You knew?'

'Of course I did. It's all totally cool. Amber and Elliot were together such a long time, they're still really good friends.'

Bianca frowned. 'I'm not sure I'd be happy about my boyfriend meeting up with his ex-beautiful-fashion-designer-fiancée.'

'Really, it's not like that.' Lizzy stood up. 'Would you excuse me? I must go to the loo.'

The Ladies were two nightclub-style cubicles that afforded no privacy, but luckily they were empty. Lizzy went into the furthest one and sank down on the seat. She felt like she'd been kicked in the stomach. Why hadn't Elliot said anything? Was Antonia making it up? Lizzy stared at the plastic toilet door. Even her boss wasn't that vindictive.

She got her phone out but there was no reception. Lizzy unlocked the cubicle and stood in front of the mirror, inhaling deep, juddering breaths to calm down. *There has to be an explanation. There has to be an explanation.*

So why didn't he tell you? the Voice of Reason chimed in. *If it was just an innocent meetup, why didn't Elliot tell you?* And then came the creeping thought: *You knew something wasn't right.*

The Kings Road was alive with Christmas action. Lizzy stood on the pavement in her dress clutching her handbag. Her coat was still in the restaurant along with her Secret Santa present, but there was no way she could go back in now. She'd just have to text an excuse to Bianca about feeling ill.

She dialled Poppet's number, but it went straight to voicemail. Elliot had told her he was going for work drinks, but as Lizzy stood on that cold, noisy, brightly lit street, she instinctively knew it was a lie. She *knew* with that sixth sense a girl sometimes got, that gut-churning, throat-tightening *I'm-going-to-be-sick* feeling, that he was with Amber. She should have trusted her instinct from the start! Instead she'd shoved the niggling doubts to the back of her mind, because she didn't want to ruin the perfect picture she'd created. Now the paranoia had been ignited with a vengeance and was spreading like wildfire through her body.

Lizzy walked right out into the middle of the road,

narrowly avoiding a passing car. The cab behind it screeched to a halt.

'Eagle Wharf please, on the Embankment,' she told the driver.

The journey through the rush-hour traffic was the longest forty minutes of Lizzy's life. Paying the driver the eye-watering fare, she started to zigzag her way down the myriad of streets towards the river. 'You'll catch your death dressed like that!' a woman dog-walker called as she ran past, but Lizzy barely heard her.

The apartment block was mainly in darkness, the odd rectangle of light in amongst the black windows. Most people were probably out celebrating, just as Lizzy should have still been in the warm, rowdy restaurant with her work colleagues, instead of standing there by the freezing Thames in heels and a little party dress.

She stood in front of the building and tried to work out which one was Elliot's apartment. Lizzy counted up the floors and found his living-room window. There were no lights on. No one was home.

Lizzy took a long, grounding breath. She was going out of her mind! She'd just hared across London on a ridiculously paranoid whim. Although it still didn't answer why Elliot had lied about going for dinner with his ex-fiancée . . .

There will be a reason, she told herself. *There's always a reason. Elliot's a good guy. He wouldn't do that to me. I bet Antonia did get it wrong.*

At that moment a light suddenly came on. Lizzy's

heart leapt into her mouth. At the same time, a figure hurried round the back of the apartments, the same way Lizzy had come. He or she was wearing a long trench coat and a black beanie hat, but as the figure hurried up the front steps and went inside, Lizzy caught a glimpse of the beautiful face. A chill went through her that had nothing to do with the weather.

It was Amber.

The next moment the blinds came down in Elliot's living-room window and Lizzy was left standing alone in the cold.

Chapter 52

Lizzy finally made it into the office the next day at 11 a.m. Bianca was slouched at her desk, studying her eyebrows in a magnifying mirror. She glanced up and did a double-take. 'Sweets, you look awful!'

Lizzy took her coat off and sat down at her desk.

'How weird only you got food poisoning and the rest of us were OK.' Bianca leant across her desk. 'OMG, things totally kicked off after you'd gone!'

'Did they?' Lizzy said listlessly.

'Antonia ended up having a massive row with Jocasta and she's lost the Zen Ten account!'

Lizzy looked at her colleague. Words were coming out of Bianca's mouth but they were making no sense.

'Jocasta phoned when we were still at the table and started kicking off about something. Antonia was pretty pissed by then and said she was fed up with being Jocasta's emotional punchbag, to which Jocasta apparently said that that was *exactly* what Antonia was there for, and while she was on the subject, Antonia was pretty shit at it. She fired Antonia on the spot!'

Bianca paused for breath. 'There was lots of shouting about boundaries and invasion issues.'

Lizzy looked over at the conference room. Antonia was wildly gesticulating on the phone to someone.

'She was in there when I came in,' Bianca whispered. 'I heard her going mental about something to do with Karen Jones as well. What's that about?'

Lizzy didn't even bother turning her computer on. A few minutes later the door to the conference room opened.

'A word, Lizzy,' Antonia said coldly.

Both company laptops were open and the table was littered with files and invoices. Antonia sat back down in her chair.

'Would you like to explain why Karen Jones is still only paying fifty per cent of her monthly retainer?'

'I lied to you,' Lizzy said dully. 'She was having money worries, so I gave her a reduced rate. I thought she'd be able to pay the money back.'

Antonia's nostrils flared. 'And you didn't think to consult me about this?'

'I knew you'd say no.'

'Of course I would have said no!' Antonia shouted. 'We're running a business here, not a fucking charity!'

Lizzy looked at the floor. There was a bit of gold foil scrunched up by her feet: the telltale evidence of someone's illicit chocolate snack.

'Well?' Antonia demanded. 'Aren't you even going to defend yourself?'

'There's nothing to defend.'

'I'm suspending you with immediate effect.' Antonia gave Lizzy a long hard stare. 'It goes without saying how shocked and disappointed I am. You're meant to be a trusted senior member of staff.' She shuffled some papers. 'We'll be in touch on how to proceed with your disciplinary, but it goes without saying that your future looks *extremely* bleak at Haven PR.'

Lizzy gazed at the woman she'd worked her arse off for for the last two years. 'You don't have to suspend me.'

'I don't think you're in any position to tell me what to do,' Antonia said loftily.

'Yes I am, because I quit.' Lizzy turned and walked out, leaving her boss open-mouthed at the table.

Lizzy emerged into bright sunlight outside the Haven office. Everything looked the same, but Lizzy had the strangest sensation that she was on a stage and that the familiar landmarks were props and the Christmas shoppers scurrying past with bags were actors, all taking part in the production. Nothing felt real. She was in free fall and there was nobody to put their hand out and catch her.

What do I do now? Where do I go? She was in a horrible dream that she had no way of waking up from.

She went into the park across the road and sat down on a damp bench. Her mobile started buzzing in her bag. Lizzy knew who it was. Elliot had left her two voicemails last night and he'd called again this morning.

Lizzy almost let the phone ring out before answering. 'Hi.'

'You're alive!' He did a good impression of sounding relieved. 'I was about to send out the search and rescue team.'

'My phone died,' Lizzy said.

'You could have at least sent me an email. I was starting to get worried.'

The sheer casualness of his deception took Lizzy's breath away. 'How were your work drinks?' Each word lodged painfully in her throat.

'Nothing special.' He sounded utterly normal. 'I was tucked up in bed by eleven.'

Lizzy stared across the park. A small dog was running across the grass after the ball its owner had just thrown. A weird, detached part of her wanted to smile at the absurdity. Was she really sitting here on this bench, having this conversation with the man that she'd fallen in love with? It was so clichéd it was almost comical.

'Where were your work drinks?' she asked.

Elliot paused for a fraction too long. 'At a bar in the City.'

'What was it called?'

'I can't remember.'

A steady anger started to build inside Lizzy. 'You can't remember the name of the bar you had your work Christmas drinks in?'

Silence. Lizzy could almost hear his brain whirring, going on the defensive, looking for an escape route.

'What's this about, Lizzy?' he asked.

'Do you want to tell me where you really were last night?'

'I just told you. I was out for work drinks.'

'No,' she said very slowly and deliberately. 'You were at your place with Amber.'

More silence. 'How do you know that?'

'I saw you through your living-room window.'

'You were spying on us?'

'I wasn't spying! I just had this gut instinct, which as it happened turned out to be right.' Lizzy stopped. 'Hold on a minute, *I'm* not the one who's done something wrong here. Don't you dare turn it back on me!'

She expected a blustering denial from Elliot, or at least him begging forgiveness. The lack of any reaction was damning.

'So you're not denying you were with her?'

'No,' he said simply.

Lizzy's heart started to pound. Was this really happening?

'Where are you?' he asked. 'We need to talk.'

'I've think I've heard all I need to hear!'

'Lizzy, please.' Elliot lowered his voice. 'Let me see you face to face so I can explain.'

She gripped on to her phone. 'Just tell me one thing, Elliot. Have you been meeting up with Amber since you and I have been together?'

Lizzy was willing him to give her an explanation, a way out of this nightmare. *Tell me it's not how it looks.*

'Yes, but—' He started blustering. 'Lizzy, just listen for a moment . . .'

'You *bastard*.' She hung up and burst into tears.

Chapter 53

The last week before Christmas had descended into the usual festive chaos. People were staggering from one drinks party to the next with the exhausted look of marathon runners at mile twenty-four. The exodus had started out of the major airports as millions headed off on their well-earned breaks. It had become perfectly acceptable to see grown men going to work in the mornings with Santa hats on, and there were urban myths about commuters offering their seats to each other on the Underground. Everyone had been infected by the happy, silly giddiness before they waved goodbye to work for ten days and entered a world where calories ceased to have any meaning and it was acceptable to start on the Prosecco at breakfast.

Everyone that was, except Lizzy. She had lost her job, she had lost Elliot, and for the first time ever, she had lost her faith in the human race. After putting down the phone on Elliot, she had packed her bags and gone to stay with Poppet, and she'd been there ever since, drifting round in her pajamas like a ghost.

Lizzy had never been (knowingly) cheated on before, and she'd been shocked by her physical reaction. When she'd watched a moment of betrayal in a film or, say, in *EastEnders*, there had been lots of tears and shouting and one person would storm out of a room or throw an ornament or something, but that was nothing compared to what she'd experienced. When Elliot had admitted his infidelity (or *hadn't* admitted it, the cowardly bastard), Lizzy's heart had started beating so fast and so painfully that for a moment she'd honestly thought it had been about to pack up. Her whole body had been invaded by pins and needles that felt more like stabbing knives. It was like developing sudden frostbite, and she'd been frozen ever since.

To make matters worse, Elliot had started to call her incessantly. He obviously wanted to exorcize his guilty conscience, leaving rambling voicemails about how he'd messed everything up. Lizzy had started deleting them without even listening. She'd given Elliot every opportunity to explain himself, and he'd had nothing to say. There was nothing *to* say. How do you defend the incontrovertible truth that you're in love with another woman and always will be?

She spent hours going over little things Elliot had said or done, tormenting herself even further. He was a private person and Lizzy had always respected that. But now, when she thought about it, there was never any accidental *stuff* that had spilled out of his life the way it normally did when you were seeing someone. Elliot had only ever given her what he'd wanted to. For example, wasn't it funny how he never left his iPhone lying around? Or how he always seemed to be cutting a call short as he walked up to her? When he'd been on his iPad all those times in the coffee shop, Lizzy had never really known what he had been doing. Had he and Amber been instant-messaging each other while Lizzy had been sat there blowing on the froth of her latte like a clueless fuckwit? What about all the evenings he had worked late, the times he had turned his phone off because he was in meetings or interviewing somebody? Lizzy had worked with enough journalists to know that they *always* had their phone on. That time she'd caught him on his phone in the corner of M&M's World and he'd fobbed her off and changed the subject. Hadn't fifteen years of reading women's magazines taught her *anything*?

And yet, in amongst all these dark thoughts, there was a tiny part of Lizzy that still wanted to believe. Still wanted to believe that Elliot *had* genuinely felt something for her, that he'd meant some of the things he'd said. She wanted to believe that she hadn't imagined the way they'd grin at each other like a pair of idiots for minutes on end, or the way Elliot had held her in bed after sex, or that annoying protective-man thing he did when he took her hand at the side of the road, as if Lizzy wasn't trusted to get across by herself. The way he'd made her *feel*, even when Lizzy hadn't been with him. It had all felt so *real*. Maybe Elliot had convinced himself that he had felt something for Lizzy, but when the love of his life had clicked her fingers, he'd gone running. *Because if you want to trick yourself that something is there with someone, it's easier to do than you think.*

*

Poppet came back at seven o'clock to find Lizzy still lying in the same position on the sofa that she'd left her in that morning.

'I thought you had your work Christmas party tonight,' Lizzy said dully.

'I wanted to see if you were all right. You haven't been answering your phone.'

'I had it on silent.' Lizzy was staring mindlessly at an episode of *The Hairy Bikers*. She bet Dave and Si didn't take women's hearts in their dependable, floury hands and smash them into smithereens on the kitchen floor.

'Is Elliot still trying to get hold of you?'

Lizzy nodded miserably. 'I wish he'd just leave me alone.'

'Do you think it would help if you did see him? It might give you some closure.'

'What's the point, Pops? It's for his benefit, not mine. Mr Bloody Principled has been caught with his hand in the cookie jar, and now he wants me to forgive him so he can walk away with his decency intact. I'm not giving him the satisfaction.'

Poppet sat down next to her. 'You're worth ten of Amber. You do know that, don't you?'

'Amber is a beautiful, world-famous fashion designer who once helped ship two thousand stray puppies out of North Korea,' Lizzy said dully. 'I used to peddle suppositories for a living. I'm not exactly catch of the century.'

There was a silence. 'Right, I'm staying in tonight,' Poppet announced.

'Don't be daft; you can't miss your work do.'

'I'd much rather stay in with you. Besides, I've been

402

drunk eleven nights in a row and I can't do up the top button of any of my work skirts.' Poppet patted Lizzy's leg. 'We'll have a lovely night in together watching schmaltzy Christmassy films and I'll cook you something nice. Oh no!'

Big fat tears were running down the side of Lizzy's face and plopping on to the embroidered petal pillow.

'We don't have to watch schmaltzy Christmassy films if it upsets you.' Poppet looked round for the remote. 'I think there's something on with Jean-Claude Van Damme in it.'

'It's n-n-not the schmaltzy Christmassy films,' Lizzy gulped.

'Oh sweetheart.' Poppet looked close to tears herself. 'I'm so, so sorry.'

Lizzy let herself be scooped up into Poppet's arms and cradled like a child. 'Why am I always the girl who nobody wants?' she sobbed.

Chapter 54

The Three Crowns at the end of Poppet's road had to be one of the only pubs in London that hadn't been given the gastro facelift. At midday Lizzy was sitting in the gloomy saloon bar with a Baileys in front of her. The only other customers were a heavily tattooed skinhead with no teeth, and two old men in flat caps sat at one of the round tables by the door arguing about horse racing. The smoking ban obviously hadn't reached the clientele of the Three Crowns, because everyone apart from Lizzy, the barman included, was chain-smoking.

She gazed through the fug of nicotine around her at the peeling flock wallpaper and stained seats. The only concession to Christmas decorations was a single paltry line of tinsel along the bar. The place had definitely seen better days, but Lizzy had needed to get out of the flat. There was only so much internal monologue a person could take. Besides, Poppet's dad was coming over to fix the flickering light in the hallway and Lizzy couldn't face the inevitable questions. Poppet's dad was a very nice man, but he'd once asked Lizzy if she'd ever considered learning to sew to make herself more attractive to men.

'Another one of those, love?' the barman asked.

Lizzy looked at her glass. A treble Baileys went down so quickly. 'Better make it half a lager,' she said gloomily. Now she was unemployed she didn't have the money for such luxuries.

A loud noise suddenly blared out from nowhere, interrupting the funereal quiet. Lizzy reached for her phone. Poppet had changed her ringtone to Destiny's Child's 'Survivor' to try and put Lizzy in a more positive state of mind.

It was her mother. 'I just tried you at work and they said you weren't in.'

'That's because I've been sacked for misconduct and I'm now sitting in an old man's pub, getting drunk by myself.'

'Ha ha, very funny, darling. Quick question! Do you think Elliot would like a pair of leather gloves?'

Lizzy gazed at the wallpaper. Was that a blood splatter, or was it meant to be part of the pattern? 'What?'

'I *said*, would Elliot like a pair of black-leather driving gloves for Christmas? I ended up buying two pairs for your father, and if you think Elliot would like them it would save me a trip back to Bluewater.'

'Mum, I can't really talk about this now.'

'Getting an answer out of you kids about Christmas is like getting blood out of a stone! Robbie still hasn't got back to me about whether he wants a stocking this year. I know Hayley always told us not to bother because she liked doing one for him, but do you think he'd like one from us again now? Or is he too old? And what are your thoughts on a chocolate yule log?'

One of the old men blew his nose violently into a grubby tartan handkerchief. Lizzy watched him open it and inspect the contents, his eyes widening in wonder as if he'd discovered a priceless treasure.

'Is that a trumpet playing in the background?' Mrs Spellman asked. 'Are you at a Christmas concert?'

'I have to go,' Lizzy said. And for the first time in her life, she hung up on her mother.

The toothless tattooed guy had been loitering by the fruit machine shooting Lizzy looks. Sensing an opening, he sidled over.

'All right darlin'?' said a raspy voice.

Lizzy gazed up at the walking Etch A Sketch standing in front of her. The man had 'Candice' tattooed on his neck, 'Mayhem' across one sinewy bicep and 'Mad in Britain' across the other. And wait, was that a mermaid bleeding from the eyes on his forearm?

'What's a pretty girl . . .' He clocked Lizzy's pajama bottoms. 'What's someone like you doing in a dump like this?'

'I wouldn't come too close if I were you. I can't remember the last time I brushed my teeth, and my breath could melt pavements.' Lizzy blew on her hand for confirmation. 'Whoa!'

Toothless Tattoo Man's smile faltered.

'How can I help?' she asked briskly. 'Have you come to chat me up?'

'Well babe, I wouldn't put it exactly like that . . .'

'Because I may as well tell you first, I'm a woman on

the edge. I've just lost my job. And I've just found out that the man I was in love with – actually, can I really say that?' Lizzy sat back and pondered it. 'I mean, I *thought* it was love because every second with him felt like I was floating on air, and I wanted to burst into hysterical laughter at everything – even when I tracked dog poo into the flat and thought it was the bins for two days – because everything was so bright and beautiful and so bloody *brilliant*, and every second we were apart it was like I was holding my breath until the next time I saw him, and I could start living again.' Lizzy drew a breath. 'That sounds very dramatic, doesn't it? But that's what it felt like. Have *you* ever felt that with someone?' she asked, not waiting for an answer. 'But while all that was going on with *me*, it turns out that *I* was just a stop-gap to him! What one might call' – Lizzy winked at him horribly and did the quote marks – '"a filling-in-the-timer".'

Toothless Tattoo Man shot the barman a nervous glance.

'Never mind!' Lizzy said brightly. 'Where were we? Ah yes, the man I was in love with, who has just run back to his beautiful fashion-designer fiancée.' She took another slurp of her lager. 'So now *I'm* falling apart,' she announced. 'With no idea how to proceed with my life from now on, or even how to get in the shower in the morning and get dressed and go about my business like a normal person. Look!' She stuck a bare foot out of her UGG boot. 'I've even stopped shaving my toes!'

Tattoo Man's face dropped. 'Sorry, babe, I've just remembered I've gotta go and meet a man about a dog.'

Lizzy watched him leave with a morbid self-satisfaction. So now she even repulsed men who looked like they'd just escaped from the lifer's wing at a high-security prison.

An hour and two more halves of lager later she trudged back to the flat. *You will get through this*, she told herself. *You just don't know how yet.*

There was a strange trilling noise as Lizzy let herself in. Did Poppet have a burglar alarm that she hadn't told Lizzy about? A few moments later Lizzy realized it was a landline phone ringing. Good Lord, did anyone under the age of sixty even own one of these any more?

She located the phone next to the cabinet of vintage teacups. It had to be one of those old-fashioned ones with the round dial that took about two days to call a number. Lizzy lifted the receiver to her ear. 'Hello?'

It wasn't someone trying to sell Lizzy life insurance. 'I told you to take your phone off silent!' Poppet exclaimed.

'Sorry, my mum keeps calling and I just can't face telling her anything yet.' Lizzy eyed up the bottle of amaretto on the top of the cabinet.

'Do you follow Tiana Dawson on Twitter?'

The supermodel with the crying baby Lizzy had gone up to? It seemed like another lifetime ago. 'Yeah, why?'

'She's just tweeted about Night Night Baby!'

'What?' Lizzy ran over to her bag and pulled out her phone. Bypassing the missed calls, she went straight on to her Twitter account. There it was, Tiana Dawson tweeting to her 1.7 million followers.

Happy baby means happy mummy! Can't say how much this product has saved my life!

There was a shot of a bottle of Night Night Baby lavender oil next to an adorable sleeping child.

'The *MailOnline* have already picked up on the story and are calling it a miracle for stressed-out babies and mothers!' Poppet said excitedly. 'This is really good, isn't it?'

It was better than good. Lizzy rang off and listened to her voicemails. There were three from Karen, each one increasingly more excited.

'Phone ringing off the hook . . . orders flooding in . . . can't keep up . . . Oh Lizzy, this has saved us!'

There was another voicemail by the time she had finished listening, this time from a very contrite-sounding Antonia. 'Bianca mentioned about your chance meeting with Tiana Dawson. Maybe I've been a little hasty about the . . . situation. I'd very much appreciate it, Lizzy, if you could give me a call about coming back in.' Antonia emitted an over-hearty laugh. 'The sooner the better! The place isn't the same without you.'

More like she hadn't got anyone to do her donkey-work for her, but Lizzy couldn't stop grinning. They'd only gone and got the PR miracle she'd been praying for! Now she could balance the books at Haven, and Karen wouldn't lose her house after all.

Her phone buzzed again. 'Karen?' Lizzy said joyfully. 'I can't believe it! Didn't I tell you it would all come good?'

'It's me.' The voice was so husky it took a moment for Lizzy to realize who it was.

Her temporary high drained away. 'What do you want, Elliot?' she asked coldly.

'I need to see you. Please, Lizzy.'

'Well, I don't want to see you! Just leave me alone!'

Before he could say another word Lizzy hurled the phone across the room. Narrowly missing Poppet's *Home Sweet Home* tapestry, it hit the wall and bounced off with an ominous crack.

Lizzy stood there breathing heavily, shocked at what she'd just done. *I've turned into the woman who throws things across rooms.* If that's what it took to get Elliot Anderson out of her life, so be it.

Chapter 55

Worried about Lizzy's state of mind, Poppet had offered to take the day off work, but Lizzy had insisted it wasn't necessary. She was still wandering round the flat wearing three-day-old knickers and spending hours staring out of the window. It wasn't fair to inflict that on another person.

Lizzy spent the morning watching a special edition of *The Jeremy Kyle Show* ironically called 'Xmas Cheats!' She had briefly pondered whether to ring up the show to ask if they had any episodes planned for the future called 'Hairy-toed and Alone – Girls Left on Love's Scrapheap,' before deciding it was probably too niche.

As well as having no company, she now also had no phone. The two times Lizzy had been phoneless before (both, embarrassingly, when she'd dropped said phones in glasses of wine – try passing *that* off as water damage), it had felt like her right arm had been ripped off, but now it was a blessed relief. At least she could put off explaining to her family that she'd messed up her love life again. More importantly,

Elliot couldn't get hold of her and Lizzy could be left alone to grieve.

She still had contact with the outside world through email at least, on Poppet's ancient old Dell computer that weighed about three stone. Ironically, at a time when Lizzy didn't want to speak to anyone, everyone wanted to speak to her. Her inbox was full of requests from journalists for samples of Night Night Baby products and interviews with Karen Jones. Lizzy had forwarded them all on to Bianca to take care of. Even her ditzy colleague couldn't balls up this one.

She'd also had a message from her mother, who used email so rarely that Lizzy had forgotten she had a Hotmail account. It read like a wartime telegram with imaginary STOPS.

> Your father and I are worried. Robbie can't get hold of you either. Please call home. Love Mum.

Lizzy had just forwarded another glut of emails to Bianca when a name popped up in her inbox that made her heart lurch. It was from a member of the Anderson family, but it wasn't Elliot. It was Cassandra.

> My dear Lizzy, I hope you don't mind me emailing. I feel so dreadful about this whole business. Elliot has explained to me briefly what has happened. I know you must be feeling terribly hurt and betrayed right now, but please, won't you consider meeting up with him so he can tell you what really happened? I know he's hurting terribly as well.

Lizzy deleted the message. Anger burned in her belly. He was getting his *mother* to email on his behalf?

Did the man have no dignity? Why didn't he stop prolonging the agony and just concede that he was a duplicitous, lying, cheating bastard?

That afternoon she swung wildly between brief moments of cynical defiance and longer periods of black despair. She retired back to the sofa with the amaretto bottle to watch *The Polar Express* in the hope that if she gorged herself on Christmas films a little of the goodwill would transfer over, but all she could think about were the presents she hadn't bought and the job she didn't want to go back to and, surpassing all of that, the huge void Elliot had left in her life. *I'll be OK tomorrow*, she kept telling herself desperately. *I'll dust myself off and get on with things. Tomorrow I'll wake up and feel better.*

Except she didn't feel better. Every time she thought about Elliot's stocking fillers, wrapped at home in three-pound-a-sheet paper from Paperchase, the knife twisted in Lizzy's heart a little further. Or the hard-won tickets she'd got to the Young Vic to see the play Elliot had been raving about, followed by dinner at the new Ottolenghi place. The night would have cost her a fortune, but Lizzy had been flush with love, and money had meant nothing. Now she'd been left with tickets to a three-hour Chekhov performance, and a redundant table booking at the hottest restaurant in town. Christmas had always been her favourite time of year. Now it loomed before her, joyless and empty.

Day turned into night without Lizzy even being aware of it. She was sobbing at the John Lewis advert for the umpteenth time (she'd hit a new low when she'd welled up at the Iceland one earlier), when she thought she heard a knock on the front door.

Lizzy didn't pay much attention, but then she heard it again. She sat up and a half-eaten mince pie fell off her chest. Had it been the wind? A more disgusting thought: had it been *her* wind? There was another knock this time, louder. There was definitely someone there. *Poppet's dad again, perhaps?*

Lizzy got up and wrapped the blanket protectively around her. At least she knew it couldn't be Elliot because he didn't know where Poppet lived.

As she ventured into the hallway a shadow was clearly visible through the frosted-glass door panel. Oh God, it wasn't Poppet's pervy neighbour who always came round to ask her to put suncream on his back in the summer, was it?

Lizzy pulled the door open, ready to blast any amorous advances off with her dishevelled appearance, or failing that her unwashed odours, but it wasn't a seventy-plus pensioner waving a piece of mistletoe with a hopeful look on his face. It was Nic.

She stood on the doorstep in a new green duffle coat that Lizzy hadn't seen before, clutching a Tesco bag that looked full of wine.

'Hello,' she said in a small voice.

'Hello,' Lizzy said in a small voice back.

There was an awkward silence. 'Poppet's not in,' Lizzy said.

'I know, I came to see you.' Nic held up the carrier bag and grinned briefly, a flash of her old self back. 'I don't know about you, but I need a drink.'

414

Back inside they stood in the middle of the living room like two long-lost exes. 'I'm sorry the place is such a mess,' Lizzy said. 'I would have tidied up if I had known you were coming round.'

Nic made a small gesture, as if to say *that's the least of our worries*. 'Poppet told me. About you and Elliot. Are you OK?'

'Not really,' Lizzy admitted. And then: 'Are *you* OK?'

Nic shook her head wordlessly and burst into tears. 'Oh Lizzy! I'm sorry I've been such a bitch!'

They sat on the sofa together, arms round each other. Nic was inconsolable, her chest heaving with great gulping sobs. Lizzy had never seen her like this before.

'I've g-got something to tell you. You're g-going to think I'm a really bad p-p-person.'

'Nothing you could do would make me think you're a bad person,' Lizzy said tearfully. 'You haven't murdered anyone, have you?' she added, half-joking.

'It's only just below that.' Nic blew loudly into a tissue. 'I've been having an affair with Simon.'

It took a moment to digest the news. 'As in your boss Simon Hargreaves?'

'As in married Simon Hargreaves, who has two young kids and a lovely wife called Marcelle who lent me her lip gloss in the toilet at a work party.' Nic burst into floods of tears again. 'And I'm the home-wrecking cold-hearted career bitch!'

'Nic, you're not.' Lizzy looked at her distraught friend. 'Don't say that.'

'I never thought I'd be the girl who had the affair with her married boss. It just *happened*,' she said helplessly.

'How pathetic does that sound? Can you imagine me saying that to Simon's wife? "Sorry for breaking up your marriage, but these things just *happen*, yeah?"'

'What *did* happen?' Lizzy asked softly.

Nic started to cry again. 'We just spent loads of time together. It wasn't anything to do with him being powerful, or being a replacement father figure or anything, but because he was kind and funny and he listened to me. Stuff I *never* thought I'd wanted – he had moobs and a paunch for Christ's sake, but there was just this connection between us. He was my *friend* more than anything; the sex wasn't even that great. I just felt like I could tell him anything and he'd understand.'

'Pops and I are your friends, Nic. You could have told us.'

'I couldn't. I felt so ashamed. And then you had all that stuff going on with Elliot and it just brought out this misplaced guilt and rage in me, and for some reason I put it all on to you. I'm so sorry, Lizzy,' she said wretchedly. 'I cut you off because I knew I couldn't keep on pretending everything was fine, and I didn't want to face up to myself.'

Lizzy took the soggy tissue out of Nic's hands and gave her a new one.

'I did try to break it off a few times,' Nic said between sniffles. 'Simon said he loved me and that he wanted to be with me, but he couldn't leave until the kids were older. Jesus, listen to me! I've always thought I was so bloody clever and I ended up falling for the oldest lines in the book.'

A drip of snot fell off the end of her nose. 'The worse

thing of all is that I think Simon really does love me, the dickhead.'

'*Do* you want to make a go of things with him?' Lizzy asked tentatively.

Nic shook her head. 'I mean it this time. How could I ever look at myself again? How could I look at him, knowing what we'd done? S-s-so there you go,' she stammered. 'My dirty secret is out in the open. I don't blame you if you hate me. I'd feel the same.'

Lizzy gazed at the distraught, puffy-faced mess sitting beside her. 'I don't hate you,' she said simply. 'You're my friend, Nic, and I love you. That's never going to change.'

Nic stared up at Lizzy through reddened eyes. 'You really mean that?'

'Of course I mean it. Don't start crying again. Oh come here, you idiot, I've missed you so much!'

And that was it in a nutshell. Who was Lizzy to make a moral judgement? Could she one hundred per cent categorically state that she wouldn't have done the same thing if she'd been in Nic's position, and Elliot had still been going out with Amber? Until you were standing in a person's shoes, you never really knew what you would do. All Lizzy knew was that Nic was her friend, and she'd always been there for Lizzy. That was all that mattered.

'What are you going to do now?' she said after they'd had the world's longest hug.

'Look for a new job. Simon and I are being very sensible about it.' Nic allowed herself a wry smile. 'I suppose that's one positive thing about having an affair with a proper grown-up.' She gave a deep sigh.

'I don't know, maybe I need to take time out and take up knitting or something. Join this "home-spun revolution" Poppet keeps talking about.'

'It's "home-grown". And you'd be terrible at knitting.'

'I know, but something's got to give. I spend half my life in luxury hotels and I'm never on holiday. My hair's falling out with the stress, but I can't take the time off work to go and see a trichologist. We walk round thinking we're owning it when actually we're just other people's puppets. Well I did, anyway.' She sighed again. 'I dunno, I might start my own business.'

'Do you need anyone to come and work for you?' Lizzy thought about it. 'Scrap that, if you were my boss I'd be terrified of you.'

Nic gave her a rueful smile. 'Poppet told me about what happened at work. And all that stuff with Elliot. Lizzy, I'm so sorry I've been wrapped up in my own stupid crap.'

Lizzy gave a desolate shrug. 'It's OK. There's nothing to say really.'

Nic's phone started ringing. 'It's probably Poppet,' she said. 'Making sure that we haven't torn each other apart.'

She pulled it out of her handbag and looked at the screen. 'I don't recognize the number.'

'Oh God, do you think Pops has got so pissed she's lost her handbag again? I don't think I can go through the trauma of hearing how much it costs to replace her make-up collection!'

'We'll soon find out.' Nic put the phone to her ear. 'Hello?'

Lizzy watched her friend's face as she listened to the person on the other end. First Nic's eyebrows shot up, then she looked angry, and then she opened her mouth as if she wanted to jump in and say something, before shutting it again.

'OK,' she said eventually. 'I'll ask her.'

Nic put her hand over the mouthpiece. 'It's Amber. She wants to talk to you.'

'What?! How the hell did she get your number?'

Nic shook her head. 'She has to speak to you urgently.'

'Well, I'm not talking to her!' It was lucky Lizzy wasn't standing up because she would have been knocked off her feet by the woman's front. Had Amber actually rung up to rub Lizzy's nose in it?

Nic went back on the phone. 'She doesn't want to speak to you.' There was another long pause as Nic listened.

'She says she has to speak to you in the next five minutes,' she told Lizzy.

'Well, I don't want to speak to her, like, ever!' Lizzy whispered violently.

'She says you've got it all wrong and things aren't what they seem!' Nic whispered back. 'You know what, Lizzy? Six months ago I would have told the girl to take a running jump, but I've realized that things aren't always in black and white. Maybe you should give Amber the chance to explain?'

'Oh for God's sake!' Lizzy snatched the phone off Nic. 'Yes?'

'Lizzy?' It was Amber's well-spoken voice, slightly breathless.

'This is Lizzy,' she said, determined to keep an icy

composure even though she felt like being sick. 'What do you want?'

'Look, I realize that Elliot and I aren't your favourite people right now . . .'

Lizzy snorted mirthlessly. 'What gave you that impression?'

'Oh God. He's handled this whole thing *so* badly.' Amber gave a nervous laugh. 'He's always been like this when it comes to anything emotional. Turns into a complete mute.'

'I don't need you to ring up and tell me Elliot's handled this badly,' Lizzy said coolly. 'Now, if you don't mind—'

'Please don't hang up, Lizzy,' Amber pleaded.

'Give me one reason why I shouldn't.'

'Elliot's asked me to pass on a message and it's imperative that you listen. You have to turn on your television right now.'

Lizzy glanced at Nic. 'Why? I don't understand—'

'There's no time to explain! Turn to the ITV News now. Just trust me, OK?'

'She's saying she wants us to turn over to ITV!' Lizzy whispered faintly.

Nic grabbed the remote control. The *News at Ten* was on. Lizzy's heart skipped a beat as she saw Elliot sitting across the desk from the presenter Mark Austin.

'That was our economics correspondent, Elliot Anderson, on the latest controversy over mortgage debt. Thank you, Elliot.' Mark turned back to the camera. 'Coming up . . .'

Lizzy watched as Elliot leant across the desk. 'Mark, if I could just interrupt.'

The newsreader's eyebrows momentarily shot up.

'It won't take a moment.' Elliot gazed straight into the camera. 'This is a message for Lizzy Spellman. I really hope she's watching the news for once and not *The Kardashian Christmas Special*, because otherwise I'm going to be making a real idiot of myself for no reason.'

'Oh my God,' Nic breathed.

'Lizzy.' Elliot's green eyes gleamed brightly. 'I know you don't want to talk to me right now and I don't blame you. But please believe me when I say it's not how it looks, and I love you, Lizzy, and I want to explain. Will you meet me at the place I said I'd only go to over my dead body? In say, thirty minutes?' He gave Mark Austin an apologetic smile. 'That's it. Thank you.'

'Well, that was a bit unexpected,' the ITV anchor said smoothly. 'Lizzy Spellman, whoever you are, I hope you'll go and meet Elliot. Coming up next . . .'

Nic clicked the TV off.

'Oh my God!' they both screamed at each other.

'What do I do?' Lizzy shouted.

In her excitement Nic had dropped the phone and switched it on to loudspeaker. 'Hello? Is anyone there?' Amber's disembodied voice crackled into the room.

'Go!' Nic urged. 'I'll deal with the ex-fiancée!'

'But . . . what . . .'

'What are you waiting for?' Nic grinned. 'Go and find him, Lizzy!'

Lizzy jumped up. 'I'm going!' she said ecstatically. 'Oh Nic, what does he mean, it's not how it looks?'

'You'll have to ask him!'

'He said he loved me!'

'I know!'

'He hasn't been having an affair with Amber!'

'So it would seem.'

'Oh, I am going to *kill* him. Why didn't he just tell me that?'

'In his defence, you haven't been the world's most contactable woman lately,' Nic said dryly.

'I've got to get out of here!' Lizzy rushed over to the door.

'Lizzy?'

She stopped and turned round. 'Yes?'

Nic waved her hand in front of her nose. 'You might want to clean your teeth first.'

Chapter 56

Lizzy's heart was pounding as she came out of the tube station. Had she understood Elliot's message? Was this the place she was supposed to meet him?

Leicester Square was like the Notting Hill carnival in full swing. Lizzy fought her way through the hordes of tourists, drunks and rickshaw drivers towards M&M's World. She couldn't see Elliot standing outside the entrance. All she could do was wait.

Ten minutes later she was beginning to lose hope. Either she'd got it wrong, or Elliot wasn't coming. Her BlackBerry was still currently in three pieces on Poppet's sideboard, so she couldn't even call him. *Note to future self: being a drama queen is pointless and completely inconvenient.*

Lizzy scanned the jostling crowds again. There was no sign of him. She was about to start trudging back to the tube when something caught her eye. A familiar, unmistakable sight was bobbing towards her above the sea of heads. 'Oh,' she breathed. 'You have got to be kidding me.'

Elliot walked up to her wearing a pink Happy Halo on his head. The Halo clashed horribly with his hair.

He smiled cautiously. 'Seeing as these things brought us together in the first place, I was hoping they'd work their magic again.'

He looked so adorable and ridiculous that Lizzy felt herself starting to melt, but she had to be strong. She stayed where she was, keeping distance between them. 'What the hell is going on, Elliot?'

He sighed heavily. 'I've got a lot of explaining to do.'

'You certainly have,' Lizzy said icily.

'Can we go somewhere quieter to talk?'

She folded her arms. 'I'm perfectly fine standing here.'

Elliot looked like he was about to protest, but then thought better of it. 'OK. You're right. I have been seeing Amber behind your back. But not like that,' he added hurriedly when he saw Lizzy's face. 'Oh God,' he muttered. 'I've made a right pig's ear of this.'

He took a deep breath. 'I have been seeing Amber.' He corrected himself again. 'I've been *meeting* with Amber, but just as friends. She was in trouble and she needed my help.'

Lizzy didn't say anything. The stage was all his.

'The thing is . . . the thing *is*, Lizzy.' Elliot looked Lizzy straight in the eye. 'Amber's pregnant.'

Lizzy stared at him. 'I'm sorry, could you run that past me again?'

'Amber's pregnant.'

There was a long drawn-out silence. 'You . . . *bastard*,' Lizzy hissed.

'Wait, it's not mine!' The deelyboppers wobbled violently.

'What do you mean it's not yours? Whose is it then?'

Elliot took a deep breath. 'The baby is Marcus's.'

Lizzy was speechless for a moment. '*What?*'

Elliot had a rueful smile on his face. 'I thought you were going to revert to form and headbutt me.'

'This isn't a fucking joke, Elliot,' she snapped. 'Friends or not, you've been meeting your ex-fiancée behind my back. That is not cool when we're meant to be in a relationship!'

By this time all the diners in the Aberdeen Angus restaurant opposite were watching them through the window.

'You have every right to be angry,' Elliot said. 'I should have been honest with you from the start, but Amber swore me to secrecy until she'd worked out what she was going to do.' He looked directly at Lizzy again. 'I didn't want you to start worrying that something was going on. It was a really bad call.'

She acknowledged the apology with a tiny nod. 'So what about Amber and Marcus?'

'They slept together a few nights after we'd split up. Amber was distraught, and Marcus was just waiting there on the sidelines. A few weeks later she found out she was pregnant.'

'Sorry, but where do you come into all this? If I was Amber, I would have gone to one of my friends, not my ex-fiancé.'

'Amber *was* my friend. She still is.' Elliot sighed heavily. 'That's how this whole sorry mess started in the first place.'

'What do you mean, this whole sorry mess?'

'I always thought Amber was what I wanted. But as soon as we finally got engaged I knew things weren't right. But instead of talking to Amber about it straight away, I withdrew from her. I thought if I bottled things up then somehow they'd just go away. I should have finished it then, instead of letting it drag on.'

Lizzy couldn't quite believe what she was hearing. 'Sorry, you're saying that *you're* the one who called off the engagement?'

'Yes,' he said simply.

'Why let everyone think you were the one who got dumped? The *MailOnline* was calling you "Angsty Anderson"!'

'I didn't want to say anything out of respect for Amber. I'd put her in that position by not being honest with her sooner; I'd do what it took to get her out of it. Her people wanted to put out the line that it was Amber who'd finished things, and I wasn't going to start shooting my mouth off about it.' Elliot shook his head. 'I certainly didn't want to get caught up in all that gossip mag crap.'

But you did get caught up in all that gossip mag crap, Lizzy thought. *You took all the name-calling and speculation to protect the person who had always been your best friend.*

'I don't get it, Elliot. You always said that Amber was the kind of woman that every man dreams about being with.'

'Everyone, it would seem, except me.' He smiled tiredly. 'Amber is an incredible woman, but we work better as best friends. We should never have got into

426

a relationship in the first place. Both of us can see that now.'

'So let me get this right,' Lizzy said. 'You're saying that all these years you *thought* you wanted to be with Amber, but when you finally got with her, you realized that you didn't want to be with her after all? Why get engaged then?'

'I was in this stupid state of denial. Everyone was gunning for us, and I thought it would make things better. All it did was make things a hundred times worse.'

'And they say us women can't make up our minds.' Lizzy let out a long sigh. 'Why on earth didn't you just tell me all this in the phone call?'

'I just panicked,' he admitted. 'All I could think about was how badly I'd handled it. By the time I'd got my wits about me you'd put the phone down.' He gave Lizzy a wry smile. 'And you've been refusing to speak to me ever since.'

Lizzy wasn't letting him off just yet. 'But I saw Amber going up to your apartment!'

'She came round to tell me that she and Marcus had decided to make a go of things. I was happy for her. For her and Marcus. I always told her he wasn't good enough, but what the hell did I know?' Elliot shook his head. 'Marcus has always loved her. It's more than I could have ever given her.'

'So you and Marcus have kissed and made up?'

'I wouldn't go that far. I still think he can be a prick, but he probably thinks the same about me.'

They exchanged their first smile. 'I cocked things up,' he told her. 'You don't know how sorry I am.'

'I think I do now,' she said softly.

A drunken man stumbled past and glanced off Lizzy's right side. Instinctively Elliot put his arm out to protect her. 'The last few days have been the worst of my life. I can't imagine being without you.' He gazed at her. 'There's just this . . . *magic* about you. I never believed in all that crap about fate and the thunderbolt moment until I met you. You've taught me so much, about walking on the lighter side of life and seeing the good in people. *I'm* a better person because of you.' Elliot shook his head in disbelief. 'Do you know that I emailed a BuzzFeed link about giggling penguins around the office the other day?'

The darkness that had descended over Lizzy's life over the past few days vanished like a puff of smoke. She got that weirdly intense tunnel vision again. Like she and Elliot were the only two people who mattered in the entire universe.

'Amber will always be a big part of my life. But she's not the love of my life.' Elliot put his hands round Lizzy's face. 'Don't you get it? *You're* the love of my life, Lizzy Spellman. You wonderful, infuriating, intoxicating, animal-print-wearing madwoman.'

He went to kiss her. 'Hold on a minute,' Lizzy said. She pointed at the deelyboppers. 'Take those off. I can't take you seriously.'

'Now you know how I felt.'

'Oi! Any more of that and I'll set Shaman Ron on you!' Elliot pulled his Happy Halo off and chucked it away. 'Now come here and kiss me.'

'Hey! That Headbutt Girl!'

Lizzy opened one eye. They'd been kissing so deeply

she hadn't realized a gang of Japanese tourists was standing round them.

One woman waggled her camera at them. 'Can I get picture?'

'I'm very sorry, we're off duty,' Elliot told her. Amongst cheers and wolf-whistles he pulled Lizzy in to finish what they'd started.

Chapter 57

Where there were people, there were camera phones. 'Girl Who Gets Jilted at Friend's 30th and Headbutts Boyfriend Gets Her Man After All' was put up on YouTube that night, and by Boxing Day evening it had received over two million hits. There were intense Twitter debates about whether it was better than the John Lewis advert in terms of feel-good Christmas schmaltz. In a BBC interview Prince Harry was even asked if he thought redheads were the new sex symbols. 'Not that you need much help in that department,' the interviewer had cheekily added.

It was a surreal, exhausting, happy time. The days passed by in a whirlwind for Lizzy, and before she knew it, she and Elliot were dressed up in a cab on their way to a New Year's Eve party.

Having barely had an appetite over Christmas, for the first time she could remember Lizzy was wearing something that didn't have an elasticated waistband. The midnight-blue dress with the plunging back (a daring last-minute purchase from ASOS) hugged her body like a second skin.

'Stop wriggling.' Elliot was beside her looking very debonair in his black dinner jacket. 'You look gorgeous.'

'It's so tight I feel like you can see my organs.' Lizzy tried to unsuccessfully tug the skirt down.

'No one can see your organs and tight is good.' He leaned in and gave her a smooch on the lips. 'I'm already thinking about taking it off later.'

'Road's closed, mate,' the cabbie announced at the top of High Street Kensington. 'You want me to do a U-ey and try another way? Everywhere is going to be pretty jammed, though.'

Elliot looked down at Lizzy's strappy heels. 'How do you feel about finishing the journey on foot?'

Amber had invited them both along to the party she was holding at the iconic Kensington Roof Gardens. A hundred feet above the concrete streets, the sprawling site was famous for the four pink flamingos that lived in the grounds, as well as some of the most spectacular views in London.

'Are you *sure* Amber's cool about me coming?' Lizzy asked again as they walked to the venue.

'Of course. Why wouldn't she be?' Elliot had his arm firmly round her. It was more of a practical gesture than a romantic one; Lizzy had already gone over on her ankle twice.

'I didn't know if she'd find it all a bit weird.'

They walked past the entrance to Kensington Palace.

'Amber's happy that I'm happy,' he told her. 'She's really looking forward to getting to know you.'

People kept passing by and giving them knowing little smiles and looks. A flower seller outside the tube station stopped the pair to give Lizzy a red rose. 'I'm so pleased you've got together. You make a lovely couple.' The old man tapped Elliot warningly on the arm. 'You make sure you treat her right, now. This one deserves a happy ending.'

'I hadn't realized I was going out with a national treasure,' Elliot commented after they had walked off. 'I'd better watch my step.'

A line of black cabs was pulling up outside the venue, depositing their glamorous fares on to the pavement.

'I'm not sure I'm going to fit in here,' Lizzy said.

'Don't be so ridiculous. Amber hasn't just got friends with their heads up their own arses.'

They had just turned the corner to the discreet side entrance when someone stopped in their path. 'Lizzy?'

She stared at the man. He looked a bit like Justin, except that somebody had taken a bicycle pump and blown his face up, and then added a rather unattractive beard. The next moment she realized it *was* Justin.

There was a look of astonishment on his face. 'I thought it was you.'

Lizzy tried not to show her shock. Her ex had put on quite a bit of weight since she'd last seen him, and he was dressed in a pair of scruffy tracksuit bottoms. Justin had only ever shopped at Reiss when they'd been going out.

His gaze wavered towards Elliot. 'You look nice,' he told Lizzy. 'Going anywhere good?'

She pointed up at the building. 'A party up there.'

He looked envious. 'Wow, I bet that will be amazing.'

Lizzy felt Elliot gently squeeze her hand. 'Have you got any plans?' she asked.

Justin held up the Sainsbury's bag with a four pack of beer and a pizza box. 'My mate's house-sitting at his aunt's. I said I'd go and keep him company.' He looked down at his trainers. 'I don't know if you heard. Me and my, er, girlfriend split up. Well actually, she dumped me.'

This was the moment Lizzy had fantasized about. But now, looking at him standing there, all she felt was pity.

'I'm really sorry to hear that. I hope you're OK.'

Elliot squeezed her hand again. Lizzy gave Justin an apologetic smile. 'We'd better get going.'

'Of course, don't let me keep you from all the fun. You're looking really good, Lizzy,' Justin added.

'Thanks, Justin. I'll see you around.'

'Lizzy?'

She turned back round. Justin was still standing there under the street light. The bags under his eyes looked huge in the lamplight. 'I am sorry,' he said. 'For the way I ended things, I mean.' He smiled poignantly. 'I'm pleased it all worked out for you.'

'Thanks, Justin. I really hope things work out for you as well.'

*

'The bloke looked in complete shock,' Elliot said afterwards.

'Well, the last time he saw me I did nearly break his nose.'

Elliot slid his arm round Lizzy's waist. 'I bet he's kicking himself now.'

They ended up getting into the lift with a gorgeous creature who looked like she'd just stepped off the set of *Made in Chelsea*. When the doors had closed the girl turned to Lizzy.

'I've just got to say, you're a total inspiration.'

'I am?' Lizzy said in surprise.

'You give all us single girls hope.' The girl looked sad for a moment. 'I got dumped by my boyfriend at the start of December. He said he couldn't see me as a board director's wife.'

'What an idiot. You're much better off without him.'

'I hope so.' The girl hugged her clutch bag to her chest. 'I hate walking into places by myself.'

'I know exactly what you mean. You can walk in with us if you like.'

Elliot got quite a few envious glances as he walked in with the two women on his arms. Their glamorous companion gave a shriek. 'Petra! There you are!' She fluttered off into the crowd like an exotic butterfly.

'Another deed done for the good of mankind,' Elliot remarked. 'I'm going to have to start calling you Lizzy Mandela.'

Amber had very kindly extended the invite to a couple of Lizzy's friends and Nic and Poppet were already at the bar. They both looked fantastic, Nic in a black asymmetric dress that showed off her toned shoulders and Poppet was wearing a strapless red cocktail dress that revealed an indecent amount of cleavage. When Lizzy clocked the dapper, clean-shaven chap standing with them she nearly fell over.

'Robbo! You scrub up all right!'

'I could say the same about you, Sis.'

'Where's the beard gone?'

He rubbed his chin. 'The maintenance levels were getting too much. So I've gone back to being boyishly handsome.' Robbie shook Elliot's hand. 'Mate, it's good to see you.'

'Have you guys been outside yet?' Elliot asked the others. 'The gardens are spectacular.'

Poppet shook her head. 'Nic's a bit scared of running into one of the flamingos.'

Nic drained her glass. 'Another one of these and I should be OK to go outside.'

While Poppet and Robbie placated Nic, Lizzy and Elliot went to the cloakroom. She'd just handed over her faux-fur stole when Amber rushed up in a cloud of Chanel No. 5.

'Guys, you made it!' Elliot's pregnant ex was radiant in a flowing red gown, her hair in an elaborate fishtail plait down her back.

'Nice kaftan,' he told her. 'The earth-mother look suits you.'

'Cheeky sod, this is new-season Marchesa!' Amber touched Lizzy on the arm. 'I love your dress. Blondes always do carry off navy the best.'

'Thanks for inviting us,' Lizzy said, suddenly feeling rather shy.

Amber gave her a radiant smile. 'Thank you for coming. I wanted to have one last big night out before I get too enormous to move!'

Even six months pregnant the fashion designer's stomach still looked smaller than Lizzy's did after a blowout at Giuseppe's.

Someone came up to say hello to Elliot, leaving the two women alone for a second. 'Lizzy, I'm so pleased it's all turned out OK for you and Elliot. And I'm so sorry about the big misunderstanding and all the heartache it must have caused you.' Amber's expression looked heartfelt.

'It's fine, really,' Lizzy smiled. 'I get it now.'

'Elliot and I – we were never meant to be together. And when I hear the way he talks about you, I know you two were meant to be together.'

Lizzy blushed. 'Does he talk about me?'

'He never stops!' Amber laughed. A mischievous look entered her dark brown eyes. 'You and I can gang up on Elliot now. I'll let you into all his horrible little secrets.'

Lizzy pulled a face. 'I've already experienced the sneezing.'

'Oh my God! The squealing pig thing? I used to get *so* embarrassed when he did it in public. I'm telling you now, he could clear whole rooms in seconds.'

'What's so funny, you two?' Elliot was looking at them with a quizzical expression on his face.

'We're talking about your sneeze-squeal,' Lizzy told him.

Elliot rolled his eyes. 'I do not squeal when I sneeze.'

'Yes, *you do*,' Amber and Lizzy both fell about in giggles.

Marcus joined them, looking very impressive in a sharp tuxedo. 'Anderson,' he said gruffly, putting a protective hand on Amber's shoulder.

'Marcus,' Elliot replied equally stiffly.

It was Amber's turn to roll her eyes. 'Will you two just get over yourselves? Seeing as both of you play an important role in my life, you're going to have to learn to get along together.' She winked at Lizzy. 'Now shake hands like you mean it.'

The two men gazed at each other unwillingly. Elliot stuck his hand out. 'Marcus.'

He accepted the handshake. 'Elliot.'

The handshake seemed to go on for ever. Lizzy looked at Elliot's whitened knuckles. It looked like he was squeezing really hard. She gave him a subtle nudge.

'Well, it's good to see you,' he told Marcus.

'Darling?' Amber said pointedly.

Marcus swallowed, as if it was a massive effort. 'It's good to see you.' He nodded at Lizzy in a semi-friendly fashion.

'Twat,' Elliot muttered as they walked away.

Despite Lizzy's fears that the party would be a load of stuck-up fashion folk, there was actually a really good mix of people. Amber's generosity knew no bounds; the champagne and canapés kept coming round all night.

Lizzy came back from the toilet to find Elliot

standing at one of the windows, looking out into the night. He looked so tall and dashing she felt her heart fill up.

'There you are.' He put his arm round Lizzy's shoulders. 'Fancy taking a midnight promenade?'

'But it's not midnight yet.'

He put down his glass. 'Do you have to kill anything romantic I say stone-cold dead?'

They wandered out past the marquee where the swing band was playing and further into the gardens. Ducks floated past on the stream, although the famed flamingos had yet to make an appearance. Everywhere they turned was another little bridge, or a flower-strewn pond. It was like being in their own enchanted forest, high up on the rooftops of London. They wandered into the Spanish garden with its vivid red walls, and sat down on a bench.

'So,' said Elliot after a few moments. 'We're definitely going to be business partners then.'

Something rather remarkable had happened. Between them, Lizzy and Cassandra had persuaded Elliot to take Beeston Hall off the market, with a view to turning the stately home into a viable business. Lizzy was setting up meetings in the New Year, while Elliot was going to approach investors for the funds they needed to get the thing off the ground, as well as putting in his own money. In time they would need to think about hiring a team of staff, but one thing at a time. In the meanwhile Lizzy was going to do the PR and travel between London and Dorset. She was both excited and terrified about what lay ahead.

Antonia had already offered Lizzy a significant pay

rise to come back, but it was too little and too late. Lizzy had already decided to go freelance, and had the added bonus that Karen Jones wanted to come with her. Technically of course, Karen was still a Haven PR client, but since Antonia had never bothered to draw up proper contracts, Karen was free to go where she wanted.

'I feel sick every time I think about it,' Elliot said. 'You do know we could end up going bankrupt and having to sell the Hall anyway?'

'So you keep reminding me,' Lizzy said dryly. 'It's good to know you're going in with such a positive attitude.'

'Sorry,' he sighed. 'I'm hoping some of your relentless optimism will start rubbing off.'

They sat together looking up at the stars. Lizzy couldn't remember when she'd seen such a crystal-clear night.

'By the way, I've got you a little something,' Elliot told her. He pulled something out of his tuxedo pocket.

Lizzy stared at the small black box. Was that what she thought it was?

'It's not a ring,' Elliot said hurriedly.

'I didn't think it was,' she said equally quickly back.

'What I mean is, not to say I wouldn't give you a ring ever . . .' He started speaking even faster. 'I mean, what I'm saying is not right *now*. I'm not ruling out anything in the future . . . That's if you wanted to . . . I mean, we don't have to . . .' He trailed off. 'Oh God.'

Lizzy put a hand on his arm. 'I think I know what you mean you don't mean.'

Looking infinitely relieved, Elliot opened the box.

Inside was the most exquisite dragonfly brooch lying on a piece of navy velvet. 'It was my great-grandmother's,' he said, scooping the insect out with his finger as gently as if it was actually alive.

'Are those diamonds real?' Lizzy gasped.

'Yep, so be careful.' He fastened the brooch on her dress. 'Do you like it?' he asked nervously.

Lizzy brushed her fingers across the dragonfly's bejeweled wings. 'I think it's the most beautiful thing that I've ever seen. I don't know what to say.'

'Don't say anything. My mother wanted you to have it. Says there's no point it being kept locked up in a drawer.'

Lizzy looked down at the brooch. 'You do know this is technically animal print, don't you?'

Elliot sighed loudly. 'I think I'm fighting a losing battle with that one.'

Amber and Nic were deep in conversation as they rejoined the party. God knows what the two of them had to talk about, but she and Amber seemed to be getting on really well.

'Where's Poppet and Rob?' Lizzy asked.

Amber and Nic exchanged a look. 'Ah,' Nic said. 'I'm not sure how you're going to feel about this.'

She pointed out of the window, to where Robbie and Poppet were snogging passionately under the pergola.

'Poppet said as soon as she saw Robbie in his DJ she had *that* feeling. She's always had a soft spot for him.'

Lizzy watched her brother tenderly cup his hands

around Poppet's face. 'Oh God,' she said. 'This could change everything.'

It was like watching a film you know you shouldn't be watching but can't help yourself. After a moment Lizzy dragged her eyes away. 'OK. I am officially weirded out right now.'

'I think they make a good couple,' Elliot told her.

'I'm not saying they don't. It's just *weird*!' Despite herself Lizzy started to laugh. 'What if Poppet ends up being my sister-in-law? That could actually happen!'

'As long as I get to be flower girl,' Nic drawled.

A few minutes before midnight the DJ started to gather people in the garden. 'All right people! Does everyone have their champagne?'

In the marquee the swing band were doing a warm-up for 'Auld Lang Syne'.

Lizzy and Elliot stood under a nearby apple tree with their arms around each other. 'This is the first New Year's Eve party where I've actually enjoyed myself,' he told her, sounding astonished.

'I love New Year's Eve!'

'Why doesn't that surprise me?'

'Oh, get over yourself, party pooper.'

He laughed and kissed her. Warm in his arms, Lizzy looked round the garden. Poppet was sitting on Robbie's lap in the pergola, laughing at something he'd said. One of the flamingos had finally appeared and had hilariously made a beeline for Nic. Lizzy watched her friend nervously feed the giant bird another bit of canapé and pat it cautiously on its head.

At the front of the crowds Amber and Marcus

441

were waiting for the DJ to start the countdown. Marcus was standing behind Amber with his hands protectively on Amber's bump. He hadn't left her side all night.

'Marcus really does love her, doesn't he?' Lizzy said.

'Yes,' Elliot admitted. 'I think he really does.'

'OK, people. Ten, nine, eight . . .'

'Seven, six!' Everyone shouted.

'Five, four, three, two, one . . . Happy New Year everybody!'

A cacophony of fireworks soared up into the sky. People starting cheering and kissing anyone they could get their hands on.

Elliot pulled Lizzy into a passionate embrace. 'Happy New Year,' he murmured, just as her knees were about to give way.

'Happy New Year, Elliot.'

'Here's to the future. *Our* future.'

'Our future,' she said happily.

Elliot's green eyes searched her own. 'Are you sure you'll be able to put up with working with me? You know what they say about mixing business with pleasure.' He brushed Lizzy's mouth with his fingers. 'And you are always strictly pleasure.'

'You might think twice about that when we're stood across an office arguing with each other.'

'Arguing is what we're good at, isn't it? There's no one else I'd rather be doing it with.' He smiled. 'There's no one else I'd rather be doing anything with, for that matter.'

A rocket went off, matching the *swoosh* inside Lizzy's stomach.

'You do know that, don't you?' This time Elliot planted the sweetest of kisses on her lips. 'It was only ever you.'

Acknowledgements

Some very good people helped me with *It Had to Be You*. It has turned out to be a very different book to how I'd first imagined it, but if I haven't used your wit and wisdom this time round, it is stored up for the future. A huge thank you to Bryan Barboni, Patrick Vickers, Ben Faulkner, Freddie Lait and Jo Healey. Also to Leila Ager, Abigail Segall, Kara Williams and Dan Tyte, as well as Rob McDonald and Mike Steen. Special thanks to my special readers Jacquie and Jordan Paramor, and also a big shout to the amazing Tom Woolrich. All mistakes are my own. To my brilliant and dedicated editor Katy Loftus for all her hard work, and to the lovely team at Transworld. Last but definitely not least, my agent Amanda Preston.

Do you love talking about your favourite books?

From big tearjerkers to unforgettable love stories, to family dramas and feel-good chick lit, to something clever and thought-provoking, discover the very best **new fiction** around – and find your **next favourite read**.

See **new covers** before anyone else, and read **exclusive extracts** from the books everybody's talking about.

With plenty of **chat, gossip and news** about **the authors and stories you love**, you'll never be stuck for what to read next.

And with our **weekly giveaways,** you can **win** the latest laugh-out-loud romantic comedy or heart-breaking book club read before they hit the shops.

Curl up with another good book today.